TRADING YESTERDAY
© 2017 KAHLEN AYMES

First Edition
Version: 2017.11.12

Cover Design and Formatting by R.A. Mizer of ShoutLines Design. For more information visit Shoutlinesdesign.com.

Cover photos: iStock-692813214, AdobeStock_80009862 & AdobeStock_810022330

Published by Kahlen Aymes Books, Inc.
Amazon ISBN: 978-1-973358947
ISBN: 978-0-9967344-8-6 (E-book)
ISBN: 978-0-9967344-9-3 (Paperback)

TRADING
Yesterday

KAHLEN AYMES

Special thanks to Justine Tevis & Donna Cooksley Sanderson for your editing prowess! And, thank you to Kahlen's Book Babes, Kahlen's Super Girls, Kahlen's Angels & the amazing CATB ladies!

This book is dedicated to my parents.
Thank you for always putting wind in my
sails, and for everything you've done for me
and Olivia. You keep me on course!
I love you,
Always.

ONE *touch*
AND THE PAIN
melted away.

Prologue

CHASE

I was flying high. Disbelieving. Excited… but, torn.

This was the chance of a lifetime; one that I'd be a fool to turn down, but the timing was off. I'd wanted to play professional soccer since I was ten years old when I watched Pele' name David Beckham to the FIFA 100 greatest living players on ESPN. They, and other ballers like them, were my heroes.

I'd been playing since I could walk, and had somehow landed a full ride at Clemson. My college career rocked; my team was ranked in the top 10 nationally and had played in the NCAA championship series all four of my years at the university. We made the elite eight last season, and this year, we won the whole damn thing. If there ever was a team sport; soccer was it, but I was named MVP of the final game of this season, and it was a fitting culmination and was the rocket that put my entire career in motion.

When Coach Noonan pulled me into his office right out of the shower after the game, I was intrigued, but I about fell over when I saw Arsène Wenger through the glass of his office walls.

Call it football or soccer, every player who kicked the black and white ball anywhere on the globe knew who Arsène Wenger was; the manager of Arsenal Football Club in London. Beckham hadn't played for his team, but it was damn close enough. The man was a legend in his own right.

I took his proffered hand in sort of a stunned haze, still damp from my shower, and my hair dripping water down the muscles of my back. I was dressed only in the large white towel wrapped around me, low on my hips, and didn't know what to say in that moment; utterly amazed by what I was hearing. One of their forwards broke his leg and was benched for the season, and they were recruiting for a replacement. If I did well enough, it was a chance to earn a permanent place on the team.

It was as if the planets aligned and dropped a big golden egg in my lap. I mean, we won NCAA, by some miracle I was MVP, and I played the same position they needed to fill—it all fit. Shit like that just doesn't happen, even if you do spend twenty years working your ass off to make it so.

The whole thing took less than ten minutes, and I was walking out of that office, using the small towel around my neck to dry my hair; a smile a mile wide plastered across my face. My teammates had all been staring into the office, practically plastered up against the glass, and straining to hear what was said. When I emerged and told them what was up; the locker room erupted in a chorus of cheers, laughs, pats on the back, amid a few disappointed groans.

It was fucking beautiful.

I couldn't stop grinning while I threw on my clothes in a mad haste, already lagging behind the rest of my team. I was itching to get to Teagan so I could tell her the news. My impatience made it hard to get out of the locker room because I was constantly bombarded by questions and congratulations by my friends. A few of them had jealousy behind their eyes,

2

but I could understand how they felt. I was walking on rainbows, but I knew they had acid eating at their guts because it was me, and not one of them. I was sure that I'd feel the same way if it were anyone else.

Mr. Wenger gave me twenty-four hours to make up my mind, but seriously, there was no decision to be made. My parents were lower middle class and my dad had always worked two jobs. My scholarship had been like a magic wand opening the door to a future I could never have had without it. I was sure they'd both worry that I wouldn't finish up my bachelor's degree at Clemson, but they knew soccer had always been my dream. I didn't want to disappoint them, but their reaction wasn't my main consideration. I had only one semester left, and yeah, maybe it wouldn't be on scholarship, but I could always finish up later.

I wanted it badly, but it would mean leaving Teagan behind, and that thought alone made my heart seize painfully. For the first time since I walked out of that office, my heart paused and the happy euphoria I was feeling dwindled, literally pausing me mid-step. Life had a way of offering up succulent morsels, but there was always a price to be paid.

It would suck in a major way but I couldn't ask her to ditch her degree just to follow me halfway around the globe. Plus, I'd be playing all over the world, and she had no friends in London and I couldn't leave her sitting in England while I was gone. To expect that would be selfish.

Plus, I had enough issues with her old man. Her father didn't appreciate my career aspirations and would rather I pursue a career in business or law, and I hoped this opportunity would show him that football was a real career, and I truly was worthy of his daughter; a chance to prove she'd have a secure future with me. I understood his concern; she was his only child and he wanted the best for her; though there were plenty of times when he made it plain he prioritized a consistent paycheck over big dreams.

I had to take one of the buses back to the hotel with the rest of the team, and though Teagan had come to the game, she'd be waiting for me there. I'd never been to Philadelphia before and Talen Energy Stadium was an awesome facility right on the Delaware River, but the wind coming off the water was cold as hell. The December temperatures were a good twenty-five degrees less than what we were used to in South Carolina, and the light jacket I had with me wasn't enough. I started shivering on the short walk through the parking lot toward the two waiting luxury buses. As I climbed aboard the first one I was thankful for the heated interior, realizing this was a preview of what I could expect of English weather in winter.

More shouts and cheers confronted me as I took a seat next to my best friend, Jensen Jeffers. I smiled and waved at the guys as they started shouting more congratulations and questions about when I had to leave. "Soon," was all I'd say. "I don't even know if I'm going yet." A roar filled the small space as they all started in with incredulous disbelief that I was even hesitating on my decision to join Arsenal.

Jensen just watched me with his usual contemplative demeanor. He was logical and supportive, and we'd have plenty of time to discuss it, but it would be more like a talk-through of the pros and cons; he wouldn't try to influence me either way.

He'd been my dorm roommate my freshman year and he knew me better than anyone other than my girlfriend, Teagan. Jensen was the Tiger's senior goalkeeper and one of the best in Division I. There was no doubt the Tigers would take a huge dump with our record if it weren't for him saving our asses. Offense was only half of it, and he was good enough to play professionally, but it wasn't what he wanted. He was as

4

competitive as me, but solid as a rock, and grounded. Both of us were lean and cut; the game keeping us in top shape, though he was a bit bigger than me. He was the type of guy girls flock to, smooth and polished. He had his own plans for life after Clemson, and I was positive he'd be successful either way. Jensen always had women hanging around, but he spent a ton of time with Teagan and me.

He was casually smiling as I approached, and he nodded to the open seat across the aisle from him. I was finally feeling the exhaustion left by the miles I'd just run during the game.

"Ugh," I groaned as my fatigued body fell into the seat. I ran a hand through my hair, which was still a bit damp to the touch, but it flopped back down into place immediately. "Jesus, I'm tired."

"Want some?" He had an open bag of Crunchy Cheetos and offered it to me so I could take a handful, but I shook my head in refusal.

"Thanks, dude, but I'm meeting Teagan in a minute." Under normal circumstances, I'd invite him to go with us to dinner; that was normal at away games. There were rare occasions Jensen's "girl-of-the-moment" would carpool with Teagan to away games and we'd double, but most often, it was just the three of us; Teagan called us the Three Musketeers.

"Figured." He nodded and reached into the bag for another helping. "Dude. Wow. The MVP, the Arsenal thing, and Teags waiting for you; jackpot night ahead." He nodded wryly. "You've got it made. How do you think she'll take it? You are going, right?"

He was the first guy to congratulate me in the locker room, and he'd already heard what was said in the office; he wasn't just my teammate, and I was grateful for our friendship. I lifted my right shoulder in a half shrug and turned my head to the side so I could look at him. "She'll be happy. This will set us up for life. It's only a year until she graduates."

"Famous last words. I'm sure she'll support you, Chase, but it's a year and a half last time I checked. She'll put on a good show for you, but you're kidding yourself if you think this won't hit her hard."

I sighed, wishing she could go with me right away. Of course, I wanted her with me, but it was selfish to even consider. A dark cloud of struggle hung over a decision that should be the easiest one of my life, but one I had to make for the future I wanted for us... for Teagan.

I tried to shake off the sadness that could potentially change my mind. "You're just gonna miss being my bitch." The corners of my mouth lifted in a wry smile, and I huffed out a laugh.

Jensen burst out laughing right along with me. "Yeah, that's it, for sure," he agreed with amusement. "Because we both know, I'm such a pussy." Grinning, he shoved a few more Cheetos into his mouth and chewed, being obnoxious on purpose. "Seriously, she could go with you. She'll want to." Players were filling the seats around us, and I was impatient to get the bus moving on its way back to the hotel.

The laughter died away as I considered his comment. "Yeah, I know, but I can't let her. Her dad already has a huge hard-on for me. You know he thinks soccer is shit and I should be a fucking accountant or something."

Jensen nodded, continuing to eat. "Yup."

"Yeah. Well, this is my chance to prove it will be a career and I'll be able to take care of her. He'll respect me if I don't yank her out of school early."

Jensen's eyebrows shot up, as the bus doors closed. "You think so? He'll think you're a selfish bastard to choose soccer over his daughter and you know it, Chase."

He was right, but I'd never be happy pushing a pencil, and I didn't want to resent my life. "I know, but what can I do? I don't want to be a fucking banker."

6

"I know. It's a bitch for sure. But get one thing clear... you won't be 'letting her' do shit. You're acting as if you're the only one who gets input on this decision. Have you met Teagan Tessler?"

I could see respect and admiration for Teagan in his eyes, and I could hear it in the tone of his voice. We were all good friends and I was thankful we were friends. He'd be here to watch over her for me in my absence and it made me feel easier. He and I met her at the same party at the beginning of my sophomore year, though I'd seen her around campus a couple of times before that.

She was a nursing student and I was in business so outside of a few cores, we didn't share classes. She was happy and laughing, her dark brown eyes sparkling. Her body was softly seductive, gently curving in all the right places, and slender, but it was her face and personality that drew me to her. I spent half the night staring at her from across the room, mesmerized by how perfect she was. I'd never been nervous around girls, but I was with her, and I was determined not to fuck it up.

In the end, it was Jensen who walked up to her, tapped her on the shoulder and with his usual casual confidence, turned; pointing in my direction, said a few words, and then wearing a casual smile; waved me over. He'd cornered me, but what could I do? I wanted to crawl under a rock, but if I didn't want to look like an asshole, I had no choice to go over and say hello. Her beautiful face lit up when she smiled, Jensen left us alone, and the rest was history. We were inseparable after that night; instantly crazy for each other.

"Yes. I get what you're saying, J, but she's also the smartest person I know. Her heart might want to follow me to Europe, but her brain will know she has to finish school. We have to look at the big picture."

My friend could see the sadness behind my words, and he nodded solemnly. "You're a stronger man than me. I could never leave a woman like that."

"It isn't what I want, man. I could be selfish and beg her to come along. She would, but she deserves her degree, and to not alienate her dad. We have the rest of our lives to be together. The time will fly by." Even as I said the words, I knew I was lying to myself. Joining Arsenal and traveling would be amazing, playing professional ball against the best teams on the planet would be the experience of a lifetime, but I would miss my girl more than I wanted to face. It would be hell and I'd seen more than one long-distance relationship fall to crap.

Jensen was right, I owed it to Teagan to ask her what she felt and make her tell me the truth, and then figure it out. I told myself right then and there, that if she didn't want me to go, I wouldn't.

Teagan

My hand touched my stomach below my navel knowing it was too soon to notice anything different about my body; too soon to feel any fluttering of life.

Less than a month ago, the condom Chase and I were using broke and the entire tip of it came off inside me; Chase had to get it out using his long fingers. I prayed, we both did, that we wouldn't get pregnant. We loved each other and I had no doubt that, one day, we'd be married, but this wasn't the time. We were both in college, Chase had big dreams of a professional soccer career, and my father would never forgive me. I shuttered at the thought.

I lost my mother in a car accident when I was fifteen, and Dad and I only had each other. He'd been my whole world until I met Chase. I was not concerned about Chase's family being supportive; I knew they would be. He had the perfect nuclear family that all rallied around each other and would help out, but my dad... another story completely. My face crumpled as I sank down on the edge of the bed. I didn't want to disappoint him, but I was going to have a child, and to get an abortion was not something I wanted to consider. I knew two other girls who'd done it and were fine, and one who had a nervous breakdown a year later.

My best friend in high school got pregnant on prom night and she had her sister take her to another state that allowed underage abortions without parental consent. It was as if she'd never even gotten pregnant at all. Life went on. No one knew. Maybe it was the best decision for Shelly because the guy was a loser who left her high and dry, but Chase would never do that to me. I knew I could count on him; so much, he'd give up anything or everything to do the right thing for me. I closed my eyes and two fat tears squeezed out from behind my closed lids and tumbled unceremoniously down my cheeks.

I felt so guilty. He only had one semester left, but I had three, and I was scared what my dad would do. If he kicked me out now, Chase would have to give up his scholarship and get a job to support us. We already stayed together most of the time, but we'd need a bigger place to live with a baby, and for sure, my father wouldn't help and his family wouldn't be able to.

Dad was already so down on Chase because he dared to want a professional soccer career when he thought he should get, to use his words; "a real job" since soccer was a "pipe dream that had an ice cube's chance in hell of paying the bills." He had no reservations about pointing that out whenever my boyfriend was around.

I could see the defeat written all over Chase whenever my father would lecture him about it, and how every time he had to be around my dad, he steeled himself for the onslaught that would always follow.

I hated that this would only make their relationship worse. Already, it was so awful that it made me uncomfortable. I mean, how could my dad not see in Chase, the amazing, hardworking guy that I saw? It blew my mind. Chase was incredible in every way and I couldn't love him more, or be prouder of him. He woke up at 5 AM to work out and do extra drills to hone his soccer skills, and he kept a 3.5 GPA to keep his scholarship at Clemson. He'd graduate debt free, and he did every bit of it on his own. His family didn't have money, he didn't have the privileges growing up that I did, but he did have amazing parents that were behind him one hundred percent. He should be admired, not chastised.

And now… this. My heart was breaking. My father would place all the blame for the pregnancy on Chase, and the chasm between them would only get worse. I loved and admired my dad. It was just him and I against the world for years, but Chase was everything I wanted and needed for the rest of my life. I didn't know how I'd ever be happy without either one, but Chase never asked me to choose.

My phone rang, breaking me out of my thoughts. I quickly brushed the tears away with both hands as I ran to rummage through my purse to pick it up. I'd thrown the purse down on the desk after coming back to the hotel after Chase's game ended.

"Hello?" I answered.

"Hey, babe," Chase's soothing, but weary voice came through the line.

"Hi, there. I'm so proud of you. MVP." My heart was smiling, despite my internal struggle.

"Not a big deal," he brushed off the honor like it was nothing. "We're on our way back, now. Are you hungry?"

I wasn't really. My stomach was in knots. I needed to tell him about the baby, but he deserved a night to bask in the win. "A little. Do you want to celebrate? You have to be tired. You were up and down that field like a crazy man today." I tried my best to clear the tears from my voice. "And that one aerial kick; I was afraid you'd break your neck when you landed." He'd flown into the air to kick the ball o, and backward, into the goal and then crashed to the ground hard. The attempt was good, the crowd roared, and Chase got up as if he hadn't just dropped straight onto his back.

"I am tired. Maybe just a low-key dinner, and then an early night," he said. "Just us."

"Maybe a rub-down?"

"Mmm. Won't say no."

"Jensen isn't hungry?"

"So what if he is? I want to be with you."

I sighed in relief. Jensen was a great friend, but he was with us so much and he was sans female companionship on this trip, so I fully expected him to tag along. I was worried that I'd have no time alone to speak to Chase, and if there was an opportunity to tell him, I wanted to take it. We never kept secrets from each other, but I hadn't wanted to distract him from the playoffs. "Okay. That sounds nice."

"Are you ready? The bus is just pulling into the hotel parking lot."

"Um, I can be. I just need to retouch my makeup and run a brush through my hair. Should I meet you downstairs?"

"I'll come up for a bit. I want to tell you something. Be up in a minute."

"Okay. Love you."

"Don't I know it," he said with a chuckle.

"You, do, huh?" I couldn't help but smile at his confidence in me. "Ass," I teased.

"Yup. Hurry up!"

He hung up the phone and I flew into the bathroom. My makeup and toiletries were all over the vanity and I rushed to clear the traces of tears off of my face. Chase was in a great mood so I decided to play the evening by ear and try to find the best time to drop the bomb. Maybe tonight wouldn't be a good time at all, but I had to tell him, soon.

I grabbed the brush and quickly ran it through my long hair, trying to calm the fly-a-ways. My dark hair was straight and fine, but I had a lot of it. I put on a touch of foundation under my eyes, set it with powder, and used a bit of contouring to define my cheekbones. I used a small piece of tissue to remove the mascara smudges from under my eyes and then quickly re-lined them. That was all I had time for before the door to our room burst open.

"Where are you, Monkey?"

"In here." I barely put the eyeliner down when Chase's happy face appeared as he bounded around the corner and then leaned into the doorframe. He was always handsome; dressed casually in a black V-neck T-shirt, dark blue jeans, and boots. The light team jacket he wore wasn't enough for the weather. I'd changed into a red sweater over my black leggings. I'd practically frozen in the stands.

"Mmm," he murmured and reached for me. His expression was flirty as his arms enfolded me, only to lift me up and leave my legs dangling as he walked back into the main room. The room had two beds because it was less expensive than a king upgrade. "Monkey me," he commanded, huskily.

My lips turned up in a smile as I lifted my legs and caged his body in, using my arms around his shoulders. He'd started calling me Monkey, the first time I held him like this and now it was a thing.

In less than a second, I was on my back on the bed with Chase on top of me. He felt so good against me. I felt safe and protected in his arms, like nothing in the world could hurt me. I laughed softly. "Chase," I murmured, trying to ignore the way his body fit so perfectly with mine. He shifted against me, leaving me in no doubt he desired me. One of my feet slid down over his butt and thigh to hook on the inside of his knee.

"We fit like a glove," he said my thoughts out loud. "And not just like this. In everything." He was suddenly serious. "I love you, Teagan. You're my girl."

I slid one arm up so a hand could wind into his hair; while the other came down to brush the back of my fingers against his face. "I know." I nodded just before his open mouth brushed mine, gently teasing a response from me. My body arched and my head lifted, communicating that I wanted the kiss to deepen, and he gave me what I wanted. The kiss was slow but deep, our tongues tasting, laving, and moving deep into each other's mouths. God, it was good. I felt my body open, heat pulsing through me as he pressed his hardness against me, stimulating us both beneath our clothes. Making out with Chase, even dry humping through our clothes was satisfying because it was Chase, and I loved him more than anything. He was the beginning and the end for me.

"Uhhhh, God, Teagan. Don't start," he murmured, then came back for another kiss and then another before pulling away and falling limp on top of me. It was a thing he did, like a physical protest when he was turned on and we stopped in the middle of making love. It was cute and endearing.

"I didn't start it," I laughed softly, running a hand down his back kneading his muscles lightly. "Babe... I can't breathe." I gasped and Chase eased his weight back onto his elbows, easing the pressure on my chest, though he stayed on top of me, looking down at me. There was a brilliant smile on his beautiful face. His jaw was strong, his lips full, but not overly so, straight nose that had never been broken, and clear, intent eyes that could see right through me.

"Yes, you did. You monkey'd me. It's all your fault."

I smiled up at him, taking in his sparkling green eyes. "I guess that makes sense, in a weird way." His face was serious despite our make-out session and I sensed he needed to talk. I stroked the hair back off his face. "What is it? I can tell you want to talk."

He nodded. "Yeah. I do." He rolled to his side, pulling me with him until we were facing each other, lying with our heads on the pillows, but close together. Chase pulled my leg over the top of his thigh and hitched it over his hip. His hand rubbed my leg from my knee up, over my hip and down again. "I got an offer today. Professional ball."

I was instantly excited and I screamed. "EEEEHHHHHH!" I smiled brightly and gave him a tight hug, before pushing back and scrambling up to jump up and down on the bed. Chase laughed as his body lifted and fell on the bed due to my excitement. "Oh, my God! Yay! Yay! Yay! EEEEHHHHHHH!" I screamed again.

Chase continued laughing as I danced around on the bed, bouncing him up and down, but his eyes were intense as he trained them on my face. "My boyfriend's a professional, baller! My boyfriend's a professional baller!" I was giggling, looking down at him as he gazed up at me. He grabbed my ankle and yanked knocking me back down beside him in a fit of laughter. "Where? With what team?" He was a year ahead of me in school, so this was his last season at Clemson, and I fully expected him to be picked up. I was happy. This would mean my dad's reservations about us would tamp down with concrete evidence that Chase had a future in the sport. "I'm so proud of you! I knew you'd do it!" My heart swelled with love and admiration. "You work so flipping hard. Is it with the

14

Battery?" I prayed it would be with the Charleston team in order to keep him close. I rolled toward him and he pulled me close again, his demeanor serious. I reached out to touch his hair at his temple, hesitantly, concerned by his expression.

"That's the thing, Teag; it's not a local club," he said hesitantly, pulling the hand that had paused mid-stroke on his hair, to his mouth to kiss it. "That's the part I need to talk to you about."

The air whooshed from my lungs. I wanted to be happy for him. I was happy for him, but I couldn't help how my heart fell at the prospect of being without him. I wasn't sure what it meant for me, for us, and our baby. I nodded. "I'm listening." I fought the rising ache in my throat and the burn of tears at the back of my eyes. "Where, then?"

"London."

I gasped out loud. It was so far. "Wh—what?"

"With Arsenal. One of their players got injured and they need a forward to finish out the season, and if I do well enough, they'll hire me for real. It's a hundred times better than Charleston. I'd be playing internationally. I can hardly believe they'd even consider me."

His excitement was obvious. He wanted it and why shouldn't he. It was an amazing, impossible opportunity that was exactly what he'd worked for and more. I inhaled deeply. "Of course, they want you. You're the best forward in the NCAA. When do you leave? This spring?" I pretended not to hear what he said.

"No. They want me to go now. At the end of this semester, so in a couple of weeks."

"Oh," I offered a tumultuous smile. "But the season's almost over."

"I know babe, but their best player is out, and they need me now. Then there will be training camp, try-outs, or something."

15

I tried not to cry, and to swallow the intense pain rising up in my throat. The muscles constricted in an awful ache that got worse. "That's... amazing."

"Babe, I know it sucks that we'll be apart, but it's what we need for the future, isn't it?" He shook his head at what must have been the heartbroken shock on my face. "Tell me not to go, and I won't go. You're the most important thing to me."

My heart and mind were screaming; No, Chase! Don't go! Never go! You can't go! But, I couldn't say them. His words; you're the most important thing to me, resonated deep into my soul and I couldn't put myself before him.

He was the most important thing to me, too, and I couldn't hold him back. In that second, I knew I couldn't tell him about the baby before he left because then he'd never leave.

It would be scary to wait, scary to face my father without him, scary to be here... alone, but I couldn't let him give up what may be his one and only chance to realize his dream.

I stroked his face with the back of my fingers, staring deep into those eyes I loved so much and said the words that made my heart bleed. "You have to go."

The only light in the room was coming from the bathroom, and the television that was turned down very low and the blue shadows of the changing pictures danced across Chase's perfect face. His brow wrinkled and he swallowed, hard as he fought with his emotions. It had to be difficult to feel so happy about something when he knew it would break my heart to be without him.

"When Coach Noonan called me into his office and I saw Arsène Wenger sitting there, I about shit my pants. I mean, Arsène-fucking-Wenger, Teagan! Then, all the guys were all over me with congrats—I was so freaking happy I was beside myself, but the first thought I had was that I had to tell you about it. I was so excited to share it with you, but then it hit me that you probably couldn't go with me." His eyes locked on mine, searching for my reaction.

We kept touching each other. My hands kneading the muscles of his shoulders and arms, threading through his hair, or running my fingers along his jaw, while Chase rubbed my back and pressed his forehead to mine. My first reaction was that I wanted to give up school and follow him to London, but now, being pregnant, I couldn't be alone in a city where I knew no one, and I would just be a huge distraction for Chase. "You know I want to, there is nothing I'd rather do, but I don't think it's the best idea, right now."

"Yeah. You should finish school. And who knows? Maybe I'll suck and they'll send my ass packing."

My heart shattered like a window put into the path of a meteor. It would be seventeen months until I was finished with school, and I wished I could tell him that I planned on being in England after this semester ended. That would be long enough for him to get established with the team, long enough for me to figure out how to work it out with my dad, long enough to tell Chase about the baby. He'd be furious that I didn't tell him and let him leave the country without knowing, but I could only hope that eventually, he'd realize why I had to hide it from him for a while, and forgive me.

"We've never been separated. Will you be okay?" His long fingers closed around the back of my head, as I snuggled closer to him. His cheek rested against my head as we wrapped around each other, our limbs tangling together as we couldn't get close enough.

I could hear the struggle in his voice that echoed my own. Not telling him about the baby, hurt, and I didn't want to lie about my feelings. "No. I won't be okay, I'll miss you like crazy, but that doesn't mean you shouldn't go. You can't make the goal if you don't take the shot." I used words he'd used a million times when he talked about anything he wanted.

He inhaled and his hold on me tightened. "Teagan, goddamn it."

Tears were streaming out of my eyes as I fought the sobs I wanted to let loose. "You have to go, Chase," I said into his chest, effectively soaking the front of his shirt. "We both know it."

Chase shifted lower on the bed, so once again we were facing each other and he could look into my face. His thumbs swiped at the tears on both sides of my face at once, and then he bent in to kiss my mouth, oh, so softly. "I don't want to leave you," he whispered, gently teasing my lips with his. My eyes were closed, but I could feel his every breath, sense his every move, and feel the love pouring out of him. I had to have faith in him, in me... in us.

"I know." My chin lifted to kiss him back. "It's just how it has to be for a little while. Maybe I can transfer to an English school for my last year. I don't think I'll make it all those months, without you."

I wasn't sure how I'd work it out. My dad would protest, and I wasn't sure he'd pay my tuition at an English school. I wasn't even sure I could transfer with only one year left. Most U.S. schools required two years to get a degree issued, but all I knew was that I had to get Chase to England and on that team if it was the last thing I did.

Chase backed up and looked down at me. "You're assuming I'll make the team."

I huffed through my tears and rolled my eyes wryly. "Please."

The corner of his mouth lifted in a sad smile. "You'd do that? What about your dad? He'll want you to finish at Clemson."

I shook my head slightly. "I don't know. I don't care, I guess. Let me worry about him. We'll work it out. This is the best thing that's ever happened to you. It's your chance and you have to take it."

"It is a good thing, honey, but the best thing that ever happened to me... is you. You're part of this. If I go, I'm doing this for us. My goal is to work hard, make the team for good, and then haul your little ass over the pond."

"Okay, then, you will." I sniffed and wiped at my nose with the back of my hand, finally feeling like smiling for real. "One thing you never lack is confidence in your abilities."

He flashed a brilliant smile and then rolled over on top of me, pinning me to the bed. "I thought you liked my abilities," he said with a smirk. "Of course, if you need convincing, I'll be happy to demonstrate. You did say I was a professional baller," he teased.

I'd been crying and so knew I wasn't very sexy in that moment, but Chase's adoration always made me feel like the center of the universe. "I'm sort of yucky right now. I'm stuffed up."

"Hold up," he said and then pushed up off the bed, went into the bathroom and came back with an inordinately huge wad of toilet paper and handed it to me. "Here, Monkey."

I took and pulled a few sheets off and set the rest on the nightstand next to the bed. Chase started peeling off his T-shirt and undoing the front of his jeans, all the while his sexy gazed was trained on me, even as I blew my nose.

"Ugh," I complained. "Sexy, right?"

"Always," he said, with a smile, climbing onto the bed from the foot, to straddle my knees and begin pulling my leggings and thong down. "The sexiest woman in the world. It's safe right now, isn't it?" he asked. My periods were like clockwork and he was well aware of the cycle and when we needed protection.

All I could do was nod. I couldn't get pregnant when I already was. I watched his muscles move as he undressed me, my eyes skirting over his broad shoulders and muscular torso, his pecs, and abs clearly defined. I reached out because I wanted to touch him, but my arms weren't long enough. It would have been safe, but either way, a condom wasn't needed.

His denim-clad knee moved between mine, and he spread my legs wide with his thighs before settling down on top of me again and finally, my hands slid over smooth, hard flesh. He was so strong: his movements were smooth and deliberate. I could feel his erection pressing into me in just the right spot, despite his half-state of dress.

"Now, I've got you," he murmured sensually, as his mouth came down hungrily on mine, his tongue finding mine in a slow, desperate dance. His hands began to roam my body, careful to graze all of my pleasure centers. His curled fingers brushed down the side of my body and he slid his hand beneath me to angle my hips up so he could tease me with soft thrusts, echoing the delicious rhythm of our kisses. Every touch was magic and my heart and body opened. I wanted him to dissolve right into me because as close as we were, I wanted more.

I moaned impatiently as I pushed at his jeans to get them over his hard butt, one foot trying desperately to hook the fabric and drag it down. Chase's breathing increased as heat and an aching pulse began to increase between us.

My love for him was overwhelming and it always surprised me. It didn't matter if he was inside of me, or we were just talking, or I was watching him play or have a conversation with Jensen or one of his other friends, he consumed my soul. There was nothing I wanted more than being with him. "Chase," I said his name like a prayer when he finally pushed inside my slick heat, and it was to me. "Mmmm…"

"You're so beautiful, Teagan. I love you, so much."

He was so perfect, and I couldn't imagine ever wanting someone more than Chase. I'd do anything for him; even let him go… but just for a little while.

"I love you, more." My heart squeezed with the intensity of it, as my body pressed up to meet his, and my hands fisted in the silky strands of his hair.

His kisses paused for an instant and I felt his lips lift in a smile. "Let's call it a tie."

ONE *touch*
AND THE PAIN
melted away.

Chapter 1

Teagan

The world was ending.

Remi was getting worse. She'd been so brave, but the leukemia was taking its toll on her little body. Her little arms and legs were bruised, she had headaches, trouble breathing, she was weak and so thin. It was all the hospital staff could do to keep her eating.

No mother expects to watch her child die, and I couldn't stand to think it might happen, but my training as an RN and the consults with the doctors made reality difficult to ignore. After two rounds of chemotherapy last summer, she went into remission, but it was back again. I dreaded telling her she'd have to go through it again. She was young but could remember how awful it was. There is nothing worse than watching your child suffer.

Childhood leukemia typically had better remission and cure rate than adult onset, and the doctors were on board to keep at it, but looking at my poor little baby girl, so small in her hospital bed, shivering, rolled up on her side, and holding the stuffed elephant she named Bennie, tight to her chest as she slept; I wasn't so sure. I felt selfish to put her through it.

I moved to the bed and crawled onto it and curled my own body around my sleeping daughter, closing my eyes as tears flooded them. I felt sick inside. Jensen was out of town covering a game as one of ESPN's star correspondents, and that was another problem I didn't want to deal with. He was a good man; one who had stepped up when I needed someone, but our marriage was never what he wanted. We tried to keep it together, and he loved Remi like his own child, but our marriage was empty and we both knew it.

It seemed that my special gift was causing pain to all of the men in my life, and there wasn't a day that went by that I wasn't consumed with regret. I wished I could jump in a time machine and make a different decision.

I gathered Remi closer and listened to the softness of her breathing, taking comfort in the sound and hoping the warmth from my body would seep into her and ease her shaking.

Fucking leukemia! My mind railed.

This wasn't the first time that I'd wondered if her illness was the price that had to be paid for the sins of the past, and I railed at the unfairness that she would be the one to suffer. I'd lay down my life right now if I could take it from her.

My phone was stuffed into the back right pocket of my jeans and started vibrating on my butt. I reached for it and quickly glanced at the screen without moving away from Remi. It was Kathryn, Chase's sister. Somehow we'd managed to remain friends after the disaster, but it was just another secret that weighed on me. Just seeing her name on the screen brought Chase rushing back into my mind and heart, not that Remi's condition hadn't had me thinking about him twenty-four/seven anyway.

As the years passed, I got better at pushing the pain down and hiding it from others, but it was always there, eating away at my soul like a disease. I'd learned not to talk about it, and I'd gotten past the daily bouts of tears, but I still thought about Chase every single day.

I sucked it up for Jensen's sake; the man who'd sacrificed his friendship with Chase and put his whole life on hold to save mine. Still, it was hard to paste on a smile and pretend I was okay when I wasn't. I was plodding through life; my only real purpose had been raising and taking care of Remi. After she was born, there was some happiness and things were easier because she engulfed my world, yet every time I looked at her, I saw him, and it was like a knife carving a new wound in my heart. Two years ago, she got sick and once again, we were all enveloped in misery. My first instinct was to call Chase, but Jensen and I had a huge fight about it, and guilt won out in the end.

So time ticked on and I was certain my soul was damned, but it was clear I was already paying the interest. It was a struggle to get up in the morning and put one foot in front of the other, but what else could I do? I had to put Remi first and I did my best to keep her happy and laughing as much as possible to keep her focus off of her illness.

The whole thing was such a fucked up mess, like a snowball rolling down the side of a cliff, the lie kept growing and growing. After Chase left and my father found out I was pregnant, all hell broke loose when he vowed to smear Chase's name all over the headlines. He was more concerned about his political career than what would happen to me and threatened to hurt Chase's reputation. God forbid the scandal of a state senator's daughter getting knocked up by a professional soccer player who left her high and dry. That's how it would have landed on the headlines and his professional career could have been ruined before it even began. What started out as a decision to do what was best for Chase turned into a nightmare, and I was trapped. Ugh! It still made me sick to think about it.

When Jensen swooped in and claimed responsibility, all of my good intentions to come clean and tell Chase were flushed, but my father calmed down. Everyone ended up paying a huge price. If only I could go back in time, I'd be honest with Chase, lying on the bed in that hotel room in Philadelphia, the consequences be damned. My heart knew that's what I should have done.

My father finally knew the truth, because Jensen spilled it all in a drunken haze after a trip back to Rochester. It was a tortured confession, and it turned uglier when my father railed at me that I was a selfish brat letting Jensen clean up the mess I'd made of my own life. He didn't want to hear my reasons for any of it and especially how he was a big part of the decision.

But, you can't rewind your life just because you know you made the wrong choices. My dad always said hindsight was 20/20 but it didn't do anyone any good to think about what might have been, or what should have been. I'd wanted to make it right a million times in the years since, but how? How could I hurt Jensen after all he'd done, and how could I face Chase, and admit what I'd kept from him? But, Remi might need him and now, I had no choice.

I put on a strong front, but there were times, in private, when I let myself wallow in a pit of self-pity and despair, knowing every bit of it was my fault. No one saw me fall apart anymore, but it still happened. I used to pray that the deep-seated loss would go away, but over time, it became part of me that I needed to survive. The pain and our daughter, who looked so much like him, were the only tangible proof he and I ever existed at all. Every little piece of happiness that I was ever granted had become smeared with guilt, pain, and loss... first Chase, now Remi and Jensen.

In the weak moments when I still thought about Chase, or I saw his expressions on Remi's beautiful little face, I felt like I'd die; as if a giant vacuum sucked all the air out of the atmosphere to suffocate me. It hurt like hell, real physical pain, but as much as I suffered, I knew it didn't compare to what Chase went through when I left him, and what Jensen had suffered since. God, I hated myself and I'd give anything to make her well, and to fix things for Chase, and Jensen.

About a year after my horrific break-up with Chase, and my quickie wedding at the Clemson Municipal Courthouse, Kathryn confronted me with what I'd done. Chase was still destroyed, and she wanted answers. She, along with her entire family, expected Chase and me to live happily ever after. I couldn't blame her for being hurt and confused. After listening to how much he was still suffering, I broke down in a sobbing heap and revealed the entire sordid thing. At first, she was furious and threatened to get on a plane to England to tell Chase. The memory and the misery that went with it were still as vivid as the day it happened.

I had fallen to the floor, while she loomed over me with disgust on her face. "How could you do that to him, Teagan?"

I was crying so hard I could hardly speak, my body shaking violently. "Puh-please, do-don't! Do you thu-think it will he-help Chase?" I begged in ragged gasps. "It won't. Telling him won't change anything. It won't change the fact that he's there and I'm here, or that I'm married. Don't make him suffer more by making him relive it." I reached up and grabbed her hand, my eyes pleading with her. "Please, Kat."

"You selfish bitch!" she screamed at me. "Do you understand what he's gone through not knowing why you dumped him? Don't you know what you've done?"

My heart was already shredded but somehow managed to break even more. I did understand. I played it over and over in my head since the day it happened. "It's not that simple!" I pleaded. "Do you think this has been easy for me? Do you think I haven't regretted it every second of every day? Chase wouldn't have gone to London. He wouldn't have his career if I told him I was pregnant." I bowed my head and cried like I'd never cried, leaning over my knees and the pain in my torso threating to rip me open. *"Then when my father found out he threatened to drag Chase through the mud. Like he knocked me up and left because he cared more about his career than he did me, because, God forbid, his only child would do something so irresponsible to sully the family name. I was going to risk it anyway, Kat. I bought a plane ticket, but before I could leave, Jensen went to my dad behind my back and claimed the baby was his and my father suddenly backed off Chase."*

"So what? What could your father have done to him? I don't understand you!"

"I was stupid and scared. Playing professionally was all Chase ever wanted, I couldn't take a chance he'd lose what might be his only chance. I couldn't tell him about the baby."

She shook her head angrily, her blonde hair whooshing around her slender shoulders. *"Do you think he can't count?"*

I lifted my hands and let them fall to my sides in defeat. *"I wasn't thinking straight and I just shut myself in. I didn't think he'd find out."*

"So, instead, you let him think you screwed his best friend the moment he left?"

"It was better than letting him think I betrayed him before he left, wasn't it? If he found out about the pregnancy and at the same time it became known I married Jensen, he'd think we were fooling around before he left."

"No! I saw what he went through!"

"No? Are you kidding? I know him better than anyone and I know what he wanted and I know what would hurt him the least!"

"Nothing could have been worse for him than thinking he meant so little to you, or to Jensen that you'd both betrayed him. Except this. This is a million times worse!"

"No, it isn't. He's got his career, and he's rocking it. The whole world calls him ACE. He's dating. He seems happy. Kat, please don't

tell him in a fit of rage. Please, just think about the repercussions before you do something that will only hurt him more."

"You have no right to lecture me on the rights and wrongs of hurting Chase! You should tell him the truth!" She pointed her finger at me, her voice dripping venom as she paused to consider my words. I deserved her hatred and I nodded in defeat.

"You're right. I should. I want to… but would it take away anything he suffered?" I pushed off my knees and landed on my butt, leaning up against the couch in defeat. My eyes were tired, and tears still leaked out, but I shrugged. "Would it change anything? It would only make him relive it, and you know it. He'd throw away his career, the whole thing would be a scandal in the papers, and he'd still hate me."

She sucked in her breath and her head fell back as both hands went to grasp her hair. "What the fuck am I supposed to do? He's my brother! I have to tell him! He deserves to know about his daughter."

I shrugged again, pushing back the long strands of hair that were stuck to my face by the saltiness of dried tears. "I understand, but why? If you think it will help him or make his life easier, then tell him. But please, not if it will only hurt him. Do you think the headlines will be kind to him? It will sell more magazines and get more hits if they paint him as deserting his baby mama for his career. The media only cares about hits, not the truth! Jesus, think about it!! I know he's moved on. Just let him be. I've wanted to go to him a hundred times. I've died over this, but I know it's too late! He'll never forgive me, now, and he's the star of Arsenal, he's always traveling… do you think he has time for Remi now?"

"Teagan, he'd want his child."

I knew she was right, but I said the only thing I could think of; what I knew would make Kat pause. "Would he? It was his decision to go! I didn't tell him to leave." I knew I was twisting the truth, but I didn't know how else to make her see my side of it.

What I didn't tell Kat that day was that I'd already decided to drop out of Clemson and go to London to tell Chase the truth, to let my father do his worst to both of us, political and professional football careers aside, but a woman answered his phone when I called to tell him my flight number, and I learned a few things that I didn't want to know. Against all I believed about Chase and me, it was clear that he'd already moved on. The woman left me in no doubt of her relationship with him.

After that, what options did I have? Chase was screwing some bimbo in London, and Jensen had offered to stand by me. Next to Chase, he was my closest friend. After that conversation, Kathryn didn't contact me for months, and I was scared every day that I'd get a knock on the door and it would be Chase, standing there, muscles coiled with hate simmering in his green eyes. Living without him was hard, but living with his hatred would be worse, and it wouldn't help Remi. That's how I fooled myself, how I justified it in the time since.

I followed Chase's career like gospel and used my sporadic contact with Kathryn to fill in any blanks though I barely asked, and she didn't volunteer very much. At first it was awkward and painful, but I just wanted to know he was okay. From the little she said, he struggled for months, but then, maybe she didn't know about the woman who'd told me they were lovers.

Ugh! It was all so fucked up. I should have still gone to London to confront him, but I was so fragile, heartbroken, and physically sick being pregnant, I didn't have the strength, but more, I was afraid I'd get there and he'd tell me he didn't want me to be tied down. I didn't care if I lived or died, and if it weren't for the baby I was carrying, Chase's baby, I might have done something stupid to end the incredible pain.

The phone in my hand vibrated again, breaking into my thoughts. I sighed before I answered. Life never turns out how you expect; Kat and I were friends, and Chase wasn't part of it.

"Hi, Kat."

"Hi, sweetie," her soft voice came through the phone. Kat was beautiful, her voice was pretty, her demeanor was perfect; even when she was mad at me, was always so level-headed. She was three years older than me, two years older than Chase and worked as a receptionist in a local doctor's office in Greenville. Chase's family wasn't well off; his brother, Kevin, was an electrician, like their dad, and they had both stayed close to home. "How is Remi?"

Remi was always the topic of our conversations, and I understood why, but the sound of Kat's voice asking about her always flooded me with guilt.

I realized I would never have even a moment's peace, ever. The guilt I felt at the pain I'd caused others was devastating, and Kat was another casualty in all of this. I was the worst person in the world and many times, I considered that Remi's illness was some cruel get-even scheme from God. I was at the end of my rope, and without a miracle, I'd have no choice but to contact Chase. Kat's call was just a gentle nudge to bring up, what I'd been trying to avoid.

"She's sleeping," I said softly. "She's weak," my voice cracked. "They want to give her another round of chemotherapy and I'm not sure if I can watch her go through it again."

"Oh, no." Concern laced her voice. "I'm so sorry to hear that. Are there alternatives?"

"Just one. A marrow and stem cell transplant, but to do it they have to radiate her and kill all of her own marrow. If it doesn't work, she'll have no immune system and could die right away." My throat was thick and full of pain. Tears started to stream down my face as I whispered into the phone. "I'm so scared, Kat."

"Should I come? I'm sure David would be okay with it, and Mom and Dad can help with the twins." Kat and her husband David had a modest home, not two miles from where

Kevin, Chase and she grew up. Her parents still had that house, one that I remembered well. A few months after we started dating, Chase took me home over a weekend in the spring semester of my freshman year, so I could meet them. He was supposed to sleep on the couch, but he snuck up into his old room and we had sex all night. I was scared to death they'd catch us and hate me for life, but he'd managed to get his way with me. Like always.

"Um… I'd love to see you, but I don't want to impose."

"You should have someone with you. Jensen's gone on assignment, right? I was making dinner last night and I could have sworn that I heard his voice on the TV. Alan was watching Monday Night Football in the other room."

"Yes. I don't even know what team is playing. Dallas is playing in San Francisco, I think."

"What's going to happen with Remi? Do you have a donor?"

"Not yet. I tested, but I don't have enough of the markers. There are national donor banks and they're looking. If we don't find one, we'll have no choice but to put her back on chemo."

"I thought that parents would be an auto-match."

"I wish. There are all kinds of antigen markers that measure how your immune system works and in order for it to work there are several levels that I don't match her. The best matches are usually siblings, so…"

"Teagan… what about Chase?"

I sniffed and sat up in the bed at her words. "I know, I have to call him…" I closed my eyes and drew in a shaky voice. "He'll hate me even more than he already does and I'm not sure I'll be able to stand that."

"He doesn't hate you. You have to do it for Remi."

"I know, but there's no guarantee Chase's marrow would match, either."

"You can have another baby. Would the cord blood work instead?"

I felt my face flood with heat. I'd already considered it. "Maybe, but it's a risk to wait that long. It could be a year. Besides, a baby with Jensen wouldn't be a close enough match."

"I wasn't thinking about Jensen."

My breath rushed out of my body at the speed of light. I knew I had no choice. Chase was my last hope to save Remi but my heart fell in anticipation of his reaction. It would be hard enough just learning he had a little girl and that she was sick.

"Oh, God, Kat. I can't believe you're even suggesting such a thing. How would that go? Hey, Chase, I know I lied to you and broke your heart, but by the way? We have a sick kid I didn't tell you about, and I need your sperm to make another one? Right. This will be hard enough."

"I know it won't be easy, but— it's unavoidable."

I knew where she was going and I interrupted her in panic. "You promised not to tell him," I said emphatically. "You can't just drop a bomb like this. He'll be pissed at you, too."

"Yes, he'll be hurt, but more than that, he'll be mad. I have struggled with this ever since I found out about Remi. And since she's been sick, I've picked up the phone a hundred times. He'll probably never forgive me."

I sighed, the air filling my lungs so full it almost hurt. More tears squeezed out from closed eyes as my face crumpled. "That's why I have to tell him, myself."

"Yes, you do. I should have had my head examined to keep quiet this long."

"It's not your fault. You only agreed because I convinced you it would just rip him open again."

"You were so hurt, Teagan. You both were, but now I can't see another way."

I ran a nervous hand through my hair and looked at the sleeping form of my little girl. Kat was right, but I'd sell my soul if I had any other options. I started crying in heartbroken sobs. "It's such a mess. I do—don't know wh—what to do. I'd give anything to go back and have a do-over."

Kathryn sighed heavily on the other end of the line. "Okay, I'm coming to Atlanta as soon as I get things arranged so I can be with you. But, put on your big girl panties and don't wait to tell Chase. I think he's on a short break and this would be a good time for him to come."

"Yeah. His next game is in Brasilia in three days."

"Teagan," she said knowingly.

"I can't he—help it, Ka—Kat." I slumped over my lap, one leg hanging off the edge of the bed, and the other curled under me. I knew how pathetic I must seem as I wiped at the tears on my cheeks with both of my hands. I hadn't seen Chase in almost six years, and while I wasn't sure where Jensen was traveling, I always knew where he was. He was dating some woman who used to be one of the team trainers and he looked happy, finally. I'd seen her with him in pictures at events and in some of the industry and entertainment articles, and the last thing he deserved was having me screw up his life. "I don't think I'll be able to take him looking at me with contempt on his face."

"He doesn't talk about you, so I don't know how he feels, but I do know that you need to tell him, for Remi's sake. This is about her, not you, or even Chase."

I listened to her in silence, and then glanced down at my little girl. She was shivering so I scooted closer again and pulled her blanket tighter around her little body, laying down but still holding the phone to my ear. I started crying hard enough for Kat to hear me. "I know."

34

"Oh, honey. What about Jensen? How is he?" Kat asked, hesitantly.

"We're both dealing with the illness. I think he appreciates his time away. He gets to be normal."

"No, I meant, between the two of you."

"Not much has changed. He's always been a very good friend. I owe him everything and love him, but it's not the same. I've tried so hard to open my heart."

"How will he take calling Chase?"

"Sore subject. He won't even talk about Chase."

"Doesn't he realize—?"

"Yes, he knows it has to be done, but he tends to internalize. It's like if we don't discuss it, it's not real, and it's become easier not to."

"The whole thing is so goddamned tragic for all of you. Jensen was always a great guy, but you never forget your first love."

I closed my eyes as her words made my heart break all over again. "Especially when his eyes are looking up at me every single day. She's so like him, and not just her face."

"I can see that," she added sadly.

"Do you have Chase's phone number? The old one I had for him is assigned to some woman named Brenda." I sensed Kat's question in a couple of beats of silence. "I tried it on his birthday, once," I admitted.

Kat cleared her throat before she answered. "I don't have it memorized, but I'll look it up when we hang up and text it to you. It's going to be, okay, Teagan." Her words were stern and matter-of-fact. "Trust me. Chase isn't a monster."

My heart surged at the thought of having his number in my possession and I doubted I'd be strong enough to resist calling him, even if Remi wasn't at the core of it.

"I know. He's perfect." I switched hands on the phone, half holding it in place with my shoulder, and then started to stroke Remi's silky dark hair off of her face. Finally, it was back and long enough that she didn't look like a cancer patient. I didn't even want to tell her she might have to start treatment again because I knew she'd be scared and hysterical.

"No, he isn't. Don't think about what will happen once he arrives. You'll deal with it as it comes: just call him."

"What if he won't come?"

"I think he will. I gotta get back to work. My break is almost over and I have to have a couple of minutes to send you that number. I'll call you as soon as I have things arranged to visit. I love you."

"Okay, love you. Thanks, Kat."

I didn't have any siblings, and I was thankful she was still in my life and such a good friend. Fifteen seconds after the call ended, the number came across in a text.

+447 1264 53427

My heart began to pound. I felt like it would fly from my chest. I got a slight reprieve when my daughter stirred beside me.

"Mommy?" her sleepy voice called softly. I turned back toward her, leaving my phone lying on the bed behind me. "I'm cold."

"I know baby. I'll get one of those warm blankets you like." I stroked her hair back with gentle, repetitive strokes that I knew she liked and leaned down to place a kiss on her forehead. She smelled sweet; like shampoo and powder. "Are you hungry? Do you want a snack?"

She shook her head and my heart fell. "Will you watch TV with me when you come back?"

"You need to eat more, baby."

"I don't feel like it."

Remi was so grown up for her age. She was only five, but we played a lot of games designed to teach her many things. She could read before she went to kindergarten, and I'd continued to work with her when she got sick and couldn't attend school.

I'd been lucky. When Remi got sick, Jensen insisted I quit my nursing job to devote all my attention and care to her.

Guilt washed over me. There was so much that I could never repay him for, and his kindness only increased my shame. I should divorce him for no other reason than to give him back his life, but as long as Remi was sick, I needed him; she needed him. He deserved so much better than I could give; someone who could love him with her whole heart. I knew he loved me, and I knew he loved Remi. I wasn't sure which would be worse for him; leaving or staying. He deserved the type of love I used to have with Chase. Everyone deserves that, at least once in their life.

I got up and walked to the door of Remi's room, opening it and searching the stark halls for a nurse. The hospital was new and modern, but it was still a hospital, sterile and cold. They kept the temperature down to kill germs, but the patients suffered for it. I knew where the warmer was at the nurses' station and made my way toward it. It was hard to keep track of all the nurses. Remi had been in the Children's Hospital several times, but there were so many nurses, and she never seemed to be on the same floor, I couldn't keep track.

"Hello, may I please get a warm blanket? Remi is shivering."

A pretty young CNA smiled at me. "Of course. Is one enough?"

"May we have two, please?"

She nodded and disappeared around a corner. The nursing assistants all wore blue, the nurses a dark olive green, and housekeeping and food service staff had to wear dusty pink scrubs. It was always obvious who had what job.

When the young woman returned she handed them over. "Is Sally her nurse?"

"I'm not sure," I murmured, taking the blankets from her. They felt wonderfully warm to the touch. "I can't remember what the names are on the board. I'm a bit scattered today."

"That's okay," she said; understanding. "I'll find out. Should I bring some juice or a cookie if the nurse says she's allowed to have it?"

I offered a tired smile. "She said she wasn't hungry, but maybe if it's in front of her, she'll want it. Can you bring some hot tea, two cups and a couple of cookies? Maybe if we have a tea party, she'll try."

"That's a great idea!"

I glanced at her name badge. "Thank you, Alissa. You're very sweet." I turned to go back to Remi's room before the blankets cooled.

"You're so welcome. Your daughter is so beautiful. Such a gentle soul and so brave."

I nodded and smiled again, though sadness rocked every cell in my body. "Thank you. I'm grateful for her every day."

Remi had turned over in her bed and had the TV on. She was still shivering, her teeth starting to chatter, but she'd managed to turn on SpongeBob and was smiling up at the screen. "Mommy, this is the chocolate show," she explained the episode. "SpongeBob is so silly."

I unfolded the blankets and put them around her, taking the remote so I could cover her from the neck down. I pushed the blankets around her. "Get warm. Mommy ordered a tea party for us."

Her eyes lit up as she studied me. "Mommy, do you need a nap?"

I nodded and sat on the bed next to her. "Probably. I'm a little tired, baby."

"Why don't Cindy and Wally come to visit me this time?" she asked about her best friends?

It had been my rule to always tell her the truth in a way she could understand for her age. "Well, your leukemia makes it hard for your body to fight off infection, so the doctor's don't let anyone but Mommy and Jensey visit. That's why we have to wear these funny yellow dresses." I smiled. I was thankful we didn't have to wear masks like we had done on more than one occasion. They were awful and used to scare her.

"When can I go home? I want to play with Cindy and Wally. And I want to make cupcakes and sleep with Jewel." Jensen gave her a stuffed black lab for Christmas two years earlier and promised her that when she was better, we'd get a real one. It took her five days to name a stuffed animal because she wanted it to be the name of the actual puppy when it was possible to get one. She insisted it had to be perfect, and I thought it was.

"That reminds me. After the tea party, you'll have a nap and Mommy will run home and get Jewel for you? Would you like that?"

She nodded. "I miss Jewel the most of all."

"She misses you, too, baby girl." I reached out and ran a hand over her head.

Alissa, dressed in the required yellow gown and blue rubber gloves knocked on the door. "Knock, knock!" she said happily. "Special delivery for Remi's tea party! These cookies look yummy!"

Smiling brightly, she wheeled in a grey plastic cart with cookies, two cups, tea bags, and miniature pot of hot water.

Remi clapped her hands three times. "Yay! Are they chocolate chip?"

"Is there any other kind?"

"Yes. Peanut butter and oatmeal," Remi answered with a pronounced nod. Alissa transferred the offering on the bedside table and pushed it closer until it was situated across the top of the bed, then pressed the button that raised the top half of the bed so Remi was almost sitting up.

Remi pushed the blanket down and then reached across to place the tea bags in the cups. "There are only two, but if you want some, I can share mine." Remi looked at Alissa hopefully.

"I'd love to, doll, but I have to work. Maybe next time, okay?" She leaned over and patted her hand.

"Darn. Okay."

I picked up the pot of water and carefully poured them into the two cups as the nurse left.

Remi picked up a cookie and took a bite. "Mommy, am I gonna die?" She was serious, exuding a calmness that I'd never manage to echo.

I almost gasped out loud at her bluntness, but amazed at how grown up she seemed. "Goodness, no!" I said emphatically. I didn't know for sure what was going to happen, but I couldn't tell her.

"It's okay if I am."

"No, it isn't okay, Remi! What would Mommy do without you? The doctors are working hard to make you better."

"I thought I was better. I thought that bad medicine put Leuky to sleep." She took another small bite of her cookie.

I nodded, trying to figure out a way to have this discussion with a five-year-old.

"You were, honey, but Leuky is very naughty. It doesn't always do as it's told. We have to fight it some more to get rid of it for good." I hated that she gave the disease a name, but leukemia was too long for her to say when she was first diagnosed at three years old.

Her green eyes, so much like her fathers, filled with tears. "I don't want the mean medicine, again, Mommy. I don't want my hair to fall out again. Jesus doesn't want my hair to fall out. Can't he tell Leuky to leave? Like he fixed that blind little boy in the book?"

I'd been reading her a book filled with stories from the new testament of the bible told in a kid-friendly way. She particularly liked the stories about Jesus. My heart broke inside my chest.

"He's trying, honey. Sometimes Jesus asks other people to help him. All of these nurses and doctors are working very hard to help get you better, too." It was harder than hell not to burst out crying. "Do you understand, sweet pea?"

"Yeah, but do I have to have the mean medicine?"

I shook my head. "We hope not. We're going to try something else. There is someone out there who has the same type of bone marrow you do, so they are going to give you some so you can start growing healthy blood. It won't hurt except a needle, but you're a big girl about those."

"Who is it? Is it another kid who is all better already?"

"We don't know yet, baby. There is a big list of people who offered and they all have to have a test first. Don't worry, Remi, we'll find someone, okay?"

She smiled wide. "Okay. Mommy, you're not eating your cookie!"

I picked it up and took a bite to appease her, but it tasted like cardboard in my mouth. Chase might not match either, and if I called him it might backfire and blow up all of our lives. It was a chance to save her and not have to wait for a match.

I didn't even have the phone in my hand, but my heart felt like it would fly from my chest. My prayers would be answered, or the world could end. I glanced at the silver frame sitting on the nightstand next to her bed and knew that I had no choice. I took out my phone…

Chapter 2

CHASE

Six years since I left her.

Six fucking years.

It seemed like I had no choice at the time; like it was the start of a dream, not the beginning of a nightmare. It was the biggest mistake of my life.

The offer from the English Arsenal Football Club was a once-in-a-lifetime opportunity that I couldn't pass up, no matter how much it ripped me apart to leave Teagan behind. Our plan was for her to finish college then come over there, too. It never happened.

Somehow, it all got fucked up. Royally fucked up. I spent years trying to figure out why it happened without finding any logical answers and then, I was determined to forget about her. I threw myself into the game, booze, and numerous women, but nothing helped most of the time. If I were honest, the pain never really went away and I felt the loss every goddamned day. I knew I should never have left, and that only made it worse. It was Teagan, and not soccer, who was my once-in-a-lifetime everything, but I thought we were madly in love and I completely trusted that we'd make it through it… I completely trusted her. We knew it would be a difficult couple of years, but I had no reason to doubt that things wouldn't go as planned. I thought we were invincible. Yet, not six months after I left, she married my best friend behind my back.

Some best friend. Anger cut through me like a red-hot knife and settled in to sear my gut and tighten my chest. There was no one I hated more.

My heart ached whenever I allowed myself to think about it. She called and tried to explain once, but I didn't want to hear it. No words could justify it. I felt betrayed; too devastated to find the will to function, let alone listen. Looking at her would have sliced me open to bleed out right in front of her, and after a betrayal like that, I'd be damned if I'd let her see me suffer.

Jensen tried to talk to me, too, but I was afraid if I saw him, one of us would die. What did it fucking matter anyway? There was no reason that could make it better, more believable, or easier to accept. I'd closed down, focused on the team, and stopped corresponding with either of them. It was the only way to breathe.

My eyes burned and my throat tightened. After all this time, it was still killing me. So often, I ached to call her, my soul crying out for hers, my mind railing that it was all a bad dream and if I could only hear that sweet voice, my reality would be righted. Over time, I realized keeping as busy as possible was the only thing to keep the memories from eating me alive. I was lucky that most of the places I played, and in London, I had zero memories of Teagan to haunt me, but Arsenal and its world-class program wasn't worth it. A huge career and being one of the top ten soccer players in the world meant nothing. Nothing was worth losing Teagan, but I'd made a life for myself despite her. In spite of her.

Somehow, I moved on. I breathed in and out. I waited, prayed for, and crawled toward the day when it wouldn't hurt.

I was still crawling on the inside, but I'd learned how to camouflage it so no one could see it anymore. I was sure part of me was dead inside.

My parents and siblings knew not to mention her after the first few attempts. The rage and drinking binges that resulted had finally kept them quiet. Kat looked at me with a sort of incredible sorrow, and even Kevin stopped badgering me.

"Just leave it alone, Kev! I can't fucking stand thinking about what she's doing with Jensen. Nothing will justify it! If Jensen was bleeding out in the street, the reason still wouldn't be good enough for her to be with him. It makes me fucking sick!"

I'd flung my mother's Ming vase at my brother and it barely missed his head; shattering in a million pieces against the wall behind him. He stood there stunned for a split second as my chest heaved and his image blurred behind a haze of fury and tears. Then, he rushed at me, tackling me to the ground. He beat the shit out of me, leaving me broken and crying her name, asking God why she wasn't mine, begging for relief that never came, wishing I could die right there because I couldn't see any other way to end the horrible pain. I didn't know if I was hitting at Kevin or Teagan's memory, but afterward, he dropped to his knees and held on to me as I fell apart. The whole family looked on in stunned shock, all of them powerless to help me. It was New Year's Eve and I'd gotten drunk off my ass to try to forget. Everyone left me alone ever since. My mother never even mentioned that vase. She found it at a garage sale and it was probably fake, but she loved to pretend it was real, and I had destroyed it. One more thing I shouldn't have done that piled on the guilt. I'd ruined my own fucking life by leaving and I had to live with it.

As time moved on the devastating pain eased little by little, and faded into a dull, ever-present ache. I came home to the States less because being there surrounded me with

Teagan's essence, her memory, and people who knew her and might talk about her. Not knowing where she was, or anything about her, made it easier and possible to survive.

Now, I was on a plane on my way to Atlanta fucking Georgia, because of a few well-scripted words that came across my phone via text message.

Chase, Kat gave me your number. Don't be mad. I need you. It's an emergency.

Please come ASAP.
Teagan

I ran my hand through my hair. Kat. My mind screamed at her betrayal. My sister, Kathryn was tight-lipped, telling me nothing beyond where I could find her. Apparently, she'd kept in touch with Teagan all these years, and that enraged me. Goddamn, traitor.

"Hmmph!" I huffed in disgust. So much for blood being thicker than water.

When I called Kathryn to confront her, all she'd say was that Teagan and Jensen had moved to Atlanta three years earlier when Jensen got a job with ESPN, and I'd have to wait for Teagan to explain the rest. He must not be very high on the ESPN food chain or I'd have known about his job there.

I didn't understand why, but I was pissed at my sister. Why would Teagan leave her family...and mine, to live in a strange city with a man who was probably gone more than he was home? It made no sense. But then, none of her decisions made sense since I left. Not since she chose to marry someone else.

The burning ache I'd thought I'd buried flared anew twenty-four hours earlier when her name appeared at the end of her message. I'd felt like a sledgehammer just flew at high velocity into my gut, and left me gasping as the air left my lungs. I could hear that voice saying the words on the screen as if she were standing right next to me. My heart exploded and blood rushed to my face like liquid fire.

I'd thought nothing would separate us; not distance...not anyone, or anything. Ever. I was so in love I must have been blind to what was really going on behind my back. And yet, years later, all she had to do was crook her little finger and I was dragging my sorry ass halfway across the world without knowing why.

"Welcome to Atlanta, Georgia. We thank you for flying with us today. We know you have many choices for..." The mad rushing of blood in my ears muffled the flight attendant's words. My skin vibrated as anticipation throbbed through me, and I mentally shook myself. I needed to get my shit together. I couldn't allow Teagan to see how much this still mattered. I had to be cool, calm... blasé'. She couldn't know how she'd destroyed me. I'd worked hard to build an aloof persona off the field, and a superstar one on it. When I started to stand out, the sports world shortened my name from Chase to Ace, and I embraced it.

As I gathered my carry on, I braced myself for what I would see in a few short minutes. Would Jensen be with her? Could I take that? I wasn't sure. I rubbed my hand over the back of my neck in agitation and then held it out in front of me. I was visibly shaking, so I curled my fingers into a fist in an attempt to steady myself. I was a bad motherfucker, solid as a rock, on top of my game and in the best shape of my life, so why the hell was I shaking like a pussy? As I started to walk out of the plane, I willed myself to calm down. I settled a cold mask into place over my face, praying to God it would remain unmoved when I saw her.

The seconds pounded in my head as my footsteps closed the distance to the main terminal, heavy and suffocating. I struggled to fill my lungs with air; sure I'd lose my breath forever the minute I laid eyes on her. Would she be different? I wanted her to be unrecognizable... resistible... no longer the woman I fell in love with... no longer my Teagan.

Please, God... let me not give a shit. After everything I'd suffered, would that be so much to ask?

Somehow over the years, the bitterness and anger lessened and most of what I remembered was the intense love and longing. She haunted my dreams more times than I could count, and every time I woke up in a cold sweat missing her or wanting her, I wanted to scream.

I dug down deep for the anger I'd need to make it through the next couple of days. Two days was all I would subject myself to. Then I was gone and I'd put her in the past where she belonged. I had a game in Brasília on Saturday that I couldn't miss and I was thankful for my contract.

What the hell am I doing here, anyway? I argued with myself. I should have used the game to skip it all together, but what if she was in trouble? My lips pressed together in anger. What the fuck did it matter to me? I shouldn't care at all. I sighed heavily. Taking care of Teagan was Jensen's fucking job now, not mine.

Against my will, I searched the countless faces, looking for those soft brown eyes that used to own my soul. I stopped in the middle of the terminal, as my phone buzzed in my pocket.

"Yeah?"

"Hey, lovie. I got your message," Bronwyn said casually.

"I sent it twelve hours ago. Thanks for the prompt response." Sarcasm dripped from my voice. She didn't notice.

"So you're in the U.S.? Ace, I mean... why?"

I was distracted as I kept searching for Teagan. "I thought you said you got my message. I told you that a friend needs me."

"For what?" She sounded pissed, but then, "pissed" and "I don't give a shit" were her two most prominent gears.

"I don't know, Bronwyn. I'll call you when I know more."

"I'm going to bed, so don't call until morning, hmm?" Her voice was bored and unconcerned; her whiny voice in her English accent was suddenly annoying as hell.

"The time difference is six hours, so hopefully I'll be sleeping when you wake up. Remember, my body is on London time."

"Oh, yeah. Well, then just call when you can. Good night, lovie."

"Bye." It annoyed the hell out of me when she called me that, and she knew it. I shoved the phone into my back pocket of my dark jeans, my mind immediately dismissing the woman on the phone.

Where was Teagan? I scratched my stomach through the fine linen of my dark blue button down. I'd left it un-tucked, only taking time to change my pants and shove three changes of clothes and my running shoes into a small bag before rushing straight to the airport. I left the club immediately after speaking to Kat.

I was tired and impatient as I put my hands on my hips and turned, stopping dead when I saw her moving slowly in my direction, weaving through the crowds. She looked thinner and more fragile; her skin seemed more translucent against the darkness of her flowing hair, still as long and luxurious as I remembered. My breath caught in my throat at the sight, my heart thudding sickeningly in my chest as time rewound in an instant. I wanted it to stop beating. I didn't care if it killed me or if I had to rip it from my chest; I just wanted it to fucking stop.

Her brown eyes were huge as she looked up into my face, still owning me as much as she ever had, as she closed the last few yards between us. The sadness surrounding her was so heavy I could almost taste it.

"Hello, Chase." Her voice rocked through me. The same voice that still haunted my dreams on occasion.

My hand moved to my chest, seeking to ease the tightness that prevented me from speaking. I swallowed hard as I took in her smallness in jeans and summer top that left her shoulders and arms completely bare, except for the thin straps. The yellows and oranges in the floral print made her hair appear darker and emphasized the faint flush on her cheeks.

My arms ached to reach for her and drag her against my body. The pull was tangible and I could see the same battle flash across her beautiful features. She was still so goddamned beautiful.

"Teagan…" Her name fell from my lips unwillingly as emotions I'd tried to ignore, surfaced.

We stood there, staring at each other until finally, my left hand reached for her right one. Our fingers entwined as easily as if we'd never been apart, and her eyes filled with glistening tears and then two fat drops rolled down her cheeks. The years fell away as, unable to help myself; I pulled her to me, and gathering her close then turned my face into her hair. She still wore the same perfume… still felt perfect pressed close to me. My breath left my lungs. Her arms flew around my neck as I lifted her easily into my embrace as a deep sob broke from her chest.

"Chase. Oh, God. Thank you. I honestly didn't think you would come."

My hand cupped the back of her head and protectiveness filled every cell in my body. No matter what happened, I couldn't stand to see her in pain. "What is this about? Why now?" I asked softly, despite the loud noises of the terminal around us.

"Not here. I'll explain everything, but can we go?" she asked brokenly.

I released her reluctantly, nodding as she wiped her fingers under both of her eyes at the same time and attempted a weak smile.

I nodded. "Okay. I don't have any other bags. Let's go."

Somehow we ended up near an SUV I didn't recognize. I didn't know what I expected… that she'd have her old beat-up car from college? My heart fell to my stomach when I opened the back door to stow my bag and I came face to face with a booster seat.

She has a child. I felt like I'd just been slammed into a brick wall at high speed.

My knuckles turned white as my fingers tightened around the edge of the door until I thought they would break. I wasn't prepared for the possibility that she'd ever had a child that wasn't mine. The years of ignorance had been more of a blessing than I could have possibly imagined.

My chin jutted out in painful defiance, trying to steady the shaking that had overcome my hands, again. I slammed the passenger door as Teagan slid behind the wheel, her head snapping toward me at the sound.

I was pissed, hurt, dying. Just… fucking dying. Again. I was right back in the hell that had taken me years to crawl out of. I couldn't believe I'd subjected myself to this bullshit again. I was insane to drop everything, and leave my girlfriend behind. For what?

"Chase, I—" she began.

My head snapped in her direction, and I knew my expression was harsh and hateful, but I couldn't do anything to mask it. "Teagan. I'm here, okay. I don't know what the fuck possessed me, but I'm here. What is it you want from me? Why now?" My voice was hard, a sharp contrast to how I'd been inside the airport, but I chalked it up to shock and longing for something that no longer existed between us.

"Wow. I guess I deserve this."

"Probably, yeah." I swallowed and turned forward to stare out the windshield at the concrete wall of the parking garage.

She sucked in her breath and left the keys in the ignition and the motor running, turning in her seat toward me as cool air began to pour out of the air conditioning vents. I leaned my elbow on the window, my forehead on my hand and I willed myself to keep my eyes straight ahead. I wouldn't be able to think if I looked at her and I needed to hold it together. The backs of my eyes burned and it disgusted me that I still cared this much about a woman who broke my heart without a word.

"I'm sorry, Chase. I didn't know what to do. I was young and stupid..."

I couldn't argue with her so I didn't utter a sound.

"I wanted you to go to England and not worry about me."

As if that were even possible, my mind screamed. I didn't want to talk about the past. "It's moot now, isn't it? Ancient history."

"No, I need you to understand..."

Something inside me broke and all my good intentions to keep calm were lost. "I needed to understand six goddamned years ago and you didn't fucking care! In fact, you married my best friend in just a few months. Thanks for that, by the way. It really was the cherry on top of losing you. It kept my focus razor sharp." Sarcasm and pain dripped off every word I spat out.

Her forehead dropped to her hands on the top of the wheel, shoulders shaking gently as she wept quietly. "Jensen took care of me when I needed someone."

"You never gave me the opportunity to take care of you, Teagan."

"That's not fair. Yes, I wanted you to have your dream, but you were the one who left. It was your choice to go."

"We talked about it after I got the offer, Teagan! For the two weeks before I left! I thought it was our choice! You knew…it was for us. For our future!"

She snuffled and put the back of her hand to her mouth as her face crumpled and her eyes closed. Her chin began to tremble and tears started to flow. I could no longer keep my eyes off of her. She nodded through her crying. "You're right. But… thu-things happened and I cuh-couldn't tell you. You would have…"

"Couldn't tell me what? That you were screwing Jensen behind my back? That you couldn't even wait until I left? Was it going on before I even left the country?"

She cried harder, shaking her head in a silent plea. "No! Chase, please! Jus-just listen…"

"Teagan… no. The time to talk was six years ago. Now, I just want to know why I'm here right now. I have a life, a job, a woman! Tell me what's going on, right goddamn, now!"

She gasped and her eyes widened in surprise.

"Did you think I'd cry over you forever? That I'd never touch anyone else after you?" I knew my words were like a knife in her heart, and part of me wanted her to suffer like I'd suffered.

I recognized the pain on her face. It was my pain, too.

She wiped at her eyes and drew in her breath, shakily. "No." She shook her head, still looking at me with pleading eyes. "I didn't expect you to be alone."

I felt guilty for wanting to hurt her and tried to shove it down. Fucking hell. I ran a hand over my face.

"Just tell me what you need," I said wearily. I was tired from the flight, tired of arguing, tired of hurting.

"Are you married?"

I didn't answer, but looked away, the muscle in my jaw flexing against my will. How dare she ask me that?

"My little girl is very sick. She has Leukemia."

I paused, suddenly sorry that I'd yelled at her. "I'm sorry, Teagan." I was, but I still didn't understand why I was there. "But, what does that have to do with me?"

"I wanted her... I mean she's..." Teagan cleared her throat. "Uh, she needs a transplant. A bone marrow transplant could save her and we can't find a donor match. She's gone through chemotherapy twice and she went into remission last year, but it's back. It was so horrible watching her go through treatment." Teagan was crying brokenly, struggling to talk and wiping at her nose and eyes with a wadded up tissue. "I don't want to put her through it again and we're running out of time. I couldn't bear to lose her, Chase. She's been so brave, but she knows how sick she is. My dad and I were tested to donate for her, but, uh..."

My heart ached for her, despite how much she'd hurt me. No one should be faced with losing a child. No matter what, Teagan didn't deserve that.

"Do you need money?" I was playing professionally and one thing I had, was money. My father and mother were retired and big into philanthropy. Maybe one of them knew someone at a national registry and could bump the little girl up on the list. "I'll call my dad, and maybe he can help find a donor..." My father's electrical business was modest, but he donated to many charities and knew a lot of people in high places.

"Um..." She reached out and grabbed my hand so hard it hurt. My fingers threaded with hers. Despite it all, I wanted to ease her pain. Tears fell in silent rivers from her eyes. "Chase, will you test? Please?"

"I will, but what about Jensen and his famil—" I began.

She shook her head, her fingers almost crushing mine as her eyes closed. "No."

"No?" I was confused. "He won't test?" I couldn't wrap my mind around it. Jensen might be a lot of things, but he wasn't heartless.

"They won't match. Jensen isn't her father."

The air left my chest. "What?"

"Jensen isn't Remi's father."

My mind raced and my lungs constricted. Did Teagan screw some random man?

"Chase, please don't be angry." She handed me her phone the screen illuminated with a picture of a beautiful little girl with two missing front teeth, glossy deep brown hair, and white porcelain skin like her mothers with a healthy pink flush to her cheeks. Laughter danced in the dark green orbs… "I'm so sorry."

I started to shake again as my vision blurred as I looked at the photo. "Those are my eyes," I said flatly. "My eyes."

She nodded as her voice broke on a sob. "I know. Isn't she just beautiful?"

"You kept this from me all this time? You married Jensen and let him raise my kid? How could you do this to me, Teagan?" An invisible vacuum sucked the air from my lungs. "I can't fucking believe this is happening." I felt like I was a spectator watching some nightmare unfold before me. If it weren't for the insatiable burn that ate up all of my oxygen, I wouldn't have believed it was real.

"I didn't know what to do, Chase. I knew if I told you I was pregnant, you'd leave London and your team behind."

"Damn right I would have, Teagan!" I yelled the words so loudly she jumped in her seat.

"It was my right to know! Jesus Christ! I'm…" I shook my head in disbelief. "It should have been my choice! What right did you have to keep this from me? What fucking right?"

55

Rage filled me at the same time that my heart broke into a thousand pieces. I had a daughter that I'd been robbed of and she was very sick. "Why in the hell didn't you call me when she first got sick, at least?" Tears rolled down my face. "You gave my child to another man! How could you, Teagan? I thought we loved each other!"

"We did. I thought I was doing the right thing. I loved you enough to... let you have your dream. I still love you, Chase!"

"My dream... was you! You were the goddamn dream! Soccer is a game. A career, and that's all! How could you not know that? Nothing meant more to me than you!" I swiped at the wetness on my face as my heart shattered. "When you married Jensen, I didn't care if I lived or died! I couldn't fathom why. My whole world ended; I hated everything! I didn't think you could hurt me more, until this moment. You sit there and tell me you still love me when you kept my child from me?"

She was sobbing full force as I tried to pull my hand from hers, but she tightened her hold. "No, Chase, pl-please," she cried. "Remi could die. I can't go through that without you. Chase!" Her head dropped to my shoulder above our joined hands. "Please. I didn't give her to Jensen. I didn't. She knows he's not her father. She kn-knows..."

I leaned my head back in the seat. I was drowning, my heart exploding. I'd never hurt as bad but hearing her anguish only made it worse. "But you could let her go through her life without me? I'm so mad at you, Teagan," I spat out, even as my arms closed around her shaking body. "I want to hate you, it hurts so goddamn much!"

Her hands found their way into my hair at the back of my head, clutching as she cried into my shoulder and I found myself smoothing hers down her back as we both sobbed into each other. I wanted to hate her, but somehow holding Teagan eased the devastating ache. Finally, her tears subsided and I found my voice. My instincts wanted to comfort and kiss her, to let myself feel, but my heart was still breaking.

"I want to meet her."

Teagan nodded and pulled back. The tears still clung to her lashes as she searched my expression. "Of course. Can you forgive me?" She held both sides of my face in her hands and I wanted to lean into one of them. Again I resisted and pulled away abruptly.

"I don't know yet. What you've done is…"

"Unforgivable." It was the truth. "I know." She nodded. "I'll understand if you can't."

I ran a hand through my hair as she moved awkwardly back into the driver's seat to put it into reverse. "Is her name short for something? It's unusual."

"Yes. Remilia Victoria."

I sat in silence as it sank in. "Roma and Amelia?" I asked incredulously.

"Yes." Teagan's response was whisper quiet.

"You named her after my mother and you didn't let me know her? Didn't let any of us… know her?"

"After I found out I was pregnant, I was scared and alone. I knew I would lose your family, too. And I love your mom as much as I did mine. Naming her Remilia Victoria was a way to keep her close, and a connection to you."

Roma and Amelia were my mother's first and middle names, and Victoria was after Teagan's mom. I shook my head in disbelief. "Why would you name her after my mother and then not tell me about her?"

She shrugged, her voice breaking. "You were half a world away."

"I didn't have to be," I said quietly. I was numb now. This couldn't be happening. It was a nightmare.

"Yes, you did. You had a contract."

Anger exploded and replaced the numbness in an instant. "So what, Teagan?" I yelled. "Fuck the goddamned contract! I still can't believe this!"

"Jensen took care of me. He married me because my father was furious and I..."

"It wasn't his place! It was mine! Do you think I give a damn why he did it?" My expression twisted in anguish and I glared at her. "There is no excuse for what either one of you has done. Right now, all I know is I'm not ready to deal with all of the crap between you and me. I'd just like to meet my daughter."

She blinked and I could see her throat visibly tighten as she tried to swallow, as she nodded and started to back out of the parking space to begin navigating toward the exit of the garage. "Okay. I'll take you."

We didn't speak; the air between us tense as I retreated inside myself, and my conflicted thoughts. I was anxious, excited and terrified of meeting the little person that I had made with Teagan. My heart eased slightly as I tried to get my head around everything I'd just learned. At least I didn't have to be tortured by the thought of another man's child growing inside her. How much that had fucked me up left me staggering.

We walked side by side into the hospital and rode the elevator up in silence. What would I see when I went into the room? My heart sank to my stomach. I was more nervous than I'd ever been, and scared as hell she'd look sick. I knew it would kill me, but I was going to fall in love for the last time in my life. I knew it for certain.

The hospital smelled sterile and it was stark; white everywhere except the few dull brown tiles scattered among the white ones on the floors. It felt cold until we entered the room. There were balloons and flowers everywhere, butterflies made out of construction paper lined the walls around the big bed with a small form lying in the middle. I recognized Teagan's artistic handy work.

My daughter was sleeping and I was drawn toward her. My eyes blurred as I fell, stunned, into the chair by her bedside; I gazed upon the smaller version of Teagan in the bed. She was so tiny, her features perfect as her chest rose and fell softly. I only saw the incredible little face, too caught up to notice the IVs or the machines. Her hair had grown back and was just past her ears, curling softly around her face. She didn't look that sick, except that her skin was pale and she had light purple shadows beneath her eyes, partially hidden by arcs of full, dark lashes.

"Teagan…she's just… gorgeous. Oh, my God."

"She's you, Chase."

"She looks like you. So beautiful." My hand reached out to stroke back her silky hair as the first tear fell.

"When she wakes up, you'll understand. She's like you in so many ways. Every time I look at her; I see you." Teagan's voice was tight and barely a whisper.

My finger touched a petal-soft cheek, just below the dark fan of lashes. "I'm… overwhelmed. I wish you would've told me. I wish I'd seen her born and how she grew into this. I wish I could have been with her when she went through her chemo. Oh, God." My voice cracked on the last word as my throat tightened uncomfortably. "You had no right…" I began.

Teagan's voice was shaking when she spoke, her tears constricting her words. "I know. I'd give anything to change it." Her hand came down on my shoulder from behind and squeezed and instantly my big hand covered her smaller one. I couldn't stop myself even if I'd wanted to.

"Mommy…" Remi's eyes fluttered open and she blinked, searching the room for her mother's face.

"I'm here, baby girl." Teagan moved to the other side of the bed and bent to kiss the child's forehead and brush her soft hair away from her face. "You have a visitor. Can you say hello?" She nodded in my direction with a tremulous smile, trying to hide her tears.

The little girl turned; her eyes on me for the first time and smiled softly. My heart swelled with pride. She did have my eyes and they were wise and knowing beyond her years.

"Hello," she said bravely as she examined me. Her eyes widened and she glanced at her mother and then back to me.

"It's very nice to meet you, Remi. I've been waiting a long time." I tried desperately to keep my voice from breaking.

"Me, too, but it's okay, Daddy. I knew you'd come someday."

The little angel voice shook me to the core and my eyes flew to Teagan's face. Her chin was trembling as she lifted her hand to her mouth and blinked to let the tears that flooded her eyes tumble down her cheeks. She nodded in affirmation. She'd told our daughter about me.

I smiled in joy as I turned back to the little girl, dwarfed by the hospital bed. I laughed through my tears and cleared my throat. "Yes. I'm sorry I wasn't here sooner, but I'm with you now, and I'm not going anywhere. How do you know who I am?" I asked incredulously.

She pointed a little finger at the bedside table where a picture of me wrapped around Teagan at a party sat. I remembered that day like it was yesterday. We were so happy, then. "Mommy tells me stories about you all the time. Lovely stories. And we watch you on TV." She leaned toward me and put her hand to her mouth intent on telling me a secret. I leaned in to hear her as my heart exploded with joy. "I think she loves you a lot," she whispered with a soft giggle.

My chest tightened, my emotions practically choking me. "Remelia…" I said her beautiful name for the first time, "would it be okay if I gave you a hug?"

She smiled and nodded, raising her little arms toward me. As gently as I could, I gathered her close, lifting her onto my lap as I sat on the edge of the bed, so careful of her IV, and pulling the blankets around her. She was fragile, and I saw some purple bruises on her arms and legs, which hinted at her awful illness but felt perfect in my arms. Love like nothing I'd ever felt, rushed over me.

Teagan wept silently a few feet away from us, frantically brushing the tears off of her cheeks as I held an arm out to her and she joined us on the bed. Remi wound one arm around each of our necks. Teagan kissed one cheek while I dropped my lips to the top of her head, memorizing the scent of my child. My child. With Teagan. Could anything be more amazing?

"I'm so sorry, Chase." Teagan's voice cracked on my name.

"We'll talk later, Teagan, okay?" I couldn't help it; I reached out and brushed her chin with my fingertips before returning my attention to our child. "I'd like to hear one of Mommy's stories, sweetheart. Should we ask her to tell us one?"

The little one giggled. "There are lots and lots to choose from! My favorite is the one where you stole her heart. Are you gonna give it back now?"

"Should I?"

She laughed happily, despite her paleness and the tubes and wires. "Nope!"

"Good. I don't think so either. I think I'll keep it forever!"

In a matter of ten minutes, I now shared Teagan's desperation over this little life. The mess between us would have to wait. Remi was what mattered right now. Whatever it took; money, asking my father's help, and if possible, donating marrow, I'd do whatever I needed to do.

ONE *touch*
AND THE PAIN
melted away.

Chapter 3

Teagan

"Mommy!" Remi patted the bed on the opposite side from where Chase was sitting on the chair.

I was amazed at how easily she'd taken to him, and equally fascinated at how incredible he was with her. It was as if she'd known him her whole life, and had been her father from day one. I'd been telling her stories about him since before she could talk, but this... was more than I could have hoped for.

I studied them, watching the way they engaged with each other; Remi's rapt attention, and the adoration on Chase's face as he looked at her. I swallowed at the regret that threatened to overcome me and closed my eyes, my brow furrowing with my effort as I tried to fend off the tears that burned in my eyes. I could only pray that they would both forgive me. Especially Chase. Remi had a piece of him her whole life, but I'd robbed him of so much. I could see the consequences of my decision so clearly now, and how given the choice, Chase would have given up his career. Damn my good intentions.

I was sitting near the window, just watching them and struggling to hold back my tears, and when my little girl called me. I sat up a little straighter and blinked rapidly.

"Mommy, tell Daddy the story!"

My heart seized in panic. How would I ever be able to hold it together, or more, how would I be able to keep from Chase that I loved him, and had never stopped, not even one day since the last time we saw each other almost six years before? If I told that story right now, I'd fall apart. I tried to make Chase real for Remi by letting her know him through my memories, always knowing that someday, whether I chose it or not, she'd want him in her life.

I flushed, heat seeping up under the skin of my face and neck in embarrassment. There would have been a time when I had nothing to hide from Chase, but now, after so much time had passed, with so much pain and betrayal between us, I was feeling vulnerable. "Um…" I faltered. "Daddy knows the story, honey. He was there."

Her face fell in a bit of a sad pout. "But, I love that story! Please!

I swallowed hard. The tightness in my throat was a culmination of the overwhelming emotion of just seeing Remi with her father, and the embarrassment that telling the story would cause. I felt ashamed. How could I tell the story that openly showed my love for him at the same time he was grappling with the way he was denied his daughter. It made me even more vulnerable, and my insides were already quivering like a house of cards in the wind.

Chase's eyes flashed up to mine and locked; in that moment my breath lodged in my throat. He was tan and his hair was a just a bit shorter, but those soulful eyes still read me like a book. He knew how I was struggling, just like I knew the internal battle he was waging. I could tell he was wondering if

Jensen would walk through the hospital room door because he kept glancing at it and then looking at his watch.

The much-needed reprieve came when one of the nurses came into the room to take Remi's vital signs and gently suggest she rest. Chase stood and backed up from the chair, raised his arms and laced his fingers on the top of his head. He was tall, towering over the barely 5'4" nurse.

She was young, and I couldn't help but notice the way her appreciative eyes looked Chase over. "Who's this?" she asked Remi, who instantly smiled brightly.

"That's my daddy!" she announced proudly. "He plays football across the ocean."

The nurse paused briefly while putting the blood pressure cuff around Remi's little arm. It was obvious she was judging something she knew nothing about.

"Oh, I thought—" she stammered, looking up at me as she continued pumping up the rubber bulb on the cuff, "Um, how nice."

I wanted to crawl into a hole. "Daddy sometimes plays in America and Canada, too, honey." Remi was smart and we'd looked at a globe when I told her where Chase was, but I said the words more to divert the subject than anything else. "Shush, now," I said, so the nurse could count her pulse as she slowly let the air out of the blood pressure cuff.

"Why don't you have one of those electronic blood pressure things?" Chase asked abruptly when the nurse was finished removing the instrument from Remi's little arm.

"We do, but her arm is so small, we get a better reading this way."

He nodded and remained quiet by the window as we waited for the nurse to take her temperature. "All this is good, but you know what comes next," the nurse said sympathetically as a phlebotomist dressed in another of the yellow gowns, walked into the room, "but afterward, we'll get you some dinner and maybe ice cream."

Remi's little eyes filled with tears and her chin quivered, though she didn't cry out loud.

I was already on my way to my purse sitting on the ledge by the window to pull out my iPhone when Remi's shaky voice said, "Mommy, get the music." Chase was close; watching me and once again our eyes met before I turned back to our daughter.

I showed her my phone by lifting it up and wagging it at her, I forced a happy smiled. "Got it, honey bun."

I walked to the bed, and called up a Justin Timberlake song she liked from "Trolls" and then scooted on and pulled her back against my chest. I wrapped both of my arms around her little body and held on tight as the music began.

Remi hated getting her blood drawn and she'd been in the hospital often enough that all of the nurses on the pediatric oncology floor knew our routine when she had to have any procedures involving needles. The young girl who was now in the room wasn't any different. I felt guilty that I couldn't remember her name when she started bouncing to the music and humming along. Remi and I started singing along as her arm was sterilized, the piece of rubber was tied around and a vial of blood was quickly drawn. Remi's face grimaced but we both kept on singing, pushing through it as we'd learned to do.

Chase watched us intently. He wore a gentle and understanding smile on his face and hope began to bloom inside my heart that maybe, he might at least try to understand that at the time I hid Remi from him, it was a huge sacrifice for me. And just maybe, he'd let me tell him what really happened.

"You're so brave, little one. I've always hated these things," he murmured, walking close so he could cup her head.

She pursed her lips and nodded, looking up at him. "Yeah, they hurt, but when Mommy sings with me, it helps a lot."

"Yes, I can see that. Smart Mommy." His thumb brushed her cheek then her chin before his eyes moved up to my face. "Good job."

I still held Remi against me and she leaned her weight back, to snuggle into my arms. I rubbed the arm that just got poked and lifted her little hand up to kiss it. "Let's order dinner for you, then you'll need to rest, sweet pea."

The rest of the evening consisted of watching *Frozen* on my laptop while Remi had her dinner. Her nose wrinkled distastefully at the bland burger and limp fries. "Yucky." She said, pushing at her tray.

Chase, who was sitting on the chair again, holding the laptop so she could see it, leaned forward and grabbed the hamburger, taking a big, exaggerated bite designed to encourage Remi to follow suit, but his face crumpled and he balked. "Gross," he agreed. I shot him a look, silently pleading that he not make the situation worse. His brow furrowed and then he scoffed. "Ugh, no wonder. Have you tasted this sh— uh, thing? She's not on a restricted diet, is she? This is awful!"

My eyes widened at him as Remi's face lit up in delight. "See! I told you, Mommy. It's waffle!"

We all laughed out loud and I rejoiced in my baby's tinkling laughter and the brilliant sparkle in Chase's green eyes. He loved her already. I could see it and I was never more grateful for anything in my life.

"If only it was a waffle," Chase said wryly. "There'd be syrup."

Remi had quickly taken to Chase, and the natural way they were with each other made my heart sing. His agreement that the hospital food sucked wasn't going to help my cause to get her to eat, but he was amazing with her. After everything, and the way he found out, it was more than I could hope for.

"So, Mommy," Chase's face wrinkled wryly. "This is crap. Are there any restaurants near here? I'm starving, too."

"Oh, I'm sorry. I should have realized. There's a Wendy's a few blocks down. I can go out and get something."

"I want that," Remi added, enthusiastically. "Can I have a Frosty, too?"

"I'll go. It's only a few blocks on the same street? North or South?"

"South, but you've traveled so far, Chase. I can go."

I started to rise and move off the bed from behind my little girl when Chase stood, removing the offending meal tray from the rolling table that fit over the bed, and settled the laptop down in its place with the other. "It'll be faster if I go. I'll just jog. It's faster than dealing with the car and the garage. Right?"

He was right, it would be. It was rush hour and people would be flooding in to visit patients, and the roads were overly congested. "Yes, but I feel bad, making you go."

"I volunteered. Anything to get our baby girl to eat." He ruffled her hair and turned his attention away from me to Remi. "So a Frosty, a burger and fries?"

"Cheeseburger!"

Chase laughed. "Okay, a cheeseburger it is."

"And a Coke!" she added.

"Please," I admonished. "7-up."

"Please," Remi added. "Thank you, Daddy."

Chase's face beamed, though his eyes glassed over and he cleared his throat. "That's right. Every kind of soda is Coke around here. I'll be back in a flash."

When Chase was gone, I snuggled Remi next to me and pulled the table closer so she would have a better view of the movie and bent to kiss the top of her silky head.

"Are you okay? I know it's been a big day."

Her little head nodded beneath my chin. "I love Daddy, very much. He's nice and very funny. I wish he could never go away again."

My own eyes welled with tears and I was thankful Remi couldn't see the reaction her words were having on me. "I don't think he will, baby." I knew Chase and I could see the instant bond between the two. "I mean, he has to play soccer and stuff, but I'm sure you'll see him a lot."

"Can he move in with you, me, and Jensey??"

I sighed, inhaling as much as my lungs could hold and letting it out slowly. It was all so complicated and a huge mess to be sorted out. "I don't think so, honey, but we'll figure it all out, I promise. Right now, Daddy, Jensey and Mommy just want to get you well."

I'd told Jensen from the start that Remi would know about Chase and so we agreed we'd have her refer to him as Jensey, and that extra special little girls get an extra daddy. He wasn't happy about it, but at the time, we had no way of knowing where our lives would end up. If only I'd had a crystal ball. Regret was a futile emotion with nothing to gain from it, but I couldn't seem to push it away.

It wasn't long until Chase came back laden down with a bag of fast food and a full drink tray. His hair was damp and stuck to his forehead, but he wasn't out of breath, though he must have run the whole way to get back so quickly.

"The ice cream might be melting a bit," he said upon entering the room. "You may have to eat that first, honey." He set the drinks down and dug into the bag for the straws and a spoon, before pulling the smallest cup from the tray.

"Can I, Mommy?" Remi asked, reaching for the Frosty Chase was offering.

"Yes, it's fine this time."

"Yay!" Her little hands started to remove the lid and I helped her so she wouldn't spill it, while Chase continued to unload the food and spread it out in front of all of us.

I wasn't that hungry, but I made an effort while Chase and Remi talked together and enjoyed their food. I had moved away from the bed to sit in the chair by the window and was able to observe the two of them. Chase took a seat near the foot of Remi's bed and shared the table with her. He asked her about her friends, if she had a dog, about what her favorite thing was about Kindergarten. She tried to eat but was getting tired and weak. It was time to clear the food away and get her ready to sleep. I could tell she wanted to stay awake, not wanting Chase to leave, but I also knew from experience, that she was hitting her wall.

"Chase," I murmured softly. "She's tired."

His head snapped in my direction and he nodded as he started to stuff the empty food wrappers and remnants back into the fast food bag.

Remi reached out with both of her little hands and clutched at Chase's larger one, interrupting his task; her eyes imploring. "Are you going away, now?"

The corner of his mouth lifted slightly and his features softened as he shook his head. His other hand came out to stroke Remi's silky hair. "No, sweetheart," he answered gently. "I'm not going anywhere."

There were several of Remi's favorite books lined up on the window shelf and I went over and chose The Giving Tree and held it out for Chase. "We usually read a book to get her settled. Would you like to read tonight? I can clean this stuff up. It's time for the last round of meds, and I want to make sure they get it done before she nods off."

"Hospitals aren't a great place to sleep," he added, knowing what I meant.

"Exactly."

Remi let out a big yawn, and I could see she was fighting hard to stay awake. I doubted she'd make it through the story.

Intense green eyes locked with mine and he nodded almost imperceptibly. In the midst of the mess and the anger he must surely feel, he was so gentle with both of us. My heart thudded like thunder in my chest. This was still Chase. My Chase. My soul cried out for his and I wished I could touch him, fall into his arms, and cry my heart out. Instead, I handed off the book to him and gathered up the trash. "Okay," I said.

"Teagan, I'd like to talk to you after Remi is settled."

I expected he would, but I had apprehension over what he'd say. Whatever it was, I deserved it. "Of course, Chase."

"Good," he said and turned his attention back to Remi. "The Giving Tree, huh? I used to love this book when I was little."

"I think it's sad," she said.

"It is a little bit, but it's also about unselfishness and love."

"Yeah. It's still sad."

"Sometimes sad stuff happens to teach us what matters the most, right?"

"I guess," Remi said, yawning again and snuggling close to Chase who had settled on the bed next to her, one arm behind her so she was cradled against him as he opened the book in front of them both.

"The tree gives everything she has to that dumb boy."

Chase laughed. "I thought you liked this story!"

"I do, but that boy is dumb."

Chase chuckled again. "Yeah, I guess. But in the end, he realizes he still needs the tree and isn't that really all the tree wanted? The boy to need her?"

"But why? He's dumb. And mean."

"Hmmm," Chase murmured. I could tell he was searching for a way to explain it. He sighed heavily, searching for the right words. "I think you'll understand better when you grow up, but you don't get to choose who you love, even if they don't love you back or love you in a different way than you love them."

"Why?"

"I haven't figured that one out yet, baby."

Shaking, I took the trash to the wastebasket by the door to her room thankful my back was turned and neither of them could see how much I was struggling to hold it together. All I knew was that I had to get out of there.

"I'm going to talk to the nurses. I'll be back," I said, hoping there were no telltale signs of distress in my voice, and then left without looking at either one of them.

When I hit the hall, I bowed my head and rushed to the bathroom at the other end of the floor. Tears were streaming down my face and I prayed the curtain of my hair would hide it. When I burst through the door to the bathroom and locked it behind me, I turned on the faucets and leaned over the sink just before the dam burst and I was sobbing my heart out.

My heart was shattered. I wasn't sure if I was overwhelmed with how Chase interacted with our daughter, if I was afraid of the confrontation in front of me, or if Remi's precarious health issues had finally broken me. Or maybe, I was like the dumb, selfish boy in the book.

My broken, hiccupping cries echoed in the square tiled room above the sounds of the rushing water. I slid down the wall in a heap, pulling my knees up and burying my face in my folded arms. I cried like the world was ending because it felt like it was. I'd lost Chase, and now, could lose Remi.

My choices were ignorant and careless of the possible consequences. Despite my noble intentions, despite all the other shit that happened that made it impossible to take it back or change it; there was nothing to justify it, and no amount of atonement great enough to make amends. This was the biggest mistake of my life, and if I spent every second of every day trying to figure out how I could make it up to Chase, Jensen, and Remi; there was no going back.

ONE *touch*
AND THE PAIN
melted away.

Chapter 4

CHASE

Remi was amazing. She was a smart and beautiful, precocious, and brave little angel. It was love at first sight for the second time in my life. And Teagan... there was no denying she was an incredible mother. I always knew she would be.

I was still reeling from the whole thing, but once I got in that room with her, held her and talked to her, my entire world changed. It was like a cosmic shift in the universe and nothing else mattered but that little girl and getting her better. I wanted to speak with the doctors and with Teagan. I was still pissed off and hurt, but that couldn't be my focus until I had my head around this thing, and we had a plan of action for Remi's care in place.

I'd said my goodnights to my daughter and was waiting in the hall outside the room while Teagan tucked her in. Leaning tiredly on the wall outside the room, propped up on my shoulder, I ran a weary hand through my hair. I felt dirty and sweaty from the traveling and the run to get dinner. I needed a shower and a few hours of sleep.

"Are you Ace Forrester? Of the Arsenal?" A short, plump nurse with a happy smile on her face looked up at me expectantly.

I quickly pushed away from the wall to stand in front of her. "Arsenal, yeah," I said simply. Americans didn't realize that there was no "the" in front of the team name. People recognized me in airports and other public places, but I never expected it in the pediatric cancer wing of a Georgia hospital.

"Oh, my God. I watched you play against that Argentinian team last season," she said tentatively, the fingers of both hands fiddled together in front of her nervously as her big eyes stayed trained on my face. "You were amazing! I don't remember the name of the team."

"The River," I answered with a nod. "They're a really good team."

"Not as good as yours."

I huffed out a sigh and smiled. "Well, not that time, as it turned out."

"I've followed your career since Clemson. I attended there, too."

I pressed my lips together in another half-assed smile. These situations were awkward and I'd rather avoid them all together. "Cool."

"Can I get an autograph?"

I rubbed the back of my neck, tiredly. "Sure." The door to Remi's room opened and Teagan appeared. She was still beautiful, but her makeup was worn or cried off, and I could see how exhausted she was. In the old days, my arm would have slid around her to let her lean on me, and I had to remind myself to stop. I nodded at the nurse. "If it's quick. We're beat."

"Sure! I'll be right back!" She scurried off behind the nurses' station a bit down the hall, as Teagan paused at my side.

"What's the plan? Is there a hotel or hotel close to the hospital?"

Her deep brown eyes flew to my face. "Ah... I don't usually leave Remi alone at night, but I can take you home. We have an extra room."

I shook my head. "No. It's not a good idea, and I'd be more comfortable in a hotel."

"Why? It's—"

"Completely fucked up if I stay in Jensen's house while he stole my girl and has been raising my kid." I interrupted abruptly. "No chance. The thought of being there makes me want to kill something. You shouldn't even be suggesting it."

I glared at her as heat rushed underneath the skin of my face and my chest felt like it had a two-thousand-pound weight on it preventing me from breathing. I was suddenly claustrophobic, and though I wanted to talk about Remi, that was all I wanted to discuss.

The nurse was hurrying back and I took the pen and paper she handed me and scribbled my name on it. "Thank you, Ace. Wow, my brother will never believe I have this."

I nodded once. "Not a problem."

"You're here to see Remi? She's such a sweet soul."

"Yes. She's my daughter." The words slammed out as more of a declaration than an answer to the woman's question.

"Oh," the woman said, shock flashing across her rosy face. "I didn't know."

"Neither did I." It was a cheap shot, but the words were out of my mouth before I barely registered what they were.

The nurse looked taken aback when I quickly brushed past her and stalked my way toward the elevators. I was embarrassed at the outburst; anger and resentment about being robbed of Remi's life resurfacing. "Teagan, are you coming?" I threw her name over my shoulder in a command that she follow me.

I could hear Teagan murmuring an apology and telling the nurse she'd be back soon as I pushed the down button. Soon, she was beside me waiting the few seconds before the elevator dinged and the stainless steel doors slid open.

I could sense her nervousness as much as she knew how pissed off I was. It was written all over her as she fiddled with her iPhone. I couldn't help but wonder if she was texting Jensen and resentment reared. When the elevator doors closed behind us, she shot me a quick glance before training her eyes back on her phone. "I'm looking for a hotel. There's a Marriott Express down about a mile from here, but it's not up to the standard I'm sure you're used to."

My face twisted and I huffed. "I don't give a shit about the hotel, as long as it has a bed. The closer, the better."

"I'm sure you're tired with the time difference," she said, tentatively stating the obvious. The difference in our interaction now and when we were with Remi was painful. I felt awkward for the first time ever with Teagan, but then, a lot of bad shit went down in the past six years. I wanted answers to some of it, and the rest I didn't want to know.

As if on cue, my phone rang from the back pocket of my jeans. I knew it was Bronwyn, but I didn't have the desire to talk to her. "Yeah. I just need a couple of hours. What time can I speak to the doctors? And will they even talk to me since they think Jensen's her dad?"

"They make rounds early. Around six, and yes, your name is on her birth certificate."

I softened slightly. At least she wasn't denying me completely. It crossed my mind that I might have a legal battle in front of me, but that would have to wait until after Remi was out of danger. My heart seized a little. What if she didn't get better? "How many of them are there?"

The elevator doors opened and we began walking through the hospital toward the main entrance that led to the parking garage. "They seem endless. There is a pediatric oncologist, a hematologist-oncologist, a dietitian, and a radiologist oncologist; though he is just on consult right now."

I sighed heavily. "This is so fucked up. How can such a perfect little person have to deal with something this horrible?" I could feel my throat tighten as emotion surged. "Ughhhhhhhh!" I yelled up into the high ceiling; the tiled floors and stonewalls echoed my agony and another person and security guard we passed, both stared. I didn't give one flying fuck.

"I'm sorry, Chase."

I swallowed and stopped, waving her in front of me to go through the roundabout that would take us outside. "Save it," I said, bitterly. As if saying she was sorry could change one goddamned thing. "All I care about right now is Remi. I want to know everything; what they've done, what's next in the treatment, and what the prognosis is."

Teagan pulled the keys out of her purse and her car honked in front of us as she unlocked it with the key fob. I almost threw myself into the passenger seat and pulled the door shut harder than was needed. The slam ricocheted through the concrete garage.

"As I said earlier, she's been through two rounds of chemotherapy, and it was awful. Every horror you've ever heard about it, it's true. She's terrified of going through that again."

"Obviously, it hasn't worked," I said shortly, leaning an elbow on the car door below the window and used two fingers and my thumb to rub both of my eyes. They felt dry and as if they were filled with sand. "The hematologist is the blood doctor, right?"

"Yes." She started the car and the air conditioner started to blow cool air. It made me feel less claustrophobic inside the confines of the car. I turned to look at her. "She and the radiologist are working together now. If we can find a match, then they'll keep her in a clean room and radiate her to kill all of her own marrow, and then we have to hope it will take."

"That's terrifying. Will she die if it doesn't work?"

Teagan nodded. "With no working marrow, she'll have no immune system or any way to make new red blood cells. She'll get blood infusions, but she needs healthy marrow."

"I want the test first thing in the morning, then."

"It's several tests, Chase, and it may take a few weeks. I know you have games and… other things to consider. I'll ask the doctors to work around it as much as possible."

I looked at her for a moment. I felt angry as hell. "Do you think I give a damn about any of that?"

She looked like a deer in the headlights as she pulled the car out onto the street and started driving south. "I just meant that the test results take time and so hopefully your games will fall in times when you might not have to be here."

"I'll be here whenever I need to be. I'll hit the games if, and when, I can."

"Won't you miss practices?"

I shook my head. "Yes, but it doesn't matter, either way. What happens if I'm a match?"

"She'll have tests to make sure she is well enough, then they'll radiate her and your marrow will be administered via IV."

I nodded slowly, my eyes trained on her pained expression. My heart and soul was screaming for all three of us, and for the injustice of it all. I felt as if I were shoved into the past and reliving the pain of how it felt right after she left me. I'd wanted to lie down and die. Literally, I couldn't breathe and that same type of misery was right in front of me again. "Okay."

"Listen, Chase." Teagan reached out and clasped my left hand with her right one. "It means a lot to me that you're here. Even without knowing why you came."

I could hear the emotion in her voice and it ripped at me. Why did it have to be so hard? Why couldn't my heart forget this woman? Why did it hurt so fucking much? I sucked in a breath, filling my lungs to capacity, and against my will, my thumb brushed across the top of her hand. "You knew I'd come," I said softly after I'd exhaled. "Like I ever had a choice."

It was a heavy admission, but I wasn't giving anything away that she didn't already know. The bond you have with your first, and maybe only love, held you to the fucking ground no matter how much you wanted to be free. It pissed me off and tore my heart out at the same time. She destroyed me, and still, I was unable to choose not to love her. People who think unconditional love is the ultimate gift must be mentally deranged. In reality, it was utter torture; a cage that holds you without mercy, for life.

Teagan sniffed and used her left hand to dash away a tear. "I'm so sorry, Chase. I know how wrong I was."

"Saying your sorry doesn't change anything and it won't erase any of it, Teagan," I said wearily and then instantly regretted pulling my hand back. "Look, I'm sorry. I'm trying to wrap my head around it and it's a lot to deal with all at once. Can we just get through this? Dredging up the past won't do anyone any good. It's about Remi, and honestly, she's who I care about right now."

By now she was pulling into a parking spot in front of the hotel, and left the engine running. "I just want to explain what happened—"

I put up my hand. "Maybe, but I don't care what you need or want! Don't you get that? I don't want to hear it right now. I have to make some calls, and then I need to crash for a few hours before the doctor's show up. Will you be at the hospital in the morning?"

She nodded. "I'm going back as soon as I run home to shower and change clothes, but I can pick you up about 5:30."

My eyes narrowed. "You basically live at the hospital, then?"

"Sometimes it feels that way. She sleeps a lot, but I'm there most of the time. I only go home to clean up."

Fury rose up inside my chest. She didn't have to work, and he was paying for everything. "Jensen is a real saint."

Teagan paused and looked at me; I could visibly see her suck in her breath. "He is. You don't know the whole story."

My hand reached for the door handle but the auto lock refused to allow me to open it. Pissed; I fumbled with the button and then flung the door open. "Don't need to know anything more than he stole my whole fucking life. I feel like killing him, so if he wants to keep breathing he will stay the hell away from me."

Teagan leaned across the seat to look out the window and then back over the front seat into the back when I opened it to pull out my bag and slammed the door. "None of it is his fault, Chase."

I was half turned to start walking into the hotel then stopped abruptly and turned around, slamming my hand down on the top of her car, so hard it stung. She flinched inside the car, and then I leaned down to talk to her through the open window. "I'm not interested in hearing about my traitor best friend being there for you and Remi when I wasn't even given a chance to do so. You made your choices; now we're all paying the bill. You didn't believe in me at all." I spat out in disgust.

"I did believe in you! That's why I didn't tell you!"

I couldn't take hearing any excuses and I was livid. I snapped. "I said, fucking save it, Teagan!" I shouted at her. "I don't need to hear about your little picket fence and knight in shining armor or how he saw my child born and acted like her father, or think about him screwing you behind my back! I don't need those pictures in my head right now! Just shut up!"

A family heading into the hotel stopped and stared before continuing on inside. "Come on, kids." The man, obviously their father, ushered his children and his wife through the door."

I leaned in toward her further after glancing around the parking lot to see if any others were around. "Nothing you can say will ever justify it." The entire afternoon I'd been able to bottle it up while I was in front of my daughter, but I was seething and now, was on the verge of losing it. "I'm not here to offer you absolution. I'm here to do what I can for Remi… and to make up for the time I lost with her."

Her face crumpled and she started to cry. As always, my heart allowed her pain to morph mine. I regretted the outburst, but it was the truth and I'd be goddamned if I'd let either of them off the hook after all I'd suffered. Year after year of pain and suffering; and for what? I still didn't understand how she could think I would ever choose my career over her, let alone the precious, innocent child less than a mile away in that God-forsaken hospital.

Teagan was sobbing by now and I steeled myself to withstand the deep-seated pull to comfort her. I straightened and squared my shoulders, turned, and then stalked into the hotel leaving her behind me to deal with her own emotions.

The part of me that had always taken care of her reared and it was harder than hell to keep walking, but I was angry as fuck. She'd robbed me of so much and I'd be damned if I'd cave at the first sign of weakness from her. I felt like shit; sad, mad, and exhausted. My body was wiped out and my mind was wasted.

I went through the motions of getting a room, and in a sort of daze flipped out a credit card and laid it down. I was thankful that though I was well known in the world of soccer, only a fraction of the population followed the sport. The young man at the desk explained about the free breakfast and then asked how many keys I needed.

"One will be fine," I said and offered a grateful smile when he handed it over. "Thank you."

"Certainly, sir. The elevators are just to the right past the desk. Your room is on the fifth floor. Just let us know if you need anything. Enjoy your stay."

I nodded. "I appreciate it."

In the hallway after the short elevator ride, my phone started ringing and I quickly pulled it out to see who was calling. It was too soon for Teagan to be back at the hospital, but still, my heart stopped that it could be something about Remi. I made a mental note to give my name and number to the nurses so they could notify me directly going forward. Bronwyn's name flashed across the screen.

I answered amidst flinging my duffle over my shoulder. "Hello?" I said, craning my neck to hold the phone to my ear with my shoulder. The key gave me some issues and took three swipes before it opened. "Fuck," I muttered before she could say anything.

"Well, okay, but I don't think your dick will reach across the ocean, impressive as it is," she laughed softly. "I was starting to wonder about you."

I pushed open the door and let the bag drop to the floor before the door had a chance to close. It banged loudly behind me.

"Sorry. I've just checked into a hotel and I couldn't get the key to work."

I kicked my shoes off and fell onto the bed. "You're just getting to bed?"

"Yes. I'm beat. Can I call you in a few hours?"

"Ace, I want to know what's going on. Why are you there?"

I closed my eyes in resignation, letting my body sink onto the bed. Either it was more comfortable than most hotel beds or I was too numb to notice. Maybe the reason it felt so good was because I was a walking zombie, but either way, I just wanted to sleep. A wave of irritation rolled over me. I shouldn't have expected my girlfriend to put her impatience on hold, no matter how tired I was.

I hesitated, contemplating how much to tell her. She would find out soon enough when I asked for a leave of absence from Arsenal. "It's complicated."

Bronwyn was one of the team fitness coaches and she'd worked with me since the day I joined the team. She knew how depressed and driven I was back then. It was only this year when we started to date when I'd shared a little of my past with Teagan, but Bronwyn didn't have a full picture of how much I'd loved Teagan. What was the point? You don't tell your current girlfriend that there is zero chance you'll ever love her because you've been completely destroyed by another woman.

The room had one small light on by the window and I lay flat on my back, my legs bent at the knee and my feet still on the floor. "Remember the girl I dated in college?"

I could almost feel her agitation through the phone. "Teagan, right?"

"Yes. She called me because her daughter has leukemia and they're looking for a donor."

"She has balls, I'll give her that," she said in disgust. "What does she want from you? Money? Ace, you can't be considering it. I mean, the woman broke your heart; brutally. You can't possibly believe her! It could all be some made-up sob story."

"It's not about money, Bronwyn. Your sensitivity slays me. She's only five years old, and she could die. I spent most of the day at the hospital; her illness is real."

"Well, sure, I'm sorry for the little one, of course, but after all this woman did to you, Ace, trotting off across the pond makes you a saint. You could have just wired her some cash."

I was sure Bronwyn had a lot of insecurity because the relationship I shared with her was not the same type of thing I had with Teagan, and she knew it. There was no point in beating around the bush. "Remi is my daughter."

The gasp at the other end of the phone was pronounced. "What? How can you be sure? She's probably just some elaborate con. You can't seriously believe such rubbish!"

Teagan may have done a lot of things wrong, but she wasn't a money-grubber. "She isn't like that."

Bronwyn's voice took on a harder, pissier tone. "No, not perfect little Teagan! She's just the bitch who suddenly married your best friend behind your back, broke your trust, and now lied about a child. Very innocent. You can't be sure the child is even yours!" Somehow her accent made her sound all the more indignant and incredulous.

"Look, I'm still reeling from it myself, and yeah, I'm pissed off, but it is what it is. There is a real little girl, and she is at risk of dying."

"At least get a paternity test, for God's sake."

"I don't need one. I can tell just by looking at her that she's mine," I said sternly. I felt as protective of her as if I'd know her since she was born and I was irritated by her words. I understood that she was in shock, but she could be a little more sensitive to the precariousness of Remi's situation. I waited for a response, but when it didn't come, I continued. "Anyway, I'm getting tested for a marrow match tomorrow, which should suffice. The DNA markers are tricky and the closer the match, the more likely the marrow donation will save her life."

She could sense my agitation and backed off. "I'm sorry, lovie. I'm just— freaking out a bit. It's a lot to take in."

"Tell me about it. But, she's amazing; so sweet and beautiful. I can't explain it; but when you have a child, you love it; the connection is instant. None of this is her fault. She's innocent, and I have to do whatever I can to help."

"I understand. How long will you be away?" There was a frustrated undercurrent in her tone.

"As long as it takes. I should know more in the morning after I speak to the doctors."

"Do you want me to speak to Arsène and the rest of the coaching staff, then?"

I shook my head even though Bronwyn couldn't see me do it. "Not yet. Let's just give it a couple of days until I have more to tell them."

"Ace, will this change anything between us?"

I could almost feel myself flush. Honestly, I didn't know. I'd be lying to myself if I didn't admit seeing Teagan again had shaken me to the core. That in itself would have been hard enough to deal with, but with Remi, it was a whole lot more complicated. My emotions were all over the fucking place. I was about to lie because I didn't have the constitution to deal with another conflict right now. "No. I know it's a lot to deal with on short notice, but please just be patient and give me some time."

"Okay," her voice relaxed. "Do you need me?"

"I'm fine for now. Honestly, I just need to focus on sorting it all out. Thanks for offering, though." The last thing I needed was Bronwyn's pushy personality thrown into the middle of the situation. I had so much to sort out, and I didn't need any distractions, and I didn't need to deal with any female-on-female drama. Even if unintentional, there was bound to be tension and resentment. It was going to get messy enough when Jensen got back from his trip, but all of that was secondary to getting Remi well.

"What about going forward? What will be involved? Will you need to retain a lawyer?"

I sighed. "I can't think about that now. Teagan said my name was on the birth certificate and Remi knew who I was the minute I walked in. She recognized me from pictures, and Teagan told her stories about me from a young age, and she named her after my mother. It was sort of this amazing, surreal, freaking gift, even though the way it happened was so screwed up, Bronwyn," I said still in awe of the entire scene.

"Your mother's name is Roma, not Remi."

"Roma Amelia... Remelia." Her tone pissed me off.

"Teagan is one clever, bitch, I'll give her that," she said in abhorrence; hatred literally dripping from the words. "Sure, tell the kid and not the bloody father, and to add one final nail in the coffin to make sure you can't hate her, she names the kid after your mother. Surely you can see through her, Ace! Why aren't you raging on and on about it?"

I shrugged. There was part of me that was still clinging to the past when Teagan and I loved each other, and I couldn't believe she had malice in her heart when naming Remi. It even eased my aching heart to believe she did it because, in her heart, she loved me. Maybe she was telling the truth about her motives for keeping it all from me. Teagan did say in the car at the airport; that she still loved me. It had been in the back of my mind all day, and just the hope it could be true made my heart sing. Even though I shouldn't care, I wanted to believe that more than I wanted to admit. Nothing hurt worse than thinking the memories I had of us were a joke.

"Because it wouldn't change anything. I'm angry and upset. This has stirred up a lot of shit and it will change a lot of things in my life, but I can't deal with all of it at once. Right now, Remi is the most important thing."

"Ace!" Bronwyn protested. "Things don't have to change. You do the medical thing and then you keep in touch with the little girl. Your life goes on."

"We'll see. I'm too tired to think about it now."

"Your career is at stake! The media will be a frenzy."

I sat up and put the phone on speaker, starting to peel off my shirt at the same time, throwing the phone on the bed, I kicked off my shoes and opened my jeans. "I. Don't. Care," I said. "I gotta get in the shower and get to bed. I have to be at the hospital in a few hours." I leaned down, ready to touch the red button that would end the call. "Goodnight, Bronwyn."

Hanging up on her was a prick thing to do, but I was done arguing and hearing hypothetical theories about the future. It was all up in the air until Remi was healed.

I stripped naked and walked into the bathroom and shut the door behind me. I reached for one of the large white towels, slapping it over the convex pole that held the white shower curtain in place, and then turned on the water. Steam soon filled the small room as I adjusted the water temperature.

The hot water felt amazing as it rushed over my skin and I let it get my entire head wet. My emotions were in turmoil. I was worried sick about Remi, and all twisted up with anger and resentment, but I loved Teagan. If I still loved her after she did this, I had to face that I always would. But loving her didn't mean I could forgive her, or even that I wanted to try.

The pain was soul deep and while she had Remi to ease any loss or suffering she felt at losing me, I was left with nothing but a black hole of despair and years of misery and unanswered questions. That type of devastation changes a person on a fundamental level and I sure as hell didn't want to relive it. The future loomed like a gaping abyss in front of me and I couldn't see beyond the moments and days ahead.

ONE *touch*
AND THE PAIN
melted away.

Chapter 5

Teagan

Chase had the first of several required tests.

It was a simple DNA swab of his inner cheek, and he was standing outside of Remi's room, towering beside me as he listened to the doctor explain all about human leukocyte antigens; the protein markers that determine if someone is a good donor candidate for a particular patient, the time involved in the process, and the many details that I'd already heard many times before.

He'd texted me at 5 AM and said he'd meet me at the hospital, and since he'd been distant informing me that he'd rather I stay with Remi than trail him during his test procedures, I obliged. I hated the invisible wall that he'd erected between us. At the airport, when he pulled me into his arms, I'd been transported back in time and melted into him. He still smelled the same and looked very much the same. He was in the best shape I'd ever seen him, though he was cut before. Now, his muscles rippled on his lean form when he moved, his shoulders were broader... but my heart and body still screamed for him in the same way they always had. Just being around him calmed me down, even when he was angry, as he was now.

My soul was in mourning that we weren't together, and I needed him, now more than I ever had. God, I missed him, and wished, more than anything, that I could rewind time and go back and undo the horrible, life-altering mistakes I'd made.

My phone pinged. I'd shoved it in the back pocket of the frayed jean shorts I'd thrown on with an old Clemson T-shirt just before rushing out of the house at the crack of dawn. I'd spent the night tossing and turning and I was fully aware that it showed in the disheveled look of my hair and lack of makeup. I pulled the phone out and turned, creating a few yards distance between us while he was conversing with Remi's oncologist, Dr. Radar. It was a message from Kat.

I've convinced David to live without me for a few days and Mom is coming to stay with the kids. Did Chase come?

Yes. He got in yesterday.

Told you he'd come. How's that going?

He's angry, but he's amazing with Remi. She adores him. He's speaking with the doctor at the moment. When will you be here?

I'm just leaving. See you in a couple of hours.

Please prep, my brother. This won't be pretty.

Okay, see you soon. Thanks, Kat.

No shit, it wouldn't be pretty. He already knew that Kat was aware of Remi, but her being here might only throw fuel on the fire. Jensen was due back tomorrow night, too. I ran a hand through my hair as my heart started to thump heavily inside my chest.

I turned back toward Chase and Dr. Radar. Both men had real concern on their faces and Chase was nodding and proffering his hand to shake the doctors. There had been a fair bit of shock on Dr. Radar's and the nurses' faces when he walked in and took charge. They just nodded when they all looked at me expectantly, as if I'd offer up an explanation. Thankfully, they were professional and went about their business as soon as the initial surprise wore off.

"Why don't we all go into the consulting waiting room?" Dr. Radar suggested as I reached the two of them again. "Will your husband be joining us? he asked in a quiet tone.

I could see Chase visibly stiffen and a muscle in his cheek flexed as he clenched his teeth. I shook my head and led the way to the little room at the end of the hall. "Jensen is traveling."

I'd spent a lot of time in this place with the doctors and Jensen discussing options, and came here at other times when I felt helpless and I needed to be alone and cry.

It was a small room lined with small couches and two reclining chairs in front of a television and one large window on the far wall. The sun was streaming in and the blue sky with its fluffy white clouds outside looked glorious. As I sat down, opposite the doctor, I couldn't help but wish that I could take Remi to the zoo or the park and that Chase could join us.

Chase sat next to me after a short hesitation. "How long will this take?" he asked, his deep green gaze intent on Dr. Radar's face. He sat leaning forward with his elbows on his knees, urgently seeking answers. "Finding out if I'm a match, I mean."

"The DNA test typically takes twelve to seventy-two hours. If it comes back that you're a good match, we'll proceed with a battery of other tests, and if everything works out, we'll move ahead with the radiation."

"Can't you do the remaining tests in the meantime? I don't want to wait for the DNA results to get started."

Dr. Radar's eyes flashed between my face and Chase's. "Jensen's health insurance is very good, but it won't pay for donor tests until we can confirm the match."

Chase inhaled and closed his eyes for a split second, before snapping them open and answering without a pause. "Thank you, Doctor, but I'll pay for the tests. I'll pay for all of it. I'm Remi's dad, not Jensen Jeffers."

It was clear that Dr. Radar knew the situation was delicate and he proceeded with care. "I understand your eagerness, Mr. Forrester. It's fortunate that we have another match opportunity. I'm hopeful this will be what our little Remi needs, but to change insurance in the middle of it will only slow the process, and that isn't in her best interest."

Chase stood up and went to the window to look out. "I don't care about the money. She's my little girl, and I want to take care of her." His words were stiff and anger-filled. I was praying to God he didn't explain how I'd betrayed him in front of the doctor, but I knew it was raging just beneath the surface. The whole thing painted a bad picture of me and I deserved any humiliation that he heaped on me, but I hoped he wouldn't feel the need to do so. "End of story."

I cleared my throat at the pain gathering; thankful Chase took pity on me. "Dr. Radar, may I please speak to Chase alone for a minute?"

"Certainly, Teagan. I have rounds to make, and I'll check in before I leave the hospital in a couple of hours." He stood, professional in a dark suit and muted tie in silver and black under the white hospital coat, with the stethoscope half-stuffed into the right-hand pocket.

"Thanks, again," Chase murmured over his shoulder. "For everything."

"Of course. Remi is one of my favorite little patients. I want nothing more than to see her well."

After Dr. Radar left the room and the door closed behind him, the silence boomed as I stood watching the tall, proud man standing in front of me. I was aching to wrap my arms around his waist from behind and press against the strong muscles of his back. He was hurting and I wanted to comfort him. Regret threatened to drown me in its intensity, and tears blurred my vision as I took a few steps closer.

"Chase, I'm so sorry."

His head dropped and his hands shoved into the front pockets of his jeans. "It doesn't matter now, Teagan. How we got here is in the past. It's over."

"I know it matters, Chase. No matter what happened, I still know you. I'm so profoundly sorry."

His voice was thick with emotion when he spoke. "How could you do this? I find out I have a baby, but only when I might lose her?"

Sorrow and guilt engulfed me. I started to shake and I clasped my hands together to steady them as the first tears of the day tumbled down my face. "I know it was wrong, and how hurt you are. I'll deserve it if you hate me forever and never forgive me, but there is so much to it, and I can explain. I'll tell you everything if you'll let me." I inched closer, my hands coming out to almost touch him.

"I don't want to hear it." He shook his head. "It hurts too fucking much, Teagan."

"Chase, please," my voice broke on a small sob. I had no right to cry at the misery I myself had inflicted, but the pain was so incredibly intense, I could barely breathe. "You have no idea how much I regret it."

He was so close I could feel the heat coming off of him. I couldn't help letting my hands reach out to wrap around his biceps. He stiffened and sucked in his breath, but he didn't flinch away. "Please listen." I let my forehead rest on his back between his shoulder blades. "Please," I almost whispered. It felt so good to touch him.

He stepped forward and twisted out of my embrace, turning to face me as he moved away from the window and back into the center of the room. "I'm not ready. And, for what? What will it change? Not one fucking thing."

There were tears in his eyes, but they didn't fall. He was stronger than I was. "I guess, I just want to be completely honest with you."

He huffed out an angry, tearful laugh. "Yeah? Well, I want to rewind the goddamned world! I want my girl to believe that I was man enough to take care of her. I want to wipe my memory clean of thoughts of you and Jensen screwing, and I want to be able to raise my kid!" It wasn't quite a shout, but I flinched as if he'd slapped me, and I lifted the back of my right hand up in front of my mouth, trying desperately not to full-on lose it. "When do I get what I want? What horrible thing did I do to you to deserve any of this?"

I stumbled, the back of my knees coming into contact with one of the couches and I sank down on to it, burying my face in my hands as I cried. "Nothing!" My heart was breaking. My body curled over my lap as I sat there softly sobbing. "Nuh —uthing."

For maybe a full minute I cried and Chase was silent. I felt rather than saw him sit down next to me. "Teagan, I'm sorry. I should have more control. We can't let ourselves get sucked into old emotions. It doesn't help any of us. Anyway, they aren't real. You're just remembering how it was between us."

My head came up and I looked at him with tearful eyes. He was so close I could feel the heat coming off of him, and I wanted nothing more than to reach out and lay my hand on his. I wasn't sure if the heart I could hear beating was mine, or his, but the connection was still tangible between us and I wanted to make it physical. I needed to make him understand because I couldn't stand the pain in his eyes. "Don't say that. There hasn't been one day that I haven't thought about you and missed you. I made the biggest mistake of my life and I've hated myself for it."

He shook his head sadly. "Teagan, there is nothing either of us can do to change the past. I'm not going to lie that this whole thing hasn't turned my life upside down, but I can't deal with it now. Right now, I have to focus on Remi. I want to spend as much time with her as I can." His hand came out and wrapped around mine, and his touch was like rain in the desert.

What I really craved was to melt into his arms, but I'd take even the smallest touch as a sign of truce. I nodded and wiped at the tears on my face with both hands and tried to offer a tumultuous smile, fighting hard against my feelings. So much had changed, and yet, so much remained the same. "I understand."

We both stood up together and headed out of the room and into the hallway to make our way back down to Remi's room.

"I wish we could go somewhere with her. It's such a nice day out."

"I was thinking that before. She loves the zoo and today would be perfect." Remi's door was cracked and we could hear her singing with the nurse. I smiled brightly at the sound. "She seems to have more energy today. I'll go speak to the nurses and have them call the doctors to see what's possible."

"We can get a stroller or I can carry her if they'll let us take her out for a while." His head cocked toward the door. "I'm going in."

I nodded again and went to speak to the day nurse and, after a brief conversation, was assured she would page Dr. Radar and the hospitalist to see what would be allowed. It would depend on when Chase's remaining tests would be scheduled."

"I'll have Dr. Radar paged, but then we have to ask the hospitalist, too." Reassured, I went into the room, anxious to see Remi with Chase. He was sitting on the chair he had pulled up close to the bed and she was propped up, the head of her bed raised. She was giggling at something he had said, and he was completely focused on her.

Dora the Explorer was playing on the television so I couldn't hear what they were talking about when I first walked in, but it was clear they were completely absorbed in each other. My heart was so grateful their connection was instant and so profound.

"Hey, you," I said when I walked in. "What am I interrupting?"

"Hi, Mommy!" She held up her arms for a hug. I went to her and leaned down to kiss her forehead and brush her hair back before I hugged her little body tight.

"I missed you, pumpkin. You look bright-eyed today!" She seemed healthier just having Chase next to her. I knew it wasn't possible his presence alone would make a physical change, but Remi was happy, and that soothed my heart.

"Daddy said I'm a princess, and when I'm better he'll take me to see some real castles in England!"

"Ooh, that would be fun. We better concentrate extra hard on getting you out of here, then, hmmm?" I glanced at Chase and he was watching me as I sat next to Remi on the bed. The close quarters of the room and the fact we both wanted to be near our daughter kept us all in a tight little group. "Did you eat breakfast, yet?"

She shook her head. "The pancakes were really yucky."

I knew my daughter and I looked at her sternly. "Oh, Remi. What is Mommy gonna do with you?"

"They were soggy and cold."

Chase rolled his eyes. "I don't how they expect kids to eat that shi—" I flashed him a warning look with a raised eyebrow. "Uh, crap?" He smiled, as he caught himself from swearing. "I know I couldn't!"

"Daddy could get me some donuts," Remi suggested with a giggle.

"Oh, no you don't, missy. Just because Daddy ran out yesterday, let's not make it a habit. He might have things to do at the hospital. For a while, anyway."

"I don't mind, Teagan."

"I know, but I can run down and grab something from the cafeteria for her. I just spoke to the nurse and she's calling the doctors."

Remi's little brow dropped into a frown, and she directed a question at Chase. "Why do you have to be in the hospital? Are you sick, too?"

Chase's features softened. "No, sweet pea. I'm okay, but they are going to see if I can help you feel better."

I hadn't told Remi much about the procedure, even though I went through the entire process Chase was about to undertake. I didn't want to get her hopes up.

"How?" she asked, her big eyes wide.

Chase and I hadn't discussed how much Remi knew about her illness, and he looked at me uncertainly so I took the lead on the answer. "Baby, you know when the nurses count the white blood cells in your blood and sometimes there are too many?"

"Yes. That's why I don't feel good."

I sidled closer and put an arm around her, looking down into her innocent expression, and the smaller version of Chase's green eyes. I nodded. "Yes, and remember how we talked about how your blood comes from the stuff in your bones called marrow?" Remi nodded, and Chase reached out to hold her hand. "Well, the doctors are looking into Daddy's bones to see if he can give you some of his marrow because it makes the right number of white and red cells. That might fix yours."

"Would it hurt Daddy?" she asked, concern on her little face.

"Not much, baby, and I'm tough. I can take it." Chase lifted her hand and kissed it.

She laughed. "Will I be all better, then? Will Leuky leave?"

"We hope so."

"Will I have to have more of the mean medicine?"

I wanted desperately to tell her that she'd never need to have chemo again, but I didn't know and I didn't want to lie to her. The back of my eyes burned, and Chase turned his head and blinked. We were both trying to hide our emotions from our little one. "We hope not, baby. One step at a time."

"Daddy?" she asked, looking at Chase. "Will you go away if I get better?"

Chase shook his head adamantly and reached for her, pulling her from my arms and into his. "No way. You're not getting rid of me."

I couldn't help the tears that escaped, and I quickly brushed them away. It was amazing how close they were in a day.

There was a knock on the door. "Come in." I got up and walked forward as the nurse came in.

"Dr. Radar called. He said that per Mr. Forrester's instructions, the rest of the donor tests are set up for tomorrow. He needs to be here at 6 AM."

"Okay," I nodded, folding my arms over my chest. "They're just having a moment. I know the testing process. I'll let Chase know."

She nodded. "Also, Dr. Radar said he wanted to speak to you both and he's coming up to the floor. He asked you to wait."

Fear made my chest tighten. "Is everything okay?"

"As far as I know."

"We were wondering if we could take Remi out for a bit?"

"That's something you can discuss with the doctor."

"Okay, thank you." I paused. She was new to this wing and I didn't know her yet. "What was your name? You're new, right?"

"Yes, ma'am. I just transferred to pediatric oncology from the regular cancer wing. It breaks my heart that babies have to go through this, and I want to help them. My name is Lucy." This nurse smiled. She had a gentle face and calming voice and was maybe five years older than me.

"Lucy. That's a nice name."

"You're little one is a peach. I've only just met her and I adore her, already. So happy; despite all she is dealing with. She's a trooper."

Pride filled me up at the same time I couldn't deny the sadness about Remi's illness. "Yes, she is special."

At that moment, a peal of laughter came from the room as Remi giggled at something Chase said and his deeper chuckle joined hers.

The nurse nodded toward the room. "Wow. Ace Forrester. Sounds like she has really taken to him. The entire floor is buzzing about it."

I inhaled deeply, irritated that our private business was fodder for discussion. "Awesome," I said shortly. I couldn't waste energy caring if people were whispering behind our backs; speculating on the situation of the famous baby daddy showing up only in a time of crisis. From the outside looking in, no one could ever know the whole story, and I didn't need others to understand.

Lucy could see my walls come down. "Oh, it's not like that, ma'am. He's just a big deal, you know? World famous soccer star right here in this hospital and everyone adores your daughter. It's news." She shrugged with a big smile on her face.

"I understand. I'm just very grateful that he's here for Remi."

Inside my mind I hated it, but I did get it. Chase's fame hadn't reached the level of David Beckham yet, but I had no doubt he'd get there. He was an amazing player, and handsome as hell. I could see how the women couldn't take their eyes off of him. It was like he was a golden magnet. I myself fell under his charisma, and it was worse for me because I knew his heart and his touch. He might look like a sex God, but he had a tender giving heart, and that made him all the more lethal. I was an emotional mess. I knew it and silently willed myself to get it together.

I cleared my throat and shifted from one foot to another in my discomfort. "Um, Lucy, when did Dr. Radar say he'd be back?"

"He didn't give an exact time, but soon."

There was a little snack room at one end of the nurse's station filled with snacks and drinks for the patients. It had the makings for toast, yogurt, cereal and granola bars. I made a couple of slices of peanut butter toast and grabbed a plastic container of orange juice, and one of milk and then took them back to the room.

Chase was reclined in the chair next to the bed dozing off, and Remi was watching the TV. She looked tired as well as I slid the plate of toast onto the table and opened the juice.

"Here, baby. It's still warm, so eat up." I didn't want to wake Chase, so I kept my voice low. He looked so peaceful, and zonked, I didn't want to disturb him.

I'd cut the toast into quarters and she reached for one piece. "Do I have to drink the milk?"

She didn't like milk much, but I wanted to get protein into her wherever I could. "I guess not. Did you and Daddy have a nice talk?"

She nodded. "Yep. Will Jensey be mad at me for loving Daddy, too?"

My heart fell that she would even consider such a question, but it was naïve to believe that a child as aware as Remi wouldn't ask. Constantly surrounded by adults: she had a more developed vocabulary and so, was much more mature than most children her age, though she was too young to be told the whole story.

"Oh, no, honey. Jensey and Daddy know you have enough love to go around. Everyone loves you."

It seemed to satisfy her and she took a bite of her toast. "Okay."

"How's my favorite patient?" Dr. Radar asked from the doorway before coming in and pushing the door almost completely shut behind him. "Is your dad sawing zees?" He smiled brightly at Remi.

"Shhh!" she said and put her finger to her mouth. "He's tired 'cause he's lagged."

Dr. Radar smiled and flashed me a glance, and nodded. "Oh, okay," the doctor lowered his voice but smiled broadly. "Have you been good for the nurses?"

"Yes," she said, taking another bit of the toast. "Except I didn't eat my pancakes."

"Ah, well, you're eating your toast, so that's okay. How do you feel today?" He ruffled her silky hair. It had grown out enough to touch her shoulders in the year she'd been in remission, and it curled softly at the ends, framing her angelic face.

"I'm okay," she shrugged. "I'm sleepy and kinda cold."

I started to pull the extra blanket at the foot of the bed up and over her, careful to tuck the material snuggly around her little body.

"Well, I'll tell you what? If you're a good girl, rest up today, eat as much as you can and take it easy, we might be able to let you go home tomorrow. Just for a few days."

Remi's eyes lit up and my heart danced in my chest. "Really? Can I play outside with my friends, too?"

He looked at her with a gentle expression. "It depends on the friends. You have to stay away from anyone who might be ill, so if you're careful. You know you can't overdo it."

"I won't!" Remi's face lit up like the sun.

"This is great news, Dr. Radar, thank you."

He nodded. "I think it will be okay, but you'll need to make sure the house is really clean and don't expose her to any unnecessary risks. Make sure she doesn't injure herself." Leukemia made healing difficult and any slight bumps or knocks could result in huge bruises.

"We'll know in a few days if Chase is a match, and if so, can move forward. We can discuss that if, and when, it's applicable. How's that sound?"

"Amazing. Thank you."

"Sure." He winked at Remi. "Okay, little miss. I'll see you in the morning, and if the nurses tell me you've been very good, you can get out of here, okay?"

"I'll be good."

"Okay, that means lots of sleep. After the toast, get some rest."

As the doctor left, my phone started ringing, and I fumbled to get it out and shut it off but didn't get it accomplished before it startled Chase awake. It was Jensen.

The first I'd heard from him since our huge fight over contacting Chase just before he left on this last trip. It was a conversation that needed to happen, though this wasn't the time, so I silenced my phone, glancing guiltily up at Chase.

Remi saved me. "Dr. Radar said I can go home tomorrow if I'm good!"

He flashed a brilliant white smile that contrasted beautifully with his tan skin and green eyes. "That's awesome news! You better be good, then!" He leaned in to kiss her forehead. His eyes flashed to mine. "Sorry I missed the doctor. I didn't realize I was so tired."

"It's understandable."

"I told Dr. Radar you're lagged, Daddy."

He huffed out a laugh. "Yeah, I'm lagged alright."

I smiled. Remi had eaten about half of her toast and it was clear that was all she was going to manage.

"Do you want me to take you back to your hotel so you can take a nap? Remi is on orders to rest up today, too, so…" My words fell off uncertainly.

"What are you going to do?"

"Well, I thought I'd go home and clean after she falls asleep."

We were standing on opposite sides of the bed and the hospital room seemed small. I reached down and pushed the button that would lower the head of Remi's bed down a bit. "Time to close your eyes." I picked up the remote and clicked off the TV and Remi nodded. "You wanna go home, so let's do what the doctor says."

"Okay, Mommy."

I bent to kiss her head, and I touched her nose with mine. "I love you."

"Love you, back" she answered automatically.

"Are you hungry, Chase? It will take a few minutes for her to nod off, and you can grab a sandwich before I run you back."

The start of a beard was starting to grow on his strong jawline and it left a subtle shadow that only made his eyes more striking. I could see he was tired.

"I guess." He hesitated, but only briefly. "Is there a way I can help you? Can we just hire someone to clean the house?"

"It's kind of short notice. I'm not sure we could find a cleaning company that is available. Plus, it's expensive. I can do it."

"When?" he shook his head. "And forget the money. I'll cover it."

It was generous and a huge part of me wanted to take him up on it. The time at the hospital had a way of making keeping the house clean impossible, and this job would be a big one.

"I don't expect you to do that."

"Look, it's not for you. It's for Remi." He dismissed my objection.

Chase's tone wasn't loud and he wasn't scowling at me, so why did I feel like he'd just slapped me in the face? When he put it that way, what could I say? He was right. I doubted I'd have time to get everything done and to the degree it needed to be done by myself. Plus, Jensen was coming home and Kat would arrive in another hour. I flushed, knowing I needed to tell Chase.

He mistook my pause for acquiescence. "Great. I'll grab us something to eat, and you can line up the cleaning company in the meantime?"

I didn't know what to say. "Chase...?"

He ignored me and got on his knees by the bed to talk up close to Remi. "Hey, princess. I'll see you later when you wake up, okay? Get some good dreams and I'll bring you some ice cream later. " His hand cupped her little face and kissed her on the temple, then rose up to leave.

"Mm' kay," Remi answered. "Love you."

It was as natural as when she said it to me, but it stopped Chase dead and a pained smile lifted his perfect lips. "I love you, too, baby." He was already walking past me on his way out the door, but I could see him swallow hard, and hear the emotion in his voice.

I love you, too, baby. Those words rocked me to the core. He'd said the same to me at least a thousand times. I never once doubted he meant every word.

ONE *touch*
AND THE PAIN
melted away.

Chapter 6

CHASE

I hated hotel rooms.

Traveling around the world; I didn't spend much time sitting inside four walls. There was always something interesting to do and see, but here in Atlanta, waiting to see if I could help save my child, I felt like I was in a steel cage. Anxiety was eating me alive and the helplessness of the situation drove me crazy.

It had taken additional money, but Teagan was able to hire an industrial cleaning company to come in and clean her house after hours. She went to line that up and I was going to get a few hours of sleep while Remi rested.

My wet hair was dripping down my back from the shower I'd just taken, and a towel was slung low over my hips. I hadn't bothered drying off so rivulets of water rolled down the skin of my chest, arms and legs as well.

I should eat, but I didn't want to. I felt sick; literally sick. My insides were hollow and I had this huge gaping hole where my heart was supposed to be. I felt empty, yet miserable as fuck. I didn't know what the hell to do with myself. My emotions were all screwed up. I was mad, hurt, lost... lethargic as hell, and confused about what to do next, how to act, or what to say to Teagan. Worst of all, I felt helpless to do more to help Remi. I had no clue about what would happen tomorrow, let alone next week.

Betrayal, jealousy, and helplessness were the three most ruthless emotions. I was conflicted and honestly, thankful for the break. I needed to center myself and try to organize my thoughts so I could make decisions that had to be made. Obviously, I had to be here, but I was still reeling. My entire life had changed whether I wanted it to or not.

Remi was surreal and so precious, but facing the past, seeing Teagan with Jensen or coming to terms with the severity of my little girl's illness wasn't something I wanted to face.

Losing the fight with her wasn't an option. Remi would beat this thing if it took every cent I had. She was the first priority, but the rest of it dug at me, too. It was as if I'd finally managed to breathe and now I was being pulled fifty feet under all over again.

Even though it was impossible to forget the pain, I'd somehow managed to move on and build a life. The last thing I wanted was to relive it. I'd lost count of the number of times I'd dreamed of seeing Teagan again, or the endless memories of her that would invade my mind when I was with Bronwyn or some other faceless woman. My hand went to my head and pulled on a shock of my wet hair. Water ran from it through my fingers and down my forearm, but I barely noticed.

"What a monster fuck," I muttered to myself.

I flopped down on the bed and, a minute later, reached for the remote that had been left on the bedside table by the housekeeping staff. Maybe the white noise of the news would blur my brain enough to let me sleep for a few hours. Jet lag was easier to shake when you traveled east to west, but this was not a normal circumstance. My mind wouldn't shut off, and the more tired I got, the harder it was to fall asleep.

The air conditioner under the window of the hotel was blowing into the room and caused a shiver across my wet skin. I used my feet to roughly pushing the blankets and sheets down until I could shove them beneath and then tugged the covers halfway up my chest; willing myself to relax.

I'd often use one of Bronwyn's training techniques when I was tensed. She taught me to start with my feet and flex every muscle moving up my body in succession and then to release them in the opposite direction. It did help, and my body felt like a wet noodle when I was done.

My phone was turned off at the hospital, and now was buzzing non-stop with messages from my coaches, who were frantic about my absence. I made one short call telling them not to worry, and I'd explain it when I saw them that weekend. After the tests tomorrow I'd need to catch a flight out for the game on Sunday, and then back again. What a relief that it was only an hour later in Brasilia than in Atlanta; at least there wouldn't be any added exhaustion. I didn't have my flight booked yet, and I didn't even care that it would triple the price; I'd deal with it tomorrow.

I scrolled through my phone and there were several missed calls from Bronwyn and one text from Kat. I didn't want to deal with either of them. Bronwyn would pelt me with questions that I didn't have the answers for, and Kat; well, she was another story. Anger boiled deep inside my chest and threatened to overflow. So much for blood being thicker than water. Her misplaced solidarity with Teagan disgusted me.

I guess having a pussy trumps blood ties in her eyes.

My eyes narrowed due to the direction of my thoughts. Did my parents or Kevin know about Remi? Was the joke solely on me? The magnitude of the possibility floored me. Surely my mother and father wouldn't stoop so low, and I couldn't believe my brother would take Teagan's side; he'd witnessed the depth of my destruction, first hand.

Somehow I'd managed to keep it together in front of Teagan and my little girl, but my emotions were simmering just beneath the surface and threatened to explode at any time. It was all I could do to keep them under control.

Poor, brave, little, perfect and sweet Remi. My heart leaped when I thought of her, and then sank at the weight of her battle. She was the innocent victim in all of this and she was the one suffering the most. I want to yell, scream and beat the shit out of something at the injustice of it all, but it wouldn't change anything. The only thing I could do was get through these damn tests as quickly as possible, keep the past in the past, and take care of Remi going forward.

From the moment I set eyes on that beautiful, little face with replicas of my green eyes and expressions staring back at me, I was done. There was no denying she was mine, or our immediate father/daughter connection. In a split second, she became the center of my universe.

Teagan's decision to tell Remi about me was unexpected, but it definitely made the meeting easier. I realized it would have been awful if Remi saw me as a complete stranger. It was an amazing relief, but I didn't understand Teagan's reasoning. Why would she keep my daughter from me, yet tell the little girl stories about me, that I was her father, and show her pictures of me? It made no sense. If she wanted me gone, then... why?

"Uhggggg!" I moaned into the room. There was nothing more frustrating than unanswered questions. If one more thing got piled on top of this shit storm, I'd lose it. I sucked in enough air to fill my lungs to the point of bursting and closed my eyes; trying to concentrate on the dull, droning voice of the local news anchor, and the rhythm of my own breathing to try to relax and, hopefully, sleep.

A knock on the door startled me awake just when I was starting to doze and I bolted upright. My first thought was that something happened to Remi. "Yeah!" I jumped off the bed and quickly noticed the towel had loosened and dropped to the floor. "Shit," I muttered. "Just a minute!" I found a pair of clean black jeans in my duffle and shoved my feet in the legs, struggling to pull them up and zipped at the same time as I hurried to the door.

I quickly unlatched the lock and swung the heavy door open. The air in my lungs exited in a rush when I saw my older sister, Kat, standing in front of me. I glowered at her. "Look; it's the traitor. What the hell are you doing here?"

I held the door open with my straight arm, and Kat, who was much shorter than I, ducked underneath and darted into the room. "Great to see you, too, little brother."

"Fuck you. I don't have a sister anymore. You have no right to be here. Get out."

She waltzed into the room and planted herself on the small chaise in the corner of the room. It was the only furniture other than a desk and a bed in the economy room. "Don't be dramatic. It doesn't suit you."

I had no choice but to let the door close if I wanted to confront her. I pulled a plain white T-shirt out of the duffle and threw it on. "Like I said, fuck you. You knew about Remi and you didn't tell me? I don't have one thing to say to you."

She sighed and the snarky look on her face softened. I wasn't just pissed; sadness and betrayal threatened to engulf me. "How long have you known?"

Kat looked at me for a minute and she leaned forward, scooting to the end of the chaise so she could lean forward. "I'll tell you if you'll listen."

I shook my head, doing my best not to yell or cry. I swallowed hard. "There is nothing you can say that will excuse keeping this from me for six years."

She shook her head. "You're right. It was wrong. I should have called you. It wasn't an easy decision."

I glared at her, standing on the opposite side of the room from her with my hands on my hips. If the heat in my face or the twitching of my jaw were visible, Kat had to see how angry and upset I was.

She put both hands up and splayed her fingers on them. "Please sit down and listen."

I didn't want to move or do anything Kat demanded. I felt as if I was a nine-year-old getting scolded by my teacher. My pulse was racing and my skin was on fire.

"I'm going to tell you the same thing I told Teagan; I don't want to hear any of the reasons any of you liars did what you did, I'm here to help Remi. She's all I care about." My voice cracked on her name and a lone tear fell from my right eye. I lifted my hand and brushed it away with my thumb. "The rest of you don't matter to me."

"Chase," Kat said softly, tearing up herself. "I know you love Remi, and I knew you'd take to her. She is so sweet and she's gone through so much."

"Do you know her? You're in her life when I'm not?" I couldn't even grasp the possibility.

"Not really. I only met her twice in person. She was little and I never intended to keep it from you. It isn't like Teagan is my best friend, but I read about Remi's cancer on one of the local news websites. Jensen was up and coming on ESPN and locally, people knew him. Their church was doing a pancake feed to help with expenses, and David and I went."

Hearing Jensen's name only made me more pissed off. My defenses were up as if a ten-foot thick steel wall had just slammed down on me. "Is that when you found out she was mine?"

"No, that was the second time. She was just a baby the first time."

"What?" I asked incredulously; stunned by what I was hearing. "Why didn't you tell me?" I shouted. I felt like my head and heart was about to combust. How could my own sister keep this from me? The level of betrayal almost equaled that of Teagan and Jensen.

"Before you lose your shit, just listen, Chase. Remember when I called you on your birthday the year after you left? I'd seen how upset you were the first time you were home from England and you were still so unhappy; I wanted to do something to help. I hoped if I reached out to Teagan maybe I could gauge how she was doing and if there was any hope for you two."

"She was already married to Jensen by then," I said in defeat.

"I didn't know that, then. I looked for Teagan on Facebook, but she didn't have a profile. I Googled South Carolina public records and that's when I found Remi's birth certificate and the marriage license to Jensen." Tears were starting to stream down my sister's face, and while part of me resisted hearing it, I wanted the answers. I couldn't stop her, and regardless, I needed to know.

"I was so damn angry, Chase. I couldn't believe they'd do that to you and I finally understood why you were so broken. I researched more and found out they moved to Atlanta, then went to confront her, but the minute she saw me at the door she fell apart, Chase. She was alone with Remi in a small apartment. The minute I saw that child's face, I knew the truth. I laid into her, but she convinced me that it was too late and a nasty custody battle would only ruin your budding career. She was already married, and you seemed better. You just got moved up to starting forward." Kat wrung her hands in a show of helplessness.

"I had a right to know!" My voice boomed in the small room as I took three steps in her direction. How could Kat think that a stupid game would mean more to me than my baby?

Kat flinched, but nodded, wiping at the tears on one of her cheeks with her hand. "You're right. You did. But what would you have done? I knew you weren't happy, but you were at least trying to move on. You were dating Bronwyn, and I guess... I just didn't want to make you suffer it all again, and I didn't want to be the one to tell you."

"Neither one of you had any right to make that decision for me!" I sank down to sit at the foot of the bed and bent over my knees, my grief overtaking my resolve. The magnitude of all I had lost was more than I could stand and misery took over. "How dare either of you? You have no idea how I was! I was still wallowing in hell! For years, I was in hell. All I was doing was drinking and screwing Bronwyn to keep from losing my mind! I didn't care about anything but getting rid of the pain."

If there were guests in the rooms around mine or beneath, they were getting surround sound as I shouted at my sister. "Teagan was destroyed, too, Chase."

"Yeah, right," I spat. "She was so broken up, she was married in a few months."

"Think about the timing, Chase. Her father threatened to disown her and drag your name through the mud. I didn't agree with her reasons, but when Teagan explained how she kept it quiet to protect you, it made sense in some naïve sort of way. She knew how much soccer meant to you; it was the only future you wanted. And look at you now. Look at the success you've had."

I sniffed, willing myself to get control of the fury surging through me. I lifted my head and met her pleading eyes with my accusing ones. "Do you think I give a flying fuck about that? Do you really believe I'd choose a stupid sport over my family? Teagan, of all people, should have known better! Is that what you all think of me?"

She shook her head sadly, scooting forward further to rest one hand on the two of mine that were folded in front of me. "No, but now you have the luxury of looking at it from an outside perspective, and everyone who loved you knew how important playing soccer was to you. She didn't want to be responsible for killing your dream. I didn't agree with her, but I understood her logic. She realized that if she told you; you would have given it all up and there would be part of you always wondering what might have been and she didn't want you to blame her. You know it's true, Chase," she said fiercely.

"No!" I flung her hand away and stood up, stalking away. "No, I wouldn't! Nothing meant more to me than Teagan! Nothing!"

Kat let out a small snort and shook her head. "Yeah? Well, she was the one here, alone, to figure things out."

It was as if she'd taken a wrecking ball and hit me in the gut with it. My mouth opened and then shut without saying anything, instead I dragged in a ragged breath. "Not alone," I spat, visions of Jensen with Teagan flooding my thoughts with misery.

She picked up her purse, clearly intent on leaving. She touched my shoulder and paused beside me on her way to the door. "Please, just take a step back and listen to Teagan when you're ready. I truly believe she thought she was doing what was best for you. If you don't think that she lost you as much as you lost her, you're not looking at the big picture."

"If she's a saint like you believe, what's stopped her from telling me in the years since? Especially when Remi got sick?"

"Money and fear. She didn't have the money to fight you if you decided to go for custody. She was scared she'd lose her baby, and she couldn't risk that."

Again, my anger and sense of betrayal railed with Teagan's twisted reasoning. Even if it was true, there was no excuse for that level of deceit. It was wrong on so many levels.

I started to speak but Kat stopped me.

"Don't say it." She walked to the door, but the part of me that had festered and died over this for the past six years couldn't keep it in.

"Why not?" Hatred dripped off my words. "He swooped in like a fucking vulture! He couldn't wait for me to leave. Every one of you lied to me!"

"Chase!" She whirled on me right just before she reached the door. "Will you stop acting like the wounded victim in everything? You made your own choices! You went to London! Was Teagan wrong in keeping Remi from you? Yes! She should have told you she was pregnant!" Her eyes were wide and she was pissed. "Or, I should have told you! I get that I'm the worst sister ever! If I could go back and change it, I would, but you need to crawl out of your pity party long enough to just think about your part in it! It isn't as if Teagan's or Jensen's life has been amazing. Neither of them is sucking on rainbow popsicles and living the life they wanted! It wasn't her dream to be without you or to have a terminally ill child. She's been punished enough, already! Remi has been sick for three years and you've been spared all of it!"

My hand clenched into a fist and I turned and slammed it into the wall, the momentum slamming through the wall and gouging a large hole. It caused a huge bang and Kat literally jumped back from me. My chest was heaving and I couldn't breathe.

"None of it is my fault! It wasn't my choice! I didn't want to be spared!" I yelled, frustrated tears flooding my eyes once again. My fist remained clenched and I gritted my teeth as I railed at her. "I missed out on her life, to see her born, to see

her grow, and now, there may not be time to make up for it."
Pain ripped through my heart like a million shards of glass.

Kat paused at my outburst, looking at the floor and
nodding in resignation, calm. "You're right, and I'm not
excusing any of it, Chase, but Teagan honestly thought she
was doing what you needed. If I didn't truly believe that she
believed that, I would have told you everything, but I knew in
order to really understand you needed to hear it from her. Out
of the three of you, which one of you has the life you
dreamed of?"

My head dropped and I watched the tears drop from my
eyes to the floor as if they were in slow motion, and they
splatted on the carpet. She was right, but it didn't take away the
magnitude of my loss. All I could do was shake my head, and
use the back of my uninjured hand to wipe at the end of my
nose and my fingers to push the tears off my face. "Do you
think the life I dreamed of, didn't have her in it?"

"I'm going over to Teagan's to help her with the laundry
while the cleaning crew finishes up. I'll pick you up at 5:30 in
the morning for your tests. Unless you need to go to the ER
for your hand, right now?"

I looked up, but the light coming from the fixture over the
mirror by the door, combined with the tears still clinging to my
lashes, threw glaring rays around my sister's form, making her
blur. I shook my head and stumbled back into the room.
Everything hurt so fucking much. One flip of a switch and
everything had changed.

I cleared my throat and walked to the built-in that I'd laid
my wallet on. "Wait." I opened it and took out five, one-
hundred dollar bills and handed them to her, trying to hide
how the bills shook as in my hand. "Please give this to Teagan.
It's for the cleaners. Since you're here, can I get a ride to the
airport after the tests? I have a game on Sunday."

"Sure. Hopefully, it will be your last for a while. If you're able to donate, you'll have to be here."

"I will be," I said adamantly, unable to accept any other answer. I had to be a match so that Remi would live. I would accept no other answer.

Chapter 7

Teagan

"Chase is in town, then?" Jensen's voice was tired, but with an angry undercurrent.

He was supposed to come home tonight, but it was the weekend and ESPN had given him another assignment, which would mean a two-day delay. It wasn't anything new. Jensen was a junior correspondent and frequently got cleanup duty when another reporter or anchor fell ill or the network decided to cover an event, last minute.

It was annoying at times, but Jensen's career was on the move and any chance to get in front of the cameras, especially given a chance to commentate on an entire event, was imperative. He worked hard to prove himself and he had started as a junior reporter in the newsroom without any live face time for the first two years. He deserved every advance he was given.

I could sense his trepidation and irritation through the phone, but it wasn't clear if he was angry at ESPN for the longer assignment or anxious about not being home while

Chase was in town. Lately, we were both stressed so much we argued more than we talked.

"I didn't know what else to do," I said, loudly into the phone. "We're running out of options."

The carpet-cleaning machine was running in the background making it hard to hear. The house was modest, Jensen's job with ESPN was still a reporter at present and without my nurse's salary, we were struggling. Jensen wouldn't appreciate Chase helping with the cleaning costs, but under the circumstances, I had to let him help.

"Yeah," he said, resigned. "Are you okay? How'd he take it?" Jensen rifled off questions faster than I could answer them.

I couldn't be honest and say it was a mixture of heaven and hell, so I offered an abbreviated version. "He was furious at first, but it was easier after he met Remi. He's totally taken with her."

"Who isn't?" His voice softened. "How is she doing?"

As usual, when the subject of Chase came up, the conversation was diverted but this time, it wasn't a clean pivot. "She's been tired, and it's a struggle to get her to eat. She's weaker."

"Fucking cancer. I'd give anything to take it away from her."

"I know you would."

"How'd she react to Chase?"

I hesitated to tell him the truth because I knew it would sting. "He does well with her and she adores him." I stuck the index finger of my free hand into my ear to muffle the background noise. "It's like she's always known him."

Jensen sighed heavily. "Figures. Chase always gets the breaks," resentment laced his tone like acid.

I was in the kitchen as far away from the cleaning crew as I could get. My heart plummeted in my chest. Not one of us had it easy. We were all in hell. "You know in your heart that isn't true."

"Right. Keep telling yourself that."

It hurt when Jensen was angry or jealous of Chase's professional success, but I could understand it. If only he wouldn't have told my dad he was the father of my baby... if only it hadn't hit the news, I might be living a completely different life; we all would. "I shouldn't have married you, Jensen. It wasn't fair."

Jensen ignored my comment and pushed on. "It doesn't hurt that you paint him as a saint. Its no wonder he seems perfect to her."

Bam. I was damned, no matter what I did. "I did it for her, you know that."

"That's bullshit, and you know it." His voice sounded as weary as I felt. "You did it for you and him! Remi has always been happy until she got sick. She has everything she needs, and I love her. You're the one who needed to keep the door open with Chase."

I closed my eyes, refusing to get sucked into another argument. "Considering the circumstances, I'm glad I did." Everything was such a mess and I was tired of this conversation. We'd had it a hundred times after he discovered I was telling Remi about Chase. Even though it was part of our agreement from the beginning, he was still hurt and guilt hit me like a tidal wave again. I couldn't deny everything Jensen had sacrificed to stand by me and take care of my child. And, he'd treated Remi as if she were his since the day she was born. "I know this is hard for you, and I'm sorry. All I'm doing lately is crying and saying I'm sorry."

"Well, it's one fucked up mess."

It was, but he didn't have to do what he'd done. "Chase is doing his best to come to terms with things and deal with the here and now. He wants to help Remi. Isn't that what we all want?"

"Yes."

I rushed on with the details, keeping emotion out of it. "The marker test has been done and we're waiting for the results, but Chase is moving forward with the doctors on the remaining tests so, we can move forward as soon as possible if they match."

"That's something, at least. What are his plans?" He asked stoically.

"I don't know that much about his schedule. He has a game this weekend and he's planning to make arrangements with his club to take a leave of absence for the transplant and recovery."

"Has he made any threats to take her, yet? Because if not, you'd better get ready."

Sadness washed over me that Jensen would be so suspicious of someone who used to be his best friend in the world, and wished he would concentrate on what Remi needed and leave it at that. "He hasn't mentioned anything close to it. Do you really think he'd do that?"

"You never know. A lot of shit has happened and he never was one to let anyone roll over him. He has the money to sue for custody if he wants it. There's no way I can lawyer up like he can, Teagan."

I was staring out the back door into the yard, a streetlight illuminating the modest swing set that was there next to a small sandbox Jensen had constructed out of one of those baby pools he'd sunk into the ground and filled with sand.

We'd discussed all of the adverse things that could happen if, and when, Chase found out about Remi and it had been a big part of the fight we had before he left. He was scared. Jensen couldn't love her more if he were her real father, and I understood how he felt, but I couldn't let emotions change what was being done for Remi. She was my first and only concern right now, and getting her well had to take precedence over custody. Even if I lost her to Chase, it would be better than losing her to cancer.

It wasn't as if I hadn't thought about all of this already. Chase might want revenge and use custody of Remi as a hammer. It was a concern, but deep down in my heart, I couldn't believe that he would. "I don't think he'll do that. He just wants to see her get well."

"Well, don't think it's beneath him. He's not as perfect as you think he is."

"I can't think about it right now, Jensen. He's here and he's doing what we need him to do for Remi. He's struggling like the rest of us, and to be fair, he's been blindsided. Please… just don't antagonize him."

Jensen let out a disgusted grunt just before the doorbell rang. The sound was faint over the din of the carpet cleaners and I ended the call on my way to answer it.

"Someone's at the door. I'll call you as soon as I have news, but I have to go help the cleaners finish up." The minute the words were out, I regretted them. Money was a sticky subject for Jensen and he'd never want to accept anything from Chase, for any reason.

"Cleaners?" I could already hear the accusation in his voice.

There were five workers milling through the house cleaning the bathrooms; wiping down every surface with disinfectant besides the man running the carpet cleaner. Three of them were men, and the furniture was left askew as it was moved to vacuum and then shampoo the carpets and floors beneath. I was grateful for their help. I wouldn't have been able to get it clean enough by myself, but I was afraid to look at the bill.

"Yes, Remi is being allowed home for a few days. It was last minute and I wasn't ready. Don't worry about the money —"

He cursed under his breath. "Of course. Chase, right? Mr. Amazing sweeps in and takes over."

My heart fell like a stone into the pit of my stomach. If I never heard Jensen say Chase's name like that again, it would be too soon. "It's a gift for Remi so she can come home."

"Is he staying at the house?"

"No, he has a room in a hotel near the hospital." I didn't volunteer that I'd invited Chase to stay in the spare room. I didn't know what the hell I was doing. Jensen had a right to feel threatened and resentful, but Chase might be able to save Remi and he was more magnanimous than I had a right to expect.

"That's something, at least" he sounded more relieved.

"Jensen, please. Chase could have told me to fuck off when I told him about Remi. He has every right to turn his back and never look back, but instead, he's more than willing to help." Emotion made my voice shake even though I tried to keep it even. "He might be Remi's last hope and I'm praying to God he's a match... no matter what happens afterward. Please, can we get through the next month?"

He sighed heavily into the phone. "Yeah."

The doorbell rang again and I tried to clear the tears out of my voice. "Thank you. I have to go finish up. See you when you get back."

I rushed to the door as the call ended, opening it to find Kat standing on the doorstep, her round face lit up when she saw me. A second later I was clamped into a tight hug. "Hi, honey!

"Hi! I was starting to get worried!" I raised my voice above the machines. I felt like I'd been yelling at Jensen on the

126

phone, and speaking with Kat in person was almost as difficult. "Sorry about the noise!"

Kat waved away my comment with casual dismissal. "No worries! I had a flat tire on I-85." Her face twisted wryly and she offered an over-exaggerated shrug before I ushered her inside.

"Oh, no!"

"Dave says if something's gonna happen, then it's gonna happen to me. It's a good thing he taught me how to swap out the donut," Kat laughed softly, pulling a small roller bag behind her through the entryway. The house was older; mid-1970s but it had been updated. When we moved in it was wall-to-wall carpet even in the kitchen, but we've installed laminated hardwood in the kitchen, dining room and bathrooms. It was a modest 3-bedroom, but it was nice. I considered Kat would get a room at the same hotel where Chase was staying, but her suitcase indicated she was planning on staying at the house. "He says I'm a trouble magnet."

I smiled nervously; mentally registering nearby tire shops so we could get it fixed the following day. "I appreciate that he agreed to let you come for a visit. The spare room is down the hall, first door on the left." Her visit was a bit sudden and being preoccupied with Chase and Remi; I hadn't thought it all through.

"We can get to that later! How's Remi doing with Chase?"

I paused to meet her eyes, unable to make light of it. "They're amazing, Kat. It's more than I could have hoped for. She looks at him like he hung the moon, and he's just— incredible with her. He's a natural."

The love I had for both of them filled me to the point of bursting, but it was painfully overshadowed by the lost time and the consequences of the decisions I'd made. The regret was intense and I knew it would never leave my heart.

"I knew he would be. He's great with my boys and Kevin's girls." Kat smiled, but seeing the crease on my forehead and the emotion grimacing my face, thankfully changed the subject. "Okay, put me to work! What can I do?" Kat was dressed in jeans, a casual white tank top, and cheap pink flip-flops. Her enthusiasm and get-down-to-business demeanor was a welcome foil for my exhaustion and helped me to push past the sadness.

"Would you like something to eat or drink, first?" I was anxious to find out if she'd spoken to Chase, but I felt awkward asking.

"Maybe a glass of water, thanks." She nodded. "I'll just stash my stuff in the spare room, then?" she asked.

"That would be great."

Kat turned down the hall and I quickly went into the kitchen to get her a glass of filtered water from the refrigerator. I'd kept in touch with her periodically, but had only seen her twice since Chase and I broke up. The day she confronted me, and once right after Remi got sick when we held a fundraiser and she and David attended. Since then, she called me about once a month. My heart was sick that she couldn't really be in my life, but how could I ask that of her? It was already a burden to keep Remi a secret, and I didn't want to add to it.

When she came back from the bedroom, she took the glass and looked at me with compassionate eyes.

"I know I look like hell," I said dully, suddenly conscious of my appearance. I pushed my long hair off of my face and shoved it behind my right ear.

"You look tired, that's all." Kat reached out and rubbed up and down my left arm. Her understanding tone was comforting. "You've been through a lot in the last few days."

"Really, it's been years," I admitted as I pulled out a chair and sat down, nodding to the one across from me. She took the hint and joined me at the table. "Seeing Chase has been emotional; topped off with the stress of not knowing that he is Remi's last hope," I stopped and put a hand to the nagging ache in my forehead. "It's just a lot to deal with."

"I understand. For Chase, too."

I nodded and bit my lip, trying not to cry. "I know. I'm such an awful person, Kat." My throat was tight and I struggled to speak over the thickness. "I can't stand seeing him in pain. The years haven't changed one damn thing for me."

"I understand," she said softly. "It wasn't just the tire that slowed me down. I went to see Chase, too."

My breath left my lungs in surprise. "Oh," I said, not knowing what else to say. I froze, waiting for a bomb to go off. She would have seen how this was affecting him and maybe he wouldn't have been so guarded with her. While I wanted to know how he was dealing with everything, I was also afraid of the answer. I was terrified she'd say he hated me. Contempt was the last emotion I wanted to inspire within Chase.

"I can't sugarcoat it, Teagan. He's reeling, and... railing, a bit. We should expect that."

My hand came up and I pressed three fingers to my lips as I fought back the tears. Her image blurred in front of me as I nodded. "I know. I'd do anything to take away the pain I've caused him— to take it all back. We haven't talked about the why or how everything happened like it did. Maybe he doesn't want to know."

She nodded slowly, one eyebrow lifting cynically. "He doesn't. He wants to focus on Remi right now, but I think eventually he'll want to talk about it. It will get easier." Her words were gentle and her expression concerned.

I was dying to ask what he said as tears started to tumble from my eyes and roll, one by one, down my cheeks. "I want so much to tell him everything, but I understand why he doesn't want to hear it, and I deserve that, Kat."

She reached across the table to take my hand and squeezed it. "He's mad at everyone right now. He's grieving a huge loss and suffering the uncertainty of the future. He's scared he'll lose Remi without having time with her."

I bowed my head and cried, squeezing her hand back as my shoulders shook. I was scared of the exact same thing. If he hated me for the rest of my life it was deserved, but just the thought of it ripped me to shreds. "I kn—ow." The phrase ripped from me as I cried. "I de—serve it, if he ha—hates me," I sobbed.

"Teagan, give him time to get used to things. He just has a lot to come to terms with."

"I know, but I have all this regret, and the need to explain to him is just kill—illing me, Kat. I can't stand having him thinking such hor—rible things about me. If I can tell him, muh—maybe it won't hurt him as muh—uch."

She scooted one chair closer and gathered me into a hug. "Oh, Teagan. I'm so sorry."

"It's such a muh—mess!" I clung to her for a good minute as I cried it out. If the cleaning people gawked or wondered what was going on, I didn't notice. "Everyone is suffering unspeakably because of me."

"Take a deep breath. One day at a time. That's all any of us can do."

I sniffed and did as she asked, trying to calm down. "You should hate me, too."

"No." She shook her head sympathetically. "I may not understand your reasons, but I don't think you had malice in your heart."

"It so hard, Kat. It's been so hard... all this time, I've missed him." Both of her hands were still holding me and started to rub my back in small, soft circles. It was similar to how I comforted Remi when she was upset or hurt.

An unasked question hung between us for a beat. I could feel it in the air. She wanted to know how Jensen played into the equation. What were my feelings for him? How could I be so screwed up over Chase and have stayed with Jensen all these years? I was about to tell her that Jensen and I were going to divorce before Remi got sick, but she spoke before I could get it out.

"Let's just tidy up for Remi, get her home for a few days, and let Chase get his results and make arrangements to take a leave of absence from Arsenal. We can go from there, okay? I'm sure he'll want as much time with her as he can get." She hesitated and took a deep breath, glancing around. "Uh, it will have to be here, so will Jensen be okay with it?" She'd figured out a way to get Jensen's name into the conversation so she could at least gauge my reaction.

I lifted one shoulder in a half shrug. "He'll have to be. What choice is there?"

"Exactly."

"Jensen knows how I feel about Chase, and that it hasn't changed. He's given up a lot to help me raise Remi when I needed someone," I stopped when she started to protest.

"Chase would ha—"

I put up a hand and nodded. "I know he would have, and I know what a mess this is. I've prayed a thousand times that someday they would both forgive me, but I can't worry about it until after Remi is better."

I was an only child and my relationship with my father was distant at best, so I was happy Kat was here. Remi's sickness had distanced me from the few friends I had because there was little time left to socialize. Remi, my precarious marriage to Jensen, and my undying love for Chase were all I had to hold on to. I could lose everyone who mattered; every piece of my world could crumble, and I was barely holding it together.... I'd be lying to Kat and to myself if I said I wasn't going through hell over every piece of it. There was no way to separate Remi from Chase in my heart or mind, now, but I silently vowed to put up a good front. I was already fragile enough.

"You're right. Come on," Kat encouraged brightly, patting my shoulder. "We need to get busy so you can bring Remi home, right?"

I lifted my head and brought my tearful gaze to her face, grateful for her strength. "Thank you for being here."

Kat stopped; her face concerned as she considered her next words. "I should have come sooner." Regret flashed across her expressive features. "It's just that I knew I'd fall in love with Remi and I wouldn't have been able to keep it from Chase."

I nodded sadly, feeling the intensity of her conflict. I'd felt it every day for the past five years. "I understand, Kat. I shouldn't have asked you to lie for me."

"It's just hard to understand how you could do it. You used to love him so much."

My eyes, still teary, started to burn again as it became almost impossible to speak over the emotion in my throat. "I still do. I can't even articulate how screwed up I was. I was scared for Chase... and for me."

Something burned inside me as the desire to tell her about the woman on the phone gnawed at me. The woman, who was the deciding factor in my decision to stay in South Carolina, shook my faith and I let my father bully me, and then I let Jensen take responsibility. That phone call influenced me even more than Chase's career, because of the blinding pain that blurred my ability to think straight.

Before that, he was more important than anything... my love for him made me willing to sacrifice my relationship with my father and my nursing degree, and run off to London to be with him... if only it weren't for that fucking phone call that broke my heart. I could tell her, but what would it change? What good would it do? I had so much pain to deal with in the present, digging up the past was just as intolerable in the moment, and Chase had already suffered enough. I didn't want to make it seem like I was trying to justify my actions or hoist the blame in his direction.

"Were you afraid he'd ask you to get an abortion?"

I felt like an electric shock ran through me. The thought had never occurred to me, though I could see why someone outside of the immediate situation might come to that conclusion.

I ran a weary hand through my hair and rose from the table and went to the sink full of dishes and started to rinse them before bending to open the dishwasher. "No." Never, my mind boomed. Chase would never ask me to do that. I shook myself mentally. My heart still felt exactly the same as it had from the minute I fell in love with him as if my heart knew his even better than he knew himself, but maybe I didn't. If Kat would even suggest it, maybe he would have, too. She was his sister, so if it weren't possible, would she suggest it? Jesus. "No, I never thought he'd ask that of me. Do you think he would have if I'd have told him the truth?"

"No, but over the years, I've considered that you might have taken the decision to put his career first out of his hands just to avoid that exact conversation. Like maybe... the possibility of him failing you like that would hurt too much."

"That's generous of you, Kat. More than I deserve. No." Tears filled my eyes as I plugged the sink, turned on the hot water and reached for the dishwashing liquid and squeezed a good amount into the water before shoving several dirty pans into it. "Chase would never fail that test."

"Then, I don't get it." Kat pulled off the dishtowel I had hanging on the handle of the oven and came to stand next to me at the sink. I blinked in an attempt to hide my tears. "I know you probably don't want to talk about it, but I can't help wondering."

I glanced at her trying to conjure a weak smile. I gave up and started to wash the dishes, plunging a clean dishcloth into the scalding water; wincing. It seared my skin and still, I persisted, pushing the wet rag over the surface of a pan that Jensen used to make macaroni and cheese, and then left it to dry. I scrubbed, ignoring the burn of the water on my flesh. Physical pain was a welcome respite from the emotional torture I dealt with.

"Sorry, Teagan," Kat said softly. "I didn't mean to make you cry, again."

"Everything makes me cry, lately. It's not you. My emotions are just a little too raw. I've never been good at hiding my feelings."

Kat took the pan from me and rinsed it, and then started to dry it before setting it aside as I washed the next one. "I will never forgive myself, Kat. Just seeing Chase and Remi together I realize how I've robbed them both of something priceless. If Remi doesn't make it, I'm not sure how I'll live with myself."

Kat reached out and laid a hand on my shoulder, squeezing gently. "She's going to be fine. You'll see. Chase will match."

"He has to, Kat." I continued my task. "He just has to."

"Well, if he doesn't, we'll start hounding people to test for the registry. We can start a campaign on social media. If you're all willing to tell the world he's her father, I'm sure thousands would turn out for it."

I nodded, unwilling to tell her I wasn't sure if we had the luxury of the time necessary. Remi had already been on the donor list for four months without result. If Chase didn't match she'd have to take chemo right away and I shuddered at the possibility. "Mean medicine; that's what Remi calls chemo and if he doesn't match we have to start it right away ..." I let my words die in despair.

Kat wrapped her right arm around me as we both leaned against the counter in front of the sink full of sudsy water. She tugged me a bit closer until our hips touched and squeezed my waist. "It's all gonna be fine. We just have to have faith, Teagan. Remi will be okay, and Chase will come around. Time heals everything."

My chin fell toward my chest and I gave an almost imperceptible nod in affirmation, though inside I was frozen with fear. I'd been praying for Remi for two years and Chase well, there'd been a hole in my heart since he left for London so long ago.

I prayed to God that Kat was right.

ONE *touch*
AND THE PAIN
melted away.

Chapter 8

CHASE

Remi was sleeping and I was slumped in the chair beside her.

The sound of her even breathing had a calming effect on the raging turmoil in my head and heart. It was only 10 PM, but Remi had been sleeping for over an hour. Teagan was working with Kat and the cleaning crew to get her house ready for Remi the next day. I'd texted to let her know I planned to take Remi some ice cream and spend time with her before she went to sleep, so she'd be able to finish the house without worrying about our daughter.

Our daughter. I was still reeling but somehow accepting responsibility for Remi was easier than forgiving Teagan, Jensen and now, Kat.

Jesus. Did my entire family know and keep it from me?

I'd left the hotel with my head full of convoluted thoughts, but still took a cab to the nearest bookstore and picked up a dozen new books, a teddy bear, a coloring book, and crayons for her; then I had the driver drop me off at the 7-11 down the street from the hospital where I picked up a carton of chocolate Ben & Jerry's. We shared it and then I read her one of the stories about Clifford the Big Red Dog. I'd adored the series when I was young and was pleased that Remi loved it, too.

The light in the room was off with only the soft blue glow from the silenced television to fall on Remi lying so peacefully in the bed. I glanced at her angelic face and my heart seized. In repose, it was a perfect replica of Teagan's, and when her eyes were open there was no denying she was mine. How could Teagan look in those eyes every day for the past five years and not tell me about my daughter? I felt utterly betrayed, furious, and so fucking destroyed I could barely breathe. I closed my eyes in anguish. I felt robbed and broken-hearted, walking around with my chest cracked open allowing the slow bleed that would slowly kill me.

My heart screamed at me to confront Teagan. Part of me wanted to yell and demand the answers I deserved, and another part was dying to pull her close to me and never let go. It was amazing, and at the same time, so incredibly tragic. She ripped my fucking heart out, and still I couldn't hate her even though I wanted to, and I wanted to with everything I had. I was tired of the pain that exhausted me. It had taken me years to even breathe, praying for the year I'd forget her birthday, yet one text and I was yanked mercilessly back into the past, helpless to stop the flood of emotions or the torturous thoughts.

I sighed and swallowed hard at the lump forming in my throat. Despite the desperation, depression, misery or complete and utter loss I'd suffered, there wasn't a second when I'd wished I never knew Teagan. Remi's existence, so small and fragile, only made her harder to regret. Remi was perfect and knowing how much she suffered was more than I could stand. I'd only just met her and the gravity of her illness was overwhelming; I could only imagine what Teagan had to go through watching her baby suffer the horrors of chemotherapy. Twice.

It had to be literal hell, and Kat was right; I had been spared all of it, but now I was drowning in sorrow. I pulled at the front of my shirt, absently trying to ease the tightness in my chest. I tried to fill my lungs, but it was like two steel bands refused to let them expand.

I leaned forward, and fell to my knees, resting my elbows on the mattress. Remi smelled of lotion and baby shampoo; the scent filling my nostrils as I studied her little face; the perfect bow of her mouth, her pert nose, the curve of her delicate brows and the dark lashes resting on her cheeks. She was thin so her cheeks weren't as plump as those of most children I'd seen of similar age, but she was still so beautiful.

Poor, brave little shit, my mind screamed. It wasn't fair! Life had a way of fucking you over and that was fine for me. Maybe I even deserved it, but not Remi.

I blinked at the burn in my eyes as I reached out to trace the curve of her face with the index finger of my right hand. Her skin was like velvet, her hair silky soft and baby fine. She was perfect; except for that bitch; cancer. Perfect, yet robbed of time. No child should have to suffer hospitals, needles, pain, or poison. She should be playing with her friends, going to school and having a dog… without any worries. The whole thing was so goddamn wrong.

I laid my head on Remi's pillow above hers with one arm laid over her. How could my entire world be altered so completely in less than twenty-four hours? I'd never considered this was what Teagan needed when she texted and asked me to get on a plane. I knew it was something big, but a child she'd hidden? Never. I never thought she'd do something like this. My mind slammed shut when uncertainty about her reasons nagged at me.

A few minutes later, my phone pinged as a text came in. It had to be Teagan, I thought, as I backed away from Remi to pull the phone from the clip on my belt. All of my teammates and Bronwyn were on their way to Brazil and probably sleeping on the plane. I glanced down at the words on the lighted screen.

Is she asleep?

Yes. I'm just sitting here with her. We had ice cream.

I climbed off of my knees and moved away from the bed so the light and the noise wouldn't wake my little girl. Within seconds Teagan answered.

That's nice. She likes ice cream. Are you okay?

No.

I typed the single word and sent it before I thought about how it would make Teagan feel, and was instantly pissed that I would care. I'd fought against caring for so long and all she had to do was show up in front of me and I was right back in it. I told myself it was because my emotions were all screwed up as I tried to wrap my head around having a kid and her being sick, but the truth was, Teagan was under my skin and in my heart and always would be. For better or worse, I couldn't change it.

I'm sincerely sorry, Chase.

I stood there, staring at the phone, not knowing what to respond; the words looming like one of those goofy cartoon gifs bounding out in 3-D.

She was sorry. I didn't need to hear that anymore. I sighed and typed out a message.

I know.

Do you need a ride? I can come pick you up and take you back to the hotel.

It's not that far. I can walk.

I always stay with Remi, so I'm coming back to the hospital anyway.

It's no trouble.

Damn my soul, I wanted to see her. I wanted to be near her. My heart was in agony and Teagan always used to make everything better just by being close. We did that for each other and though I knew it was dangerous, I still felt that same insatiable pull; not just sexually, but just in her presence. I sucked in a shaky breath, but before I could type more another text came in.

I understand that you want to keep distance between us, and I won't push you. I just want to make this as easy for you as I can.

Okay.

Okay to making it easy, or to the ride?

I don't know how easy it can get, but I appreciate the sentiment.

Yes to the ride. I'll meet you in front so you won't have to park.

I could have walked the whole way back by the time she'd be able to drive to the hospital, and I had no clue what would happen when we were together, but logical thought was on the back burner. My emotions were in charge right now; boiling like a cauldron inside of me. At any moment, I could lose it; I was aware and I was torn; so angry at both of us, yet so desperate just to lay eyes on her.

I'll be there in twenty minutes. See you then.

I shut the phone off and put it back on my belt before walking over to Remi and bent down to place a soft kiss on her forehead, brushing back her fine hair. Her skin was warm under my lips and once again the baby soft scent hit me. She was so precious and I said a silent prayer that my marrow would be a close enough match to save her life, silently promising God I'd give anything to get through this without too much upheaval for Remi. My marrow had to match... but if not, I'd move heaven and earth, and spend every cent I had to find the treatment that would save her.

The nurse at the desk right outside Remi's room looked up from the computer screen she was working on. She was not the same one from before; she was older than the woman from earlier in the day, but just as kind. She smiled warmly at me as I closed the door softly behind me. She didn't seem surprised to see me instead of Teagan or Jensen

"How's our girl?" she asked.

"Sleeping." Relief settled over me. The woman wasn't judging at all in her expression or her words.

"I see. She needs it."

"Yes. Her mother is coming back in a little while."

The nurse nodded and smiled again. She had a kind, grandmotherly face and I felt confident leaving Remi in her care. "Please call me if something happens. I've written my number on the whiteboard next to Teagan's."

"Yes, sir. I've heard all about you. There's a buzz about our patient's famous soccer star, dad."

I flushed again slightly, uncomfortable that I felt as if I had something to explain, even though it was nonsense. I wasn't someone who cared what other people thought about me. I played the game for the sake of playing. I was who I was, and I didn't make apologies, but this was different. I didn't want people thinking I'd abandoned my child when it was the furthest thing from the truth. No child deserved to be fatherless, especially one as sweet and amazing as Remi.

"I don't really think about people knowing who I am," I murmured, just to clarify. "I play for the game, not the fame."

After I explained the difference in the phone numbers and how she'd need to dial the country code because my phone was out of London, I was striding down the hall toward the elevators.

I felt as if I'd been rolled over by a tank. Physically, I was fine, but emotionally, I was completely spent. I longed for the mindless peace of sleep, but I'd sacrifice to spend time with the woman waiting in the parking lot.

I shook my head in self-disgust. I should hate her, and I wanted to; badly, but I'd come to the realization years earlier, that even if I could move on with my life, even be with other women, Teagan would always hold my heart. It was like a life sentence that I'd never be able to escape.

My thoughts dominated as I made my way down to the first floor; the ding of the elevator as the doors opened brought me back to the present. I focused on the glass at the front of the hospital and gleaming tile floors that led through the large lobby to the big revolving doors.

143

Teagan's silver SUV was parked under the covered driveway just outside, and I kept my eyes trained on it as I pushed through the doorway. It wasn't that late but it was dark outside, with just a hint of pinkish purple very low on the western horizon. The smells and sounds were different from those in London and it hit me how it was warmer, the air more fragrant and soft. Almost like a caress on my face and arms. My phone rang and I ignored it.

Teagan was bent down a little, watching me come outside through the half rolled down window of her vehicle.

"Hi," she said. She looked freshly showered; the ends of her dark hair damp and less smooth than I saw it earlier that day. She didn't have much makeup on, and she was dressed in dark leggings and an old Kings of Leon T-shirt.

She'd probably just pulled it out of a drawer and threw it on, but I remembered that concert and that night. It was shortly after we met and I'd pilfered Jensen's ticket so I could ask her to go with me instead. I had to pay him four hundred bucks for his seat, but it had been an unforgettable night. After the concert, we'd made out in my car until almost dawn.

I inhaled, trying to push away the memory as I climbed inside and shut the door behind me, reaching for my seat belt to fasten it.

"Hey," I returned. The perfume she always wore wafted around me, filling the interior of the vehicle and somehow it pissed me the fuck off. "Did you wear that shirt to stick it to me?" I asked curtly, unable to help myself.

Given the direction of my thoughts, my statement was a harsh contradiction, but any memory of the amazing way we had been together and how our relationship was ruined, it felt like a dagger to my heart and I literally wanted to kill something. I knew when I made the statement that it would hurt her, but the part of me that wanted to punish her didn't care.

144

Teagan faced forward as the car pulled away from the front of the hospital, but I could see the glisten in her eyes and her struggle in the way her lips pursed. She shook her head. "No. I often wear it to bed." She looked down at her chest, realizing why I was pissed. "Oh."

Upset that I'd shown even the smallest vulnerability, or remnant of old feelings when she didn't even realize what the shirt would mean to me, I closed my tired eyes and leaned my head back on the headrest and changed the subject. "Did Kat give you the cash?"

"Yes, thank you. I'd never have been able to get it all done alone." I could feel the car moving and mentally see the route in my head. It was a short drive. Though I needed to get to bed and I was mad at Teagan; I wished it were five hundred miles to the hotel. I could sense she wanted to talk. I could feel it boiling under the surface and the new hesitation that hung between us.

"Just say it." I turned my head toward her as I opened my eyes.

"What?" She glanced at me quickly before turning her attention back to the road.

"Just say what you want to say and get it over with."

I was studying her profile; her perfect face that I'd memorized and dreamt about. Almost six years hadn't changed her, other than the sadness that haunted her. She wasn't as exuberant or vivacious, but then, life happened to us both.

"I have way too much to say to do it in the car ride to your hotel."

I turned away and stared out the front window, seeing our destination was less than two blocks in front of us, I could see her point.

"Mostly, I just want to make sure you know the depth of my regret..." Her voice broke a little even though she spoke in a measured way. Her struggle was real, but the bottom line was even though I wanted to relapse into how we used to be together, I didn't trust her. "…and, how much I appreciate that you're here."

I didn't really know how to respond. That was it? I just offered a quick nod. "Okay."

She turned into the parking lot of the hotel but didn't drive up to the door to let me out, but parked on the edge of the lot facing away from the building, instead. It offered as much privacy as could be had away from the eyes of anyone coming or going from the building.

It was still very warm outside, so she left the engine and the a/c running, but unbuckled her seat belt and angled toward me. In turn, I released mine and rotated a bit, pressing up against the door so that I could look at her. Our eyes locked, but then she looked at her hands folded in her lap. "I know you don't want to hear any of it, but I want to tell you so much."

It wasn't that I was trying to make it harder, but I just couldn't make it easy; I had too much-unresolved angst boiling inside me. "I guess I don't see the point. I'm here to help Remi."

Her deep brown eyes flashed up and then down again. "The point is, that this is the only time I've lied to you, and I want to set it straight."

"You should have thought of that before."

"Look, Chase, you can be a dick about it if you want. I can't stop you, and I can't change the past. You'll never know the regret I feel."

"Oh… I'm pretty sure I do." My tone was defensive and snarky but I couldn't fucking help myself

"No, you don't." I could hear the tears in her voice even though her head was bowed. She shook her head. "You think that I just went and screwed Jensen and didn't look back from the moment you left… but that isn't what happened."

"Kat filled me in."

I ran both hands through my hair. I didn't know what the hell to do. I wanted to believe her. I wanted her to tell me something, anything, to change my perception and suddenly make the last six years okay. I had the urge to drag her across the car and into my lap to comfort her and then kiss her senseless… to take comfort from her.

"She doesn't know everything, Chase," she raised pleading eyes to mine.

There was no doubt I loved her. It was killing me.

"Ugggggh!" I let out my frustration. "I'm hanging on by a thread, Teagan. Part of me wants to know, but another part of me doesn't need to rip open old wounds. Jesus Christ, I just learned to breathe again. You're not my girl anymore! Do you know how hard that is to admit?" I fought hard against it but my eyes welled to the point I had to brush away a tear from both eyes. "I wanted to see you because just being near you makes things click… but everything has changed. Just looking at you: I'm… dying. I'm fucking dying, Teagan!"

"I still love you. I do," she cried brokenly, reaching for my hand with hers. There was a kind of desperation in her act as if our skin didn't connect she'd fall off a cliff. Her shoulders shook with the force of her grief as she clutched at my hand.

"I don't believe you!"

"Don't say that!" Teagan rose up in her seat and moved toward me over the console as her other hand reached the front of my button down. She was pulling me toward her with both hands, and I somehow found the strength to resist, but then she only pulled harder.

My heart was at war with my head. "Stop. Stop!" I demanded, startling her and making her let go. She fell back into her seat in a defeated heap and covered her face with her hands. She wasn't wailing, but within seconds she closed her eyes and turned her face toward the back of her seat, curling into it and bringing her knees up in front of the steering wheel. She seemed ashamed and broken as if she were trying to hide the magnitude of the sorrow she felt. Her shoulders shook violently in silence until she was forced to take a gasping breath. My own left me in a rush as if I was sucked into a black hole. Tears I couldn't stop rolled down my face and I tried to push them away.

"It's tra—rue, Chase. I'm heartbroken..." Her sobs tore at my soul and I could feel myself cracking. Teagan could touch me at soul-level the way no one else ever would. I knew that there wasn't one damn thing I could do to change it. "I juh—ust wanted to touch you. Just let me tuh—touch you. Just for a mi—inute. I mi—miss you, so much."

I should hate her, but every time I looked at her, all I could see was the love of my life. In that moment, the rest of it just didn't matter.

It was as if my arms had a mind of their own and I leaned forward, grabbed her by both of her upper arms and hauled her across the car. She scrambled on to my lap and into my arms, clinging to me as she continued to cry against me. The whole thing took about two seconds.

I wound my arms around her, turned my face into her hair and hung on for dear life. We didn't speak; only just clung together and cried for how long, I didn't know. She was small and her entire body fit perfectly against mine, curled close to me.

We just sat there holding each other in the passenger seat of her SUV, me stroking her hair down her back and her face buried into the curve between my neck and shoulder, oblivious to anything other than each other. Eventually, Teagan's sobs subsided, but I made no move to separate from her.

"I miss you," she whispered again. Her voice was thick with tears and we were both exhausted, but just having her near me settled me, and at the same time I had to acknowledge everything that had changed. It stabbed me straight through the heart.

I lowered my cheek to hers, wanting to feel the warmth… needing the feel of her skin on mine. My mouth was so close to hers that I could inhale her sweet breath. I wanted to forget; needed the years to melt away, to have the innocence of an unbroken heart, to trust that she loved me… to get rid of the fucking pain if only for a moment.

My hand slid up her back and into her silky long hair at the same time, the other cupped the side of her face, tilting her face up to mine, my mouth hovering over hers. I closed my eyes doing my best not to give in, but loving Teagan wasn't something I could control, and not loving her wasn't something I could choose. It would be so easy to give in.

She waited still as stone; except for her fingers curling into my hair and fisting into the front of my shirt. She said my name in the faintest, aching whisper. It was one word. Just one word, but it was filled with the same longing I'd always felt; magnified by the time that had separated us.

"I miss you every goddamn day," the admission ripped from me half a second before my mouth slammed down on hers. The kiss was wild and delicious, Teagan shifting in my arms to straddle my lap at the same time as our tongues tangled and laved against each other.

I groaned in a mixture of ecstasy and agony. It was like coming home and I couldn't tell if the pounding in my chest was my heart or hers. Our fingers clutched and pulled, my hands sliding down her back, around her butt cheeks and pulled her hard against my rising erection.

"Oh God, Chase," she said achingly as we broke for a breath. Over the past years, I'd dreamed of her saying my name like this, of holding her in my arms and making love to her like we used to.

My hips surged and hers pressed down. Our bodies, mouths, and hearts remembering the way we used to be as if not one day had passed. "Say it again." My hands moved up the sides of her body to the gentle swell of her breasts and closed over each one, kneading and reveling in the feel of her pebble-hard nipples pressing into my palms at the same time as her body surged against mine, in a decisive rhythm.

"Chase." Her arms were around my shoulders; her hands tangled in my hair as she bent to kiss me again. Her position over me gave her leverage to move against me; rubbing the engorged head of my cock against exactly the spot she needed it. She was so hot I could feel her through the material, and my mind imagined her slick, wet heat, naked and sliding, taking me deep inside her body.

"Christ, Teagan," I growled into her mouth, as I pulled back and ghosted my lips over hers. The kisses were wet, deep, amazing... and my mouth savored hers, brushing my lower lip against her top one, and then sucking on it softly. She wasn't satisfied and opened her mouth, her tongue coming out to tease mine back inside as the kiss intensified. I yanked her hard against me, and her fingers opened the top three buttons of my shirt to slide in over my chest. "I need..." I moaned painfully.

"Yes," she answered breathlessly. "Yes, Chase."

It felt like the night we made out all night in the parking lot at school. We were both so fucking hungry as we kissed over and over again, each one more passionate than the last, our hips grinding together in mutual rhythm. She was making soft moaning sounds that drove me crazy as we moved; trying to assuage the ferocious throb. Fuck, I was dying and I couldn't tell if I was going to heaven or hell.

I continued to kiss her because I couldn't stop myself, but a pair of headlights flashed across the car as another vehicle pulled into the hotel parking lot; causing me to remember where we were and what was going on. It was a cruel dose of reality that flashed brightly across my closed lids. I tightened my arms around Teagan to still her movements and dragged my mouth reluctantly away from hers.

"Teagan. We have to stop." I dropped my head to her shoulder as my breathing dragged in and out in long, labored pants. My fingers curled into the back of her shirt, both of us filled with regret. "We can't." The next words killed me, but it was reality. "You're not mine. We aren't us. You're married."

Her movements stopped dead but she didn't make a move to get off of me. Rather, her arms tightened and she sucked in her breath, turning her face into my neck. I could feel the hot, wetness of her tears as they fell from her eyes onto the skin exposed by my open shirt. Her hand lifted into a fist and she brought it down on my chest in agony. It wasn't hard enough to hurt, but it was a sort of lashing out in misery. "Don't! Don't say that. I can't bear it."

I inhaled, struggling to get control of my emotions and my body. I wasn't ready to let go of her completely and still held her close, rubbing her back with one hand with one arm wrapped around her hips. She was hurting and I felt the same way; regret, misery, and desperation… it was so thick around us it was impossible to deny.

Maybe there was more to the story than I knew, but my brain argued that there was no excuse good enough to justify the betrayal or the lies. No matter how much I loved her, or how good this felt to hold her, it was just a beautiful illusion. There was a huge, unfair loss that engulfed us and reality refused to let me fix it.

"I'm so fucked up over this, Teagan. I have every reason to hate you, and it would be easier if I could. I want to, but I can't. I just—fucking can't!" I let out a ragged breath, my eyes starting to burn again. My heart was content and broken at the same time. "That's the shit of it. No matter what you do to me. I'm completely screwed. You lied to me for years, broke me to the point I wanted to kill myself..." my voice cracked on emotion. "You've even kept my child from me for years... and despite all of the hell you've put me through, I still..." Her arms tightened and she pressed her forehead to my chin, her hot tears dripping onto the skin to roll down my neck. "I still love you."

"Do you think I don't feel the same way?" Her voice was laced with tears and muffled because her face was still buried against me. "That's what unconditional love is. You don't get to choose."

My heart exploded at her words. "I don't want to, Teagan. I don't want to, but there isn't one goddamn thing I can do to change it. No matter how much I want to be free of you and this life-sucking misery, I'm stuck. I don't want to love you anymore."

She covered her mouth with her shaky hand. "I know. Trust me when I tell you hearing you say that, kills me. You just have to let me explain and then maybe you'll understand. I'm begging you, Chase."

I put my head back, facing the ceiling of the car as I tried to breathe and regain control. I blinked my eyes to clear them of tears. I was tough and didn't wear my emotions on my sleeve. I never had; except with Teagan. She, and now Remi, were the only two people on the planet who could reduce me to tears.

So many things rushed through my head as I sat there holding her, arguing with myself. I loved her beyond imagining, but resentment of her also brewed close to a boil. So many things were standing between us, but most of all, the beautiful little girl who was depending on me.

"I'm not sure anything will make me understand. Even if I choose to forgive you, the pain and everything that happened isn't going away. It happened. It's been years of pain and helplessness. Nothing is worse than the helplessness I felt at not being able to stop you from leaving me, and my inability to change anything; even how I felt... the not knowing why..."

"The let me tell you."

"It might be too late."

"I understand. All I can do is tell you that I'm sorry and that I'll always love you, Chase." Her hand flattened on my heart and then slid up my chest and around my neck. "Forever."

"No matter how either of us feels, it's not about us anymore. There are other people involved, the most important of all is Remi."

"I know that. What's going to happen?" Teagan asked, finally.

I couldn't resist smoothing her hair down her back one last time. "I don't know, beyond moving heaven and earth to get Remi well. I honestly don't."

"I know I made the wrong decision."

"Understatement of the century." I couldn't get my head or heart around it and I was incapable of sugarcoating it, even if I'd wanted to. Just because I want her, and even though I loved her, didn't mean instant forgiveness or reconciliation. Too much was involved. I was totally aware that Teagan knew exactly what I was thinking.

"We don't have to figure it out all at once, Chase."

"Maybe not, but we can't let things like this happen, again. I'm not strong enough to be alone with you. We're both overly emotional and scared to death about Remi's cancer and it would be too easy to fall into—" I stopped myself and reconsidered my choice of words. Teagan wanted forgiveness and maybe she meant what she said, but the situation was already too convoluted. "Jensen and Bronwyn have to be considered."

"Bronwyn. Is that her name? What's your relationship with her?"

There it was. Whatever I said next would be as much for me as it would be for Teagan. Bronwyn helped me through some heavy shit way before we dated, and I wasn't about to lie to Teagan about her. I refused to lie about either one of them. "She means a lot to me, but you're the love of my life. Nothing will change that, but she's been supportive and helped me crawl out of hell. I can't betray her. I have to keep my focus on Remi."

"This, now... what's happening between us isn't just about Remi."

"I know that, Teagan."

It was hard for me to resist the feel of her body and the longing in her voice and even harder not to give in to what I couldn't help wanting, but I didn't know what was in our future and I had to have a singular focus. I couldn't tell Teagan how strong the pull between us still felt, or that she was my beginning and my end.

I cleared my throat. "But, one night like this doesn't change the six years that stand between us. Even if Remi gets better, it isn't black and white. You can't just decide you didn't want me and now, when you need me, think everything will go back to the way it was."

Teagan nodded in slow and sad acquiescence, and her fingers were rhythmically kneading the skin and muscles at the side of her neck. "I know. I don't."

I opened the door to the car and got out, still holding her, but as soon as I was outside, bent to set her on her feet. I could feel her start to lift her legs around me like she used to, but then stopped. My heart literally lurched in my chest. So many things remained unchanged.

"So, I gotta go." Monkey. The love nickname I used to use all the time ricocheted through my mind and I had to literally stop myself from saying it. It would be so easy to fall right back into it with her… as if not one day had separated us, but reality was a vengeful bitch that swung a huge fucking sledgehammer to wake you up from the dream. Like clockwork. "I don't know if I'll see you at the hospital tomorrow or not because I'm probably going straight to the airport."

"Kat said she was going to take you."

"Yeah, I decided to catch a cab. It's just easier and my schedule is tight. We have practice on the field tomorrow evening and I need to be there."

I hugged Teagan tight one time and bent my head to place one kiss on the top of her head. Her arms tightened around my waist. I sensed her unwillingness to let go so I gently pulled her arms from around my waist, but kept the connection by holding one of her hands in one of mine. My thumb rubbed across the top of it automatically. "Don't worry, I'll be back in time for the results and if it's a go, we'll get it done fast. Remi will be okay, you'll see."

Teagan looked up at me, her soft doe eyes glassy from tears. "Thank you."

"See you in a few days." I started to walk toward the entrance of the hotel, reluctantly dropping her hand and leaving her to watch me go.

"You're wrong. We are still us."

My steps faltered as my heart exploded, and I paused for a second before I kept moving. If I turned around to look at her again, there was no way in hell I'd be strong enough to walk away.

ONE *touch*
AND THE PAIN
melted away.

Chapter 9

CHASE

My eyes were red rimmed and felt as if they were full of gravel. I used my thumb and the index finger of my right hand to rub them both at the same time, the burning turning to a gritty itch.

I'd barely slept the night before, consumed with torturous thoughts of Teagan and the stolen moments with her in her car. My mind was full of worry over Remi, and the confrontation I knew was coming with Bronwyn. I lay there with a huge hole in my chest, feeling miserable and cheated, pissed off and heartbroken, terrified; all of it made me a mess. For years, I spent endless nights howling at the moon at the injustice of it all… and now, this…

I wished my life was different; that I'd never gone to England or left Teagan, I wished I'd never trusted my best friend to keep an eye on her for me, wished I'd known Remi since she was born and wished she wasn't sick. I knew it would take real effort to keep my feelings for Teagan under control and hidden, and I'd be lucky if I didn't completely lose it at some point. I couldn't afford to be weak. The only times in my life I cried was once when I was ten and my grandmother died, over my break with Teagan, and now; Remi.

One thing that all the suffering over Teagan taught me was how to lock away shit that was bothering me. I was a machine; in charge of my life, in charge of my team, in charge of the game, and in charge of my emotions. Keeping a wall up and not letting people in made life easier, but going to Atlanta and seeing Teagan again, then finding out about my little girl had me reeling.

I'd be able to lie to Bronwyn, the managers, coaches and my teammates, but I couldn't lie to myself. I was seriously fucked up. It was as if I was caught in this giant vortex mercilessly sucking me down to the bottom of the ocean and nothing I could do would save me, no solution that worked, no regret could be eased, no grief to be healed.

I laid in the dark staring at the ceiling that was auspiciously visible because of the crack under the door to my room and the small ray of light leaking in from the hallway; lamenting all that I had lost and could lose. I didn't give a damn about the game I had to play or that my team was depending on me. All I wanted was to stay with Remi and make sure she got better; to just be with her... and Teagan.

I shook my head, pissed that it was even an issue. I shouldn't even be thinking about Teagan.

I knew wanting her was wrong but considered it could be because I was blindsided. My emotions were so raw it was difficult to separate the past from the present but vowed I would. Somehow.

I'd managed to drag my ass to the hospital, get the tests done, and fly to Brasilia, though my head was pounding.

Thankfully, my eyes were hidden behind the mirrored Serengetis that I'd shoved onto my face. I made my way through the airport; walking out of the restricted passenger-only gates toward where I knew there would be a car and

Bronwyn waiting. She'd called twice and texted at least a dozen times, but I didn't want to respond. My heart was heavy and while I was prepared for the onslaught of her line of questioning, I didn't want to deal with it. Although she was my girlfriend and we were intimately involved, it wasn't on the same level as I'd been with Teagan.

I realized my feelings with Bronwyn were more of an act, going through the motions, and not the soul deep kind that fuck you up for life. The relationship I'd manufactured with her was something she wanted, but to me, it had been more of a survival mechanism just to get by. I'd known her the entire time I'd been with Arsenal, but for years she was my trainer and my friend. Then, one day I decided that if I was going to move past my heartbreak, I had to try to start over with someone new. She had been in front of me, and she wanted me.

Though Bronwyn knew, deep down, that I wasn't as committed as she was, my current situation put it square in her face. Knowing it might affect our relationship in the wrong way, but I still didn't feel like sharing the details. My feelings for Teagan were private and I was fiercely protective of Remi. I didn't need to complicate the situation more by letting my real feelings surface. So, I promised myself I'd keep myself under strict control.

I saw Bronwyn as I threaded my way through the throng of people. She was dressed in Nike shorts, a tight white T-shirt with "Arsenal" squarely across her breast, and white sneakers. As always, her face was made up and her red hair was piled up into a high, messy topknot. She had sunglasses on and her lips were painted with bright coral lipstick. She was one of the senior trainers and she definitely looked the part, but unlike most of the others, she had a glam factor that made her attractive. She was pretty, and she might dress for her job, but she was always aware of how she looked.

When she saw me, she jumped up and down and waved, then pointed at me shouting: "Ace! There's Ace Forrester!" It wasn't as if the event this weekend and her logo'd boobs hadn't already put people on notice to look for the players.

I felt my face flush with anger. What the fuck? Even though I liked to keep a low profile, Bronwyn preferred to be the center of attention. In a manner of seconds, several people were surrounding me in a mob, blocking my path and yammering for autographs.

Just what I needed, I thought sardonically. Today, of all days dealing with fans is the last thing I need.

I stopped and took the pens and papers thrust at me, quickly scrawling my name, one after the other, trying to smile and be as gracious as possible. It felt like a pressure cooker of Bronwyn's making, and I was about to explode. The gathering only drew more interest and more people crowded around.

Bronwyn stood off to one side, grinning. Her white teeth were a stark contrast to her bright lips and dark glasses. Business as usual. She had aspirations to get out of training and become a sports agent and wanted me to be her first client. I signed ten or fifteen autographs and then nicely told them I had to get to practice; I didn't speak Portuguese but knew just enough to extricate myself from the situation. It probably wasn't even completely right because I'd looked up phrases on Google Translate years earlier, and over time, committed them to memory in a few languages of countries we played in a lot. Portuguese was just one.

"Com licença. Devo começar a praticar. Obrigado. Obrigado."

I ruffled the head of a dark-haired boy who looked up at me with imploring dark eyes. He must have been seven or eight. He was bigger than Remi and adamant.

"Sr. Forrester! Sr. Forrester! Apenas mais um!"

"Okay, one more." I took the piece of paper from him and signed it before ruffling his head again and moving through the crowd toward a smiling Bronwyn. She was waiting, arms crossed and chewing away on the gum in her mouth.

"Thanks, for that," I said irritated. She fell into step beside me when I didn't stop to greet her.

"What, no kiss, lovie?"

"Nope. Why the hell did you do that? I'd almost made it through the airport without anyone stopping me."

"You'll thank me later," she retorted, pouting. "You're a hot commodity. We have to cultivate our brand, Ace. Mobs are free publicity. How many times have I told you that?"

She pointed to the left and I strode toward the entrance she indicated. "That stuff doesn't matter to me. It's flattering sometimes, yeah, but I have shit on my mind and I don't even want to be in Brazil."

"You should care," Bronwyn quipped. "You've got contract negotiations coming and you've become the linchpin of this team and this is a huge event."

I rolled my eyes behind my glasses so she didn't see. "How much money does any one person need?"

There was a limousine waiting at the curb with a driver holding the door open.

"A cab would have done," I muttered as I silently compared this waste of cash to Teagan not having enough to pay for her house to be cleaned so Remi could spend a few days there.

"Pish," she waved away my objection, climbing into the car before me. "This was easier."

I slid in and dropped my duffle on the seat between us on purpose. "I'm sure it was."

I could feel her eyes studying me and could almost hear the gears in her head turning. It was dark in the back of the limo, but I still kept my glasses on.

"Ace, I understand you're going through a lot, but don't I even get a kiss? Didn't you miss me?"

"I'm just really tired. I didn't sleep much and had to get up early for more tests. I just want to go to the hotel and get a quick nap before practice."

"More tests?" She huffed slightly. "Really? At hospital?"

It still struck me how the British never used words like "the" or "an" in the same way American's did. I'd asked Bronwyn about the difference soon after my move to the UK, and she explained that the omission meant going to the place for its intended function, but adding them indicated the person speaking was a visitor to the place. As in; Remi was "in hospital", and I went "to the hospital" to visit her. It made sense, but even after years in London, it still sounded strange to me.

"No, at the circus," I retorted, unable to drop my Americanism or the slight sarcasm that dripped from my words. Why couldn't she just be supportive instead of berating me? "Yeah, at the hospital." I looked out the window and watched the city streets blur as they passed, hoping she'd stop talking. For some reason, everything she did or said, was pissing me off.

"What for?" Whenever Bronwyn got indignant, it always seemed to amplify her accent.

I closed my eyes in irritation, though I was sure she didn't see my reaction due to the sunglasses and the way my posture turned away from her. "I told you already, remember? Remi needs a marrow transplant."

"Yes, but I thought that you tested already. Yesterday?"

"The DNA test was yesterday, yes, but today there was blood work and a few other routine things they needed from me. Plus, a load of consent forms that I needed to fill out."

"Before they even know if you're a match?"

Her voice was so unconcerned and annoyed as if my tests inconvenienced her. I didn't need to explain that the tests today were done in advance and at my insistence so that if we did match we could get on with it. "Look, I'm not a doctor. I just do what they tell me."

"It just seems a waste, that's all. If you're not a match, I mean."

I wasn't sure if it was a gut feeling or my heart begging God, but I knew I'd be Remi's match. I had to be. "I will be. Don't worry."

"If her mother isn't a match, then I can't believe you'd be more suitable."

"You can always dream."

"That's a pissy thing to say."

"I'm pissy? You aren't exactly gushing support," I retorted with heavy sarcasm.

She hesitated for maybe a minute, and it was obvious she was fuming.

"Excuse me if I'm not falling all over my bloody self that my man is now tied down by some woman claiming she has his child—"

My irritation was growing with each passing second. "Teagan does have my child. Trust me."

"You believe her so easily, and yet, she betrayed you and lied to you for years"

"Thanks for the play-by-play of events, but no, when I look at Remi, there is no denying it."

"Whatever. How long will you be out for this thing?"

"As long as it takes. I have to talk to the coaches and management staff. My plan is to make the games, except I might need a couple of weeks after the procedure to recover."

"You could designate me your agent and I can take care of it all for you." I had been with the same team for my entire career and hadn't felt the need to hire an agent, though Bronwyn had been trying to convince me. She wanted to get out of training. I'd had many offers to move teams, but I hadn't felt the need or the desire. A couple of offers came from stateside teams, but I'd liked the distance and the clean slate that London provided. London held no memories of Teagan or our relationship and I realized after a few months that it was the only thing that kept me sane. "I'll still train you, too, but just you."

"It's not the right time to make changes." I knew what she'd been trying to do and something kept me from allowing it. It would be another commitment, another tie, and I guess, my subconscious was weighing the pros and cons before I was even aware.

Bronwyn leaned forward, pressing down my bag as she reached across to wrap her fingers around my bicep. Her face softened. "We can discuss it another time. What's involved with the transplant?"

"They stick a big ass needle into my pelvis and suck out some of the marrow. I'll just be sore for a few days because the bone will be bruised but the marrow replaces within a month, similarly to blood after a blood donation." I ran a hand through my hair wearily. "Remi has the hard part."

Bronwyn began to knead the tense muscles of my arm. "You're tense, lovie. Isn't it just like a blood transfusion, and poof, she's better?"

"No. First, they have to put her in a clean room and hit her with high doses of radiation to kill all of her own bone marrow, then she's given the transplant, and we wait to see if it works."

"How long?"

"It can take anywhere from ten to twenty-eight days before we know if it helps her." My voice was flat and emotionless.

Her fingers paused and her brow furrowed. "Good God, that long? You have to stay there the entire time, then?"

My head snapped in her direction so I could look into her eyes at the same time I pulled my arm away from her ministrations. "This is a little girl who is barely five years old. She's spent the better part of two years sicker than hell, being pumped up with chemicals and riddled with pain, unable to be a kid because she can't get infections, knocks, or bumps and you're concerned with how long I have to be away from the team? So, did you really just ask that?"

"I didn't mean it like that, Chase." She only called me Chase when I was upset or angry with her. "I just meant that you could keep playing, honor your contract, and work out seeing her some of the time, during breaks and such."

"If the donation doesn't take, she probably won't survive. She'll have no immune system. She doesn't have much of one now, but after the radiation has killed her marrow, she'll have none. They have to get rid of all of it to give the healthy marrow a chance to grow uninhibited and take over making the blood. If you think I'm not going to be there for every second of that, you're crazy."

"Chase, I understand that you feel an obligation, but do I need to remind you that you were kept in the dark for years? You don't owe these people anything. I mean, yes, donate the marrow, but then we all go about our lives and get back to it."

"I'm sure that's the way you want it, but the fact is, she's my kid! It doesn't matter that she's five years, or five seconds old, she's mine, and I will never turn my back on her. She's innocent in all of this. She was robbed of me just like I was robbed of her, but I swear there won't be one more day that she doesn't have me in her life." I paused as fear gripped me and I realized how my voice had risen and backed it down. "However long that life is."

"But—"

I put a hand up to stop Bronwyn's question. "I don't want to discuss it. Just—give it a rest."

She flopped back against the plush leather seat and crossed her arms angrily. "You're going to have to discuss it. Like it or not."

"Not today. I've gotta get some rest and get my head in the game."

"Oh for goodness sake, it's just an exhibition."

I couldn't believe she could reduce this event to so little considering she'd been with Arsenal longer than I had. The whole team went balls to the wall, and we went in owning the win before it happened. The truth was, I was looking forward to the physical exertion, the mental focus, and the brief reprieve being on the field would afford and it was just another reason to leave it all on the field. Not to mention, it was for charity.

I'd already called Coach Noonan to request a meeting either after the game or early morning the next day. I hoped it was the former so I'd be able to catch a late night flight back to Atlanta. Leaving tonight would also avoid more back and forth with Bronwyn. Obviously, she deserved to know what was going on, but I wasn't going to ask permission and I wasn't going to justify my decision to her or anyone else.

I knew where I needed to be, and it was the only place I wanted to be. I'd do my best for the team, but I was out of here the first chance I got. I glanced at my watch, hoping that by now Teagan was able to get Remi home. I pulled out my phone, noting Bronwyn's curious glance, straining to see what

I was doing as my thumbs typed out a message, flashing my eyes up to meet hers and then back at the screen.

Landed in Brazil. Do you have Remi out of the hospital?

I'll call you guys later if I can. Will she be up?

She might not be, but we're going to watch you on ESPN.

The mention of the network had me wondering if Jensen was back in town. Just thinking about it started a slow, long burn in my gut.

Okay. Tell her I'll make at least two goals for her.

Okay, I'll tell her.

I waited for a beat to see if more was coming, wondering if she was going to mention the hot make-out session from the night before, but knew it was better to just move beyond it and not bring it up. Bronwyn sitting next to me in the car and Jensen coming home to Atlanta were glaring reminders that it was a bad idea, no matter how much my heart and body wanted it. It couldn't happen again.

Good luck! Remi is blowing you kisses.

A slow smile lifted my lips as I imagined it.

Back at her. Tell her I love her, too. I'll be back soon.

How soon?

I lifted my gaze away from the screen as my heart stopped. Damn if she didn't know how to burrow into my heart no matter how badly I tried to fight against her. I couldn't deny that I wanted to believe she was asking because she wanted to know and not just for Remi. I steeled my resolve to keep things in perspective. It didn't matter what my soul wanted, I had to deal with reality, not some romantic dream. I wasn't stupid and I wasn't going to get burned again. I typed out a deliberate response.

As soon as possible. I have to talk to the team execs and sort it all out.

I'll keep you posted.

Teagan

I'd been watching ESPN all day in between bringing Remi home from the hospital and making lunch for her, Kat, and me. I was thankful for Chase's sister's visit because hearing her chatter about her family kept the mood lighter. Remi was really taking to her, and Kat had introduced her to her son and daughter, Ethan and Emily, via Skype on her phone.

Remi wasn't feeling the best and knowing her expressions, I could read her discomfort on her little face, though she didn't complain. She was weak and mostly just wanted to stay in her room; only asking to come out for Chase's game. She played a bit with her Barbie Dolls on her bed, but otherwise, she slept most of the day. Since she'd been in the living room for the past hour, she was still dozing. I could see her going downhill without the need to be told by the doctors that if Chase wasn't a match, we were in serious trouble and she'd have to start another round of chemotherapy soon. The thought of it made me sick to my stomach. Remi would cry and cry if I had to tell her she'd have to go through that again.

I sat near my sleeping daughter on the foot of the older moss green sofa. Holding Remi's blanket covered feet on my lap; I applied gentle rubbing pressure, careful not to cause the awful bruising she was prone to.

Kat was perched on a matching chair that was angled toward the mounted big screen TV. The house was modest and typical of a young couple just starting out. The furnishings were inexpensive, and some of them had been purchased at flea markets or online apps, but it was comfortable and I did my best to make it cozy. It was a miracle we had this much considering the medical deductibles piling up, and a couple of times had faced foreclosure on the house. I didn't have a great relationship with my father, but once in a while, a check would arrive and under the circumstances, we couldn't refuse it. I still resented his help, and our relationship was still very strained, but I tried to see it as an attempt on his part to make amends.

Remi shifted on the couch, turning toward the TV and curling up, cuddling her favorite new teddy bear that Chase had given her. "Is Daddy playing yet?" she asked sleepily.

"Just about, pumpkin."

Kat glanced at me and nodded toward Remi. "How does Jensen take that?" I knew exactly what she was asking.

"Not well," I admitted. "But, I felt it best."

Kat's head cocked to one side as she considered my answer. I could see the wheels of her mind churning behind her eyes. "It's a contradiction, isn't it?" She kept her questions stoic so Remi wouldn't know what we were discussing.

"It is." I nodded and then shrugged. "Kat, I didn't know what I was doing? Honestly, I was… lost. No clue what was right or wrong, or which end was up. I was a mess."

"I do see that part. It just seems like a bigger mess, now. I know your reasons, Teagan, but do you think it was really the best thing for Chase?"

I inhaled deeply and looked at the ceiling with a slight shake of my head. "No. But he wouldn't be an international star if I'd chosen differently. And he loves that game. He's alive when he's on that field, and I just couldn't take that away from him."

"You don't know what would have happened," she said softly.

"You don't, either. I didn't want him to feel trapped. I wanted him to stay, but I wanted it to be his choice."

Her eyes softened sympathetically. "I understand, that, too."

I started to get emotional the same way I did whenever I let myself think about how things should have turned out for me, and Chase. It was hard to get the words out without Remi knowing I was upset. "I was terrified he'd start to resent me, and being without him or having him hate me, was better than having him not love me. If that makes any sense?"

"Yeah. With you two, it does. I get it, Teagan."

On the TV, the ESPN team had a desk set up above the field and three of Jensen's coworkers were talking about the tragedy of the recent plane crash that took the lives of so many of the Brazilian National Team, as well as giving bios of the various first stringers. There were several international tournaments, but most of Chase's games were in his local English leagues. This particular game was a charity event to raise money for the families of the fallen players. It was getting loads of publicity and it was a huge honor that Arsenal was asked out of the many eligible teams.

When Chase's picture and stats were posted on the screen, Kat squealed a bit as Remi pointed weakly. "Look! There's

Daddy!" My heart jumped in my chest when I heard her refer to Chase as Daddy.

"I see, honey." I smiled and squeezed both of Remi's feet.

"He's gonna win!" Her little voice was weak, but her enthusiasm was big, and my heart leaped. I nodded my agreement.

Rarely did Arsenal lose. Right after Chase and I broke up, I used to watch all of his games. I'd been starving for any news or glimpses of him even though it was extremely painful. Jensen was supportive, but after we decided to get married, he didn't want to watch with me anymore. He knew how much I missed Chase and he thought I'd feel better if I just put him in the past. I tried to keep it secret by only watching when Jensen was on assignment, or if I could somehow manage to DVR the games and sneak them in later. It was obvious that Jensen knew, but he never mentioned it anymore. It was awkward and painful for everyone involved.

Kat's eyes flashed her exuberance. "I always get so excited watching Chase play. I mean… it's still hard to believe that's my little brother!" she added. "Last season, we all gathered at our parents' house for the final Premiership game and my mom almost peed her pants when he was chosen man of the match in the final game. Oh, my God, it was epic! She doesn't even like sports, and she was jumping up and down on the couch, screaming like a teenager! It was so funny! Dad rolled his eyes at her, but I could tell how puffed up he was, too."

"I can imagine." I felt a pang of pride and at the same time was sorry that I wasn't able to be part of it. "He's amazing," was all I could manage as I stared, mesmerized, at his face, still rubbing up and down on Remi's leg from ankle to knee. I'd seen that picture multiple times since it had been updated on the roster, but still, he was so breathtaking, even a bit sweaty with his hair sticking conspicuously to his forehead and his jaw covered in scruff. I wasn't sure if he really was that beautiful or he only seemed so because I loved him so much.

Throughout the game, I stayed with Remi on the couch, even after she fell asleep. Chase had scored the two goals he promised and was still giving it everything he had. I'd always loved watching him live and remembered the many games I'd sat among the screaming fans, but the numbers, then, were a fraction of what they were now at the professional level.

My mind was drawing a blank of the assistant coach's name that always called Chase, Twinkle Toes. Apparently, because he made it look so easy, but I knew better than anyone, how hard he worked at it. That title that had spread through the university circuit like wildfire, but now they called him Ace and it suited him better. He was perfect, working the ball with effortlessness; passing to teammates with ease. The way he used surprise backward kicks, or stopping the ball on a dime, to switch its trajectory, was brilliant.

A well-known commentator I recognized was shouting his name over the television as Chase dodged and weaved his way through his Brazilian opponents, signaling his teammates. Arsenal played with polished precision as they worked the ball like a choreographed dance. Yet, changing it up with every possession of the ball.

"My money's on Ace Forrester to make this one," the man said, his excitement rising. "There's a pass to Henry Paul, but watch as Ace retreats on the field, but the Brazilian's should be worried... he can make a goal from way outside... Watch! Watch! Here it comes! Oh, my God! Boom!"

One of the other players was set up to take a shot at the goal but instead heeled it back where Chase was waiting to hammer it inside the goal line. The goalie dove one way, but the ball came in on the other side of his dive.

The crowd in attendance went wild and Kat squealed and jumped up from her chair in front of the TV. I wanted to shout, too, but I was aware of Remi sleeping next to me and didn't want to wake her.

"Did you see that?" She laughed out loud. "I've seen this team win hundreds of games and I'm always just as excited as the first time."

It was the winning goal, and Chase's fisted hands rose above his head as he turned and ran into the mob of his converging team. He looked so happy; a brilliant smile split his face, his eyes flashing; even sweating bullets from his exertion, he was beautiful.

I swallowed hard and nodded. "Yeah. They really are incredible. I thought they might lose this one, on purpose. Because of the crash, and all."

Kat's eyebrows rose and her lips pursed with amusement. "That team wins and they draw huge crowds because of it. More money is raised when more people show up."

"Sure, but still. I thought they might throw it, just this once. I mean, if Chase would have missed his goals…" I let the words drop off with a slight smile.

"Yeah, right. He knew Remi and you were watching. There's no way he'd intentionally tank," she said with a light laugh. "No way."

"I always watch him. I feel sure he knew I would be."

The clock on the cable box said it was half past ten and I shifted Remi's legs from my lap so I could stand and get ready to take her to her room. I bent to lift her, careful to keep her covered with the blanket. "I'll be back in a sec. I'm just going to put her down, but do you need anything before I go to bed, Kat?"

"No. I'll be fine. Do you need help?"

"I got her. Help yourself to anything in the kitchen, and there are extra blankets and towels in the hall closet if you get cold or want to take a shower. Jensen will be home soon, so will you be okay?"

"I'm fine." She sat back down and picked up the TV remote. "You go ahead."

"Just come get me if you need anything. I'll be in Remi's room with her."

"Should I let Jensen know if I see him?"

I lifted Remi up into my arms, shifting her so that her arms were over her chest. Her head lolled on my shoulder and her dead weight made her heavier than she normally would be. I started down the hall toward the room at the right end of the hall. "He knows. Night, Kat."

"Night."

I closed the door behind us with my hip, and then put Remi into bed and covered her up, pushing the covers tight around her. Leukemia and her thinness made her cold and I wanted to make sure she was warm enough.

The past two days had wrung me out emotionally and I was feeling it, big time. I was the type of tired that might resist sleep and considered taking one of the sleeping pills that Remi's doctor had prescribed for me.

I wearily pulled my phone from the back pocket of my jeans and set it on the nightstand then began to peel off my clothes and changed into old knit shorts and a T-shirt from the stash I kept in the bottom drawer of Remi's dresser. There was always a small nightlight on and I lifted the covers and crawled in next to my daughter and cuddled her. She smelled baby sweet from the bath she'd had earlier and I curled my body around hers, gently pulling her to me and kissing her on the temple.

"Love you, bunny," I said, knowing she wouldn't hear me. "Daddy, Jensey, and Mommy are going to do everything we can to make you better. It's going to be okay." I kissed her again and closed my eyes getting ready to pray. Somehow, wrapped around Remi was more sacred to me than being on my knees since she was the subject of my prayers.

"Dear God, thank you for bringing Chase back to us. Please watch over and keep Remi safe. Please help her heal, and let Chase's marrow match." I tightened my arms around my little girl and she made a little murmur in protest and I pressed my forehead against her silky hair. "Please, save my baby and keep Chase in her life." Silent tears started and tumbled out of my eyes, down my face and into my and Remi's hair. I was filled with grief and desperation and I wasn't even sure if the words were real or just in my head, but I felt every single one. "I won't ask you to help him to forgive me, but please help him to accept things and ease his suffering. Also, please help Jensen feel better. I'm so thankful he's with us. I know I've been unfair to him and he deserves to be happy. I have no right to ask any of this, but I'd give anything if those three could be safe and happy. Please take care of them. In Jesus' name. Amen."

I was softly crying by the time I was finished. It was a prayer I'd prayed a million times, always including Chase, even in our time apart.

I had placed my phone on vibrate and it started to buzz and I turned to grab it from the table, at the same time glancing at the screen.

"Chase" was blinking with each ring and I quickly swiped it open. "Hello?"

"Hey. Yeah, it's me. I just wanted to check on you guys."

"Remi is sleeping. We watched you, but she didn't make it through the whole thing."

"Yeah?" His voice seemed to light up. "I promised her I'd get two goals."

"I know. She told me." I sniffed and wiped the tears from my face with my free hand. "You were amazing."

"Are you okay?"

"I'm just, worried."

"It's stressful. I'm freaking the fuck out. The waiting is killing me."

"She seems tired," my voice cracked. "Oh, God, Chase. I'm scared. She gets more tired when her white count is too high."

His voice was soothing and matter of fact. "It's gonna be okay, Teagan. I'll be back late tomorrow night."

I closed my eyes and more tears squeezed out, and then I said something I had no right to say. "I wish you were here, now."

He paused for a beat and I could almost see the anguish on his face. "Me, too. I will be soon."

"I'm trying so hard not to need you, Chase," I said miserably, holding back a sob with the back of my hand to my mouth. "I know it's wrong..."

"Teagan." His voice was anguished. "Don't. You don't have a right to say that kind of thing to me."

My face crumpled and I bit my lip hard, trying to keep from losing it as pain exploded inside me. He was right, but he was the love of my life. "I can't help it." My body was starting to shake with the effort of holding my emotions in. "You are the closest person to me, even if you're half a world away. I'm trying... but can't help it."

Chase cleared his throat, obviously fighting his own pain, but his tone was determined. "Some things we don't get to choose... they just are. It's the hardest lesson in life, I think. We gotta get through this, for Remi. I can't let old feelings rule me, Teagan. You made your choices, now we both have to live with it."

I didn't realize how painful seeing Chase again would be. I didn't realize how just hearing his voice could break me. I wasn't prepared for being yanked right back into the pain or the love just as if no time had passed.

A sob broke from me as my grief washed over me and I started to cry. I turned to bury my face in the pillow in an effort to hide the gravity of it from Chase or wake Remi. My free hand fisted into the pillow as I stifled a scream. I couldn't take hearing him push me away every time I opened up and told the truth as I had in the car, and just now.

"Teagan?" Chase's voice was thicker and I could hear he wasn't left unmoved. "Teagan!"

I rolled onto my side and pulled my knees up to my chest, still holding the phone to my ear. "I'm here." My nose was clogged and I knew Chase would realize I'd been bawling my eyes out, but I was unable to mask it. "What time should I pick you up at the airport?"

"Uh…" He cleared his throat again. "I'll call Kat to come get me. Then I'm going to ask her to go home. I assume Jensen is back in Atlanta, and Kat doesn't need to witness the meltdown. I want Remi to be part of my family and I don't want any of it colored by the mess."

I understood what he meant. The fewer questions to answer and the fewer accusations hurled during the time we were fighting Remi's leukemia, the better. Suddenly, I wanted off of the phone to suffer alone.

"Okay. "I'll let you go."

"You already did."

I jerked as if he'd slapped me in the face as a giant gasp left me. It was hard to believe the Chase I loved would be so cruel. Was he the same man who held me and kissed me the other night?

"So did you," I said stoically and hung up the phone.

ONE *touch*
AND THE PAIN
melted away.

Chapter 10

CHASE

I sucked in my breath as the phone went dead.

"Fuuuuucccckkkk!" I shouted and hurled the phone as hard as I could at the hotel room wall. It created a large bang and a dent in the drywall. Shit!

Bronwyn was on her phone in the sitting room of the suite and she murmured her goodbye then rushed into the bedroom. I knew what I'd just said to Teagan would slice her open and still, I couldn't stop myself from saying it.

"What in bloody hell was that?" Bronwyn asked, astonished.

I was sitting on the end of the big king-sized bed and I threw myself back until I flopped onto the mattress; both of my hands fisting in my hair. "I don't know what I'm doing," I murmured, rubbing both hands roughly over my face. My beard was several hours old and poked at my hands. "I probably broke my phone."

She glanced at the damaged wall and bent to pick up the pieces of my phone that were scattered on the carpet at the base of the wall and some of it further into the room. "I'll say. What possessed you?"

My feet were still on the floor, so I was only halfway up the mattress when she cautiously walked closer to sit next to me, reaching out a hand to rest it on my chest. It made me feel claustrophobic and I sat up abruptly, anxious to end the contact with her. Emotions were boiling inside and I wasn't sure if I was overly sensitive because of Remi's precarious situation or if I'd still feel so fucked up if I'd seen Teagan again regardless of Remi.

Ugh! I stood and started to pace the room. If Remi hadn't happened, would Teagan have finished school and come to London like we planned? Or, would Jensen have still swooped in and stolen what was mine? I loved Remi, but I couldn't help lamenting for what my life should have been for Teagan and me. At the same time, I felt guilty for even considering it.

Bronwyn watched me from her perch on the bed. "It's not a problem. I'll get you another one."

I turned abruptly to look at her. Suddenly I resented her being there, which was completely wrong. None of this was her fault, but right now, in this moment, I was mad as hell that she even existed. "No, you won't. You're not my assistant, Bronwyn."

She stood and walked toward me, reaching for me at the same time. "Ace, what's going on? You're acting so different."

Tension boiled inside my chest, threatening to explode. "Are you kidding? I have a terminally ill kid who I didn't even know existed!" And... I'm still in love with Teagan and I don't want to be, my mind continued. "Of course, I'm different!"

"Yes, but you're doing what needs to be done. You played as well as you always do, today. I thought you'd handle this." She seemed somewhat bewildered and oblivious to the weight on my shoulders. "When life gives you a shitty hand, you deal with it. What else can you do? If it were up to me, you'd drop that lying bitch on her ass, let her deal with her own problems, and get back to our life."

My brow dropped into a frown as I sucked in a wry breath, anger beginning to simmer inside me. Bronwyn really didn't get it. Maybe it was her personality to put herself first, and in the past year that was fine, but this was serious and her attitude pissed me off.

"You clearly don't understand the gravity of the situation." I put up my hands and closed my eyes. "It's not your problem; it's mine. I am just trying to figure out which end is up."

I pulled out my duffle and took out a set of clean clothes, intent on getting in the shower so I could meet with the coaching staff and managers for dinner. I'd asked for a private meeting so I could explain things and get the time off I needed from the team.

I started to walk into the bathroom and she followed, continuing to berate me. "If it's your problem, then it's mine, too. I know it's bollocks, but it will sort out. I'll go with you tonight, and I'll even fly back to America with you. I'll do what I can to help get you through this."

There was one problem; I had no desire for Bronwyn to come to the dinner and was even less enthusiastic to have her with me in Atlanta. I was more than likely going to have to spill details about my relationship and break-up with Teagan, which up to the present, I'd kept to myself.

I didn't want the press printing lies. The media was stellar at taking a sound bite and exploding it into a sensationalized sonic boom. I knew I had no choice but, to be honest with my coaches and eventually, with the world, and with Bronwyn. The club would be accepting, but she would pelt me with questions and it would just crack open more wounds I wanted to avoid; wounds that would, no doubt, damage my relationship with her. It would drive a wedge between us that would be impossible to breach.

I was already feeling its weight; already fighting the urge to go after Teagan, her marriage, and my relationship, be damned. It was a deep-seated instinct that I'd always felt toward Teagan and it didn't go away even after the ultimate betrayal. I didn't want to love her, but I couldn't change it, no matter how badly I wanted to.

I laid my folded jeans and underwear on the vanity and then leaned on it with both hands. My head dropped in resignation. "I don't know. I think I should go alone. I just spoke with Teagan, and we decided we didn't need too many people around to complicate things. I don't even want my family there, Bronwyn. We need time to get Remi taken care of before I can think about anything else."

I inwardly cringed as I waited for her response. Who was I kidding? It wasn't as if I could forget about Teagan, our past, or all of the misery that followed. I hated that I couldn't separate the two, but it was impossible. I reached behind the curtain and turned on the shower spray, pulling off my shirt and dropping it on the floor in one motion. Bronwyn stood there, frozen in place.

I unbuckled my belt and dropped my pants, stepping into the shower and adjusting the water to make it a bit warmer. I began to rinse the dried sweat from my body and the steaming water was soothing.

"I don't think you should be alone. Teagan has Jensen. Are you prepared for that?"

I paused mid-squeeze of shampoo into my hand from one of those annoying little bottles hotels leave out for guests. She might as well have hit me in the gut. I dreaded facing Jensen more than I wanted to admit. The truth was, I'd never be prepared even though I knew it was inevitable. I wasn't sure I'd be able to stop myself from ripping his head off. When he wasn't in Atlanta the little nucleus of the three of us was somehow comforting, and it was easy to forget he wasn't part of it. Hatred for my ex-best friend boiled in my chest; so consuming and hot it felt like my soul was on fire. I should have known he'd always been in love with Teagan by the way he always found a reason to hang around with us. Stupidly, I trusted them both, and I got royally screwed because of it.

I tried to keep emotion out of my voice and answered with what an adult should say in this situation. "It was a long time ago. We are all adults with a mutual goal right now." I wasn't sure if I was reassuring Bronwyn, or myself. "Remi is all that matters."

"Okay," she agreed reluctantly. "So, is dinner formal or not?"

I huffed in agitation. Wasn't she listening?

"Bronwyn, I'm in Brazil with two pairs of underwear and one change of clothes. So, it better damn well be casual or I'm shit out of luck. They're sending a car in thirty minutes." I scrubbed the shampoo into my head and closed my eyes so that the suds wouldn't run into them as I turned to rinse my hair.

"So I can't come, then? I want to be there. What if they want to renegotiate your contract? You don't want to end up out on your arse."

Ugh, I thought. I turned off the water and yanked down the fluffy white towel I'd hung over the top of the shower curtain. "I'm taking a leave of absence, not leaving the team, and we've been through this. You're not my agent or manager. You're my trainer." I knew I sounded like a dick, but the conversation was exhausting.

"Thanks for the reminder; I'm just hired help," she snipped.

I dried off my chest and groin and then wrapped the towel around my waist, leaving rivulets of water trailing down on my arms, back, and legs. I stepped out of the shower. "I didn't mean it that way. I just don't want to drag this out or make a bigger deal out of it than it already is. I want to get in and get out. I'm gonna try and get a flight out back to the states tonight."

"What? Why, for pity's sake? It's already ten!"

I grabbed another towel from beneath the wooden vanity where the cleaning staff had stacked them, and flung it over my head and started to rub briskly to dry it off.

"I want to get back. This shit is eating me alive."

Bronwyn's irritation was obvious in the way she crossed her arms and scowled. "You can't change anything by rushing back! I was looking forward to this trip, Ace! We were going to stay in Brazil and take a few days in Rio, remember?"

I walked past her out of the bathroom carrying the stack of clothes I'd taken in with me and threw them onto the bed. I went in search of my phone. Glancing down at it, shattered screen and all, a pang of disappointment filled me that there was no message from Teagan. I shook my head, silently chastising myself for even checking. Bronwyn was still close on my heels as I started to dress. I felt crowded and if she didn't back off, I might blow.

"Change of plans," I stated the obvious and threw the phone down, starting to dress. I could almost feel Bronwyn's eyes burn a hole in my back as I threw on a dark teal button down over some blue jeans and slid my feet into my tan Vans. I quickly shoved the rest of my clothes, my leather Dopp kit, and other gear back into the duffle.

"But—"

I turned and let loose; throwing my arms wide as I got right in her face. "But—my kid is dying! Jesus Christ! What's wrong with you?" She literally jumped back a couple of feet, her face startled. I turned away and kept on stuffing my shit into my duffle as if nothing had happened. "I might not have much time with her!"

"I—I'm, sorry. I'll make flight plans for you while you're meeting with Noonan." I could hear the tears in her voice and felt like an asshole, but it didn't stop what I was doing and I didn't stop to comfort her. Instead, I kept my voice even and controlled.

"Cool, thanks. I have my stuff so I can get a cab straight to the airport, later."

"I'm thinking it will have to be two or three AM because of security," she said quietly, gathering her composure.

I was halfway to the door and was suddenly hit by a wave of guilt. This wasn't her fault, and I shouldn't take it out on her. "Look, I'm sorry. My nerves are pretty shot, but it's not fair to yell at you." I walked over and bent to place a quick, chaste kiss on her lips. Her hands lifted to grab onto my arms, but I pulled back before she could deepen the kiss. "I'll talk to you soon. Please... just text the flight information."

I wasn't sure if the car would be waiting in front of the hotel or not, but I was anxious and so made my way to the lobby after an awkward exit. I felt guilty for my coolness toward Bronwyn, but there didn't seem to be anything I could do to change how I felt, and I couldn't lie about it.

Maybe, when the transplant was over and I was sure Remi was going to be okay, things would go back to normal. Maybe if I kept telling myself over and over it might be true, but a bigger part of me was hoping there would be a new normal. With Teagan and Remi. As wrong as it was, and despite the heartache, or maybe even because of it... we were still connected. If betrayal, bitterness, heartbreak and wanting to kill myself didn't change the love, nothing ever would. It fucking sucked and yet, it left me stunned.

Taking a break from the game would put a pinch on the team, but I felt sure the managers, and Coach Noonan, would understand as long as I kept them informed. If not, then it would be bye bye Arsenal. As much as the team and playing soccer meant to me, I'd walk away without a backward glance.

* * *

The plane was finally arriving in Atlanta as the sun was setting in the clear blue sky.

Bronwyn was asleep in the seat next to me. I was annoyed when I arrived at the airport and she was waiting with two tickets in hand. I didn't have the energy to argue, especially with the flight time imminent. We had to run to make the gate after we passed through security. After an hour layover in Miami, we were finally here. It felt like ten days rather than ten hours en route.

I'd texted Kat just before we were wheels up in Miami and hoped she'd already been waiting. Bronwyn had checked luggage and so we weren't able to just breeze through the airport and out without heading down to baggage claim. I was impatient and annoyed, but it was what it was. I wasn't sure why, but everything Bronwyn did was rubbing me the wrong way. I felt like I was ready to crawl out of my own fucking skin.

"Hey," I nudged her awake. "We're landing."

Bronwyn opened her eyes and sat up slowly, in her typical prissy and deliberate manner. She'd been leaning on me as she slept and my arm was asleep. I rubbed it absently, wondering why her presence, which only a week ago would have been no big deal and expected, was somehow abhorrent to me now.

The answer loomed in front of me like an ocean that I was trying to cross in a rowboat. The ocean had a name and I couldn't deny it. No matter how I tried to dig in, or how desperately I wanted to disseminate my feelings, it was impossible. And it was more than just Remi. I couldn't shake the inevitable hold Teagan had over me. Even though I'd gone through the past couple of years trying to convince myself and everyone around me that I was over her, I knew now, that it was one huge lie; and in fact, one I needed to confront to get through it. At the moment, I was drowning; clawing for the relief that had eluded me for years.

"Did you sleep?"

"Not on this leg." My voice was flat and emotionless.

The time from touch down until passengers were allowed to deplane always felt long, but this morning it was taking for-fucking-ever. Once they shut off the systems the interior of the plane immediately became stuffy, and it was so damned annoying how people started standing up and gathering stuff before it was their turn to leave. I mean, why? Did they think standing up made the people in the rows in front of them get out more quickly? I huffed my agitation.

Bronwyn shot me an annoyed look. "You're in an awful mood."

"Yeah. It's always so great to have some stranger's crotch staring me squarely in my face," I muttered with a disgusted shake of my head.

"Ace!" Bronwyn chastised crossly.

"Bronwyn?" I shot back, my left eyebrow shooting up sardonically. "Look around, for Christ's sake." I didn't bother trying to camouflage my growly mood. If Bronwyn didn't like my disposition, then she shouldn't have tricked me into tagging along.

"I am." She glanced at someone across the aisle from me wearing an apologetic expression. It was probably the guy who'd just presented me with a birds-eye view of his junk. "But you don't have to be rude about it," she said under her breath.

"Yes, I do." I inhaled deeply and resigned myself to wait without speaking until it was our turn to deplane. Purchasing the tickets last minute precluded first class and in coach, people were packed in like sardines and impatient to deplane.

Twenty minutes later, we were finally walking through the airport in stilted silence. After retrieving Bronwyn's bags, we found Kat was waiting at the curb with her old Chevy minivan. That thing had seen better days.

Kat's surprise at seeing Bronwyn was evident in her wide-eyed assessment of the other woman as we approached. She quickly tried to erase it from her face. "Hi, I'm Kat, Chase's sister," she announced with fake enthusiasm as Bronwyn threw open the front passenger door to climb in, leaving me to hoist her luggage inside through the sliding side door.

"Nice to finally meet you, Kat! I'm Bronwyn, Ace's girlfriend." Bronwyn was way too happy for my peace of mind. "I'll never get used to the backward way your cars are in America."

"Most of the world drives on the right, Bronwyn. We've had this discussion," I added flatly.

"Well, lovie, I still find it silly."

Kat glanced over the seat, trying to catch my gaze. Clearly, she was skeptical of the logic behind bringing Bronwyn into such a volatile situation. I had no way to explain how I was railroaded at the airport with just minutes to spare before the flight closed.

With one hand, I slung the last bag onto the seat and then climbed in behind it. There were fast food wrappers, trash, a broken iPod, and toys scattered around. It looked like it hadn't been cleaned out in months.

"Jesus. Remind me to buy you a new van, Kat." The words were out before I realized they might come off as insulting. "This is trashed."

"It's fine. It's not that old, just dirty. That's what happens when you have three boys." She brushed it off.

"It looks like a nuclear wasteland."

"I guess it does," she said, putting the van in gear and gingerly pulling out into the steady stream of cars leaving the airport with new arrivals.

"Three kids?" Bronwyn asked astonished. Once again I was annoyed. She was so disingenuous I had to bite back a sharp retort. "I'd never want three kids."

"How is Remi?" I couldn't help asking; wondering if Kat felt insulted by Bronwyn's carelessly thrown statement. "Is she home with Teagan and Jensen?" Just uttering his name pissed me off, but I wanted to know if I should expect to come face-to-face with Jensen.

"Yes. She has been tired and lethargic. Teagan is keeping a close eye on her."

I ran a hand through my hair and nodded, though no one could see it.

"Poor little thing," Bronwyn said. "I can't imagine how hard this is."

I bit my tongue again. Resentment roared like a lion inside me. Half a day ago she was preaching to me that I should drop Teagan on her ass and turn my back on Remi, and now she was putting on this concerned act for my sister. I found myself wondering if I really knew Bronwyn or if she was just a master at acting. She said the appropriate thing, but with little feeling behind it. Maybe she'd had an agenda the whole time I'd known her, and now that it was being challenged her true colors were showing.

I couldn't speak because if I did hateful words would flow, so I listened to Bronwyn question Kat and gush about me in silence during the ride. I wondered if I should check out of my hotel and get one closer to Teagan's house, or drop Bronwyn at the hotel and get her a room before checking on Remi.

Kat broke into my thoughts. "Chase, should I take you to the hotel for now? I know you're probably anxious to see Remi, but it's getting late…"

Her words dropped off but I got the message loud and clear. Jensen was at the house, Bronwyn was with me, and no one needed another complication.

"Um, I think you should take us back to the hotel, and then you should go home."

"What?" Kat asked surprised.

"I just think that things are sensitive right now and it would be easier with fewer people involved in the immediate situation."

"But, I came here to help out, Ace. How will you get around?"

"I'll handle it. I can buy a car if I need to. I'm not worried about it."

The audible gasp from the front seat came from Bronwyn. "Don't be silly, Ace. There's always Uber, or maybe now that Teagan's husband is home, she can lend hers for a few days."

Kat's concerned eyes met mine in the rearview mirror instinctively knowing Bronwyn's words would sting.

"It will be longer than a few days and I'm tired of living out of hotels and depending on taxis."

"Maybe I can at least help line up everything before I go home. David is fine because Mom came to stay with him and the kids," Kat said gently.

My heart dropped into my stomach. I had hoped to tell my parents about Remi myself. "What did you tell her?"

"Only that a friend needed my help with a sick child."

"That's it?"

"Yes."

I nodded. "Good. Please keep it that way. I want to tell the folks myself."

"Understood. I'll keep it quite. This is your story to tell."

I nodded and looked out the window. "Okay. Then I'd appreciate your help scouting an apartment rental or one of those long-term hotel places. Something small will be fine."

Bronwyn turned and peered at me around the edge of the front seat. She looked perturbed. I met her gaze blankly until she turned around again.

It wasn't long until we'd arrived at the hotel and I was checking Bronwyn into her own room while Kat waited in the parking lot. Id asked her to take me to see Remi.

Bronwyn's protests echoed through the small tiled lobby of the hotel, but I justified the decision by telling her I might be coming and going at all hours of the day and night, and I didn't want to disturb her.

What I really wanted was to figure out a way to get her on a plane back to England as soon as possible. The last thing I needed was her hammering me for explanations regarding my standoffish attitude or my fucked-up emotions. And I didn't need her hovering at the hospital or arranging impromptu publicity events by calling the press.

I dragged her big piece of luggage behind me with my left hand while loaded down on the right shoulder with two others. How could one woman have so much shit for what was only supposed to be a weekend in Brasilia?

It seemed like it took ten years for her to open the door so I could unload.

I felt her hands on my shoulders and then running down my arms and back. "When will you be back, lovie? It was a nice gesture to be proper in front of your sister, but I'll move my things to your room when you get back. I'll wait up for you."

I left the bags on the floor and walked forward, effectively pulling out of her embrace. "No need. I don't know when I'll be back." I swung the heavy door open and started to walk out.

"Why are you acting so awful to me? I came all this way to be with you. The least you could do is be nice about it."

I stopped and turned around. She was right. If this were any other situation or even any other tragedy, I would have welcomed any comfort she offered. We'd become a comfortable habit and I shouldn't diss her or make her feel undervalued, no matter what I was going through. If this didn't involve Teagan and if I wasn't feeling so protective, I might want Bronwyn with me. However, I knew she was resentful and angry about current events and I didn't have the emotional energy to coddle her. The last thing I needed was her tearing into Teagan at the earliest opportunity. Teagan was far from innocent and had many things to answer for, but right now, Remi needed her mother and I needed peace of mind.

I knew both of them, and they were as different as night and day. Bronwyn had claws and Teagan was gentle and giving. At least, that's how I remembered her.

"You're right," I admitted. Stepping back into the room, I took a hold of both of her shoulders and bent to place a quick kiss on her lips. Her chin lifted and her mouth opened, clearly wanting to deepen the kiss, but it felt foreign to me now. I pulled back and kissed her forehead, instead. "I'll see you later." I couldn't get out of there fast enough.

I felt guilty; burned; on fire. I wanted out of that room and out of her arms. I had nothing to be ashamed of. I wasn't being unfaithful to my married ex-girlfriend, so why was my soul and heart screaming?

Teagan

Jensen was in the shower and clearly lingering.

He'd been home about an hour but things were awkward. We hadn't spoken other than when he asked about Remi and went in to check on her. We weren't exactly lovers, though we'd tried in the year after Remi was born. Through it all, we'd always been friends, and it was incredible how just the idea that Chase was back had changed the dynamic between us. It was clear Jensen felt threatened, and I understood why. I never lied about my feelings for Chase, but over the years we just stopped talking about him, and he'd given up trying to sleep with me.

I was pacing around the house, anxiously waiting for Kat and Chase to arrive when a knock on the door broke into my thoughts and halted my steps. I hurried to the front hall and opened the door. It was solid oak with a window at the top, but I wasn't tall enough to see through it.

Chase stood there, looking exhausted. His shirt was rumpled and his hair was mussed like he'd run his hands through it ten times, and Kat hovered quietly behind him. Instinct and habit urged me to go into his arms for a hug, but I moved back to open the door instead, my eyes locking with Chase's. They were stormy; a darker green as he and Kat stood in the yellow glow of the porch light waiting to come inside.

"Come in." When I nodded to indicate they should pass me and join me inside, I couldn't help reaching out and running a hand down Chase's arm as he passed. Electricity raced over my skin as goose bumps popped out in a wave down my entire body. Everything inside me screamed for physical contact. My body came alive and my heart ached so badly I could barely speak. I closed my eyes as he paused and squeezed my hand when it slid down to his. I wanted to melt into him and disappear. He was the love of my life and that face was burned in every cell of my body. The love and sexual tension between us was palpable. I was sure Kat could feel it when her eyes met mine as she passed behind Chase on her way into the house.

It would be easy to just fall into our old reality with Chase; loving, comfortable, passionate, even needy at times... we were still us and it was killing me. I knew it would be difficult seeing him again, but I didn't think it would feel like not a second had passed. Our fingers laced together for a split second, then Chase cleared his throat and continued into the living room. He glanced around the room, trying not to be obvious. He was wondering where Jensen was. I was thankful for his absence; I didn't feel capable of completely hiding my feelings.

"Is Remi sleeping?" Chase asked, shoving his hands into the front pockets of his jeans. He looked at me expectantly. "How has she been?"

I nodded. "She's lethargic and a bit weak. She is sleeping, yes." I swallowed. "She sleeps a lot more."

Kat's knowing gaze bounced between my face and Chase's.

I found myself wishing that Kat and Jensen would disappear from the house and it would just be the three of us. I'd dreamed of Chase, Remi, and me being a real family. There was nothing I wanted more, though I didn't want to hurt Jensen. My heart dropped to my stomach. I should stop wishing for something that wasn't and couldn't be. Jensen did exist and so did the woman Chase was dating. I ran a hand through my long hair and the heavy curtain of it dropped from my hand.

"Ummm..." I started to walk toward the kitchen feeling suddenly nervous and fidgety. "Can I get you anything? We ordered pizza last night. It's not ideal, but there is still some left, or I can make something. I think there are a couple of beers in the fridge?" I waved my hand in the direction of the sofa and chair. "Make yourselves comfortable."

Chase took a couple of steps toward me, lifting his hand to chest level to halt me from leaving the room. "Teagan, stop. It's not necessary. I just wanted to see Remi for a minute." He came closer and lowered his voice, leaving Kat to hover awkwardly behind him. "I know Jensen is here and it would be better if I just see Remi and go back to the hotel, and call the hospital to see if the results came in."

I understood why he felt that way however, I couldn't help feeling a wave of disappointment wash over me. It was stupid to expect he'd stay here. I couldn't expect him to make small talk with Jensen or vice versa. The one thing we all had in common was Remi. "Okay," I said, my eyes locking with his imploringly. "Chase, I—"

A door opened down the hall and Jensen made his entrance. He was freshly showered as he emerged from our room and came toward us. "Chase," he nodded stiffly in acknowledgment and came forward, proffering his hand. "Good to see you."

Kat moved forward and wrapped a hand around Chase's bicep and fear radiated over me like an electric current. I was shaking as I watched them both; waiting for Chase's response.

Jensen was at least trying to diffuse the situation, but Chase stiffened the second Jensen appeared; a muscle worked furiously in his jaw as he stood unmoving. Chase's fingers curled into a fist as he licked his lips and then swallowed; his steel gaze landing on Jensen. He didn't try to hide the venom that flashed across his features as he refused the handshake Jensen offered.

Ignoring Jensen completely, Chase looked at me and pointed down the hall. "Is Remi's room this way?" His voice was soft and deadly calm, but I could feel the war raging inside him. Clearly, this was war. To give Jensen credit, he was trying to diffuse a volatile confrontation, but Chase was having none of it.

"Second door on the left," Jensen answered before I could get the words out.

Chase's head cocked and his eyes closed for a split second before he pulled on his lower lip using the thumb and forefinger of his right hand. He nodded and looked at me.

"Teagan, I'd like to speak to you for a minute. Alone."

The air vibrated with tension.

Jensen stepped closer, putting himself between us. "Anything you say to her can be said in front of me." The two men stared each other down for a split second.

"I have nothing to say to you," Chase answered, his words stern. "Not one fucking thing." Chase's lower jaw jutted out and he looked coiled and ready to lay into Jensen without further provocation. "Don't push me. Every instinct in me wants to rip your head off, so back. The fuck. Off."

No one moved, but Jensen spoke. Chase didn't know the whole story but Jensen did, and he relaxed. "Look, Chase, things aren't as they seem. Why don't we—"

Chase interrupted him. "Teagan?" He walked around Jensen and past me heading into the kitchen and away from the others.

I nodded and turned to follow, pausing only to indicate to Kat and Jensen to let me go without a fuss. The kitchen was through the dining room and an archway, but without a door that could be closed to separate us completely.

"I'm going to ask you this, one time. Keep him the hell away from me. I'm not here to offer the two of you absolution."

Looking at him with pain painted all over him was hard and my own emotions threatened. I walked closer and reached out to touch him, though my hand hovered. I had no right to treat him like I used to. I was a head shorter and I had to look up into his handsome, scowling face. My voice and eyes implored him. "Please, Chase. I know this is difficult for all of us."

He gritted his teeth and leaned in so he could speak in low tones, but his voice was filled with hatred. "I'm sorry if my fury makes the two of you uncomfortable, but really, I don't give a flying fuck. You did this to yourselves... you did it to me, so now we are all dealing with it. So just keep him the hell away from me so we can do what we need to do for Remi."

My throat tightened and tears welled in my eyes, blurring his features. I reached out then, to wrap my right hand around his strong left forearm. My fingers only reached about halfway around and his muscles flexed when his hand fisted. "Chase," I begged. "Please."

"No, Teagan. You don't get to ask me for anything other than helping Remi. I don't have to listen to your reasons, and I don't have to understand." His voice wavered and he yanked away from my grasp.

He turned and strode from the kitchen, through the house, and down the hall more quickly than I could follow. Tears were tumbling down my face as I returned to Kat and Jensen. Chase had left us all there, to watch him disappear into Remi's room.

My heart was thrumming in my chest in a sickening way. I wanted to fall to my knees and scream or better, have the earth open up to swallow me whole. "Oh, God," I murmured and walked to the sofa, sinking down; my head dropping so I could try to push the unwanted tears from my face. It was futile. There was no way I could hide my agony.

Jensen stood there, looking at me and when my eyes glanced off of his, I could see his anger. "Don't waste your tears on him. If he's going to be a prick, he's going to be a prick."

"Jensen, please," I begged, looking up at him looming over me. "I can't do this right now."

"What did he say?" he asked coldly.

I shook my head and put up a hand. Fueling the hatred between the two old friends would help no one. "Let's just get through this. We can't expect him to take this well and we can't change what happened."

"What did he say?" he asked again, more forcefully.

I looked up, resigned. "That he doesn't owe either of us and to give him space to do what he needs to do. He doesn't want to relive it."

Kat looked on uncomfortably, her brow furrowed, and she folded her arms and tried to begin a conversation with Jensen so that I had time to compose myself. "Do you remember me?" she asked stiffly. "I'm Chase's sister, Kat. Um, I came to help Teagan for a few days."

My eyes burned, but I willed myself not to cry as I looked up to watch the interaction.

"I do," Jensen offered.

If the situation weren't so pitiful, it would be funny. I felt like some idiot kid on the first day of school. No friends, no idea what to do, no composure. The two of them stood, gawking at each other, both searching for words until Kat sat beside me and Jensen loomed over us.

"Teagan, Chase thinks I should go home after I help find him a place to stay for a few weeks. He doesn't want anyone around. Are you okay with that?"

My elbows were resting on my knees and I clasped my hands together. I wasn't sure how I felt about being alone with the two men and I hated the thought of Chase in one place, and me in another with Jensen. I wasn't sure I'd be able to handle any of it.

"Why would he want you to leave?"

Kat lowered her voice. "Well, Chase's girlfriend, Bronwyn, came back with him from Brazil. She's at the hotel and he doesn't want her around either."

My eyes widened in shock as reality slapped me in the face. "Oh." I should have known she'd come to Atlanta if Chase was going to be here for any length of time, but I was fragile and on the cusp.

"He has to deal with it in his own way."

"Don't we all?" Jensen threw out, pulling his phone from the clip on his belt. He was dressed in old jeans and an ESPN T-shirt, and walked to the hall closet, opened it and pulled out some slip-on Vans. "I'm going to Moe's, Teagan. I gotta get out of here. Call me after Chase leaves." He slammed out the front door without another word.

"Wow. What a mess," Kat murmured incredulously. "I guess when people say time heals all wounds, they're wrong."

My face crumpled as I started to cry again. My heart was breaking. "I can't stand seeing them both in pain. I'm an awful person. I've hurt everyone I love, and I feel guilty about them both, and guilty because all I should be thinking about is Remi right now."

Kat reached out and closed one hand over the top of one of mine, her fingers tightening. "Oh, Teagan. Love can't be compartmentalized. You might be able to choose how you act or what you say, but not how you feel. Things will work out. They both love Remi so they will learn to co-exist, even if they can never be friends like before."

"But Chase has been hurt so badly."

"He has," she agreed. "But, I feel he'll move on from this. He'll come around, you'll see." She'd scooted closer so she could sit beside me.

I wanted to tell her that there had been moments when I'd glimpsed the Chase I loved, how I felt him softening, how maybe if he'd only listen, he'd come around, but not with Jensen there. Jensen didn't deserve any of this any more than Chase did.

"Everything is so awkward," I murmured miserably. Chase's girlfriend being here was not something I'd prepared for and I wasn't sure I'd be able to handle it. Jensen would be off on another assignment and without Kat; I'd be alone with the two of them. I didn't want to watch them together, I didn't want to hear them talking like we used to, or hear him be sweet to her. My heart exploded like shrapnel ripping my insides to shreds. I wanted to let my sorrow out like rain, but I had to try to bury it inside. I couldn't make this about me, no matter how intense the pain.

"I'd feel better if you'd stay. At least until we get the results and know if we can move forward with the treatment." It was selfish as hell, but I couldn't help asking. "I know I have no right to ask, and I know Chase wants space, but I'm not sure I can handle things." I sniffed and my voice broke on a sob as emotion finally spilled over. Kat put her arms around me to offer comfort during my tearful rant. "They're both so angry and I can't stand seeing the two of them hating each other. I hate myself for ruining their friendship. They were like brothers." More tears tumbled down my face as I hugged her back and started to sob. "I'll never forgive myself."

She sighed and rubbed my back with one hand. "They both made their own choices. Chase didn't have to leave, and Jensen didn't have to marry you. Don't take it on all by yourself. It's gonna work out because Remi needs all of us."

Nothing she could say would lessen my guilt. As much as it hurt to admit, I knew everything was completely my fault. "Then you'll stay?"

"I don't know, Teagan. My brother is already furious with me. I'm not sure what is the right thing to do."

"Kat, please? The truth is; with Remi's condition so precarious, my emotions are shot. I'm just not strong enough to see Chase with Bronwyn."

Kat's expression was a mixture of sympathy and surprise. "I guess I understand that given he's your first love, Teagan, but what about Jensen?"

"It's complicated," I began. I needed someone to know the truth and if Chase refused, maybe Kat would listen. "I'll never love anyone more than Cha—"

"Teagan!" Chase yelled loudly from the other room, his voice frantic. "Teagan! Get in here!"

Both Kat and I jumped up and ran down the hall, bursting through the closed door. Chase was holding a limp Remi in his arms, wrapping the quilt from her bed around her and lifting her into his arms. "She's burning up and I can't wake her up!" His worried gaze met mine.

I was anxious, but calmer than Chase because I knew how to handle the situation. A fever spike meant her white count was low and she had an infection and it was serious. "We have to get her back to the hospital."

"Should I call an ambulance?" Kat asked breathlessly.

"Chase, make light use of that blanket; we can't risk increasing her temperature. Kat, will you drive us? It will be faster than waiting for EMT's to arrive." I ran from the room to wet a washcloth with cool water, put on my shoes, and grab my purse.

Kat darted out of the front door in a flash, and Chase appeared holding Remi, wrapped in one of her smaller blankets and with a stuffed teddy bear resting in her lap.

"Teagan?" The question in Chase's voice was clear. "Oh, my God. Will she be okay?"

"We just have to go. Right now." I held open the door and he rushed through it and out to the waiting car.

ONE *touch*
AND THE PAIN
melted away.

Chapter 11

CHASE

Breathlessly, Kat rushed into the ER. Her cheeks were flushed and her eyes held a worried look. "What's going on?"

"They took Remi back and Teagan is taking care of the paperwork," I said curtly, pacing back and forth on the small strip of tile that separated the waiting room and the glass partition. The two women who sat behind it had taken basic information and buzzed open a locked door where one male nurse and one female quickly put Remi on a gurney and wheeled her down the hall. Teagan was seated right behind that door talking to another woman, who I assume was doing intake of all the insurance information and a medical questionnaire.

I was rattled. My chest felt tight and shaky. I wanted to be in there with Teagan, but I needed to let Kat know what was going on.

"Chase?" Kat asked again, walking up to me and putting a hand on my arm to stop me in front of her. "What's happening?"

"Uh," I muttered, shaking my head and resuming my course back and forth at the edge of the waiting room. "They took her back and Teagan is filling out paperwork, but Remi just left here two days ago, so they should have everything." I was introspective, talking as much to myself as to my sister. "Shouldn't they?"

"Hospitals have all sorts of rules. The people working ER wouldn't know she'd recently been a patient or her medical history, Chase. After Teagan gives a few basics, they should be able to look everything up." Kat stood there and with the other people sitting in the waiting room and watched me pace. "Do you want to sit down?"

I shook my head and at the same time pulled out my phone and began tapping out a text with my thumbs.

Are you with her? Can I come back?

I stared at the screen of my phone willing Teagan to return the text, but she didn't respond.

I felt Kat's hand on my arm again. Her touch was gentle, but I couldn't be soothed. "Come on, honey. There isn't anything you can do but wait. Teagan will let us know as soon as she knows anything."

My heart started pounding in a fast, anxious rhythm as if I had run up and down the soccer field. "I'm her dad. I should be in there, too." I turned and walked over to the elderly woman still sitting behind the glass. She looked up from her computer screen as I approached. The younger, thinner one sitting next to her earlier was missing from her desk.

"May I help you?"

"Yes, ma'am. I'd like to go back to see my daughter."

"What's her name?"

"Remelia—" I paused for a split second. Teagan said my name was on her birth certificate, but I wasn't sure if she'd be using Jensen's last name since the medical insurance was issued through his company benefits. I felt my face flush with a mixture of anger and embarrassment. The best way to get through it was just to own it. "Forrester or Jeffers."

"Which is it, young man?" The old woman asked. Her eyebrow rose in judgment.

I leaned in close to the silver metal gadget that allowed her to hear me through the glass, so I could keep my voice down. "Look, she's my kid, but her mother is married to another guy. The insurance is under Jeffers."

The grey eyebrow rose up another notch and her pink stained lips pursed. "I see."

I wanted to shout at her but retained my low tone. "Not that it's any of your business, but I don't think you do. I didn't know I had a child until a few days ago, but Remi is mine and if it were up to me, I'd be responsible for everything. She's very sick and I have a right to be in there with her."

The woman's eyes widened as she typed away on her keyboard. I pulled out my wallet in case I'd need to show my ID.

"Hmmm," the woman, murmured, watching the results of her search pop up on the screen. "Oh yes, here it is. Remelia Forrester, hyphen Jeffers."

Kat, who was standing behind me, laid a hand flat between my shoulder blades. She knew that hearing Jensen's name attached to my own was hard to swallow and it was her attempt to comfort and make me aware that I was in a public place.

"Yes, that's her."

"What's your name, sir?" she asked sharply. My brain was starting to refer to her as "the hag", though the badge clipped to her blouse said Lois.

"Chase Forrester." I flipped out my ID and slid it through the small hole at the bottom of the glass. "See?"

"Yes, I do, but her father is listed as Jensen Jeffers, here, so I can't let you in. I'm sorry." She pushed my ID back through the hole.

I reached for the small plastic card with my right hand while my left curled into a frustrated fist. Pain exploded inside me. My throat thickened, my eyes burned and my chest constricted painfully as if steel bands suddenly wrapped around and clamped down, keeping my lungs from expanding. I was hurt and I was furious.

"I don't give a shit what it says on your computer, I'm her dad," I spat out menacingly.

"We'll have to wait and speak to her mother before I can let you in, sir."

"Look, lady," my voice rose in a shout loud enough for everyone behind me to hear. "You have no idea what I've been through! My daughter has leukemia and she might die. She spiked a fever and was unconscious which is why we're here! Let me the hell in there!" My voice cracked and my eyes welled with tears. "Please! I haven't had any time with her."

The woman's expression softened with sympathy for the first time. "I can't allow you in, sir. I'm sorry, but those are the hospital rules and I can't risk my job. Perhaps Mrs. Jeffers will be out soon."

"Chase," Kat said softly. "Let's just call Teagan. Maybe she can come out to get you."

I shrugged off her arm as I whirled around. "Don't you get it, Kat? I shouldn't need permission to see my own daughter!" Two tears rolled down my face and I hastily brushed them away in angry frustration. Ten or more sets of eyes were trained on me; nurses, people in the waiting room, the hag behind the glass and even a patient in a wheelchair being pushed in from the parking lot through the outside doors.

"This is bullshit!" I yelled, and then stormed toward the exit, leaving my sister and everyone stunned and gawking at me.

The electric doors opened and I rushed through almost running directly into a frantic Jensen. "Chase, is Remi okay? What happened?"

Something inside me snapped and I shoved him hard, all ten of my fingertips coming into painful contact with his chest.

"Why are you asking me? Huh?"

Jensen stumbled back and I kept moving forward. I shoved him again.

"I'm just her goddamned father! I ought to kill you, you son of a bitch!" I snarled before hurling myself forward and slamming my fist into his jaw. Pain shot through every part of my hand, ricocheting through the bones of my wrist and into my forearm. I grabbed the front of his shirt to keep him from falling and drew back my arm intending to land another blow.

"How dare you blame me for everything? You left, you mother fucker!"

"Shut up! You couldn't wait to go behind my back and take her! You always loved her! Admit it!" I shouted.

"Yeah, I loved her! Enough to step-up when you fell off!"

"You lousy bastard!" I hauled off and hit him again and again, landing one blow after another using his shirt to pull him forward while my other hand slammed into his face with sickening thuds. "I will never fucking forgive you!"

Jensen stumbled again but then regained his balance. He let out a sarcastic laugh. "You think I want your forgiveness? You're welcome, you ungrateful fuck!" He spat, then launched into a run and his shoulder hit me square in the gut, knocking the wind out of me in a whoosh.

"Ugh!" I grunted as he slammed me into the brick wall behind me. I couldn't breathe and I started coughing uncontrollably.

"Come on!" Jensen goaded. His lip was split and blood was dripping down the side of his mouth but he was ready for a fight. "You wanna go? Let's go!"

"Fuck you!" I pushed off of the wall and went for him, punching him again in the face, this time in the temple and then as hard as I could into his stomach. He grunted and instantly bent over in pain. "You stole my whole goddamn life! You stole my life!"

We continued to fight; pummeling each other mercilessly for the next few minutes. I welcomed the physical pain, hoping that it would replace the mental and emotional agony consuming me. However, each pound of my fist only made the pain inside my heart worse. I was beating the man who used to be my closest friend, and the pain went way beyond physical.

Finally, two armed security guards rushed out of the hospital to intervene, each of them pulling one of us off the other.

"Stop!" one of them yelled. "Or we'll have to call the police! Do you want to go to jail?"

My face and hands were throbbing, and I was certain my abs would feel it tomorrow. I was physically exhausted and an emotional wreck. Any second, I was going to completely lose it.

"Okay! Get off me!" Jensen shrugged off the other guard, while I bent at the waist and put my hands on my knees, breathing hard.

The betrayal of my girl and my best friend was the worst pain of my life, but now it was coupled with an incredible fear that I might lose any chance I had to know Remi. It was more than anyone could handle.

I pushed into a standing position, meeting Jensen's eyes over the two shorter men who stood between us. Both of us were breathing in hard, heavy bursts. I pointed at him, tears glassing over my eyes and turning all three of them into a blur. "How could you do it? You were my best friend!" My shoulders started to shake with the force of my sobs. "She meant everything to me!"

Jensen rubbed the back of his hand across his lower lip, pulling it back to look at the blood smeared there. His chest rose and fell from his exertion. "Did she? Then why did you leave her? You don't even know what she dealt with, why I married her, or why she decided not to tell you!"

"I left so we'd have a secure future. She wanted me to go!"

"That was before she got pregnant, Chase!"

"You should have told me! Instead, you used it to weasel into her life, and push me out." I coughed again, the taste of salt and iron in my mouth. I spit onto the sidewalk and it was red with my own blood. The two security guards still stood between us, listening to the whole goddamned thing.

"Maybe I should have, but no one wanted to be responsible for you losing your dream. Least of all, Teagan!"

"You always loved her. You wanted her," I accused, my eyes narrowing.

"I loved you, both, you jackass!" Jensen leaned back against the wall, trying to calm his breathing. There was pain on his face but I didn't want to see it. "You were my brother, and you asked me to take care of her. That's what I did!"

"Bullshit! I didn't ask you to take her from me."

"Like I said, you don't even know the half of it. Teagan said you didn't want to hear it."

"Do you know how the two of you ripped my guts out? The two people I trusted the most! Do you think I want to relive it? I barely survived it the first time."

"No. But maybe knowing will help you accept it and understand."

"I'll never accept it. Never!" I hissed at him.

"You sure as hell won't if you don't listen! But go ahead. Be your arrogant fucking self, Chase! Big soccer star! You got what you wanted and everyone else paid the bill!"

Fury exploded inside me. Who in the hell did he think he was? "If this is just about the money, I'll repay you tenfold!"

"That's not what I meant, you asshole! Teagan made a huge sacrifice when she let you go, and I made one when I married her. Her heart is closed to me! I love Remi as if she is mine, and I've watched her go through this fucking cancer! And, you stand there like you're the only one who suffered." He shook his head in undisguised disgust. "Get over yourself." He huffed and turned to walk into the hospital, leaving me with the guards.

Jensen's words hit me like a hammer; harder than his fists had done. I stood there stunned, and tears started to roll down my face as his meaning resonated. His statements echoed those of my sister a couple of days earlier in my hotel room.

He was right. They both were.

Everything would have been different if I would have stayed at Clemson, taking my chances that professional soccer was in my future like Teagan and I planned. Maybe I would have ended up in professional soccer, maybe I would have had to quit school and get a job to support my family; either way, Teagan and I would have stayed together and Remi would have had her dad from birth. That was the truth of it. If only I hadn't put my career before the one person I loved more than anyone else. If only...

I ran a hand slowly through my hair as I stumbled back, falling against the brick side of the building. Regret and sorrow washed over me like a tidal wave; the pain of it was as unbearable as the agony at my child fighting for her life. I still didn't know the reasons behind Teagan's decisions, I didn't know what drove her to marry Jensen, but now, I wanted to know no matter how much pain it caused. Maybe she hadn't trusted me to put her first; after all, I'd already put my own ambition ahead of her once. I swallowed hard at the hard lump and uncomfortable thickness in my throat, as I slowly wiped at another tear. Before she left me, I'd already left her. If Jensen wanted to make me feel guilty, it worked.

The older of the two officers cleared his throat and nodded toward the hospital entrance, indicating to his cohort that they should leave me alone. I slumped against the wall, bringing the back of my hand to my mouth as they went inside.

I could blame everything on Teagan, Jensen, even God... but the truth was, it had been my decision. My choice. My fault.

Teagan

It was bad.

Remi was running a fever of close to 103 and she was unconscious. The ER staff had barely gotten her hooked up to the monitors and an IV line into her port when it all went to hell.

Two of the nurses were urging me to leave the small room; two sets of hands gently but firmly on my arms and shoulders pushing and pulling me from the room.

"No! Please!" I cried, desperately. "Don't make me leave her! I'm a nurse!"

I was gasping and the floor was opening up to swallow me whole. I was used to the hospital routine and having to rush her to the hospital, but they'd never made me leave her before. The monitor hooked up to Remi's chest was screaming an alarm and I couldn't rip my eyes from the flat-line pulsing across the screen. Doctors and more nurses were throwing back the sliding glass doors and the curtains, hauling carts of instruments in.

"Get her out of here," the attending physician said firmly. "Bag her, and give me twenty units of vasopressin, then push normal saline, stat. Ready another ten units and a syringe of epinephrine as a back-up."

I couldn't breathe. The irony of own heart was pounding like a drum in my ears, while Remi's had stopped; made me sick. I heard everything as if I were underwater; even my own voice. "No! I can't leave my baby! Please!"

"Come on, ma'am. You know that you have to get out of here so the doctors have room to work," the nurse pulling on my right arm slid her other arm around my back and turned me, ushering me quickly out of the examining room. "It's best to go to the waiting room. Is there anyone to sit with you?"

I nodded absently and in a matter of three seconds, I was in the hallway and out of the double ER doors. The nurse's arm was withdrawn from around me and she was murmuring something about letting us know. She turned and rushed through the door before it had a chance to close all the way. I watched her disappear into the room where my daughter lay lifeless, as the door shut me out.

I gasped; my arms curling up until both of my hands rested at the base of my throat. I could feel my heartbeat under my hands and was acutely aware of my aching chest rising and falling. My breath left as quickly as I'd sucked it in, and my eyes blurred with tears.

Instantly, Kat and Jensen were by my side. Jensen's dark eyes were concerned and my mind briefly registered that his face was bruised and bloody. Kat was already weeping, though I could tell she was trying hard not to.

My husband tried to enfold me into his strong embrace, but I didn't want to be touched. It was if I'd crumble to dust if anyone touched me. My eyes searched the room for Chase, but he wasn't there. Kat turned quickly ran through the lobby and out of the hospital doors to the ER parking lot.

I felt numb. There was a sort of incredible pain lurking, but in that second all I wanted was to be alone. I didn't want Jensen holding me and I moved forward out of his embrace, holding up a hand to keep him from trying to keep the contact between us. I huffed out a breath, closing my eyes as my chin dropped and my head bowed. That damn heartbeat wouldn't stop its annoying thud in my chest or inside my head.

Boom. Boom. Boom.

I walked toward the window through the room of people, oblivious to all of them. Everything seemed to be playing out in slow motion as I placed my hands on the sill and leaned my head on the cold glass. It was dark outside, with just a smattering of yellow lights glowing in the parking lot and from the buildings across the street. Vaguely, I registered the yellow, red and green of a changing traffic light. It was all a blur and I wasn't sure if it was due to the tears in my eyes or the rain just beginning to bead on the other side of the window. Lightning struck in the distance; running brightly through the dark, billowing storm clouds all around.

Boom. Boom. Boom… my heart continued its unending torture.

The room was suddenly filled with a high visceral wail; like a wounded animal screaming at its predator just before it succumbed to the inevitable. I started to crumble as my mind started to wrap around the reality that my little girl could be dead. My heart was exploding, the beating finally getting the better of me, and I couldn't breathe. I was shaking violently; my knees starting to buckle.

"Teagan—" Jensen rushed up to catch me, but I shook him off, sliding to the floor. I curled into a ball of misery, pulling my knees up and as violent sobs wracked my body.

"For God's sake, what's going on?" He crouched down beside me, reaching out his hand to touch my arm. I could do nothing but sob.

"Pardon me. Excuse me. Let me though!" Chase's voice sounded frantic as he rushed to my side, followed closely by Kat. "Teagan!" In seconds he'd fallen to the floor beside me and was pulling my quaking body fully into his arms and onto his lap. "Jesus Christ! Teagan!"

I was crushed to him and soon, I was crying into his neck and chest, clutching at his clothes and skin. "Cha—Chase," I cried. Chase sat with me, stroking my hair while I shook with the magnitude of my grief. "Oh, God, Chase! Remi wasn't brea—eathing!"

His voice was thick when he spoke, and he sniffed. "For God's sake, tell me what happened," he begged.

"Her heart stuh—stopped,"

Chase's breathing started coming in shallow pants. His arms tightened and I curled into him like a child as his grief ripped through him. "No!" he said brokenly, slamming one closed fist against the wall so hard I felt the impact ricochet through both of us.

"God wouldn't be this cruel, Teagan. She's gonna make it." I felt his lips against my hair as we huddled together. I wasn't sure if the hot tears running down the skin of his neck and chest were mine, or his. "Remi has to make it. I haven't—uh, had time to be her dad, yet."

A new torrent of tears unleashed at his words. "I'm suh—so, suh—sorry." I was sure I was the one dying because every breath and shuddering gasp hurt.

Chase's hand continued its soothing, even strokes down the back of my head, smoothing my hair down my back over and over. "It's okay. Don't worry about me right now. Remi is who is important and I know she'll make it, sweetheart."

I sensed Jensen getting to his feet and then looming over us. I realized that he had to be devastated, too. I pulled back slightly from Chase to look up into Jensen's face. He was wiping his own tears; his expression was hurt and angry. I tried to scramble off of Chase's lap to reach for Jensen but he took a step back; as if touching me would burn him. "No.," he said, angrily. "I'm outta here. You don't need me." He turned to leave but Chase stopped him.

"Jensen!" Chase said loudly as he quickly, but gently, pushed me from his lap so he could stand. "Remi needs all of us. Don't go."

I sat there looking up at the two most important men to ever touch my life, watching Chase extend his hand to Jensen and wait for him to take it. Both of them looked beaten and it dawned on me that they must have fought. Another little piece of my heart broke. No matter what happened, I wanted them to be friends again.

"Come on. man." He nodded at his hand. "We gotta get through this, for all our sakes. You were right about what you said out there." He nodded toward the parking lot with his head. "It's on me. I'm sorry, brother."

Jensen looked at the hand Chase was offering and after a few short seconds took it. "I'm sorry, too. I should have told you."

"Yeah, you should have, and maybe someday I can understand it, but now isn't the time."

Jensen's left hand came up to grab Chase's right shoulder. "You're right."

The ER doors opened and the nurse who had taken me out just moments earlier emerged. I scrambled to my feet. All four of us moved toward the nurse. I was scared to death about what she was about to say. Chase's arm snaked around my waist and pulled me close to his side. I used my free hand to reach for Jensen's. Kat used both of her hands to push her short hair back.

"We got her heart started again and as soon as we're sure she's stable we're moving her to ICU. We're running a series of tests to look for the infection so we can treat it, properly. She's a very sick little girl, but we're through this hurdle."

I closed my eyes and swallowed hard. "Oh, thank God. Can we see her?" I asked.

"In a little while. She's still unconscious, so she wouldn't know you're there."

"That doesn't matter. We want to see our little girl," Chase said.

"I'll come get you when we're ready to move her, but the doctor will only allow two visitors at a time."

I was still shaking and leaned on Chase as he held me by his side. Jensen's fingers tightened on mine.

"Thank you," Jensen murmured.

"We appreciate all of you in there," Chase added.

The nurse nodded with a gentle smile. "She's not out of the woods, but you're welcome."

After she left us, we stood awkwardly. "Do you want to get something to eat or something to drink?" Jensen asked.

I glanced at Jensen and then at Chase, hoping their fragile truce would remain firmly in place, but it was clear neither of them was comfortable. I dropped Jensen's hand and stepped out of Chase's embrace, despite the calming effect it had on me. "I think I'm just going to wait. You go ahead," I replied.

Chase's phone, though out of sight, started to ring and he stepped away and pulled it from the back pocket of his dark jeans to answer it. "Hello?" He moved a few feet away to take the call in more privacy and Kat stepped forward to hug me.

"Thank goodness." She sighed heavily. "Is there anything you need from the house? Can I get it?

I shook my head. "No. I'll be okay."

"Maybe Chase will want to run back to the hotel for a shower and a fresh set of clothes. He looks a little worse for wear." It was clear she was referencing the traveling, but also the blood on his now ripped shirt. "Plus, then you and Jensen can go see Remi. I'll call and get her room number."

My eyes met hers. They were red-rimmed, as no doubt mine were, too. I felt tired, and wiped at the skin beneath my eyes in an attempt to rid my face of any telltale signs of tears and smeared makeup. Jensen had walked away and was getting coffee from a beverage station set up on the far side of the waiting room.

"That might be a good idea. I'd like to talk to Jensen, too."

Kat nodded and squeezed my arm. "This is quite a difficult situation and hard on all of you. After all this time, it's gotta be hard for Jensen to see you and Chase together."

"I'm sure it is."

"But, it's also hard on Chase."

"I know. I can feel them both suffering. I wish there was something I could do about it, but I don't know how."

Kat nodded again. "I know. Bronwyn may come back with us, so I just want to prepare you."

I drew in a shuttering breath and went to sit down on a nearby chair. Kat took the one next to me. "I appreciate that. I'm dreading it. What is she like?"

Kat huffed and half shrugged. "Pretty, but fake, mostly. She's all gooey on the surface, but I sense a viper underneath."

"Awesome. Who is she?"

"She's one of the team trainers and they've dated. That's all I know."

Jensen came back with two cups of coffee in hand and held them out to both Kat and I. "Would you like some?"

Kat accepted his offering, thanked him, and then moved over to where Chase was standing. He was just ending his call and they were out of earshot.

"No, thank you."

"I think we should talk," he said solemnly.

"I agree. I have a lot of questions about why you both look like someone beat the hell out of you."

He nodded and took a sip from the steaming liquid in the paper cup. "You already know the answer."

"Who started it?"

"Chase."

The muscles in my back tensed and I stood up a bit taller. I already knew that, too.

Chase and Kat approached, side-by-side.

"Okay, so we're going to go for a while," Kat stated.

"Teagan, will you be okay?" Chase asked.

"She'll be fine," Jensen answered for me, his tone trite.

I could see Chase visibly stiffen so I tried to reassure him. "I'm okay. I'll text if I find anything else out."

His eyes locked on mine and I could see he didn't want to leave.

"Okay." He diverted his gaze in Jensen's direction briefly, and then back to me. "Let's go, Kat." He ran an errant hand through his hair and I couldn't help but notice the angry bruise on his temple.

She jingled her keys. "I'm ready."

"Hey, if you want to go back to the house, here are my keys." I reached into my purse to grab the house key on its keychain and held it out to Kat. She accepted them automatically.

"Let's go," Chase murmured, and soon they were gone.

I turned to Jensen. His expression studied me, seriously.

"Do you want to go to the cafeteria? We can get a table in the corner. It will be better than here. We've already put on enough of a show."

"Okay." We started to walk through the hospital toward the elevators that would take us up to the fourth floor where the cafeteria was located.

We didn't talk at all until we were seated facing each other in a booth at one end of the cafeteria. Jensen had purchased a diet soda for me and set it down in front of me.

He took his seat and in seconds, bluntly told me what was on his mind.

"I think we should get a divorce."

We'd talked about it years earlier but after Remi got sick all thoughts of it were put on the back burner. I sucked in a surprised breath, and he continued, contemplating his hands wrapped around his cup, holding the now lukewarm coffee. "Wow. I didn't expect that tonight."

"We both know where your heart is Teagan. I'm not going to pretend that it doesn't sting, but it's time. Maybe you and Chase can—"

My eyes locked with Jensen's; my soul filled with sadness. "Chase may not feel the same way."

Jensen's face twisted wryly. "Right. Do you see my face?"

"He's got someone else, now."

"Maybe so, but that doesn't mean you and I should stay together."

I nodded. "I agree. You deserve someone who loves you more than anything."

He nodded sadly. "Yeah. I do."

Inadvertently, my words had said that person wasn't me. It wasn't anything either of us didn't know, but still, it was painful.

"What about Remi?"

"Of course, I still want to be part of her life. No matter what happens."

I reached a hand across the table to wrap around his, my eyes flooding with tears. "Of course. She adores you."

"We can wait to file until she's done with treatment, and I'll make sure she stays on my insurance. Of course, Chase is loaded, so I don't think money will be an issue." His voice was thick and tight. "I can see he wants to take care of her, and he can maybe save her life where I am powerless to help."

My heart swelled with love and admiration for this man. "You've given her so much. You gave her your love."

"I couldn't help it. In my heart, she's my child, too."

A tear rolled down my face and I squeezed his hand. "I know. I owe you everything, Jensen. I can't ever repay you. Especially for how you are with Remi."

"She's a gift. That's how I'm always going to think about this time with her."

"You're a gift to both of us, and there will be more time. We have to pray she'll recover enough to have this transplant and it will cure her cancer. I love you, Jensen."

"I know, but not the way you love Chase. If I'm honest with myself, I knew you never would. I just hoped, I guess."

I sniffed knowing I couldn't deny it and I didn't want to hurt him more by lying. I let go of his hand and reached for a napkin from the container on the table. If I let myself, I'd be full on sobbing. Instead, I dabbed at my eyes and concentrated on not crying.

"Can we keep this between us? Chase's girlfriend is in town and I'd rather not stir the pot."

"Aren't you going to tell him that you want to be with him?" he asked incredulously? "He's been in your head and heart this whole time, Teagan."

I shook my head, sadly. "I've already screwed up both of your lives so badly. I don't have the right to keep doing that. If he's happy now, I want that for him. Just like I want it for you. Just—please? I don't want him to trash his relationship in an impulsive moment. Can we keep the divorce between us, please? I'll tell him if I feel the time is right, but our focus is getting our baby better, first."

"Okay. Remi first," Jensen agreed, somberly.

"Yes. Remi first."

My heart knew Chase would agree.

ONE *touch*
AND THE PAIN
melted away.

Chapter 12

CHASE

A sick feeling of dread hung over me at the coming meeting between Bronwyn and Teagan.

"Do you know what room she's in?" Bronwyn asked.

We took a cab back to the hospital after I'd had a quick shower and change of clothes, and she was walking beside me through the hospital. I felt an obvious distance between us, but she tried to compensate for it by clinging to my hand. I knew why I felt this way, but I also knew I shouldn't. There should be no guilt involved regarding Teagan, no worry about her feelings, and I should be more considerate of Bronwyn, but instead, I felt withdrawn from her.

"Yes," I stated simply, not telling her that Teagan had texted it to me fifteen minutes earlier. "It's late. You didn't have to come."

"Of course, it might be awkward for a moment, but you don't have to worry about me, Lovie. I can handle Teagan."

I stopped mid-stride, pulling my hand free of hers and stopping her by grabbing her elbow and turning her to face me. "Look, don't turn this into a confrontation. Teagan is fragile right now and she doesn't need any more stress."

Bronwyn looked up at me, with a shocked look on her face. "You're still doing it." Disgust laced her voice. "You're still protecting her after everything she's done to you?"

I huffed. If I had to deal with this every second, it wasn't going to go well. I was stressed, Teagan was stressed, and the last thing I needed was more agitation. "This isn't about me and Teagan. Remi almost died tonight. Don't you get that?"

Her hand reached out to flatten on top of my chest, and her expression softened. "Yes, but I can't help feeling defensive, Ace. I mean, you came back tonight with your face a mess and blood all over your shirt."

"That was just old anger working its way out." I started walking again, not liking where the conversation was going.

"Was it?" Bronwyn fell into step beside me, her stiletto heels clicking obnoxiously on the tile floor. I was skeptical about why she'd chosen this occasion to change her dress code. Maybe it was unfair, but I was annoyed.

"Yep." My jaw set as I reached forward and pushed the elevator button. "Jensen and I worked it out. We're fine."

"Yeah, no. He shagged, and then married your old girlfriend behind your back. Things will never be fine."

"Drop it, Bronwyn. Please. Continually nagging me about it doesn't help. I just want to check on Remi"

"And Teagan," she pointed out.

The elevator bell dinged and then one of them opened. I ushered her inside and ignored the obvious dig. I didn't like how things were playing out and I didn't trust her to keep her remarks civil.

Pediatric ICU was on the tenth floor and Teagan's text had consisted of nothing but the number: 1024. The minute the elevator doors opened I scanned the walls for the sign that would direct me to Remi's room. The elevators were in the middle of the floor and there were hallways of rooms off both sides of the hall.

We walked past the nurses' station and there were others here or there along the corridor with portable carts and laptops, entering patient information on electronic charts. A couple of them glanced up and smiled as we passed. Around another corner, we found Teagan and Jensen standing halfway down the hall. They were both wearing shapeless yellow gowns made of paper and had surgical masks hanging just below their chins. They were talking quietly as we approached. Teagan's eyes widened slightly at the sight of Bronwyn with me, but then looked quickly away, resuming her conversation with Jensen.

"How's she doing?" I asked.

"They're taking her vitals, but she's sleeping," Teagan murmured softly and tried to smile at Bronwyn. "Hello, I'm Teagan and this is my husband, Jensen."

"Nice to meet you," Bronwyn reached forward to shake Teagan's hand, but Teagan lifted hers up covered in a blue glove and shook her head.

"I'm sorry. They make us wear all this stuff and every time we touch anything, we have to change them out," she offered in explanation.

"I hate these goddamned things," Jensen added, shaking his head.

"I'm very sorry about your little girl," Bronwyn offered. She sounded genuine and I was silently grateful.

"Thank you," Teagan and Jensen answered at the same time.

I couldn't help the wave of resentment and jealousy that washed over me, second only to the fear and sorrow that resulted from the situation. I ran a hand through my hair then leaned up against the wall outside the room next to Teagan. "Will we be able to see her at all?"

"You might be able to go in after the nurses come out, but you'll have to wear all of this garb," Jensen answered.

"They want her to rest and the staff will be in there a lot, so it might be better if we come back tomorrow."

Bronwyn started pacing on a short path in front of us.

"She hasn't woken up," Teagan said softly, sadness lacing her voice. "You'd think I'd be made of iron by now. We've gone through so much; I should be stronger, but I'm still a mess." She used the sleeve of her gown to brush a tear from her face.

"That's why we should go home. You need sleep, Teagan," Jensen offered. "You're exhausted."

"I can stay." My response was prompt. "I'll call you if anything comes up."

"Does anyone want coffee?" Bronwyn asked. "Is there a waiting room somewhere?"

Teagan nodded. "There's a small family waiting room about halfway down around that corner. None for me, thanks."

"You go ahead. I want to wait here," I added.

"I don't want to go alone." Bronwyn shook her head. "How long will they be?"

"A few minutes," Jensen said as he began to pull off his gloves and gown and then shoved them in a bin set aside outside Remi's room specifically for their disposal. "I'll show you where the coffee is. Are you sure you don't want to go home for a few hours?" The question was directed at Teagan. "There isn't anything you can do here."

"I can be here." It was a quiet statement that held a ton of meaning. She wasn't leaving Remi's side.

I wondered if it was possible to rent a room in the hospital so that she might at least sleep a little. I knew she'd want to stay in the same room with Remi, but who could sleep wearing one of those masks? They were suffocating.

"Okay," Jensen said. "This way, Bronwyn."

He motioned for Bronwyn to precede him and she turned in the direction he indicated, but stopped and wrapped a hand around my bicep. "I'll be back soon, Lovie."

Teagan was concentrating on her feet, even after Jensen and Bronwyn disappeared around the corner.

"Sorry, this is so awkward," I said, not knowing if I should mention the elephant in the room.

She nodded, her eyes sad. "I never thought I'd see you with someone else."

I swallowed and leaned my head back against the wall, closing my eyes. "I know the feeling. I'm sorry Bronwyn is here. I didn't know how to stop her, and I just wasn't up for a fight after what happened with Remi earlier."

"I understand. She has a right to be here with you, Chase. I have no right to feel hurt."

"Do you feel hurt?" Damn it! I hated myself for asking, but a huge part of me needed to know. It wasn't as if I wanted to punish her. At least, I didn't think I did... but I had to know.

Teagan nodded. "It's so bad, I can barely breathe."

I inhaled until my lungs were at capacity and then let it out with a heavy sigh. "How did things get so fucked up?"

Her glistening eyes implored me to understand, to love her, to take the pain away and there was nothing I wanted more. Except to save Remi.

"It's complicated. You left and my dad—"

The door to Remi's room opened and two nurses dressed up in yellow emerged, pulling off their masks and gloves. "Remi is sleeping. She's on a strong course of antibiotics and we're giving her prescription strength Tylenol to help with her fever. All we can really do is watch her, keep her comfortable, and wait... for now."

"Will she wake up soon?" I asked, impatiently. I hadn't been able to talk to her or hold her since before I went to

Brazil, and more than anything, I just wanted her to know I was here.

"We've given her a mild pain medication and it will also act as a sedative. She will feel quite sore from the CPR for a few days. We don't want her getting anxious, so the doctors will probably be decreasing the dosage little by little as she heals. As you know, leukemia patients bruise easily and her chest is black and blue. It may scare her if she sees it, so let's work together to try not to let her see her chest for a few days until it starts to turn yellow. Our first priority is getting her fever down and ridding her of the infection."

As I listened, a sick feeling welled up in my throat. It was so much for someone so innocent and small. All I could do was nod. "I understand."

"Do they know what's causing the infection?" Teagan questioned.

"Not yet, I'm sorry. The doctors are ordering a battery of tests."

"Can we see her?" I was anxious to get in there.

"Yes, but it's best to keep it short." She opened a cupboard that was just outside Remi's room, reached in and pulled out one of the yellow gowns. It was folded, but I knew from the color what it was. "You'll have to wear this," she handed it to me, and then one of the masks. "The gloves are in the box on the counter by the sink just inside the room. They must be worn at all times."

I took it and began to unfold it. It had a hole for my head that had a flap that covered half of my back and I shoved my arms into the sleeves. Automatically, Teagan began tying up the back as I lopped the loops of string designed to hold my mask in place over my ears. Instantly I was confronted with my own breath rushing hotly into the mask.

The inside of the room was dark with just one low glow of light coming from a fixture close to the ceiling. Remi was hooked up to monitors that measured her pulse, breathing, and oxygen level. There was a steady beeping coming from it that coincided with the blip on the screen. She was sleeping on her back in the middle of the bed, covered up to her neck in a white cotton blanket.

Teagan had pulled her mask back up into place and went to the opposite side of the bed. "Mommy is here, baby." She stroked back Remi's fine dark hair with her gloved hand.

I knelt down so I could be close to my daughter and laid an arm across her, laying my other in an arc on the pillow over her head. I could feel the heat radiating from her. "She's still so hot."

"They'll get the fever down. One other time they had to use ice. It was awful watching her shiver and cry, but knowing she had to go through it." Teagan's voice shook. "At least now she's sedated, so she might not realize it."

"Jesus Christ." The words ripped from me as emotion threatened to choke me. "She's so little to have to go through this. I'd give anything if I could go through it for her."

Teagan's hand reached out for mine on the pillow. "I'm glad you're here."

I couldn't help the tears that fell onto my cheeks. "I'm not going anywhere. I told my coaches and the team manager that I'm taking leave indefinitely." My eyes met Teagan's in the low light and she nodded her understanding.

I leaned in closer so I could lean my head against Remi's and my arm tightened slightly so I could pull her closer. It was the best I could do to hug her in her prone position. "Remi." My voice was soft but urgent. I wanted her to know I was with her. "Daddy is here and I won't leave you, ever again, I promise."

Teagan reached out and laid her arm over mine, so we were both holding our daughter. Her hand squeezed my shoulder and I looked up at her again. "I never thought I could love anyone as much as I loved you."

"The world changes when you become a parent; your focus shifts."

"Mommy?" Remi's eyes fluttered, and her voice was hoarse and laced with sleep. "I'm thirsty." Her little face crumpled in a whimper when she tried to move. Her little hand raised to her chest. "It hurts."

"I know. Try not to touch your chest, okay, sweet pea? I'll get you some water and then you can go back to sleep. Look who's here." Teagan pointed to me before she stood and went out of the room, I presumed to ask a nurse to bring Remi a drink.

Remi's little eyes looked at me and she tried to smile. "I saw you on the TV, Daddy." Hearing her address me as Daddy with so much ease was the blessing in this whole mess.

"You did?" I grinned and brushed back her hair.

She nodded. "You run fast, and you almost fly."

My eyebrows rose. "Fly?"

She nodded again. "When you go high up in the air to kick the ball." Her right foot moved under the covers and I put my hand down on her leg over the blankets.

"Don't move too much, sweetheart." I knew she meant the overhead back kicks that had taken me years to master. "Would you like to learn that when you're feeling better?" My face was close to hers and my hand continued to stroke her hair. She was so small; my hand could cup her entire head.

"I don't think so."

"Really?"

"It looks like it hurts when you fall down."

I laughed softly, so happy to be talking with her. "It does sometimes, but it's worth it. It helps me win."

"You win a lot. Mommy and me like to watch you."

Pride filled me from head to toe. Teagan may have kept Remi from me, but I was grateful she didn't keep me from Remi. "I'm happy you do. It makes me want to win even more. How about you and me make a signal so you'll know it's just for you when I'm on the field?"

Her little bow mouth curved into a smile of genuine happiness that exposed two missing teeth. "Yeah!"

"Hmmm. What should it be?" I teased.

She lifted one shoulder lightly, bewildered. "I don't know."

I laughed lightly, noticing how the slight movement made her wince. She was the spitting image of Teagan, but I could see myself around her eyes. I couldn't believe how devoted and deeply in love I was with this little girl, already. "Well, you make my heart happy, so why don't I touch my heart, like this?" I placed my hand on my chest, my fingers splayed out.

Remi nodded, "But you gotta do it twice. Like this."

"Careful, honey. You're sore, remember?"

Remi nodded then she copied my movement gently, but then lifted her hand and patted her chest a second time. "Once for me and once for Mommy, because she loves you, too. Kay?"

My heart felt like it would explode with emotion. I felt elated, flying, amazing... full to the brim with love. "Are you sure?" I teased.

"I'm sure. Please?"

I nodded. "Okay. Deal. Two pats over my heart."

"Don't forget, 'cause she'd be jealous and stuff." Her eyebrows rose and she looked at me pointedly. She was so damn cute that I could barely stand it. Sick and sore as she was, she was happy.

"Never. You'll see," I agreed adamantly.

"Okay, you two, what's going on in here?" Teagan said skeptically as she came in carrying a plastic mug with the hospital name on it. It was overly large for someone as small as Remi.

My face twisted wryly and I winked at Remi, silently telling her this was our secret. "Nothing."

Teagan's head cocked and though I couldn't see her face behind her mask, I knew she was wrinkling her nose. "Uh huh. You're up to something," she admonished, wagging a blue latex covered finger at me.

I put both hands up. "Hey, don't look at me."

"Yeah, don't look at us!" Remi added, smiling.

Teagan laughed lightly and I realized how good it sounded to me, and how much I missed it. "Okay. Here's your water, babes."

I moved to the chair and watched Teagan maneuver around the hospital equipment, the IV bag, and the adjustable table that was a constant fixture next to hospital beds. She pushed a button that lifted the head of the bed and brought Remi up into a sitting position before she sat next to her, put one arm around her and helped her take a small sip from the big straw.

Teagan's movements were practiced and second nature. It was obvious much of her time with Remi was spent in hospitals caring for her. I was even more determined that Remi would heal and we'd move past this. I used to think I'd give anything to erase my memories of Teagan from my mind so I wouldn't have to suffer losing her, but in this moment, I wouldn't trade a thing. In this room, like it or not, was my entire life.

Teagan

Despite everything, tonight had been a mixture of heaven and hell.

I was glad Jensen and I had some things settled, but sad because I knew he was hurting. The interaction between Chase and Remi was amazing and somehow healing, but I had been unprepared for meeting his girlfriend.

His girlfriend.

Just the thought of it killed me. Knowing she was in town was one thing, but actually being confronted with her and seeing her try to keep touching him, was another. She was pretty, and I could see she was athletic. I was thin, but I wasn't muscular like her. I guess it was to be expected of a professional trainer, but I thought she'd be a bit more tomboyish. Instead, she was feminine through and through. Funny how you imagine things turning out one way, and then reality makes it worse. Being able to actually picture her in Chase's arms hurt worse than any image my imagination could conjure.

I had no right to presume that Chase would want to be with me, even if I did get a divorce, but it was my heart's highest wish. His presence filled a void in my heart and in my life; one that couldn't be filled with anyone else. Not Jensen, and not even Remi.

Love for my child was engrossing, but I loved Chase in a different way, and the loss I felt without him was debilitating. You learn how to function day-by-day, especially when you have something as serious as Remi's illness to face, but having him back ripped open how much my heart bled without him. I missed him like a damned soul misses salvation. I didn't know if he could ever forgive me, but I at least needed the chance to explain.

Remi had been given her nighttime meds and was drifting back to sleep as I sat beside her bed and held her hand. Her fever still lingered and it was obvious how crappy it made her feel. I stood to pull the covers up and tucked them around her and leaned in to kiss her forehead. I realized I couldn't kiss her properly through this damned mask, but I wanted to feel close to her, and more, I didn't want her to feel isolated.

I was exhausted and the thought of spending another night in a chair in a hospital room was less than desirable. Jensen had already gone home because he had to pack for an assignment in L.A. over the weekend. Remi's illness had become a sort of normal for us and we'd gotten so used to hospitals and tests. In the beginning, he called out of work a lot, but we needed the medical insurance, and he had to make sure his job was secure. It was hard on him, but Jensen was a good provider and since I no longer worked, we had little options. A fresh wave of guilt washed over me as I checked Remi one last time to make sure she was asleep.

I wasn't sure if I'd find Chase and Bronwyn outside the room or not, but it was late, I was tired and I needed something to drink. I wanted Chase to be there but wasn't sure if I could handle the English woman. She hadn't been rude, but it was uncomfortable as hell, and the situation was hard enough already. I pushed open the heavy door to the room and shut it behind me before pulling off the latex gloves, mask and paper gown and shoving them in the waiting waste bin. The lights in the hospital halls were dim due to the lateness of the hour, and still, there were a few nurses here or there, but no sign of Chase.

My heart fell in disappointment. I didn't know what I expected, but I'd hoped he be here, without Bronwyn. Maybe they were in the cafeteria getting something to eat. I pushed both hands through my hair and shoved it behind both ears. I knew I looked a mess, and I didn't care. I started a slow, weary walk around the corner and down the hall to the beverage station that was put there for patient family and friends. There were a couple of small couches with a TV in the sitting room across from it, and I filled a paper cup with ice and water and went in, intent on stretching out on the couch. I could hear the television but hoped there wasn't anyone in there. I needed just an hour or two of sleep to feel better.

I stopped dead in my tracks as my breath hitched. The only light was from the television but I could clearly see Chase's long body stretched out across one of the couches. He had one arm over his eyes and his legs hung off one end so far they were bent at the knees. It reminded me of the many times we'd fall asleep studying in my dorm room the year we met. He still looked so boyish; lying there all rumpled, even with the heavy shadow of a beard that was starting to show on his jaw. I wanted nothing more than to be close to him, to feel him next to me, to smell his cologne and skin.

I momentarily closed my eyes, then moved across to the other couch and sat down. I took a drink from the cup, sat it on the nearby table before curling my legs under me and leaned my elbow on the arm of the sofa. It was hard and uncomfortable and even though my intentions were to sleep, I was sure two things would prevent me. The awful couch and my desire to stare at Chase, unobserved; to drink in every bit of him I could.

When we were together, I used to catch him staring at me like this and it made me smile, but for me, now, this might be my last chance. He must be dead tired to sleep so soundly on such an uncomfortable piece of furniture. His jeans were ripped on the left knee, and the skin on the knuckles of his right hand were broken and bloodied. Once again, the two men who I loved were hurt because of me.

I couldn't help wondering if they both wouldn't be better off without me. At the moment, I needed them because of

Remi, but when this was over, I knew I had to let them both go. I was so tired of crying but unable to stop. Everything seemed so hopeless. I looked down at my lap, willing the tears to stop, willing myself not to fall into self-pity, but my heart was broken.

Chase inhaled suddenly and his body jerked. I quickly wiped the tears from my face as he sat up slowly. He seemed a bit out of sorts as he glanced around and his eyes landed on me.

"Did something happen to Remi?" The urgency in his tone was reflected in his panicked expression.

I shook my head. "No. She is sleeping."

He ran a hand over his face. "Shit." He inhaled deeply.

"Bad dream?"

"Something like that. Are you okay, Teag?"

"Not really," I admitted honestly; hesitant to bare my soul. I was struck by the shortening of my name. He hadn't called me that since we broke up. "Where is Bronwyn?"

"Kat took her back to the hotel. Are you planning to stay here all night?"

"I usually stay with Remi most of the time. Hopefully, she won't wake up because of the sedation, so I don't know if I'll stay tonight. You don't have to stay, either way."

"It doesn't feel right to leave you here alone, and I'm terrified something will happen. I'll never be able to forgive myself if I wasn't here when something happened."

He was already an amazing dad and I was thankful he wasn't holding any of this against our daughter. His instincts were right on, just as I'd known they would be. "Do you want to talk about what happened with Jensen?"

Chase huffed and leaned forward; his elbows on his knees. He didn't look at me. "Isn't it obvious? Did you think I wouldn't still be pissed as hell? The pain doesn't go away. It may have dulled over the years, but this— I knew it was going

236

to be hard to see you again, but it's just—" He paused. "Torture. Magnified by the lies and Remi's illness, I have to remind myself to keep it together ten times an hour."

I knew how deeply Chase felt things and he was being ripped to shreds. I could see it on his face, hear it in his voice, and sense it in his agitation.

I got up and moved over to sit beside him. I wanted to be closer, to touch him, to take some of his pain away. "I know. I can say I'm sorry a million times, but I know it doesn't help."

His green eyes were trained on mine and I reached out hesitantly and pushed a lock of hair that had fallen across his face back; then threaded my fingers through the soft hair at his nape.

"Don't touch me unless you're prepared for what comes next. I'm not made of stone, Teagan." He swallowed and looked away.

"Chase." My voice throbbed out his name. I left my hand on the back of his head, but my fingers stilled.

He pulled from me and stood, towering over me with a scornful frown on his face. "Do you know how hard this is for me? When I'm with you, I want to forget all the bullshit and just be us. Like we were! But how can I get past the betrayal? This is killing me! You have no right to treat me like we're still together!"

"I'm trying not to, but I can't help it! Do you think it was easy for me to walk away from you?" I was openly crying now, pleading for Chase to understand.

He pointed an accusatory finger at me. "If that were true; if you loved me like that, we'd still be together. Don't lie to me!"

I covered my mouth with my hand, gasping at the depth of my pain. I was trembling, my shoulders shaking with sobs. "There's muh—more tuh—to it! Puh—please listen!"

"What do you want?" A muscle worked in his jaw as his teeth clenched. He glared at me with pain and determination written all over his handsome face.

A time machine, my mind screamed. "I can't have what I want. I'll probably never have it, and I've spent all these years trying to accept that, but I can't."

"Welcome to my world," he spat bitterly.

I didn't know if I what I was about to say would release him or make things worse. "I want you to know that I love you, and how very sorry I am. I know I don't deserve your forgiveness, but I need to tell you the truth. All I can do is hope you'll understand why things happened the way they did, and why I made the decisions that I did. It was never to hurt you."

Chase's head dropped and his voice thickened as he fell into the chair at the end of the sofa. I could hear the tears in his voice and my heart seized. Again, the urge to put my arms around him and hold him close overcame me, but I had no right to do so.

"Do you know how it feels to be so goddamn helpless? You cut me off at the knees. You and Jensen ruined my life without telling me why! It's the unanswered questions that kill me. Now, we have this huge crisis and you've only called me because you need something from me. I have to wonder if you would have ever told me about Remi if she weren't sick. What about my career? Will I look like the dick that abandoned my child just to play the game? What do I tell my parents?"

I tried desperately not to lose it. Pain tightened my chest and made it hard to breathe. I slid down to the floor and crawled the few feet to be near him, between his thighs and I could sense his hesitation in the way he went rigid. I wrapped both hands around his biceps and I leaned into him, letting my forehead fall to his shoulder, praying he would listen. He was stiff but didn't push me away. "Please let me explain."

In an instant, his hands wrapped around both of my arms and pulled me closer. I was startled, but after our faces were a breath apart and our eyes met, he stilled. "Explain this. Why do I still want you? Why can't I hate you?"

My heart exploded in my chest. "Oh, Chase," I reached out a hand to touch his face. The shadowy stubble on his jaw was softer than I expected. "You can't choose who you love."

"So you think I love you unconditionally, so I have to accept what you did and forgive you. Is that it?"

"No. I know you can choose not to forgive me, just like I could choose to marry Jensen, but I can't choose not to love you, and I don't think you can either. At least, I hope not—"

In a flash, his arms gathered me close and he turned his face into the curve of my neck. My fingers stroked his jaw and my other hand slid up his solid chest and around his neck. He felt so amazing and I didn't care if this was all I'd ever have with him, I needed to be in his arms. I could feel the tension between us. His muscles coiled and his hot breath rushed over me causing an instant and white-hot reaction at the core of my body. Heat pooled and began to throb. He was the only one who could affect me with this incredible, desperate want. My heart felt like it would explode it was so full of emotion and all I could do was hang on to him for dear life.

"Teagan," he breathed. "What are you doing to me?"

He pulled back enough to kiss me, his mouth swooping in to take mine in a hard, hungry kiss. I opened my mouth to him; completely surrendering as my body came alive, reveling in the feel of my soft curves being pressed so tightly against his muscular torso. His shoulders were broad and he was solid as a rock and so familiar. Nothing ever felt this good.

We kissed deeply; again and again, lips tasted, tongues explored each other's mouth and hands roamed over each other, pulling and pressing each other closer. My hands threaded through Chase's hair to deepen our kisses. I couldn't get close enough and I was starving to have his mouth and hands on me. My chest heaved and ached for him to explore the soft swells. One of his hands fisted in the back of my shirt and another slid down over the curve of my hips and bottom, intent on plastering our bodies together.

I was getting lost in him, the feel and taste of him, and our past. It was always this intense between us; unstoppable passion and love flowed like an electric circuit that only became stronger the longer we touched. His tongue was wild; laving and twisting together with mine.

A low groan erupted from deep inside Chase's chest. He was panting hard when he ripped his lips from mine and pressed his forehead to mine. "Jesus Christ. I'm so done, Teagan."

"Chase," I protested, lifting my chin for more kisses. He rewarded me with pulling my top lip between his to gently tug on it. All it did was frustrate me. "Please," I begged as his lips hovered over mine. He began gently nudging and then nipping at my lower lip with his teeth. I found it irresistible. "I'm starving for you."

"Teagan, remember where we are," he murmured breathlessly between kisses.

I nodded, sucking in the breath he had just exhaled. "Take me somewhere."

Chase's forehead dropped to my shoulder and he paused. "Let's think about this. Are you sure? It's not just about us anymore."

Part of me panicked for a brief second. Maybe he didn't want me. Whether he did or didn't, regardless if I could be humiliated by his rejection. He deserved to hear the truth. He deserved everything I could give him. I had to take the risk.

"I know," I said painfully. I did feel guilty, but the love I had for Chase ruled anything I owed to anyone else.

"You're sure then?" He asked, still breathing hard. "There's no going back."

"I'm sure I love you, and that's all I can think about, right now," I whispered. The words were so full of emotion they hurt to say. "If you never touch me again, I'm sure I'll love you, forever."

I couldn't see his face, but his arms tightened around me and his face turned so he could press an open-mouthed kiss on my neck, softly sucking like he used to, one hand moved up to cup the back of my head.

He held me tight for at least a minute. I knew he was struggling with the rights and wrongs of making love to me, but my body was buzzing with wanting and my heart was breaking with love. In that moment all I wanted was to be in his arms and never leave.

Our eyes locked as Chase stood, lifting me with him as he set me on my feet. "Let's get out of here."

ONE *touch*
AND THE PAIN
melted away.

Chapter 13

CHASE

I'm sure I love you, and that's all I can think about, right now.

Teagan's words reverberated through me like an earthquake. The air was charged around us, and the inevitability of what was about to happen rocked me. I couldn't stop it, even if I wanted to. It didn't matter that my mind argued that if I betrayed Bronwyn with Teagan, I was earning Teagan's betrayal of me with Jensen. It didn't matter. Either way, I was screwed. All I knew was that now that I'd given in to the want, I couldn't stop it, and I didn't want to. My heart wanted to pretend we were still us and that all of the misery of the past could evaporate, and we were healed. My heart needed hope. It needed healing.

Sex with Teagan wasn't about lust. I wanted her and my body was on fire in anticipation, but my heart was full of her and for the first time in years, I felt whole. It was about love. It was about healing. Mostly, it was being honest with Teagan, and with myself.

On the drive through the night, our hands clung together without either of us speaking a word. I couldn't stop touching her and it was evident she felt the same way because she held on to my arm, even when I was digging out my wallet and signing for the room at this random hotel that I didn't even remember the name of. My hand shook as I ran the keycard through the lock and waited for it to flash to green and click.

My heart was pounding; my body was buzzing. I wasn't sure if doing this would save my soul or damn it; I didn't know how I'd feel afterward or what would happen. The only thing I was sure of was that no matter what happened, I was powerless to stop it. Teagan and I were inevitable.

I pushed open the door and threw the card on the floor, turning to Teagan and yanking her hard against me as the door slammed behind us.

Her hands slid up my chest and around my neck as mine slid down over her ass and between her legs to separate them and lift her against me. She wrapped her legs around my waist and pushed her pelvis tight against my cock. I was engorged and so hard, if the pressure didn't release soon, I was sure I would explode. The blood rushing wildly through me made my heart pound and my dick ache.

I almost slammed Teagan against the wall in my need to thrust against her. She was hot as hell; heat seeped through our clothes as our bodies heaved against each other.

We kissed passionately and her hands pulled at the front of my shirt, her fingers frantically trying to work the buttons free. I could feel her frustration because it echoed mine. We were already panting in our excitement, as the need between us throbbed like a living thing. My hands pushed up her shirt so I could cup and then knead both of her lace-covered breasts.

"You're still my monkey," I whispered between kisses. "God, Teagan, I want you."

There was no one else who could make me feel this way; so desperate to bury myself in her hot, slick flesh, and pour all of my love into her, just like I always had.

244

She let out a soft whimper as she finally freed three of the buttons of my shirt so her hands could splay out on my chest. Having her hands on me felt incredible, but I wanted more. I wanted every inch of her skin on mine, I wanted to touch her and make her come, to taste her, and remind her that she belonged only to me.

"You're still mine," I insisted because I couldn't tolerate anything else. One touch from her and the maelstrom of pain that always hung over me, melted away.

"Always," she whispered urgently.

I gloried in hearing her admit it even though we both knew it. My heart ached that I'd missed even a minute with her, but I pushed away the implications of everything that happened since. I wanted this time with her to be completely unmarred, to lose myself, to pretend, for just a for a few hours, that all that shit never happened. I needed it like I needed air.

Her teeth gently tugged at my lower lip and her tongue slid along the top one. Every touch was driven, sensual, designed to bring me to my knees. She knew what I liked, she knew what turned me on, and she knew my heart like no one else ever had.

"Chase, please." The urgency in her voice went straight to my dick. It pulsed and pushed against the confines of my jeans even as I continued to push against her, aiming for just the right spot to make her crazy with wanting. "Take me to the bed."

I took her weight easily and turned toward the king size bed, laying her down gently. We'd continued to kiss all the way down, but when I pulled back so I could look into her face, she protested my absence. Teagan's lips clung to mine, her head lifting off the bed in an attempt to prolong the kiss as her hands slid down my arms. She shook her head. "No, don't stop, Chase."

"I'm insane to be inside you, but I want to go slow. I want to look at you. Who knows what will happen tomorrow, but I don't want to think about anything outside of these four walls tonight. I never thought I'd ever be with you like this again, and I want to remember every second." I kissed her again because her neediness for it was irresistible, but this time it was with a slow, languid thoroughness that communicated my intentions.

I moved back to look down into those amazing eyes. I was hovering over her and caging her in with my body.

Teagan's eyes flooded with tears and her hand reached for my face. "Chase—"

I shook my head. "No. Don't promise me anything. We'll deal with the other shit when we have to, but not tonight. I don't want to think about anything but you and me right, now."

Our eyes locked and tears overflowed, rolling down the sides of both sides of her face at her temples. She got a little crinkle between her brows and nodded without speaking. I knew her heart was screaming, just like mine. It hurt to look at her because deep down, I couldn't shake the heartbreak; but I had to be with her because it would kill me not to.

I tried to swallow, to push down the lump in my throat caused by the emotions that ruled me. I pushed off of the bed to close the shades even though it was dark and we were several stories up. I adjusted the thermostat and turned out all of the lights except the light in the bathroom.

I could physically feel Teagan's eyes follow my every move from where I left her lying on the bed. She made no move to remove her clothes other than kicking off of her flip-flops because she knew I enjoyed removing them myself. A new surge of desire rushed through me like fire; so intense it made my body literally shake, my breathing shallow and my heart felt like it could fly from my chest. The feeling was exactly what I expected; euphoric agony.

Her hair was splayed out on the white comforter. The small stream of light cast from the bathroom allowed me to find the TV remote and easily navigate to Music Choice, and search for a soft rock or love song station.

We used to make love to music and candles all the time; regretfully, we had no candles, but I'd do the best I could to create the ambiance that would take us back to where we were so we could forget everything but each other. Tonight was not the time for guilt or regret. It was for love, and love alone.

I walked the few feet to flip off the bathroom light, leaving the room cast in a soft bluish glow from the music station on the television. My eyes never left Teagan as I kicked off my shoes and unbuckled my belt. I pulled it from my jeans and dropped it on the floor. I pulled the button loose and the zipper down. My cock was still hard and ready, the tip pushing through the waistband of my boxer briefs, and there was nothing hotter than the way Teagan's eyes lingered on it before her eyes snapped back to mine and bit her lip. She wanted me; it was written all over her; the way her mouth dropped open, her half-lidded gaze, and the way she moved slowly, provocatively as she lay there, running her hand down her body; tempting me to the point of insanity. She knew exactly what she was doing.

"You're killing me. I want you so much it hurts. It fucking hurts." My voice was low and dripping with need.

"Come over here," she beckoned softly, and I couldn't resist her soft command.

"My movements were slow and deliberate as I lay down beside her, sidling up close so I could lean over her so my hands could explore her body in a slow caresses and still allow me to watch her expression. Instantly, she turned toward me and slid her leg between mine to slide up the inside of my thigh, pressing and teasing against my groin. She closed her eyes in satisfaction when my head fell back and I groaned in surrender. It was a slight touch, but so provocative. The fingers of her left hand ghosted up the arm I was using to touch her. Two could play the teasing game.

My knuckles grazed the swell of her left breast and then around and over the erect nipple. I watched her face, taking in the way her gorgeous eyes closed and her perfect mouth fell open as her breath left her. She was so goddamned beautiful.

"Chase," she moaned softly. "Stop torturing me."

"You know I give as good as I get."

"I do."

Reaching down, I opened the fastening of her jeans and pushed them open. Her stomach was still as flat as ever, and I flattened my hand over it and slid upward under her shirt. She sucked in her breath as her leg pulled at mine and her hand kneaded and tugged at the bare skin of my shoulder. It was hard to resist her silent plea that I move on top of her.

I leaned in and took her mouth hard as my hand easily undid the front fastening of her bra and pushed it aside giving me full access to her soft swells. Her breasts were still firm and maybe just slightly larger than I remembered; her skin was still as smooth as silk.

I kneaded first one, then the other, being careful to tweak and tug on both nipples, pulling the hard buttons gently until her hips started to push forward in slow thrusts. I began to echo her movements with thrusts of my tongue into the deep recesses of her mouth.

My body protested at my slowness, but I wanted to make the most of every second. I needed to hear her panting my name and feel her body arch as I pleasured her. I would make sure that she'd never forgotten who owned her; heart, body, and soul.

She tasted amazing, as she kissed me back with abandon. It was clear what she wanted, and I was going to give it to her and more.

"Chase," she whispered again. "I want you inside me. I'm… uhhhhh," she let out a sigh. "I need—"

"I know what you need, babe. Me, too. Be patient," I whispered against her open mouth.

Her fingers tightened on my wrist and pulled my hand down her body to the place that ached the most. My lips curved into a slight, satisfied smile, as I obliged; pushing my fingers under the waist of her bikini panties and further. Her body was ready, already slick with need.

"Mmmm," she murmured and bit her lip, arching into my hand. My fingers slid through her folds, over her clit to slide my middle finger inside her.

"Jesus," I murmured against her mouth, withdrawing my fingers to slowly push in again and again.

Teagan's legs fell open and her hips began to undulate in sync. Her reaction was abandoned and super sexy and my own body reverberated with want. My hips pressed into the side of her leg, pressing my hard cock against her thigh. I wanted her to feel what she did to me and know how much I wanted her. I knew exactly how she liked to be touched with a combination of stimulation of her clit and deep thrusts of my fingers and I concentrated on making her come, but I wanted to give her a slow build and a hard orgasm.

"My God, Chase. Why are you waiting? It's been so long."

Her hand moved up my arm and over my shoulder to fist in the back of my hair. She wanted to be closer, but also, needed to give me the access I needed. It was amazing to just be able to touch her, but knowing that in minutes I was going to make love to her, kept me from losing it.

"That's why. Because it's been so long." I thrust against her, rubbing back and forth to get some of the stimulation I craved when she reached down and grasped the shaft. "Uh, God," I panted.

"Chase." Teagan's hand moved down to stop mine from its slow torture, though I wasn't easily persuaded to stop before I gave her an orgasm. "Make love to me."

"I am."

Her forehead pressed against my jaw. "I know, but I want to hold you, feel you on me. In me."

I could feel her body tighten around my fingers and her words rocked me. It would be easy to give in to what she was asking, but it was more important to me to make her feel amazing. "You're so close."

She swallowed and nodded. Her hot breath rushed over the skin of my neck. "I know. But, please?"

I sighed and did what she asked by pulling my hand free of her body and immediately pushed on her pants to slide them down her hips. My lips found hers in a desperate attempt to stay connected while I completed the task. Teagan struggled to undress me at the same time, using her feet to drag my jeans down when her hands couldn't reach any further. It reminded me of the first frantic time we made love in college.

"Oh, screw this," I smiled and moved off the bed, leaning over and pulling her jeans and panties completely free and dropping them on the floor. In seconds, mine had joined hers in a pile. Teagan peeled off her top and her bra, then flung it and her bra off the side of the bed by the wall, leaving us both completely naked.

It would have been easy to assuage the incredible need by crawling on top of her and pushing my cock inside. She was ready and she wanted it as badly as I did, but I wanted to savor every single second of our time together.

Teagan's body was still just as perfect as it had always been. Having Remi hadn't changed the slimness of her waist or ruined the skin on her stomach. I realized it wouldn't have mattered either way, but my eyes ran over her in slow appreciation.

"Teagan," I sighed and shook my head. My heart was so full of joy and sorrow I felt choked up. "I'm not going to regret this, and I'm not going to feel guilty about it."

She lay on the bed naked, but serene. Her hair splayed out like a glorious halo and her expression full of desire. She was sensual and beautiful. "I don't want you to. I won't either."

I came to her then, letting my hands slide up her legs and body as I hovered over her, hungry to kiss her; to devour every inch of her skin. My knee parted hers and I used my thighs to spread her wide open. I loved the taste of her skin as I kissed her jaw, down the cord of her neck, and over her collarbone. My fingertips slipped behind her head and tangled in her glorious dark hair.

I lowered my body to the bed next to her to free up both of my hands to explore her body. "I can't believe you're in my arms. I never thought it could ever happen again."

Teagan reciprocated the exploration. I listened to her breathing, felt her heartbeat, and sensed her excitement building. I was rock hard and ready and couldn't help letting out a low growl as she worked her hand up and down on my flesh. Years of practice made it easy for both of us to find all the secret places that excited us most. I surged against her in slow thrusts, dying to feel her slippery heat around me.

I let myself kiss down her body, worshiping her breasts with my mouth at the same time teasing her sex with my hands. Teagan's back arched and her head fell back as she lifted up off the bed. My hand moved down her body, over the side swell of her breast, her trim waist and the womanly curve of her hip, down her thigh, and my lips followed suit.

251

The scent of her desire surrounded me and my cock bobbed with the force of the blood pushing into it. My own breathing was shallow and fast, and I could feel a drop of pre-cum leak from the tip. Teagan used her thumb to spread it around over the head making me more determined to draw the same pleasure from her.

"Uhhhh," she breathed as I moved lower, pushing her thighs apart so I could kiss her in her most private places. She was perfect, the intimacy of the act a measure of my love for her. I used my lips and tongue to make her writhe.

"Chase," she sighed. "Uhhhhh." She let out a soft moan threading her fingers through my hair as I made love to her with my mouth. "Chase, come up here. Now."

I sucked in my breath and moved up as she commanded, kissing her hard. Teagan opened to me and sucked my tongue into her mouth.

Rolling onto my back, I pulled her up the bed with me, so I could lean on the headboard and watch her every move. My eyes narrowed, my lids dropping in passionate anticipation. Teagan met my gaze, unflinching as she straddled me. I held my dick up so she could slide her body onto mine with one, long, slow push.

A hiss left me as her tight heat surrounded me. It was everything I remembered and more. Her body hugged and pulled on mine. I was buried deep and she started to rock her body on mine. It felt incredible. My hands slid down to cup her butt and leverage her as tightly against me as I could, halting her heady movements.

"Don't move yet, babe. I want to look at you, and feel you on me." I sat up and leaned my forehead on her shoulder, and used one arm around her waist to pull her as close as I could. Emotion overflowed between us. I was with Teagan. Inside Teagan. The love of my life. The only woman I would ever love in this lifetime.

My throat hurt and my eyes burned with tears. For years I'd fought to bury my feelings, but since seeing her again, feeling seemed to be all I could manage. I couldn't speak, letting out a pained "Ugghh" from deep inside my chest.

She wrapped her arms around my shoulders and head. "I love you, Chase." She was crying softly as she held me. "It's only ever been you."

I looked up at her, reaching up with one hand to push back the curtain of her hair. "I know," I said truthfully because anything else was impossible. It was like no time had passed. All I had to do was touch her and the pain went away.

In my heart, Teagan would always be mine and I didn't care if being with her was wrong or if our lives would implode when the sun came up. All that mattered was that she was in my arms and that she still loved me. I could deal with anything else that got in our way.

"Make love with me. Just like always." I tilted my chin up to capture her lips with mine at the start of a deep kiss. Kissing her had always been amazing and so intimate, and nothing had changed.

I cupped her face and ran a thumb over her high cheekbone. Our mouths and bodies moved in slow unison. Desire licked along every inch of my skin, there was an intense urgency between us to get closer, push in deeper as we surged against each other. I was going slow, controlling Teagan's movements with my hips and hands, but it had been so long since we'd been together. My balls tightened and the pressure in my dick increased to the point of pain. Teagan's muscles squeezed around me; trying to milk me. It felt unbelievable and unstoppable: I could come at any second, but I didn't want to.

"Teag, go slow baby. It's hard for me not to come. It's been so long and you feel so good."

"I want you to."

253

"I can feel you're trying to push me over, but I don't want it to be over, yet."

Her hips undulated against mine in sensual circles. As hot as it was, every movement, every touch was about showing love. The pleasure was more intense because of the feeling surrounding and motivating us.

She continued to move on me, and I willed myself not to flip her over and take control. My fingers ghosted over her chest and breasts, only to move up and cup them both. I rubbed her tight nipples between my thumbs and forefingers. Our position allowed her to take me in deep, but it still wasn't close enough. She leaned forward and bit the side of my neck, while I sucked on hers. "It's never over," she whispered.

I closed my eyes, letting my senses fill with her. Her perfume surrounded me, mixed with the essence of our sex; every touch was magic and the way she was working my body with hers, pushing, pulling, squeezing was impossible not to lose myself in. Sensations enveloped me, emotions overflowed; I was getting close, and I could feel she was, too. Her movements were more urgent, the sounds she made higher pitched and her breathing faster. I couldn't fight the urge to put her beneath me any longer. I wanted total control and to make her feel as amazing as I felt, I wanted to see her face as I made her come. I rolled over, making sure my body didn't slip from hers.

I pushed in hard, intent on using my pelvic bone to put pressure on her clit with every thrust. She gasped and arched against me and met my movements with her own, still clenching tightly, then released around me.

"Uhhh, uhhh. Mmmm."

"That's it, baby," I said. I was leaning on my elbows and I felt Teagan's nails dig into the flesh of my back "It feels so amazing. Come on, babe," I urged, feeling my orgasm on the brink.

Her legs wrapped around me and her heels dug into the back of my thighs as the uncontrollable pulsing of her orgasm made her muscles flex around my cock. That was it; I was done. Three thrusts later, I was pouring into her and groaning her name. "Teeeaagan." I came hard, jerking against her as she clung to me. Her fingers gently stroked the hair at my nape and she pushed on my ass with the other hand. "Oh, babe."

It took me a second to recover, then I pulled back to look at her, still breathing hard. Wisps of her hair clung to her temple by a slight sheen of perspiration, her eyes were heavy and her mouth swollen. I used both hands to push her hair back and frame her face. I traced her jaw with my thumbs and brushed along her hairline with my fingers.

"You're still perfect."

I could see her swallow and tears flood her eyes as she ran one finger down the side of her face. Every touch between us was reverent. "Will you let me tell you now?"

I studied her face and still found pain there. "I don't want to ruin this. It's too incredible to be with you. I never thought I'd touch you again."

She pushed her fingers through the damp hair on one side of my head and fisted her hand in the back of my hair. "If I had my way, you would have never stopped."

I slid out of her and rolled onto my side to face her. Her words made me uneasy. If they were true, why did it stop?

"We have time to talk about the past, but I think we need to talk about Remi."

"I just need to tell you the truth, first. Please, Chase."

I was flying and I didn't want to spoil the moment by digging up painful memories.

"Okay, but not now. Not when we've just made love."

She closed her eyes then opened them again. "When we're close is when I should tell you. When you can feel how much you mean to me."

I didn't say anything, just continued to meet her eyes. I was gently kneading the flesh of her upper arm. She had a point, but I still hesitated.

"I don't have to tell you everything right now, but a piece of it. Please."

I sighed deeply. "Okay. Just answer this: Did you know you were pregnant before I left?"

She nodded. My jaw jutted forward in anger.

"Just before you got the offer from Arsenal. I was going to tell you after the championship game, but you were so excited about the offer, I just couldn't do it. I knew you wouldn't go if you knew about the baby."

It made sense in a way, but it still didn't explain the rest. "I might have. At first, it was just to fill-in as forward for a while. We knew that."

She shook her head sadly. "No, we didn't. We both knew once they had you, they'd keep you, Chase. You were the best forward in college soccer."

I huffed and tried to smile. "You were my girlfriend. You had to think so."

"It was the truth, and you know it."

I half shrugged. "Saying it out loud makes me sound like an asshole."

It was Teagan's turn to smile. "Being honest doesn't make you an asshole."

Honesty. The word hung between us like a storm.

I wanted to get this over with so, hopefully, we could get past it. "Okay, so you couldn't tell me before I left, but why not later? Why not just come to London?"

"When my dad found out, he threatened to destroy you! Your career—"

Anger exploded inside me. Then, and I sat up and moved back from her. Her father never thought I was good enough for his little girl. He made it clear he held disdain for my middle-class roots and felt that I wasn't good enough for his daughter. He was a pompous bastard and he'd done his best to break us up. Obviously, in this case, it worked. I felt some of the anger over her betrayal weasel its way back into my heart. "What could he do?" I spat.

"He was going to tell the press. He said you were a deadbeat to leave your pregnant girlfriend here to deal with this mess while you went about your life," she admitted, climbing on to her knees, but keeping the sheet around her naked body. "It's not what I thought, Chase," she added, knowing I was about to blow.

"I know that! You knew I went for us! For our future. A professional career pays a lot more than a high school soccer coach. He knew that, but he just used it against us. He was always against us, Teagan. His fucking hatred of me only drove me to prove him wrong."

"I know."

I was getting more pissed by the minute and pushed off the bed to grab my pants and throw them on. I towered over the bed with my hands on my hips. "So why didn't you tell him to go straight to hell?"

"Chase, he's a U.S. senator. He knows people all over the world. I couldn't take the chance he'd get you thrown off the team."

"That lousy bastard. What about you? What did he do to you?"

I was furious and could feel the heat of it seeping up like a flame beneath the skin of my chest, neck, and face.

"He wanted me to have an abortion. He said I was staining the Tessler name and he didn't want his legacy to be that his daughter was a whore, rather than his contributions to Congress."

"That contemptible fuck! I could fucking kill him, right now!" I was almost shouting, but Teagan was still calm.

"That's part of the reason I didn't tell you. He'd already hurt you so much when we were dating. I couldn't stand anymore."

"Who needed him?" I started to pace back and forth. "You should have just come to London."

She moved in my direction, scooting to the edge of the bed. Her eyes implored me to understand. "It wasn't that simple."

"Jensen." My back stiffened. "How does he fit into this?" Was she already with him? Was that why she didn't tell her father to fuck off? Was his reaction just an excuse to legitimize her relationship with Jensen?

Teagan stood and walked toward me. She seemed so small and fragile. "Jensen was my friend, just like he was your friend, Chase. He was the only person I had to talk to about you and about the baby; about what my father threatened. I didn't know what to do. All I knew was that I had to protect you, no matter what."

"You did a hell of a lot more than talk to him!" I was upset that the evening was now tainted with this conversation.

"You don't understand, Chase." She walked forward to lay her hand on my bare chest. "Just listen before you jump to conclusions. He went to my dad without telling me and said he was the father and he planned to marry me. It was in the paper before I even knew it happened. He thought he was protecting me, and you."

"I didn't need either one of you to protect me! I needed my woman and my baby!" I yelled, rapidly dipping to pick up my shirt and shoving my arms into it.

"I know that now, but I didn't then. The most important thing to me now is that you know neither of us wanted to hurt you."

I huffed angrily, picking up her clothes and throwing them at her. "Hurt me? You goddamn killed me." I wasn't yelling anymore: I was stating the obvious.

"I know. I killed me, too. And Jensen has also paid a huge price." She quickly dressed, turning her back like she was embarrassed.

I was incredulous. "Why is everyone always trying to make me feel like shit? You made a choice! Jensen made a choice! You didn't have to do what you did! I wasn't asked what I wanted!"

As mad as I was, I was still heartbroken and the strength of my grief rocked me. "You stole Remi from me, and what if she doesn't make it, Teagan?" My face crumpled and I fell against the hotel room wall, sliding down to the floor in anguish.

For the first time, I let myself face the possibility of losing Remi and all my misery flooded free. I hadn't cried like this in front of anyone since that time with Kevin right after Teagan left me.

Teagan, now fully dressed scrambled onto the floor next to me and put her arms around me as sobs wracked my body. I couldn't help it; I leaned into her and held on tight as the torrent of tears flooded out. I cried my heart out; my body shaking against hers.

"I love you, Chase. I never stopped, loving you. You have to believe me. I'm so—sorry."

Somehow Teagan ended up sobbing and crying into my chest, soaking my white button-down with her tears, and clutching at the front of it. My head dropped and I turned my face into the curve of her neck.

"Jesus Christ." The words were ripped out of me. "How in the hell am I supposed to deal with that? You can't say that shit to me, Teagan. Not anymore. This is hard enough. Not unless everything changes."

Her arms snaked up my neck and my fingers laced in the soft hair at the back of her head. I felt her desperation.

"Chase, please hold me," she begged. She had no right to ask, or for me to grant her request, after what she did. Even after our lovemaking moments before… but I couldn't deny that I needed her as much as she needed me. "I'll die if you don't right now."

It was as if time melted away as I stood up and lifted her with me. My arms tightened, crushing her to my chest, her feet dangled off the floor and I held Teagan as close as I could. Her breasts crushed to my chest felt incredible, and her body wrapped around mine was like a balm to a mortal wound. It was glorious and miserable at the same time.

Never would my heart be unbroken, never would I stop mourning the loss of that precious time with my child, or this precious woman, but even so, I couldn't stay away from her and I couldn't waste any chance I had to be close to her.

She clung to me and buried her face against my chest, her body shaking with sobs like mine had been.

"Please forgive me. I'd gah —ive anything to tuh—ake it all back."

I sat down at the foot of the now love rumpled bed and lifted her to sit on my lap. "Hush." I wiped the tears from my face and kissed her forehead. "It'll be okay." She curled into me and laid her head on my shoulder.

The truth hit me. I had to forgive her or I'd ruin the rest of my goddamned life. "We'll be okay, Monkey."

Teagan's arms slid around my shoulders and her fingers grasped at my hair and shirt as a new torrent of tears started. It was obvious her heart was just as broken as mine. The one thing I could trust was that she still loved me, and I would always love her. Whether I wanted to or not.

Chapter 14

CHASE

Early in the morning Teagan texted that Remi was in surgery to replace her port. After her text, I frantically called her back as I threw on my clothes and rushed out the door to the hospital.

Remi had been placed on a heavy course of IV antibiotics to combat the infection and was being closely monitored, but she wasn't recovering well. Finally, it was discovered that the infection that had caused her fever spike originated in her chemotherapy port and it needed to be changed out with a new one.

"I don't understand how it could take them days to figure that out," I said shortly. "Seriously?"

Teagan's weary sigh could be heard through the phone. "I know, but I'm grateful that now that they have, they're treating it as an emergency."

"Because it is one, Teagan!" I retorted, angrily. Remi had a life-threatening illness and she could have died because the doctors didn't know what they were doing. "Jesus Christ."

"Calm down, Chase. This isn't a major procedure and she'll be out of surgery soon."

I nodded, though Teagan couldn't see it. "Where are you?" My strides became longer as I quickened my pace.

"In the surgical waiting room on the first floor of the hospital. On the west end."

I chastised myself that I hadn't stayed with Teagan at the hospital the previous night, but the air had shifted since our night together. The air was charged between us and it was all I could do not to fall into old habits. There were times when I almost touched her hand or went to put my arm around her and had to stop myself. I was still struggling with things and sensed there was more to it. I couldn't reconcile that Teagan would acquiesce to her father's demands without at least talking to me first. My suspicion nagged at me, but I decided to wait to ask her to elaborate.

We hadn't been allowed to stay with Remi in her room for more than a few minutes at a time anyway, and we'd just spent days filing in and out two-by-two for a few minutes every few hours. It didn't make sense to hang out in the waiting room hour after hour, and the rules that required we wear those god-awful masks, gloves, and gowns made us look like yellow aliens that seemed to scare Remi. She was startled awake once when a nurse knocked over her IV cart. She cried, and it broke my heart.

Later, Teagan told me that Remi was used to the gowns and masks from previous occasions and it must have been a bad dream. Either way, it had been Teagan's soothing voice and her tender mothering that calmed her down. It was plain that Remi was Teagan's whole world.

The whole thing terrified the shit out of me, but at the same time filled me with pride, admiration, and love. It was hard to hate her or even be mad at her when the love she had for that child, my child, was so palpable, yet the past week had been hell. I was constantly on edge.

The fragile truce between Jensen and I held, but the air chilled whenever we were in the same room together. Teagan became increasingly quiet and introspective when he was around and I hated how different she became from how she was when it was just the two of us, even if I did understand it.

I was agitated as hell when Bronwyn was near Teagan, too. No matter how I felt myself, the situation was bad enough without a potential confrontation between them. Bronwyn was as cold as ice to Teagan, and her claws were beginning to show more and more through her snippy tone and standoffish demeanor. Resentment almost dripped from her and I used it to ease my guilt over my night with Teagan.

As if reading my thoughts, Teagan's voice tensed on her next sentence. "Is Bronwyn with you?"

"No. It's just me."

"Oh."

"Is she feeling alright?"

I could almost hear her wondering if Bronwyn knew what happened between us. "Yeah, sure, but she isn't a morning person."

"I see."

Did she? My heart dropped as I realized the implications. I gained nothing by hurting Teagan, but despite our night together some things hadn't changed. I reminded myself that she was married, and she had no right to feel anything one way or the other about my relationship with Bronwyn. This awkward distance created by the past would be a problem until we could talk again, but the incredible need to be near her hadn't changed.

I never thought I'd be having a discussion with Teagan about another woman. Not in ten lifetimes, and not after admitting we still loved each other. I sighed heavily. "Okay, I'll see you in a few minutes."

"Bye."

To be fair, Teagan had done her best to maintain civility with Bronwyn, but the strain showed around her eyes and in the way her lips pressed firmly together whenever Bronwyn entered a room or when her name was mentioned. I'd just heard that cautious tone in her voice on the phone. It was uncomfortable as hell for all of us and I could only think of one way to make it better.

Jensen would be on another assignment soon and Bronwyn needed to go back to London, so I could really talk to Teagan. My not-so-subtle hints weren't working, and I was getting close to the point of bluntly insisting. It was either that or tell her I was still in love with Teagan. I'd be forced to admit that she was the only one I could see a future with and I was willing to do anything to make that happen. It wasn't going to be pretty, but Bronwyn had to have suspicions because I rebuffed all of her attempts for sex since we'd arrived back from Brazil the prior week. It felt wrong.

Kat had gone home three days earlier, but before she left she helped to find a small basement apartment in a converted old house just three blocks from the hospital. It wasn't much, and I'd certainly gotten an earful from Bronwyn about how awful the place was. Either way, it was all I needed. I didn't care that the appliances were twenty years old, or that the carpet had seen better days. The landlord was a widowed elderly man who lived on the middle floor. He was quiet, it was cheap, and had the three things I required the most: a bed, a shower, and it was clean.

I didn't care about the lack of luxury in the apartment and I didn't care about Bronwyn's objections, in fact, I was hoping it would make her leave. She was still sleeping when I left the apartment, and I didn't bother leaving a note. I was in a hurry and she'd know where I went, anyway.

The sun was shining and a light breeze rustled the trees. The sky was amazing, dotted with fluffy, cottony clouds, and the morning traffic was bustling. Stores were opening and there was the smell of bacon and pancakes in the air from a coffee shop on the corner. If it weren't for Remi's illness and my fucked up emotions, the quaint charm of the neighborhood could have been a more modern version of a fifty's sitcom.

My steps were brisk as I walked to the hospital, anxious to see Remi after her surgery, anxious to get the results of my DNA test and anxious to comfort Teagan. The test results had taken longer than we expected and the delay made me nervous.

What if I didn't match? The question was constantly nagging in the back of my mind, but I never spoke it aloud.

I'd spent most of the previous night researching Remi's type of leukemia, the treatment options, and the likelihood of a marrow match. Chemotherapy, radiation, and marrow transplant were pretty much the only treatments available, and as I poured over page after page of information I'd discovered that the best donor matches were siblings, typically, and that wasn't an option for Remi.

The sick hollowness that started to ache inside my chest was becoming familiar. If I'd stayed with Teagan, we'd no doubt have another child by now and Remi would have a better chance of survival.

My heart sank into my stomach at the direction of my thoughts.

One decision. One shitty decision followed by more shitty decisions. It was like a domino effect that fucked everything up from that moment on.

I shouldn't even be thinking about having another child with Teagan, but if my marrow didn't match Remi's, then every option would have to be explored. It could get messy, but a child with me had a better chance of matching than one with Jensen. It seemed almost cruel to an unborn baby to try

265

and conceive it just to save the child you have, but last week when Remi lay lifeless in my arms and I wasn't able to wake her settled into a crystal clear perspective. It got worse when her heart stopped in the ER and Teagan fell apart right in front of me. Witnessing that created a deep desperation worse than any I'd ever felt before; even more than when Teagan left me for Jensen.

I'd be damned if I'd sacrifice any chance that Remi had of surviving, no matter what I had to do. I was sure Teagan, and even Jensen, would agree but the question was whether we could keep Remi alive long enough to make it happen.

I shoved my hands into the pockets of my jeans, silently shaking myself. One of my teammate's wives had trouble getting pregnant and he'd confided that they were trying In Vitro. IVF was expensive and it could take months or even years to result in a viable pregnancy. It would mean a lengthy process of Teagan taking fertility drugs, harvesting eggs, implantation, and then waiting to see if a pregnancy happened. If it didn't take, the process would need to be repeated, cycle after cycle. I knew in my heart, Remi didn't have that kind of time. We'd be lucky to eek out the nine months to a year it might take if she managed to get pregnant the natural way. Plus, I was worried how the numerous drugs Teagan would have to take would affect her health and that of an unborn child. And after the other night, I selfishly wished Teagan was already pregnant. I couldn't help thinking it would be hypocritical to use IVF after what happened between us.

I took a deep breath, expanding my lungs to capacity. After making love, all I wanted to do was touch her. When she was sobbing in the ER waiting room, I had to get her into my arms or felt like I'd die. The love I still felt for her for was so damn amazing, and I believed her when she said she felt the same way. It emanated in every glance or touch... I felt it with the same magnitude as if I was standing near her or looking at

266

her across a room. It was there whether I saw her or not as if nothing had changed between us. Still, her betrayal still stung; so utterly surreal that someone you love that deeply could have done something like that, but everything that she said put it all in perspective.

Since the night Jensen and I beat the hell out of each other, I'd replayed the words he yelled at me in the parking lot over and over in my head. "You'll never know the truth if you don't listen. Do you think you're the only one who suffered?"

No, I didn't think I was the only one who suffered, but I sure as hell was the only one who wasn't given a choice, and that was the one thing I didn't know if I'd ever be able to get over it. God knew I wanted to, but it was as if a white-hot knife was twisting in my gut whenever I thought about it. I wasn't allowed to decide my own future. I felt robbed and that might even be worse than thinking of Jensen making love to my girl, and I never thought anything would make me feel worse than imagining that. I was broken hearted and resentful, but howling at the moon for what should have been, didn't change one damn thing.

I felt helpless, sad, and furious all at the same time, and yet my heart remembered only the incredible love. Even though Teagan was the cause of all of the pain, I realized that having her back in my life and having her love was probably the only hope I had of resolution. I wasn't sure I'd be able to forgive her completely, but being close and letting each other in was a step in the right direction.

I pulled my sunglasses off and made my way through the lobby of the hospital to the information desk and asked for directions to the surgery waiting room, then readily set off in the direction the receptionist had indicated.

It was a large room filled with several families but as I walked in, my eyes were instantly drawn to Teagan sitting at the end of one row of upholstered chairs in front of a big window. The sun was streaming in and even though her back was to me, it gave her hair a soft auburn glow as it flowed in soft dark curls down her back. She was sitting up, her back straight and I ran my eyes down her slender form registering everything about her. She was dressed casually in a white jersey top and blue jeans. I couldn't see her feet, but knowing Teagan, she had on black Vans. She didn't look a day older than when I left for London six years before.

I paused briefly to drink in the sight of her. My hand came to my chest and my head cocked to my right as I registered how beautiful she was, even in her sadness. I inhaled deeply as the inevitability of Teagan was to me. I was never going to stop loving her and I needed to know she was okay. Even if we couldn't work everything out and be together like before, I needed her in my life in some way. I swallowed at the lump forming in my throat and blinked at the tears burning my eyes.

Her head turned as if she felt me standing there and our eyes met. I couldn't help the small smile that curved my lips as I looked at her beautiful face. I took a few steps toward her as she rose from her seat, using her hand to indicate the empty chair beside hers.

"Hey," I said, as I approached her. I took her hand in mine and leaned in to place a gentle kiss on her velvet cheek. She smelled of vanilla and sunshine and I breathed in her essence, pulling back just enough to move and press another kiss at her temple. Her fingers tightened on mine as a gasp escaped her mouth. I felt her free hand curl into my shirt above my belt. It felt involuntary and desperate. It felt emotional and it felt right and expected; it felt like us.

My pulse quickened and I was sure she could feel my heart beating through our joined hands, where my lips touched her skin, and in the air around us: one pulse that kept us both alive.

268

"Chase," she whispered.

I paused, letting the moment linger, savoring her nearness. I didn't want to pull away. My fingers tightened around hers and I pulled back just enough to look down into her beautiful dark eyes. Those unique eyes haunted me and always would. I didn't want to let go of her fingers but couldn't stop myself from brushing the knuckles of my free hand against her jaw. Her lids closed slowly and she leaned her cheek against them.

Teagan dropped my hand and stepped forward, sliding her arms around me and pressing close against me and in less than a second, I enfolded her close and pressed her tight against my chest. I sucked in my breath and pulled her closer still.

"Will you hold me? Just for a second. Don't be mad. I can't help it."

"I'm not mad at you."

"You should be," her voice was barely a whisper, but I could still hear the break in her words. "It's so hard to hide how I feel when you're around."

"Me, too. Are you okay?" I had to ask.

Her silky head nodded beneath my chin. "Better now that you're here. The procedure is pretty routine if it weren't for the infection."

"I understand." We separated reluctantly and sat down side-by-side in two of the chairs. I reached for her hand again, unwilling to end the easy contact and automatically her fingers threaded through mine; so familiar and somehow comforting. I could only hope Teagan felt the same way. "Remi will be fine."

Teagan's brow furrowed even though she nodded in agreement. I could see the worry and the pain written all over her. "I know."

"She will, Teagan. I can't have it any other way." I glanced at my watch. It was just past 8:30 AM. "I'm hoping I'll hear something about the DNA results today because if I don't, I'm ready to beat the shit out of someone."

"Even if we do get positive results, it might be days before Remi is free of infection. They won't do the transplant until then."

"I know, but in case I'm not, the sooner we know the better, so we can consider options. We can't just sit here; we have to find another donor or something." My eyes involuntarily filled with tears. "I read up on things. Chemo is literally poison."

Teagan's fingers tightened again. "I know. It's bad, Chase. Remi calls it the mean medicine."

"Well, this is going to work," I said matter-of-factly. I got a knot in my stomach knowing this was the time to bring it up. "If it doesn't, we have to have another baby."

"I've already considered that."

I tried to gauge her reaction as my eyes skimmed her face.

She got a scared look in her eyes and her hand reached out to wrap around my forearm. "That isn't why I let the other night happen, Chase. That was about us."

I wanted to ask her if it were possible she could get pregnant or if she was on birth control, but that would only dig up shit I didn't want to deal with. Birth control pills would mean she and Jensen were sexually active, and while it was completely plausible, it was abhorrent to me. "Look, until we get things figured out between us, can we promise each other we won't sleep with anyone else? Even if we aren't with each other; I just have to have that promise, Teagan. Especially, not Jensen."

She nodded, squeezing my arm and leaning into me. "That's easy."

270

I sucked in a deep breath. "So, no matter what we have to do, Remi will get better, grow up like a normal little girl, and have everything she's supposed to have, I promise."

Teagan's red-rimmed eyes were evidence of tears and her face showed a lack of sleep. Still, she was so mesmerizing to me. The way she loved Remi, and how devoted and loving she was as a mother only made me love her more.

She nodded but didn't speak. We sat quietly, leaning gently against each other our shoulders touching. "You're tired," I murmured. "How long have you been here?"

"All night. I went home to shower and change clothes when they took her down to prep at six. Surgery was supposed to begin at 8, but they never start on time."

"Yeah." I slouched in the chair a little, settling in to wait for the unknown amount of time.

Teagan's head dropped to my shoulder and she sighed but recoiled quickly. "Oh, I'm sorry." I held fast to her hand even as she tried to pull it free. "I shouldn't have presumed. I wasn't thinking."

"Hey, it's okay. It's easy to slip back into it." I stared into her eyes, glistening as she blinked and swallowed. She was nervous and I understood. "It's fine to lean on me. I want you lean on me. It's how we are supposed to be."

A tear tumbled down her cheek, and then another on the opposite side, as her face crumpled.

"I have no right to." Her voice was fragile and trembling, threatening to crack over the next word. She shook her head again, shortly.

"It's you and me. Old habits die hard."

"I know, but it's not fair."

I could deny it. It wasn't. We continued to sit there looking at each other, Teagan brushing the tears briskly off of her face, and my throat aching. My lower jaw shot out and I closed my eyes. I wasn't sure if I was fighting telling her I loved her, or just losing it right there in front of everyone.

"I should have told you about Remi, Chase. I'm so sorry. I'm not apologizing because I'm trying to feel better, I just… I would do anything in order for you to feel better. There isn't a day that goes by that I'm not consumed with regret, and even if you hate me forever, I still want you to be okay."

I knew she was telling the truth because it was written all over her. I cleared my throat trying to get beyond the overwhelming emotion threating to overflow. "Regret is a useless emotion."

"If I could just decide not to feel it, I'm not sure I would. I deserve it."

She thought she deserved to feel pain. I spoke softly, trying to soothe her with my words. "It's useless for me to tell you not to feel like shit when I feel like shit, too. And, I regret everything after I got that fucking offer, Teagan. It's my fault, too. I shouldn't have left."

"Professional soccer was your dream."

I shook my head. "No, I told you at the airport; you were the dream."

Teagan sucked in her breath in an audible gasp. I placed my free hand over hers to engulf it between both of mine. "I know how bad this is, but we can't fall into our own misery. We have to be strong for Remi. If I fall into that trap, I'm not sure I could come back from it, and she doesn't need to see her mom and dad sappy and sad. It will scare her."

She sniffed, nodding, and her voice was full of tears. "You're right, but there's more to tell you, and I'm not sure I have the right, but I'm asking anyway. It might not change anything, but at least you'd know why things happened the way they did. I need to tell you, Chase. I know you think it will hurt you, but I don't think it will. At least, I hope it won't."

Honestly, I didn't know how anything could add to the pain I'd already been subjected to, and I'd already decided I wanted to know.

"The other night changed things. We'll find some time to talk. Not here, though." I glanced around and noticed a plump woman in a blue velour tracksuit listening to every word we said, and she wasn't the only one. When our eyes met she knew I'd caught her and she jumped up and rushed away as if her ass was on fire. "People are listening."

"Excuse, me, Mr. Forrester?" a woman came over and touched my shoulder. It startled me out of my intimate conversation with Teagan and I turned to look at her. She was in her late thirties or early forties, dressed casually and without makeup. She pushed a few strands of her straight, shoulder length hair behind her ear.

"Yes?"

"Of Arsenal?"

"Yes, ma'am." I nodded and stood to speak to her.

"I'm sorry to intrude, but I saw you at the reception desk in the hospital lobby and I was wondering—" She clasped her hands in front of her as I wondered if she'd followed me through the hospital and hovered the whole time I was in the waiting room with Teagan. Her expression was pained and she hesitated. "My son is a huge fan and he loves soccer. He was in a car accident and he might never walk again. I was hoping... well, I was hoping you could stop in to see him? I know it would mean the world to him."

My heart dropped. If this was a kid who dreamed of playing soccer and now was faced with his dream ending, I wasn't sure if seeing me would help. It might only make things worse. "I'm very sorry to hear about your boy, but are you sure it won't make him feel worse?"

Teagan stood by my side and slid her hand around my elbow. "Chase, you can help him see nothing is achieved without hard work so he won't give up hope of getting better. Nothing is worse than no hope." Instinctively I covered her hand with mine. She was right.

I nodded and looked back at the woman. "Okay then, sure. I'll be happy to. What room is he in?"

"342. This will mean so much to him. I can't thank you enough."

"My pleasure. I have to wait a bit because my daughter is in surgery. It might be this afternoon."

"Thank you!" she said with tearful exuberance. She leaned in to give me a loose hug and I returned it.

"You're welcome. I'll see you later, then."

"Okay. I hope your daughter is okay."

"Thank you. I do, too."

The woman walked away and out of the waiting room as I stood to watch.

"That was nice." Teagan's hand slid down my arm and I threaded my fingers through hers.

My phone started to ring in my back pocket and I hoped it wasn't Bronwyn. I pulled it out and glanced at the screen. "It's Dr. Radar's office."

"Oh, my god," Teagan said. "Maybe they have the results."

"It better be," I answered the call. "Hello?"

"Mr. Forrester?"

"Yes, this is he," I said impatiently. "Do you have the DNA results?"

"Yes, sir. If you'd like to come into the office—"

"Just tell me the results, please," I answered shortly.

"Can you please verify your identity by giving me the last four digits of your social security number?"

I didn't hesitate. "3791."

"Thank you. It's good news, sir. You're a good match for Remi's marrow."

I sucked in a shaky breath and exhaled. Teagan was fidgeting next to me, and I slid my free arm around her and smiled, nodding. "Oh, thank God. When can we do this?"

"I'm afraid that is something you'll have to discuss with Dr. Radar, but I'll put it on his schedule to give you a call when he's finished with his rounds."

"Thank you," I murmured. Teagan's arm, now around my waist tightened.

"Your welcome. Enjoy the rest of your day."

"You as well. Goodbye."

I turned and lifted Teagan into my arms, swinging her around. She squealed in surprise and hugged me tightly. "It's happening!" My tone was loud in my exuberance, and I didn't care that everyone in the room looked at us. "It's happening, Teagan!"

I set her down and kissed her hard on her mouth. She was laughing and crying all at the same time. I laughed with her and then brushed the back of my knuckles against her cheek. "This is no time for tears."

"What in bloody hell?"

I heard Bronwyn's snarky English accent behind me and turned to see her marching toward us. Teagan pulled away as if she was being burned by my touch. Guilt was written all over her.

"We just got the DNA results. Chase is a match." She said quickly, rubbing her lower lip with the back of her wrist. "We were just happy."

Bronwyn's eyes narrowed and her lips pursed for a split second before she smiled wide. I saw her blatant animosity, even if Teagan didn't, but I wouldn't let her ruin the moment. "That's excellent news! We can get on with it, then?"

I was acutely aware of the difference in Teagan's demeanor and the literal space that suddenly separated us.

"When Remi's infection clears, I think, but we have to talk to her doctors."

"Good. Well, here's hoping it's bloody soon. We can all get back to normal."

I huffed at Bronwyn's barely veiled jibe. If I had my way, there would be a new normal.

Chapter 15

Teagan

Remi was out of surgery and in recovery. She wouldn't be in her room for another hour and Chase suggested we get a late breakfast in the hospital cafeteria, but what he really meant was that he was going to buy breakfast for Bronwyn and I and then call Dr. Radar's office to make an appointment to set up the transplant.

I knew him well enough to understand that he saddled me with Bronwyn so he was able to make the call in private. I was nervous about being left alone with the other woman but was confident that Chase would include me in the appointment regarding the transplant.

I picked at some mixed fruit while the other woman devoured a bagel with cream cheese and lox, scrambled eggs, and bacon. I couldn't help being jealous at how much she could eat and still stay so fit, but then, I had spent the better part of the last three years in a hospital room with my daughter.

She eyed me as she chewed a bite of bagel. It was awkward; even more, after what happened between Chase and

I. I shifted uncomfortably in my seat and forked up a piece of fresh pineapple.

"So, lucky Chase is a match, eh?" Bronwyn said bluntly.

"Yes," I said, putting a hand over my mouth as I answered, due to the fruit in my mouth.

She nodded and sat back in her chair, assessing my reaction to her words. "I know Chase is anxious to get back to England and his football club."

I swallowed, my eyes snapping up to hers. She looked on smugly; her eyes daring me to contradict her.

I didn't want to get into an argument, but she was begging for one. "That's nice," I said, laying down my fork. Suddenly, I had no appetite.

"Yes, isn't it. Don't get any ideas about using the girl to keep him here. He's putting on a great show, but his heart is on the field. You've got him by the balls right now, but don't think it will last."

I huffed in mock amusement as my jaw jutted out involuntarily. I feigned nonchalance and incredulity at the audacity of her remark. "Chase makes his own decisions."

"He always has, hasn't he?" She picked up her glass of orange juice and took a sip. "Chase is all man, that's for sure, but he's mine. He has been for years. And he's already chosen football over you once. You'd best be remembering that."

I cleared my throat. Her words stung, I couldn't deny it and I was sure the skin on my face was flushed. The conversation was embarrassing and painful.

"How gratifying for you," I returned. "I'm not trying to influence anything Chase decides, Bronwyn. I'm grateful he's helping our daughter."

Bronwyn was pretty, but it was marred by her bitchy expression. "I have to hand it to you. It was one savvy move to trap him with a kid."

I laughed out loud. Who did this bitch think she was?

278

"Obviously, he hasn't shared the whole story, or you'd know that I didn't trap him. If that were my intention, I could have done so six years ago. I wouldn't have had to, though. He loved me." I was angry with her, but also at myself for allowing her to bait me.

"You sure about that?" She leaned forward, placing both elbows on the table, trying to intimidate me. "Didn't take him long to bed me, though, did it?" She was almost sneering at me. "I thought you'd have gotten the message already."

My eyes widened in recognition. She was the woman on the phone that day I called to let him know I was going to leave Clemson and go to England. "It was you, on the phone."

"Love, it's always been me ever since the moment he came to London." For the first time since I'd actually seen Bronwyn in person, I saw her as a selfish bitch. "As soon as I saw him, I made up my mind he'd be mine someday and no stupid little twit across the pond was going to stand in my way. Then, idiot that you are, you went and broke his heart. Thanks for that, by the way," she quipped. "What could possess you to let a man like Ace Forrester walk away from you?"

"My past with Chase is none of your business."

"Whatever you think you mean to him; let me assure you, you don't. He told me last night in bed that he feels sorry for you, so any soft feelings he's exhibiting are due to the situation, only."

I huffed again and threw my napkin on the table next to my still full plate. I'd witnessed Chase's emotions first hand, and I wasn't buying what this bitch was selling. "Look, I don't know what I've done to you to make you so hateful, but I'm grateful that Chase is here for Remi. I'm not trying to make him do anything he doesn't want to do."

"Uh huh." She sniffed and licked her lips. "Let's not forget that I'm the one thing that you're not; single. I'm sure your husband would love to hear about how you're crying on

Ace's shoulder. Serve you right if he booted you out on your arse. Then where would you be?"

I sat there seething, unclear what to say to her but wanting to slap that egotistical look off of her face. I wasn't sure if she was referring to the insurance situation or if she thought Jensen and I had a real marriage, but whatever it was, her audacity pissed me off. I took a deep breath and unclenched my fists, determined not to let her get the better of me.

Bronwyn's pleasure with herself was obvious as she pulled out a compact from her purse and deftly reapplied dark pink lipstick, rubbed her lips together and preened in the mirror. "I've got to find the loo." She replaced the lipstick and compact in her bag and rose to pause beside the table. "You just concentrate on keeping your man happy and keep your paws off mine. If you do that, we'll get along splendidly."

"You act like he's your puppet. I know him better than you ever will," I said calmly, pasting a sweet smile on my face.

"Hmm." Bronwyn glanced coolly at her watch. "Are you certain? One thing I'm positive about is that he'll never get over what you did." With that, she turned and stalked away.

After she was gone, I let out the breath I wasn't even aware I was holding. I felt a new and profound hatred for Bronwyn after discovering that she was the real reason I didn't go to England. I'd tried to move past that part of it; to forgive him his indiscretion that was as much to blame for my decision to marry Jensen as my father's blackmail. The whole thing was a big ball of pain and it resonated that maybe all of the bad stuff would always stand between Chase and me. The uneaten fruit on my plate blurred and I starred at it, struggling with my thoughts.

"Where's Bronwyn?" Chase's voice broke into my reflection.

I blinked and looked up at him as he pulled out a chair. "Oh, uh…" I sat up straighter in my chair and tried to keep my tone even. "I think she went to the bathroom."

He watched me, trying to gauge what had just happened in his absence. "What'd she do?" he asked, accusingly.

My shoulder lifted in a half-shrug and I tried to smile. "Nothing."

Chase's brow dropped into a frown and I could almost see his mind working it out. "Why don't I believe you?"

"What did Dr. Radar's office say?" I asked, hoping to change the subject.

"His receptionist said he usually makes rounds at 6 AM but he was going to stop by this evening before dinner to check on Remi."

"He's an awesome doctor. I'm just hoping switching out the port will work to rid her of the infection soon so we can move forward."

Chase nodded. His hair was gelled, but obviously, he'd ran his hands through it several times already today and a lock fell forward over his brow. I wanted to push it back. The urge to touch him was strong, but I couldn't forget what Bronwyn just said.

Chase reached over and picked up an untouched toast triangle from my plate and then took a bite. "You didn't eat much. Are you sure you're okay?" His expression was concerned.

"I'm fine," I answered shortly. I was never one who was able to hide my feelings, especially from Chase.

He took another bite of the toast, and I pushed the plate toward him. "Do you want to order something?"

"This is good." He chewed the toast and grabbed my fork, stabbing a strawberry with it and popping it in his mouth. "Tell me what's wrong," he insisted. He was in a good mood and why wouldn't he be? The marrow matched and Remi came through her surgery with ease.

"Nothing, I'm good. I'm just..." I shrugged again, searching for something to say to hide the real reason I was upset. "Nervous, I guess."

"About the radiation? I understand; me, too. It's terrifying to kill her immune system."

"The hardest part will be that she'll be in isolation and I won't be able to comfort her."

Chase paused and looked at me. "You're an excellent mother, Teagan. Remi doesn't lack love, and she adores you."

My heart squeezed in my chest. I wanted to tell him I could already tell what an amazing father he was going to make, but I couldn't without making him remember what he'd lost, or rather what I'd stolen, and that was the last thing I wanted to make him feel.

"Hopefully everything will work out and you can get back to your life." There it was. Damn Bronwyn and the way she'd reminded me that he'd been unfaithful before anything else happened. I couldn't help blurting the words.

He stopped eating and locked eyes with me, reaching out to lay one of his hands on mine. "I want to talk to you about that."

I pulled my hand out from under his, involuntarily, my emotions overruling my head. "There isn't anything to talk about. Let's not let old baggage get in the way of keeping the focus on Remi."

Chase was taken aback; frozen for a split second before he shoved his chair back and threaded his hands together, resting them on the top of his head. "What are you talking about? Old baggage? I thought we'd turned a corner."

"We have," I answered stiffly. "I'm sorry, Chase. I just don't want to be presumptuous and you can still be Remi's dad without changing your life. I'll never keep you from each other again."

"Okay, what the fuck just happened?" he demanded.

I felt pensive and sad in the face of his anger. "Nothing. Just a reality check."

He shook his head angrily, huffing out of his nose. "Tell me what Bronwyn said to you right goddamned now, Teagan!" His voice was low and controlled, but fierce. "I thought we were moving forward."

I sucked in a deep breath. "We were. We are. It's just that when I'm with you, I forget a bunch of shit that muddies the waters in real life, but there is so much to deal with."

"I know, and we will."

"Will we?" I asked.

His eyes narrowed and he ran a hand over his mouth and jaw. "Yes."

"I just don't want to pressure you into anything. I know you're feeling—"

"Don't fucking tell me how I feel! I already have one woman trying to do that."

"I'm not trying to, Chase!" I felt panicked, feeling any progress we'd made slip away. It was my fault for letting Bronwyn needle me. No matter if he did have sex with her while he and I were still together, it was ancient history, even if it still hurt. "I just want you to know for sure what you want."

"Yeah, well obviously, we need to talk."

"When do you suggest we do that?" I was exasperated. With Bronwyn here and hovering, I couldn't see how it would be possible unless he lied to her about any time he spent with me. Jensen and I had come to our conclusions and it was just about logistics, but Chase didn't know that yet, either.

"We had some time the other night. We can again."

My heart literally fell into my stomach and my eyes implored him to think about what he just said. "Making love doesn't solve the problems. It just lets us forget for a little while."

"Yes, we should have talked, it's just that—" Chase paused and leaned in toward me so he could lower his voice. The hospital cafeteria wasn't any better to have a meaningful conversation than the waiting room had been. "I can't ignore what's happening between us, Teagan. I don't want to."

"What about Bronwyn? I don't want you to have to lie to her to spend time with me. Even to talk." There. I said it. I looked down at my lap and then my eyes flew up to meet his.

"Uhhhh," he said urgently. The hand he'd laid on the table curled into a fist. "I didn't plan for her to be here. I didn't ask her to be here, and I don't want her here."

"Even if she wasn't in Atlanta now, she is still an issue."

"You mean, like Jensen?" he threw back.

I opened my mouth to speak and then shut it. I nodded. "Yes. We can't forget they exist and just fall into a little fairytale world where Remi is fine and we can be a family." My throat felt thick and my words broke. "Even if I want to."

"Teagan," his hand reached for mine again and this time I didn't pull away. "I don't know how this bullshit is going to work out, but I love you. I want us to be together. I want Remi and more like her."

His words were like a magic balm and I wanted desperately to believe him. But after what Bronwyn had just said and knowing that he wouldn't have seen me again if it weren't for Remi, I had to wonder if his feelings weren't confused.

"Chase." His name throbbed out of me and it was all I could do not to throw myself into his arms right then, and there. "I want to tell you something, but it can't be here."

"Just tell me what it is. I can't take more of this. You said you don't want secrets between us now, so don't keep any."

He was so beautiful, and I could see the love in his eyes. I drew in a shaky breath.

"I want to tell you everything, but not here. Bronwyn could come back any second. I don't want the interruption." My heart ached at the anguish on his face, and I wanted to wipe it away with my confession right then.

"Okay," he nodded, his tone resolved. "Tonight, after Remi is asleep, we'll go someplace. Is it about something Bronwyn said to you while I was calling Dr. Radar?"

"In part, but what I need to tell you is partly about the past, too."

"Fine, but tell me what Bronwyn said to you. I need to know, right now."

The fact was I wanted to tell him. I needed to see his reaction so I could gauge his real feelings for the other woman. "She just reminded me that I'm married, and you're with her. She said you'd never be able to forgive me."

Chase's features hardened and he started to speak, but I stopped him.

"No, Chase. I was hurt and angry, but she was right. As much as I want to be with you, it's wrong; you said it yourself the night we made out in the car. And worse, I'm scared that you'll be with me because of Remi and even if you do love me, I'm terrified it could all come back and ruin us later if we can't move beyond everything. There are things I need to ask you, and things I need to tell you. I want to be completely honest; I want us both to be. Even if it hurts."

"Alright, I can do that, Teagan."

I still felt apprehensive, but I'd had my conversation with Jensen, and I needed a come-to-Jesus conversation with Chase. We both needed it.

"I don't really feel comfortable around her because my emotions are shot. I'm just not strong enough to deal with her jabs. I have no right to ask, but I'd appreciate it if she didn't come around me, especially when Remi is there." I didn't want her around my daughter, period. Remi's condition had made it impossible for her to meet her so far, and if I had my way, she never would. "She doesn't need to be thrown into the middle of this."

"I agree. I'll talk to Bronwyn, Teagan." He said, letting go of my hand as the other woman appeared in the cafeteria entrance as if on cue. I wasn't sure exactly what he meant, but I knew in my heart that I could trust him to protect Remi and me.

"Remi will be waking up soon, so I need to get upstairs to be there when she does."

Part of me was scared of Chase being alone with Bronwyn; afraid she'd spew lies about me or misconstrue something I said, but all I could do was to give Chase a chance to make his own decisions and then respect them. I owed him that much.

"I'll be up soon, too," he said quietly. "Just give me a couple of hours."

The pull that always existed between us was strong and I was reluctant to rise and leave him alone with Bronwyn.

"Okay." I nodded slightly, pushing my chair back to stand, readying to leave.

Chase rose with me and ran a hand down the length of my arm and it was all I could do not to slip my arms around his waist and press a kiss to his clean-shaven jaw. "It's going to be okay," he reassured. "Don't worry. Just concentrate on our daughter."

My heart flip-flopped inside my chest at his words. It was like a dream to hear those words come from his mouth.

I picked up my bag and flung it over my shoulder at the same time that the other woman reached the table. Her eyes shot from Chase to me and back again. "I will. See you later, then" I murmured and started to walk away, but still able to hear the start of their conversation.

"Yes," Chase answered.

"Hi, lovie. Is everything okay?" Bronwyn's voice was decidedly sweeter in tone when directed at Chase. "You look a little frazzled."

"Let's go back to the apartment."

"Ooh. An afternoon delight," she cooed.

"Not exactly."

I couldn't help smiling as I walked out of the cafeteria. My heart was soaring, feeling as connected to Chase as ever, and glad he was willing to hear the whole story and anxious to tell him.

For now, I had to trust him and let him handle Bronwyn. I was anxious to spend the rest of the day with Remi. My beautiful little Remi with her daddy's gorgeous green eyes.

CHASE

Bronwyn sensed my anger as I led her from the hospital, and out into the sunlit day.

"Chase, what is it? What's wrong?"

I felt completely disconnected from her and I let go of her arm the second we were out of the door and we started across the parking lot. I didn't bother asking if she wanted me to get a cab or Uber. The walk was perfect to talk without her being confined within four walls and she'd be less able to whine or wheedle me. I didn't want her to try to touch me or try to initiate sex. She was prone to do that whenever we had an argument and I intended to avoid it entirely. Not that I'd ever be able to touch her now, but I just didn't want to deal with it.

"What did you say to Teagan?" I asked pointedly.

"Nothing, Ace."

"Bullshit!" I shoved my hands into the pockets of my jeans as I strode down the sidewalk. Her legs were shorter and she had to walk faster to keep up. "I know when I've been lied to."

"Oh, do you? That's rich!" Bronwyn exclaimed. "You're taking her side over mine? No one has lied to you more than she has!"

We both had sunglasses on, but I could see by the frown and firm line of her mouth that she was furious. The thing was, I didn't give a shit. I faced forward and kept walking. "Just tell me what you said."

"I've been here for you the whole time. Where has she been? Marrying some other bloke and letting him raise your daughter. You've got your loyalties misplaced!"

I stopped and grabbed her arm, turning her to face me. I didn't care that there were people walking past us, I didn't give a damn if others overheard us. "The stuff between Teagan and me is between her and I. Right now, I'm asking you what you said to her."

"I said the truth, Ace." She said, yanking her arm free and scowling at me. "What she did is unforgivable, she's married, and you and I are together so she should stop trying to play on your emotions!"

All things being equal, there was a ring of truth to her words and I'd have to be an idiot if I hadn't said the same thing to myself ten times, but my emotions were dictating every goddamned thing. I ran a hand through my hair and put one hand on my hip. "Fuck," I muttered. "She isn't trying to play me. She hasn't asked me for one damn thing other than to help save Remi's life if I can!"

"We both know that's utter bloody rubbish! This whole thing is a scheme to get you back. Open your eyes, for God's sake!"

I barked out a cynical laugh. "Right. Remi's leukemia is all made up and the entire hospital is playing along!"

"That's not what I meant, and you know it!"

All I could do was stare at her. The trip to the U.S. had shown a new side of her and she'd killed anything I felt for her. I found myself wondering if she was even my friend. "It's not fair to you, but I need you to go back to London until after Remi's transplant is over. I need to take some time to get my head on straight."

She snorted angrily. "You're letting her get to you!"

When she didn't respond, I continued in a calmer tone. "Look, I still love her, okay? I can't lie about this. Teagan was everything to me, and I can't help how I feel about her. She needs me right now because she is suffering unspeakably. We could lose Remi!" Just staying it aloud cracked my chest open and left a gaping, sucking hole.

"And yet, Teagan uses her dying kid to yank your chain," she spat bitterly, shaking her head ruefully. "You're pathetic. What happens if Remi doesn't make it? Are you going to give her a sympathy shag? Give her a chance to trap you once again?"

The second her words were out, I saw red. Heat infused beneath the skin of my neck and face. I could literally feel my face flush. "Wow," I said in disgust, starting to walk away from her. "You are one. Cold. Bitch. You need to pack your shit. Let's go."

I left her standing there with no choice but to follow. "Chase! Chase, I'm sorry, Lovie."

I ignored her pleas and kept on walking, trying to get control of myself. It took less than five minutes for us to arrive at the apartment. I went straight to the closet and pulled out her suitcase, flung it on the bed and unzipped it; flinging open the flap. "I'll call you a cab."

She followed me slowly into the bedroom and leaned her shoulder on the door jam. "Are you really doing this?"

I wanted to leave the room, but she was blocking the doorway, so I decided to put it out there. "I am. I'm not going to bullshit you, Bronwyn. I never thought you coming here was a good idea because of what I'm dealing with. I don't have time or energy to expend trying to placate you or listen to you complain about this place or about Teagan, but I absolutely will not tolerate you talking that way about Remi. She's the innocent victim in all of this, and if you can't see that, there is no way I could be with you, even if Teagan wasn't an issue."

"But, she is an issue," she said in defeat, finally beginning to open the old dresser that sat against the wall to pull out her clothes.

I lifted both hands, palms up and dropped them again. "I just said it. I can't help how I feel, and like I said, I'm not going to insult you by lying. My heart has a mind of its own when it comes to Teagan, and I can't do one damn thing about it. I wanted to, and I tried, but she's the only one I'll ever love in that desperate, all-consuming way."

"Are you sure it isn't about Remi? That your emotions are raw and the two of you are re-bonding over a mutual tragedy?" Bronwyn seemed upset, but she wasn't crying or heartbroken. She wasn't sobbing her heart out over me like Teagan had done, and it gave me a sense that I was doing the right thing; for all of us.

"I am," I stated simply. "Being in England without any memories and having you around to take the edge off helped, but I've never really moved on. I didn't know it at the time, but I was probably using you and it was a dick thing to do."

"It didn't feel like you were using me."

"I didn't think I was, but I also knew I would never feel the same way about anyone else. I'm not trying to hurt you."

"I don't know how you can forgive her or trust her."

I was reluctant to share the intimate details of my conversations with Teagan, but maybe if I were honest, this would be over and done with. I laid a hand flat on my chest over my heart. "I don't know how to explain it, but if you need to hear it, here it is: there is something palpable and alive between Teagan and I. We're connected in a way I've never been with anyone else, and I have to face that she is the only one who can heal the wound I have over her. I don't know if we'll be able to put the past to bed, but I do know that no matter what happens, she'll be part of my life, one way or the other."

Bronwyn looked at me, and I read the skepticism in her face. I instinctively knew what she was about to say.

"Don't say it, again. Remi is going to survive, Bronwyn. Even suggesting otherwise slams the door between you and me and we won't even be able to be friends. I've been beating myself up, thinking how being pissed and resenting your presence here was unfair, but when you said that, you killed every iota of feeling I had for you."

"I care about you, and it would be nice if you weren't such a prick right now."

I sat down on the bed as she finished packing, feeling bad for her. "It isn't like I don't care about you, I just can't believe you could say something like that."

"That's just a sorry excuse, Ace! You're letting her manipulate you!"

"That's not true." I shook my head in pissed off exasperation; so much for my attempt to end things civilly. If anyone knew about manipulation, it was Bronwyn. "I don't need an excuse!"

"You're looking for anything you can to alienate me and run back to your poor little, manipulative Teagan."

I stood up and reeled on her. "It doesn't matter what you say, it isn't going to change anything!"

Bronwyn's eyes narrowed and she nodded knowingly. "You're already shagging her. That's it, isn't it? I don't know why I didn't see it before. So she's made you a cheater, too."

I had the grace to flush and for a moment, I was speechless. "We didn't mean anything to happen, but Teagan is where my heart is and she has been for more than nine years. Pretending otherwise was the only way I could get on with my life. But, pretending I was over her didn't make it the truth. Being with her isn't even about sex, Bronwyn. It's about being able to fucking breathe. That's as honest as I can be. I'm sorry."

I walked around her and left her to finish packing alone.

Chapter 16

Teagan

I watched Chase's sweet interaction with Remi. He'd come back to the hospital mid-afternoon and it was close to dinnertime.

The residual anesthesia from the surgery kept her drifting in and out of sleep, but he never left her side, speaking in soft tones and brushing her hair back lovingly. We still had to wear the yellow gowns and masks and we did the best we could to talk to her and hold her. I was lying on her bed next to her and she was cuddled next to me as I felt Chase's eyes on us like a physical touch.

He was sitting back in the chair; his hands tented in front of him and his expression contemplative as if he was thinking about something hard.

"What is it?" I asked softly. My arm was draped over Remi's small form and she was warm, but I was on top of the covers and shivered slightly.

"Just thinking about things," he murmured, then got up and went to the cupboard close to the bathroom, pulled out one of the extra blankets and unfurling it, he placed the white cotton over me in the same loving manner he had Remi.

"Thank you." Instantly, the chill from the air conditioning vent in the ceiling was blocked. "Are you regretting your decision about sending Bronwyn home?" Guilt nagged at my subconscious but I also felt a huge sense of relief. Chase and I hadn't discussed the future beyond his impassioned revelation that he wanted us to be a family the other evening. Hope bloomed, but a few words said in the heat of emotion were fragile and until we had a real discussion, I had to keep it in perspective. I still had to tell him about Jensen and our plans to divorce and make him understand the decision was made years ago. It wasn't something I wanted to blurt out casually.

His lower lip came out in a little pout as he shook his head. "Not at all."

The blanket wasn't very substantial, but warmth started to seep through me and I pulled it up around my chin and was slightly worried when he didn't elaborate. Instinctively, I felt there was more to it. How did he leave things with Bronwyn? "Are you scared about Remi?"

Chase had been so strong; adamant that she'd get better after the transplant but the past week had been a hard reality that showed him just how delicate her condition had become.

He ran a hand through his thick tawny hair. "Yes. She's gotten so much worse in such a short time. If the transplant doesn't work, then what are our options? We don't have time to have another baby. I'm terrified."

My eyes widened slightly. "I know." I nodded and reached a hand out from beneath the covers beseechingly. Chase leaned forward and took it on his own, but the rubber gloves we were both wearing kept us from really touching. He dropped to his knees beside the bed to get closer; leaning his other arm over the pillow to cradle around Remi's head. "I've thought of that, too. I couldn't ask that of you," I said honestly.

"You should have called me sooner."

"Believe me, that's all I've thought about. For years."

"That isn't how I meant it, Teagan. Stop blaming yourself, and concentrate on Remi. The would've, should've, could've bullshit won't help any of us. We can't change the past, and somehow we have to deal with it." We were holding on to each other under the covers, and over our little Remi. Chase bent to kiss her forehead. His brilliant green eyes met mine. "I'm glad I'm here now, and I'm not going anywhere."

My eyes burned with unshed tears and my throat constricted painfully. "You're so incredible. I don't deserve you." I wasn't sure exactly what he meant, but it didn't matter. For sure he'd be with Remi, but would he be with me after I told him the entire truth?

He smiled. The mask hid his mouth, but his eyes crinkled at the corners. "That's for sure," he teased. His hand wrapped around my upper arm and squeezed gently.

A single tear dripped from the corner of my eye and over the bridge of my nose to plop on the pillow. "I can never make it up to you. I know that."

"I'll think of something," he let out a small laugh that should have comforted me, but I was still so worried about Remi. What if we lost her? The thought made me want to die myself.

"Over the past month when Dr. Radar mentioned the transplant, he said Remi will be isolated after radiation and for a few days after she gets the marrow. She'll be frightened and I won't be able to comfort her."

His hand rubbed up and down my arm. "She knows you love her. She's a smart little shit; we'll explain it to her in advance. It will be tough but we'll get through it. All of us."

My phone started to ring from my purse sitting on a counter just inside the door to the room. "That's probably Jensen," I explained, pushing back the blanket and starting to rise from the bed. I regretted having to untangle from the comfort of Chase's arms. "He's calling to check on Remi. I talked to him after the surgery when you were with Bronwyn, but he wanted to know what we found out about scheduling the procedure."

"Understandable. He's a good guy." He said the words, but they were stilted and I knew deep down, he was struggling to mean those words. It was another reason we needed to talk.

I paused and looked at him. He was pushing off the floor and settling back into the chair. "I'm glad you think so." The phone continued to ring until I was able to pull it out of my bag and answer. "Hello?"

"Hey, it's me. Have you heard from Dr. Radar?" Jensen asked.

"He hasn't been in yet. I can call you to fill you in later after we speak to him."

"I should be there." His tone was weary.

I could tell he was worried that Chase would replace him in Remi's heart. "You will be."

"Of course; Chase is there." It was a statement, not a question.

"Uh huh. He's very concerned about Remi."

"When will you know if switching the port worked to get rid of the infection?"

"Probably tomorrow, but her fever has already dropped, so I'm optimistic. She's still groggy, but I think they'll try to wake her up to eat dinner soon."

"Okay. My producer knows what's going on and I can be there within a few hours if I'm needed. Don't do this without me. I need to be there."

"I know that. I'd never do that to you."

"Okay, good. Well, I have to go. The pre-game show starts in ten minutes and I have to get hooked up. Tell Remi I love her and I'll call her tomorrow morning."

"Okay. Have a good show. If she wakes up I'll put it on for her."

"Thanks. See ya."

I replaced the phone in my purse and turned back to Remi and Chase. My breath on the inside of my mask was starting to make me feel uncomfortable. I wanted to pull it off so I could breathe. "Jensen is commentating tonight. The Rams are playing the Giants in New York." I felt like I had to explain. "He feels bad that he's not here."

I hoped mentioning Jensen wouldn't be painful to Chase. The whole thing was still awkward, but I had to figure out how to deal with it. Jensen and I might be getting a divorce, but Remi loved him and needed him in her life.

"I understand that he loves Remi."

"I think he's worried you won't want him to see her, but he—"

"Even if I hated his guts, I'd never do that to Remi, Teagan."

"That's what I told him yesterday."

There was a knock on the door. "Come in,"

I turned as Dr. Radar pushed it open slowly and peeked inside before entering when Chase waved him in. He and the nurse following him in were also dressed in the yellow gown and masks. "How's my little patient? The surgeon said the procedure went well and we're about ninety percent sure that the infection originated in the old port. The good news is that her vitals are good and her fever is down. I think we've turned a corner."

Chase stood and moved to the foot of Remi's bed with me as Dr. Radar looked her over. He listened to her heart and felt her forehead, and glanced at the last set of vitals another nurse had written there an hour before. "Her white count has gone down a bit."

"When do you think we'll be able to proceed with the transplant?" Chase asked anxiously. His voice was soft, but I could sense the urgency behind his words.

Dr. Radar nodded. "The infection should clear up relatively quickly, but I'd like to wait to commit until the morning. Let's see how she does tonight."

"How long will it take to know if it works?"

"The process of Remi's body accepting your cells to seed her marrow and grow new is called engrafting. It can take a month or more before the process is complete, but if it's successful, she'll get stronger and stronger, though she is at risk for infection until she's fully grafted. You're a good match so I'm hoping she won't have too many side effects. She may need some anti-rejection drugs for the rest of her life."

"What kind of side effects are possible?" Chase was firing off the same questions that I'd already discussed with Dr. Radar.

"Some pain, headaches, shortness of breath, coughing, chest pain or fatigue. There's quite a list and she may get only some that aren't pleasant, but we'll monitor her very closely. Some patients don't have to stay in the hospital the entire month of engrafting, but each case is different. We'll have to play it by ear. She's just had a rough go, but I'm optimistic."

I sucked in a ragged breath; relief flooding through me at Dr. Radar's words. Chase automatically reached for my hand. "Thank you, doctor."

"I'll want to do the transplant very soon after we radiate her. That will be the scary part for you and for her. Remi will have to be in clean room isolation so you won't be able to be with her for a few days. I feel if we do the radiation about the same time you're in surgery, she can receive it soon after."

Leaving Remi alone would be the hard part. My heart broke for her, but we had no choice.

"Will Chase have any side effects from donating?" I asked.

"We'll put him under general anesthesia, so he will be able to leave about eight hours after the procedure. Only about one percent of donors have serious complications, so don't worry. Usually, it's just being sore as hell for a few days, and some bruising. You won't be able to play soccer for at least a week."

"Do I have to be out cold?"

"We could do a local or an epidural, but we'll be sticking huge needles into your pelvic bone in about four places and to say it's extremely painful is a bit of an understatement. General anesthetic works better for the patient and the team drawing it. There are risks with GA, but it's rare. You'll be asked to refrain from food or water after midnight the night before and also, stay away from anyone with colds or flu. We'll test you before we take the donation. Remi can't afford any second-hand infections."

"Sounds logical," Chase answered, nodding. He still held my hand and I couldn't help wrapping the other around his arm.

He turned back to the little girl. "Remi, it's Dr. Radar. Can you open your eyes for me, sweetheart?"

She stirred in her bed and she tried to open her eyes. "Mommy?" she asked. She always called me the second she woke up and I stepped forward to let her see me behind the doctor.

"Mommy and Daddy are both here, baby. Jensey said to tell you he loves you and he'll see you tomorrow afternoon."

Remi tried to look at me, but her heavy lids dropped sleepily. She reopened them halfway once more, but couldn't wake up, and they fell closed again.

"Is it okay to let her sleep?" Chase wanted to know. "She seems like she needs it."

The doctor nodded. "If she wakes up and wants to eat, the nursing station has snacks. Anesthesia has lingering effects."

Remi's numerous stays in the hospital made me acutely aware of the little room with refreshments set up on every floor. I'd be able to find something she liked if she was hungry.

"I'll go out and get her a cheeseburger," Chase stated. "She'll eat that for sure."

Dr. Radar nodded with a smile on his gentle face. "This is one lucky little lady to have so many people who love her. She's a good little patient."

"We can't thank you and the staff enough for everything you've done for Remi, Dr. Radar."

"We all adore her." He took the three steps necessary to reach me and patted the side of my upper arm. "We'll get her through this."

Chase offered his right hand to shake the doctor's hand. "Thank you. Is there a cot or something that can be brought in here so Teagan can get some sleep? If not, would it be possible to rent out one of the empty rooms? I'm happy to pay whatever is necessary."

"I'll get an orderly to bring up a cot," the nurse said. "Don't worry about that."

"Thank you."

When Dr. Radar left and it was just Chase and me in the room again, his stomach rumbled loudly.

The sound surprised us both, and he put a hand on his stomach. "Wow."

I chuckled. "Speaking of eating, it sounds like you need food. When was the last time you ate something?"

"That piece of toast and your leftover fruit this morning. Why don't we both go get something? It will give us a break from these awful masks. I can't stand these damn things."

I looked down at Remi and ran my fingers down her arm. "They are terrible, aren't they? I don't like it when I can't hold her or kiss her."

"I hate feeling my breath on my face every time I exhale. It's suffocating," he said. "As far as Remi... I just want time to play with her and get to know her."

I glanced in his direction, nodding sadly. I was unsure if I'd be able to get past the guilt of keeping them apart. "I know you do."

Chase bent down and pressed his cheek to the top of Remi's silky head. "She's so precious. Teagan." When he straightened, he ran his blue latex covered index finger down her cheek. His eyes were glassy when he looked up at me. "I'd do anything to save her." Chase was always so strong, so adamant that Remi would be fine, but I saw fear behind those tears.

I wanted nothing more than to comfort him and walked around the bed and instantly into his arms. I hugged his waist to hold him tight. I pressed my cheek to the front of his hospital gown and the steel chest beneath it when he enfolded me in a warm embrace. "You will. I know you will."

Love rushed and overflowed my heart. I hugged him tighter, trying hard not to burst into tears. I loved this man more than anything. Once again, he'd become the center of my universe... and not just because of how much he loved Remi.

"I love you, Chase," I choked out. "So much."

He cleared his throat and I knew he was struggling. "You know what you mean to me, Teagan. That won't ever change." His words were the miracle I didn't deserve but had been praying for.

All I could do was nod, my throat too tight for words. I did know; now that he was here, with me. In the years apart when he would cross my mind, I wondered if he missed me in the same desperate way I missed him and my heart always came up with the same answer. I hoped he did, but after the phone call that broke my heart, I had to accept that he'd moved on, and it was the only thing that motivated me to make an attempt at a real marriage with Jensen. There was a lot of evidence to support that Chase was happy, but Jensen and I couldn't conjure a relationship just because we thought it's what we should do. It never worked, and Chase's ghost was always between us.

I was still wrapped up with Chase and he rubbed a flat hand up and down my back. "Let's get something to eat and have our talk, then we can come back and spend the night with Remi later. If I'll be able to stand this fucking mask," he added with a wry chuckle.

"What was that?" Laughing softly, I poked him in the ribs with a pointed finger then used it point at our sleeping child.

"Oops, sorry. No cussing in front of the kid. Got it."

CHASE

I was anxious for the conversation I knew was coming, but I was just as anxious to be alone with Teagan.

I would have preferred to take her to a nice restaurant like a real date, but we were both tired and not dressed for it. Instead, we went through a Chinese drive through and I took her back to my shitty apartment with the food. It was barren and small, but it was clean. I'd barely been there, and now that

Bronwyn was gone, her things wouldn't be strewn around in a mess.

"This place reminds me of college," she murmured as she followed me into the kitchen. "Not what I expected you to have now."

"Why?" I threw Teagan's keys on the small wooden table in the corner and walked past her. "You think now that I'm not dead broke, I would turn into David Beckham?"

Teagan moved up behind me and slid her arms around my waist, pressing her hands flat on my chest and stomach. "You're better than David Beckham ever was."

I smiled, huffing. "He wouldn't agree." I pulled out four red and white cartons, fortune cookies, and packets of soy sauce, sriracha, and sweet and sour sauce and set them out on the table.

"You are." I felt her kiss my back through my shirt. "Bronwyn isn't exactly Posh Spice in sneakers."

My heart surged at the tinge of jealousy I heard in her voice. I took one of her hands and pulled it up to kiss the inside of her wrist. I was deliberately sexy in the way I used my open mouth to caress her. Her arms flexed, tightening around me in response.

"Mmmm…." She sighed.

Suddenly, I wasn't hungry for food.

I turned inside the circle of her arms and easily lifted her up. Instinct had her legs and arms wrapping around my body like she'd done so often when we were together. One of my hands wrapped around her ass cheek and the other slid up her back under the curtain of her hair to cup the back of her head. She was dressed casually in jean shorts and a light pink blouse that suited her dark hair and brought out the blush in her peachy complexion.

She bent so that her lips were hovering over mine and she was playing with the hair at my nape.

"There's my monkey," I murmured, against her lips and she smiled. My tongue snaked out to slide sensuously along her upper one and her thighs flexed on my hips. My dick was already hard, and I wanted her so much it physically hurt. I sucked in a breath laden with her shampoo, perfume and the scent of her skin as our mouths collided in hungry abandon. Memories flooded my mind and heart. It was as if we'd never been apart.

The apartment was small and there was an old, ugly brown sofa less than six feet away. Somehow we ended up there, Teagan straddling my lap. I wanted her beneath me so I could press into her and so she could literally feel how much I wanted her.

The kisses were wild and we were hungry. She made passionate little moans that drove me insane. This was how want and starvation felt. My body throbbed painfully and I was dying a blissful death. Her mouth was frantic with mine and I sucked her tongue inside mine to slowly lave and suckle it.

"God, I want you so bad," I panted in shallow breaths between kisses. My heart was thundering against hers and my hands roamed up and down her body, along the side swells of her breasts, over her slim waist and down the gentle swell of her hips. My pelvis surged into the cradle of hers. "You're mine."

I ripped at the front of her shirt, my fingers and mouth in search of the creamy white skin and the erect pebbles of her rosy nipples beneath. Buttons flew across the room as I exposed her lacy bra. Their clatter and the material giving away were the only sounds except our mouths kissing, soft moans and soft, but heavy breathing. It was beautiful, painful agony.

My mouth dragged down the side of her neck in a light lick and sucking pattern that I knew made would cause her to melt in my arms. She opened like a flower to me. My hands wrapped around her full breasts after I'd freed them from her bra, kneading and teasing, lifting them so I could go to work on the tips with my mouth. Teagan's head fell back and she arched in my arms. I used the momentum to move just enough to lay her down on her back using one arm around her waist and my thighs to hold her weight.

We kept kissing and petting hotly. I pressed the head and shaft of my dick hard against her, thrusting through our clothes. I thrilled in the ravenous way her hips met mine, the way her fingers clawed at my clothes and her heels dug into the back of my thighs to give her leverage. "Christ," I groaned into her mouth.

I sat back on my knees and tore my own shirt off, looking down at Teagan in the half-light coming from the light over the stove. I unbuckled my pants and ran my hands up her legs from her knees to her hips. Her dark eyes were intense and filled with desire as she looked at me.

"I thought we agreed we wouldn't do this again until we talked," she murmured, reaching for my left hand and threading her fingers with mine.

I sucked in a breath and let my head fall back. "Talking is overrated. I can't help it. I'm starving for you."

"I missed you."

I raked my free hand down her body, between her bare breasts and to the button and zipper of her cutoff jean shorts. I deftly freed the button and zipper, pushing them open and getting a good glimpse of her flat stomach and the top of her lace bikini panties. "You're so beautiful, Teagan." My heart swelled to bursting, so full of love I thought it would kill me.

"Chase," she said. Her voice was thick with passion. I bent to kiss her beneath her bellybutton, and Teagan sucked in her breath. She still held one of my hands and I pulled free long enough to pull her shorts down her thighs. She had to help me by pulling first one her leg free and then the other due to my position between her thighs.

The couch wasn't the perfect place to make love, but nothing would stop me. The touch of my hands and mouth were soft as I kissed along the top band of her panties. Every inch of her skin was like velvet. I slid a hand up to cup and tease one of her breasts, while I hooked her panties with a finger and moved them aside to give me access.

I inhaled her arousal and the moist heat coming from her body beckoned. I kissed and slowly licked and sucked on her sensitive flesh, parting her slick folds with my fingers. My soft, pulsing sucking made her body arch involuntarily. I pressed a flat hand on her stomach to control her movements. It was like we'd never been apart. I knew exactly what to do to make her body sing.

I wanted to go slow, but her body moving against my mouth and her low moans of pleasure drove me to the edge. My dick was screaming for release. I knew she was close when the silken little nub began to throb on my tongue and I imagined her clenching and milking her tight body around my cock.

"Uhhhh." Her soft sigh was like a purr and her hips rose in slow thrusts as I made love to her with my mouth. I knew if I slid one finger inside her, it would push her over the edge.

"Chase, stop. Make love to me. Come with me."

"No, I don't want to stop," I said, determined to make her come hard. Both of my hands pressed on the back of her thighs to spread her wider and hold her there. I alternated between soft flicks of my tongue too long laving strokes. When her legs began to tremble, I sucked her clit softly into my mouth and I knew I had her.

"Cha—Chase, oh God." She moaned, threading a hand through my hair. "Uhhhhhhh."

The hand in my hair twisted as her body arched violently while her orgasm overtook her. I kissed her softly then laid my forehead on her stomach and willed my throbbing cock to stop its painful demands.

Teagan gently stroked my hair over and over. She sighed softly. "Come up here." Her hands slid over the muscles of my shoulders and back as I did as she requested, pulling me closer and turning her chin up to capture my mouth with her own. Her hands reached for me, pushing my jeans down just enough to free my cock. My erection bobbed free and both of her hands closed around it, pulling up and pushing down in slow torture, squeezing tighter over the head.

"Teagan." I still hovered over her and my head dropped; my forehead pressing against her bare shoulder. "Uhhhh." My breath left me in a rush. "That feels amazing, babe." My eyes were closed and I was afraid I'd come in her hands. My fingers found her opening and she was still slick and wet from her orgasm. I pushed a finger inside her and she gasped in pleasure as I pressed up, finding the hard g spot, still overly sensitive from coming. Her hands continued to work on me and it took all I had not to explode in her hands.

I swooped down to kiss her and at the same time grabbed my cock to slide the head up and down through her slick heat and into her. Her legs fell open and I pushed inside her tight, heat. She clenched around me, making it even more incredible. The kisses were glorious, deep and sensuous. I settled down on top of Teagan and began slow, deep thrusts, getting as close as I could; so intimate. I registered every touch, every sigh, every sensation, and every breath as we made love to each other.

It didn't matter that the couch was as hard as a rock, that this apartment was older than dirt, or that we had problems as big as Mount Everest to climb over, all that existed to me was Teagan and the love between us. I wanted her to feel it from me like I needed to feel it from her.

My hands cradled the side of her head as I rested on my elbows, and her body wrapped around mine. There was nothing like being inside her and having her arms and legs caging me in possessively as her fingers lovingly stroked my jaw as I kissed her. With every passing second, our mouths and bodies worshiped each other. I'd already resolved to forgive her because there was no way that I'd ever feel this close to another human being as long as I lived and I knew it.

* * *

We lay together naked on the couch; Teagan curled against me with her head on my chest and wrapped up in my arms. I was absently running the back of my knuckles up and down her bare arm. I knew we had to talk, but I was reluctant to ruin the bliss of the moment.

"What are you thinking about?" she murmured. I could hear the sleep in her voice and I felt it myself. I would be content to lie there for the rest of my life. Despite the love I felt for Teagan, and the mistakes of the past, part of me worried about Jensen. Stupidly, I felt guilty. She was mine first; but still, I couldn't help wondering what this would do to him.

"Just that I love you."

"But?" she asked knowingly.

I sighed, my chest rising beneath her cheek. I turned to place a kiss on her forehead. "But," I spoke against her skin. "I worry about Jensen. How is this going to affect him? My head says I have no reason to feel guilty. We were together first, but..."

Teagan turned and started to get up. I was instantly regretful. "Baby, don't..." My hand slid down her back as she rose and started to get dressed.

"I'm not going anywhere, Chase. I'm just cold and we do need to talk about this."

She was frowning and I wanted to lighten the mood. "Well, my mouth works when we're naked. I thought I just proved that."

I smirked when her eyes shot to mine. Her left eyebrow shot up in challenge. Teagan couldn't help but smile as she threw my pants at me. "Hmmm, my blouse is destroyed." She put it on and tried to tie it shut at the bottom but it left a wide expanse of skin showing at her waist and plunging between her breasts. I couldn't help appreciating the view it afforded.

I'd thrown on my pants and walked into the other room to grab one of my white T-shirts from one of the dresser drawers. I realized, with more guilt, that Bronwyn had unpacked my suitcase and put the few pieces away. "I like the way that looks, but this might be better when we go back to the hospital."

I walked to her and bent to kiss her mouth softly, tilting her chin up with the crook of my index finger. I had a hard time not touching her. Teagan's hands settled on both sides of my bare waist as my lips ghosted over hers intent on another kiss.

"Chase," she said, tensing. "I thought we were going to talk."

She was right. We did need to talk. Her reaction just now when I mentioned Jensen nagged at me. I threw on my shirt and left it unbuttoned over my bare chest, padding into the kitchen to get the food. The small three-room apartment was sparsely furnished with a bed, a couch and chair, and a small kitchen table with two chairs. There were also a few utensils, pots, pans and dishes. I opened three drawers before I found the forks but then closed it without taking them out, realizing we weren't going to talk about our relationship and future over crappy Chinese food.

I turned back into the living room. Teagan was sitting on the couch, and dressed in the T-shirt and her shorts; she looked so young with her love-tousled hair. I went to sit beside her and took her hand in mine. "So, talk."

"I've told you a lot of it, but what you don't know is that despite my father, I was going to drop out of Clemson and come to London. All of this happened before Jensen took it upon himself to approach my father."

Her words were soft but held the weight of a sledgehammer. My eyes widened in surprise. "What?"

"After I found out I was pregnant, I was scared you'd give up Arsenal and I panicked. I didn't tell you in Pennsylvania because you were so excited about the offer, and I couldn't ruin it. But, after you left, I was so sad and I knew you'd want to know."

"Then why, Teagan—?" I wanted to tell her that when I left I had no intentions of a life without her. Ever.

"No, let me finish. I was a total mess without you already, and my father refused to pay my tuition anywhere but Clemson for the last year, and worse, he swore to ruin your career if I followed you, until Jensen took the heat. He's your friend, Chase. He really thought he was helping us both. He told my dad Remi was his, all on his own. I never asked him to do it, and I didn't know until it was done."

"You have to know that Jensen has always been in love with you, Teag. If you think he married you for any other reason, you're kidding yourself. And you gave your dad way too much power. He couldn't have done shit to my career. Rumors go away."

"Maybe. I don't know." She pulled her hand free and a scowl settled on her face. "I'm trying to take responsibility, Chase. I'm not excusing what we did, and I'm not trying to paint Jensen a saint, but he was trying to save me from being left alone and took care of me."

I ran an exasperated hand through my hair. "Why would you be alone? You knew how much I loved you. It was me who should have taken care of you." Anger started to well up inside, despite my intention to remain calm. "You had to know in your heart that I'd want Remi."

"No, I didn't."

I huffed indignantly. "Why in the hell would you doubt me?"

She inhaled sharply. "Because. I was going to surprise you in London, but when I called you the night before my scheduled flight, a woman answered your cell phone! It was the middle of the night there, Chase. Bronwyn admitted to me in the cafeteria, this morning; it was her."

"What the hell are you saying? You're accusing me of cheating?"

"It broke my heart and it broke— me. It hurt so badly I didn't know what I was doing. I didn't care if I lived or died. I was pregnant, my world was about to implode and you were apparently taking the first chance you had to be with someone else." She threw her hands in the air and let them drop into her lap, her eyes leaving mine to stare at her hands.

I stood and reeled on her accusingly. "How could you believe I'd do that?"

"I was in so much pain, maybe I wasn't thinking straight. Jensen was the closest friend I had and I called him crying my heart out. He stayed with me and I told him about the phone call and the baby. He wanted to confront you, but I begged him not to. The next day, he went to my dad and said the baby was his."

"That's tied up pretty neat, except I wasn't sleeping with Bronwyn, Teagan! She was one of the trainers. She was constantly with the team. The whole team!"

"I know that now, but I didn't then."

"I didn't start dating her until this year, for Christ's sake!" Her eyes widened and I started to pace back and forth in the small space as pain and fury exploded inside me. Both hands clenched into fists at my sides. My expression had to be twisted with agony and flushed because I could feel the heat rising under my skin. "You should have called me! You should have trusted me!" I accused. "Jensen should have known better, too! Neither one of you trusted me enough or thought enough of me to fucking ask me for the truth?"

Tears welled in her eyes. "We should have, you're right, but after the first call, I was terrified to go through that again. I couldn't deal with hearing you say you didn't want me, to hear that it was true from your own mouth. So... I let you go."

I stopped and faced her, stunned by those four words. "You let me go," I repeated her statement and it was laced with misery. Tears overflowed my eyes and helplessly ran down my face. I brushed them away in frustrated anger; pissed that I was incapable of hiding how I felt. She let me go. Just like that.

"You think you fucking let me go? That was the farthest thing from the truth!" I railed at her; yelling at the top of my lungs. My heart was exploding inside my chest and I felt like an iron band was constricting my chest. "You killed me! You let me think you and Jensen were fucking behind my back for God knows how long!"

She scrambled off the couch and came to me crying. Her fingers wrapped around my forearms as she pleaded with me. "Chase, please listen! I didn't know that's what you believed, or I would have made sure you knew the truth. I thought you were happy in your new life and that it wouldn't matter to you about us! I had no reason to think otherwise. I watched you play and..."

"How could you know anything? We weren't talking! You weren't taking my calls. Neither of you did. Do you know how it feels to be completely cut off from the two people you trusted and loved the most?"

"It hurt too much and as I said, I was scared of hearing you say it was over between us. I knew I wouldn't be able to take it, and I had to think of the baby. I waited almost until she was born to marry Jensen… waited for you, but you never came after me."

I looked down at the woman I loved more than my own life and realized that the intense debilitating pain that I was experiencing myself, was smeared all over her, too.

"Yes, I did!" It came out in a hiss. "I came back that first Christmas, but you were already with Jensen and I lost my shit. I had a fucking nervous breakdown in front of my family. Kevin kept me from coming to you and making a complete fool of myself, but I got so drunk I almost killed myself from alcohol poisoning!"

"Oh, Chase. I'm so sorry. Please forgive me."

She was crying softly against me and I had to hold her. I was pissed; at Teagan, at Bronwyn and Jensen, at myself, and yet, I loved her more than ever. The undeniable bond between us demanded I go to her and I pull her close into a tight embrace or we'd both only suffer more.

Teagan was a good head shorter than me, so to bring her as close as I could, I lifted her off the floor into my embrace with her feet dangling off the floor. As hurt as I was, I'd already reconciled that I needed her and we'd have to put all of this shit behind us, one way or another. "Hush. It's over now."

Teagan's head fell so that her forehead was on my shoulder and she sobbed harder. "I'm so sorry. You're the last person I ever wuh—wanted to hurt."

"Me, too." I kissed the side of her face, tasting her salty tears on my lips, my own heart breaking. "We were both idiots, but it's over now."

I bent to put one arm under her knees, lifting Teagan bridal style so I was able to move to the couch. I sat and situated her easily onto my lap. She curled into me and I wrapped my arms around her. I knew I loved her and I'd admitted it to myself, and to Bronwyn, that I wanted Teagan in my life. "Here's the thing; I love you, so I can be stubborn and try to hate you, and lose you all over again, or we can figure this shit out."

Teagan slid her arm up around my chest and hugged me. "Oh, Chase," she said tearfully.

"Even when I wanted to hate you, I couldn't. It's like the most painful, damning, amazing and beautiful fucking thing on earth."

"I know. It's the same for me," her tear-laced voice was soft and trembling.

"But, it's still wrong to be together. I convinced myself that being with you wasn't wrong; that it wasn't cheating because you are the love of my life, but the fact is, you're married and I don't want to sneak around. It's killing me to say it out loud, but as long as you're with Jensen, we have to stop this."

Teagan pulled back to look into my face. She laid a hand on my cheek. "We already talked about being a real family. I thought it was understood that I'd leave Jensen."

"You never said it, for sure."

"Chase, you need to know that Jensen and I were going to get divorced three years ago, but then Remi got sick and everything went off the rails. I had to quit my job and he stayed with me because we needed to keep her on his insurance, but we knew it wasn't right between us."

"He loves you. It's written all over him."

"He does, but I've never lied to him about how I feel about you. I tried, but I couldn't pretend I had feelings for him that didn't exist... Worse, I couldn't pretend I didn't have feelings for you. I told him I wouldn't marry him unless we could always be honest and that included telling Remi the truth as soon as she could understand."

I sat back and pulled her with me. My anger calmed with a couple of deep breaths as I considered what she'd said. I wanted to believe it because it would end the torturous acid eating away at my heart and soul for years. I closed my eyes and pressed my forehead against the warmth of Teagan's temple.

"Remi is the saving grace in all of this. The one thing that makes it possible for me to even deal with this at all is that you told her about me. Having her know about me; saved us, Teagan. Walking in to meet her and having her know who I was, was the most amazing gift."

Teagan's arms tightened around me and she kissed the skin beneath my ear; her hands softly stroking the back of my head and the skin on my forearm that was draped over her knees. "There was no way I could keep it from her. I was bursting with it, and I prayed for the day you'd know her. Finally being able to tell you everything is a relief. For me, having you know, finally, is the gift, Chase."

ONE *touch*
AND THE PAIN
melted away.

Chapter 17

Teagan

The next day, Remi was doing much better.

She was awake and Dr. Radar scheduled the transplant for the next day. Chase decided to go back to South Carolina on a day trip to see his parents after his dad called and asked him about an upcoming game and he had no choice but to admit he was in Atlanta.

Chase didn't want to lie to his parents about Remi. Given that Kat knew, he felt it would be better for Remi if everyone knew the truth and she was able to meet his family. She deserved her family, and I couldn't argue.

I was concerned that his family would have a deep-seated hatred for me after finding out I'd kept Remi a secret, but no doubt, they'd be hurt by the deceit; especially hiding her existence from Chase for all this time. I understood his need to tell them, but I was apprehensive. I could only pray that any hostility they might have for me wouldn't be exhibited in front of my daughter. I wondered how Roma would feel finding out Remi was named for her.

My mother died when I was young and I no longer had a relationship with my father, so my little girl had no grandparents on my side. Jensen's parents adored her, but Chase was close with his family, and I had no doubt they would all embrace Remi.

I was sitting next to Remi, with one of her favorite books; the Green Eggs and Ham by Dr. Seuss. I was still enrobed in the hated paper gown, mask, and gloves, but happily reading her the rhyming story. She's had a good breakfast of, fittingly, scrambled eggs, ham, and toast, and was anxiously waiting for Chase to arrive. We both spent the night in this room, me on the cot and Chase in the recliner in the corner, but he'd only complained about the mask three times in eight hours. I left early to shower and when I arrived back at the hospital, Chase told me about his decision to go to Greenville.

Chase and I agreed that we'd talk to her about the transplant together. Jensen would have been included but he wasn't scheduled back until late evening, and she would no doubt be sleeping. I'd spoken to him on the phone earlier and he agreed, she needed to be prepared. He was glad that Remi had a chance to get better; elated like the rest of us… but I knew he was still worried he'd be cut out of Remi's life, despite my reassurances. I doubted he'd believe it until he heard it from Chase.

"Mommy?" Remi asked as I closed the book and laid it aside.

"Yes, sweet pea?" I lay down beside her and turned propping my head up on my fisted hand.

"When Jensey comes home, will Daddy go away?"

Her question took me aback. "I'm not sure exactly what will happen, Remi, but I do know Daddy will never leave you."

"Not even for soccer?"

"Well," I said thoughtfully. "That's his job, just like talking at the football game is Jensey's job. So he will have to do that sometimes. But that doesn't mean he'll go away for good."

She nodded. "Okay."

"Do you like Daddy, Remi?"

Her face brightened with a big smile and she nodded again, this time more vigorously. I couldn't help smiling back, though she couldn't see my face through the stupid mask.

"He's funny and he likes cheeseburgers and Clifford, just like me. He said we could do lots of stuff when I'm better. He said he'd show me some real castles and he's gonna teach me to play soccer with him."

I didn't hear Chase enter because Remi held my attention. She was so happy talking about Chase and it filled my heart to bursting. I was completely unaware he was listening until he laughed from the just closing doorway. "And why are we going to visit castles?"

Remi giggled with delight at seeing him and the sound was music to my ears. "'Cause all princesses need castles!"

"That's right!" His voice was full of joy and his eyes were sparkling above the mask. "Look at me! How lucky can a guy get? I'm surrounded by princesses!"

He was openly flirting with me and making Remi squeal in delight. He walked to Remi and ruffled her hair. "How are you feeling, sweetheart?"

"Fine. Mommy was reading Dr. Swiss."

"Wow! I love Dr. Swiss!" He deliberately pronounced it like Remi.

I cocked my head and shot him a wry look. He only laughed out loud.

"Which story?"

"Green Eggs and Ham. I wanted it for breakfast, but they didn't make it green like mommy."

"Mommy makes green eggs and ham?"

"Sometimes it's only eggs, 'cause her green ham turns out sorta brown." She wrinkled her nose and Chase laughed again, gleefully.

I couldn't help but laugh with them. I cleared my throat and changed the subject because Chase had to get on the road if he wanted to be back and get a decent night's sleep before the transplant. "Remi, Daddy and I want to talk to you, okay?"

"Okay." The head of her bed was elevated and I was sitting on her right, and Chase sat down on her left and reached for her hand with his blue latex covered one.

"Remi, I'm going to give you some of my bone marrow tomorrow, so tonight the doctors have to put you in a big machine to get you ready, and afterward, your body has to stay really clean, so you'll have a new room for a while. Mommy, Jensey or me won't be able to see you for a few days, but the doctor says we have to do this right now, to make sure we don't bring in any germs. We don't want you to be scared because we'll be very close, okay sweetheart? Dr. Radar and the nurses will be able to visit, but we'll all be just outside the room where you'll be."

My arm slid around her. "I know how brave you can be, Remi, and this is what we need to do to get you better. We talked about this, remember?"

Her eyes were wide and I was afraid she was about to cry. I kissed her forehead as best I could through the mask and held her close to me. Chase's thumb rubbed the top of her hand. "Yes," she said quietly.

"Daddy will give his marrow to another doctor and then Dr. Radar or one of the nurses you know will give it to you through your port and after a few days, he'll let us all be with you."

"Will it hurt?"

"No, honey," I answered. It wouldn't hurt going in, but it wasn't certain if she'd feel any pain as it seeded in her bones. "If it does, Dr. Radar will make it stop. He promised. It won't hurt like the mean medicine, though."

She seemed to consider this. "Okay." She looked at Chase. "How do you get it out of your bones for me? Do you have to break your leg to get at the inside stuff?"

"No, honey. Big needles."

Remi frowned and recoiled as if the needles were a worse prospect than breaking the bone. "That will hurt, Daddy."

"It might, but I'm tough, I can take it. Don't worry about me." He winked and touched her chin.

"Why do you have to go away today? Mommy said you have to go somewhere."

"I'm going to get you a big present." His voice wavered and he blinked. "But you've gotta get better before I can give it to you."

"What is it?" she clasped her hands together, her expression lighting up.

"It's a secret. Nice try, though," Chase teased.

"Is it a cheeseburger?"

Chase and I both laughed softly, both of us fighting our emotions. "No, baby. It's better than a cheeseburger."

"Hmmm. I really like cheeseburgers." She looked at him coyly, with a tilt of her head.

"We'll go somewhere and get an amazing cheeseburger when you're better. I promise."

His answer seemed to satisfy her. "Will your trip take all day?"

"Most of it. I'll try to get back in time to say goodnight, okay?"

She nodded. "Don't forget."

"I won't," Chase promised.

TRADING YESTERDAY

"Daddy has to go, baby girl. He's got a long drive in front of him." I nodded toward the door, silently telling Chase I was going to walk him out. Chase stood and kissed the top of Remi's head, cupping it when he was done. He seemed reluctant to leave and I understood how he felt. Remi was going to be vulnerable as hell after the radiation and it was happening late tonight. It would be a race to get back in time.

"Remi, you be big and brave for Daddy, okay? Jensey will come see you later, and Mommy will stay with you." She held up her arms to him, and he didn't hesitate to scoop her up until she was completely in his arms.

Remi hugged him tight in return. Jensen and I had always shown a lot of affection to Remi and we never left her without showing love. "I love you, Daddy."

Chase's eyes widened and then closed. He held our daughter tighter and kissed her temple and then her cheek. "I love you, pumpkin. Don't be afraid. I won't let anything happen to my best girl." He sniffed and his voice cracked when he set her down then turned toward the door to her room and started to walk out.

"I'm going to go say goodbye to Daddy, honey. I'll be right back." I handed her my iPad that was loaded with games and books for her. Her illness meant she wasn't able to attend Kindergarten last year, but Jensen and I had decided to homeschool her with K12, an amazing online school program in South Carolina. Remi was smart and it was easy to engage her, except when she was in the throes of chemotherapy. "Do you want to play AniMatch until Mommy gets back?"

Remi took the iPad from me. She was smart and though we had to keep her out of school, I had a lot of learning games loaded for her. "Kay, Mommy."

Chase was ripping the god-awful paper gown from his body, exposing muscled arms and biceps, the outline of his chest visible under the fine material of his expensive V-neck t-shirt. The olive-green material emphasized his eyes and sun-kissed strands of his hair. His face was mottled and he pulled the mask off and clenched it in his fist.

"Maybe I shouldn't go."

There were two nurses, one male and one female, who were outside of Remi's room discussing another patient's case and their conversation stopped for a brief period as they observed us. Discretely they turned away and pushed the computer cart they were working on farther down the hall to give us privacy.

I was suddenly calm, even though my emotions were a mess. I laid a hand on his chest and tried to keep my voice steady. "Chase." I looked up at him and his eyes locked on mine. We were both teary eyed and I could see a muscle working in Chase's jaw as he struggled with leaving. "It's okay. I know you need to do this."

"Yeah. They need a chance to know her, but it might be too late. What if—" He shook his head adamantly. "I don't want to be away if—"

"Hey. You had faith that your marrow would match and it did. You said she's going to get better. She will. Have that same faith she's going to be okay. I trust you."

Inside I was just as terrified and part of me didn't want him to leave, but I didn't want to stop him. He brushed a loose tendril of my hair behind my ear. "Jensen said the last years had been hell and I had been spared, he wasn't kidding. This is brutal."

It was. After three years of dealing with it, I wasn't much better at handling the unknown or the stress. The strong façade, necessary in front of Remi, was exhausting. "It is."

"I'm proud of you, Teagan. I don't know how you do it day-in and day out, year after year. You amaze me."

"I do it because I have to; for Remi. She can't see how scared we are or she'll worry about dying. I can't let that happen."

"I know." His arm snuck out around my shoulders and he pulled me into a hug. I melted into him. His cologne surrounded me, and it was all I could do not to kiss the bare expanse of chest at the collar of his shirt. "I wish you were coming with me."

"I think it's best if you drop this bomb without me. They're going to hate me."

"It'll be okay. I won't let them hurt you."

He released me and I stepped back. "I'll walk you out."

Chase nodded and we started moving toward the elevators on the far end of the floor.

"What reason did you give your dad for being in town?"

"The truth. I told him I was donating marrow to save someone I cared about." He grabbed my hand and threaded his fingers through mine with familiar ease. "Don't worry about this. I'll take care of it. I know they can't meet her before the procedure or for a while afterward."

When I'd gone home to shower, I'd brought back a few pictures of Remi as a baby and since, and had them in a small white envelope in my back pocket. When we arrived at the steel doors of the elevators, Chase pressed the down button and I pulled it out, offering it to him.

"What's this?"

"A few pictures of Remi. I thought you'd want to show them, but don't look at them if it's going to hurt you."

He took the envelope in his hand and stared down at it. "It's going to hurt, but I'm going to look at them. I want to see everything I missed," he said thickly.

My head fell in defeat. It hit me, that even if Chase could forgive me, the past would always be there to torment him. I reached for his hand again, and my chin snapped up so

324

I could look at him. "I'm sorry, Chase. Will we ever be able to put it behind us? You can forgive, but this will always stand between us. I don't know how we'll get over it." Sorrow laced my voice. I was sad, worried, tormented so much of the time, and I didn't know how my eyes could produce any more tears, but they never seemed to dry up. "Is there ever a moment when you don't think about it?"

"Here or there. When we're making love, I don't think about it. When I'm with Remi, I am just glad to be with her."

He shoved the envelope into the back pocket of his jeans and used that hand to cup my face, his thumb grazing back and forth on my jaw. I couldn't tear my eyes off of the beautiful miracle that was Chase, and his didn't waver. "We'll get this behind us, and make new memories. Then the bad stuff will fade. We have our whole lives in front of us; with Remi."

He bent and brushed my lips with his in a soft kiss as the elevator doors opened. Thankfully, no one was inside. "I love you. See you tonight."

He walked into the open elevator and his fingers untangled with mine as he went. I felt bereft at his leaving, like part of me was going with him. "I love you, too."

"I know that in my gut, Teagan. That's why we'll be okay."

I nodded. "Be safe."

"I will." The doors started to close. "I'll call you later."

I took a deep breath as I slowly walked back to Remi's room.

The nurse was leaving as I gathered another of the gowns and methodically re-garbed to keep my child safe. Pulling on the gloves and the mask, I prayed that a month from now Remi would be free of the horrible cancer and our lives would be moving in a better direction. My mind and heart were flooded with so many things, not the least of which was the little angel in the middle of the hospital bed, happily engaged with the tablet, and talking to the stuffed black lab Jensen bought her.

"Look, Jewel. See this big grey thing? It's an elephant," Remi explained seriously. "We gotta find another one on here somewhere. Where do you think it is? "Right here? Me, too." She touched the screen and smiled big when the match materialized. "Yay!"

"Jewel is a big help," I smiled and sat down beside Remi.

"Yep. Do you think Daddy likes dogs?"

"I do." I nodded.

"That's good, 'cause remember Jensey promised we're getting a real Jewel when I'm better."

"I remember."

"When will Jensey come back?"

"Tonight. Want to call him?" She nodded and went to retrieve my phone from my purse, pushing the button that was Jensen's number on speed dial. I handed Remi the phone. The situation was complicated but Jensen was a huge part of Remi's life and that was one thing that couldn't change. Somehow, we had to make it work. The phone volume was loud enough, and I was close enough, that I could hear Jensen's voice coming across the phone Remi held to her head.

"Hi, squirt," he said. He'd called her that since she was just a baby and it stuck.

"Hi, Jensey! I miss you. When are you coming?"

"I'm on my way back now. I miss you, too, and can't wait to see you."

"Me, too. Daddy and I got an operation."

"Mommy told me. I'll be there, I promise."

"Okay."

"Are you having fun with Daddy?"

I knew it pained Jensen to ask, but I was glad he did. We had to treat the situation as normal and make her feel secure that all of us were here for her and united in putting her first.

"Yes. He's not here right now."

"That's okay. I'm sure he'll be back, and I'll play with you when I get there."

"Okay!" She was happy and unconcerned.

"Can I talk to Mommy, squirt?"

"Okay. I love you, Jensey."

"I love you, too, babes."

Remi handed me the phone. "Here, Mommy."

"Hey."

"Where did Chase go?"

I turned away from Remi and moved to the other side of the room. I made sure my voice was low. "He went to Greenville to see his folks."

"Today?" His voice was accusatory.

"His father called and found out Chase was in Atlanta. He wanted to know why and Chase thought it best to tell them in person."

"I see. Did they tell you when she is getting the radiation?"

"Tonight. They'll put her out so she won't be scared, but after that, we can't be with her until the transplant starts to work."

"Let's pray this works."

"It has to."

"I know. I'll be there in about three hours. My plane is about to take off."

CHASE

I drove into the driveway of the small acreage my parents owned outside of Greenville. It hadn't changed since the last time I was here.

It hadn't really changed since I was a kid. I'd called Kat and Kevin and asked that they be here, too. Kat knew, but Kevin didn't, and I didn't want to explain this shit more than once. My mother would be furious with Kat for not telling her, and so, even though I was still angry with her, decided we didn't need more family friction and it was better to keep her cover-up a secret. No one would benefit from throwing her under the bus.

The tires crunched on the gravel driveway as I pulled up to the house. It was a nice two-story that my dad had built for my mother when his business started seeing success and saved a shit load by wiring the whole thing himself. We'd lived here since I was eight years old, and most of my childhood memories were built in this house and on this land. The tree house my father built for us was still in the huge oak tree to the left of the house. It, and the tire swing hanging from a branch below it, probably got a lot of use from Kat's three boys and Kevin's twin girls. I couldn't help thinking how much fun Remi would have playing with her cousins and being doted on by my parents. They were the epitome of indulgent grandparents.

Kat's minivan and two of the company trucks sat in the drive by the house. Everyone was here. I took a deep breath and gathered up the photos of Remi I'd left strewn on the passenger seat after I'd looked through them before I got out of the black Nissan I'd rented. My mother came running out of the house with open arms, and the other's followed behind.

I was body slammed as my mother threw herself into my arms. "There's my baby!"

"Mom, please." I laughed and hugged her back.

"I'm so happy to see you!"

I hadn't seen my parents since they came to London last Christmas and it had been longer since I'd seen my brother. My dad came out and offered his hand. He was old school and in his book, men didn't greet each other with hugs. His other hand came out to pat my shoulder, though. I could see myself, and Remi reflected in my father's eyes. Kat and Kevin looked more like my mom, though I also had her coloring. "Good to see you, Son."

"You, too, Dad. Kevin," I said, shaking my brother's hand. Both of the other men's hands were rough with callouses and stained with evidence of the manual labor they did on a daily basis.

"Hello, Chase."

My brother was heavier than me, no doubt because I spent my whole life on the field running, and his wife, Jodi, was an amazing cook. They were high school sweethearts and got married before they were twenty-one. Kat's husband David was the produce manager at the flagship store of a local grocery chain, and they had an acreage that wasn't far from my parents.

"Are you hungry? I made lunch," my mother said, wrapping an arm around my waist as we all made our way into the house. The day was nice, and out of the city, it was cooler with a breeze. The air was clean and I realized how much I missed being home.

"A little." I wasn't, but it would crush my mother if I refused her food. The knot in my stomach hurt and I just wanted to get this over with.

Inside the house, Kat shot me a look and I mouthed. "It's fine," to her when I thought no one would see. My mother was busy cooking and talking about the grandkids and asking me questions about Arsenal and how long I'd be home. "You know the town will be buzzing when word gets out you're back."

My dad, however, just watched me. He knew me and knew what I had to tell them was a heavyweight. "Roma, let the boy breathe. He just got here." He was leaning up against the counter with his arms crossed.

I was thankful for his intervention. "Mom, Dad, I need to talk to you. I need to talk to you all. I know you have lunch going, Mom, and I'm sure it's delicious, but can we go into the living room for a few minutes?" I asked. I didn't have much time and after lunch, I'd be turning around and driving right back to Atlanta. "I have something pretty big to tell you."

My mother wiped her hands on a dishtowel as her brow dropped. She was clearly concerned. "What is it, Chase? Is Arsenal releasing you?"

"For Christ sake's, Mom. He's their star forward. No way they're releasing him," Kevin said, exasperated. He took off the billed hat that bore the logo of Forrester Electric and put it right back again.

Kat was conspicuously quiet.

"Please?" I motioned with my hand toward the other room. "Can we all sit down? I'll explain."

They all preceded me in with a mixture of concern and confusion on their faces and took positions on the leather sofa and loveseat. I was nervous and didn't feel like sitting, more like climbing the walls. "Look, I don't know how to pussyfoot around this, so I'm just going to say it. You can ask me a question, but please, just let me get it all out, first."

"Chase, you're worrying me. Dad said you were in Atlanta to donate bone marrow. Is that the truth? Is it you who is ill?" my mother asked.

"No. I am donating marrow. To my daughter."

My mother gasped and Kevin said, "Holy shit!"

My dad sat back and rubbed a hand over his face letting it all sink in before he responded.

"She's five years old and she has leukemia. Two rounds of chemo put her in remission for about a year, but it's back. A transplant is probably our last hope to save her."

"Oh, my God," my mother said, stunned. "Why didn't we know about her, Chase?"

"It's a long story."

"Who's her mother?" my brother demanded.

I paused, unwilling to have them think poorly of Teagan.

"Teagan Tessler," my father stated without hesitation. "If the little girl is five, it must be her."

Kat was sitting on the couch and held her head in one hand, watching my parent's reaction.

"Yes. You didn't know because I didn't know."

"The bitch that married your best friend? Has he been raising your kid? That's soooo fucked up," Kevin murmured under his breath.

"Kevin, let your brother finish," Dad admonished. "Go on, Chase."

"Yes. I'm not gonna lie, it hit me like a Mack truck. I'm still figuring shit out, but right now, my first priority is helping Remi."

"Remi?" Mom asked. "That's a unique name."

Kat cleared her throat.

"Her name is Remilia Victoria. After you and Teagan's mother, Mom."

"How... wonderful!" My mother was a bit stunned; her eyes flooded with tears and she covered her mouth with her hand. "It's a beautiful name."

"She's a beautiful child. It suits her." I pulled out the pictures and handed them to her. My dad looked at them with her as she shuffled through them one-by-one. The picture that Teagan showed me at the airport was among them.

"She has your eyes," my dad said. He wasn't one to get emotional, but he was not left unmoved.

"Yeah. Yours too. She's amazing. Sweet and smart, and so brave." I could feel my voice begin to crack and I cleared my voice. "She's been through so much, and she's still happy. Teagan is a very good mother, and Jensen loves her as his own."

"How can you say anything nice about that bitch after what she did to you? Or that no-good friend of yours?" Kevin hissed angrily.

"Kevin!" My mother's voice was as harsh as I'd ever heard it. "Chase needs our support."

"Who said I wasn't supportive? But keeping him in the dark about his kid? That's unforgivable." He shook his head in disgust.

"It does no good to talk like that, Kevin. Chase has enough to deal with," my father's voice was stern.

My mother stood and came to me, putting her arms around me, concentrating her gaze on my face. "Chase, I'm sure it does hurt."

"It does. I can't deny that." I accepted her hug but then stepped back. "The thing is; when I walked in to meet her, Remi knew exactly who I was. Teagan and Jensen told her the truth all along. She had pictures of me and her mom by her bed in the hospital; she called me Daddy as if I'd always been with her."

"Well, that's… pretty unexpected." My mother's face was perplexed.

My emotions would not be held at bay and I broke down, tears starting to stream down my face. "She's the most amazing thing to ever happen to me, and I love her dearly. Teagan wasn't a match for her marrow, and so she called me to

332

see if I could be. Thankfully, I can give to her and the transplant is scheduled for tomorrow morning. I wanted to tell you because the minute I check into the hospital tomorrow, the press will be on me. I'm sure it will be all over the web before I'm even out of surgery. I didn't want you to find out that way."

I pinched the bridge of my nose and sat down next to Kat. Immediately her arm came around my shoulders, and she dropped her forehead to my shoulder.

"I notice you're awfully quiet, Kathryn," Kevin accused. "You knew, didn't you?"

"For a while. I didn't know what to do. Chase seemed to finally be happy and that's why I didn't say anything. There is more to the story, and Chase doesn't need you to hate on Teagan, right now. She thought she was backing off so he could have his dream career."

"When you left for a week, that's where you were? In Atlanta?" Clearly, my mother was hurt that no one told her.

"Yes, Mom. I'm sorry," Kat admitted. "I didn't know if Chase would be there, and Jensen was traveling. Teagan needed my help. I couldn't tell you about Remi because it was Chase's place to do that. I gave Teagan his number so she could tell him, and I thought they needed time to work it out before the family was told. Please don't be upset."

"Well, what's done is done. What can we do for you, Son?" Dad's voice was comforting. He'd always been the voice of reason; ready to deal with shit that can't be changed. "Do you want us in Atlanta? We should be there."

"Remi has to have massive radiation to kill her own defective bone marrow before she receives the transplant. It's extremely dangerous she'll be extremely susceptible to infection, so no visitors will be allowed to see her; not even Teagan or me. At least, not until we see if the transplant is working and the doctor gives the okay."

"Oh hell," my dad said.

My mother, now back sitting next to him gasped loudly. "Will this cure her?"

"No guarantees."

"Damn, that's rough," Kevin added. "I'm sorry, Chase."

"This is the last shot. It has to work." My heart was aching in my chest. I hadn't admitted that to anyone before, not even Teagan. Remi might not make it. I had to be strong for Teagan, but in that moment, I was helpless to my own grief.

"Oh, my god!" My mother sat with a look of stunned disbelief on her face. She quickly brushed a tear away in an attempt to keep me from noticing she was crying.

My dad came to sit beside me and took me into a strong embrace. He patted my back hard. "Remi will be fine. She's got one hell of a father. You don't lose, Chase. You won't lose at this." He patted my back again and I hugged him back hard. It was all I could do not to lose it, my hands fisting in the back of his company work shirt. "And a Granddad wants to meet his new baby girl."

Relief rushed through me at my family's acceptance and support. Even Kevin seemed to be coming around. "Thanks, Dad. That means a lot." My father's confidence helped. I'd relied on him to put shit in perspective my entire life and so far, he'd pretty much nailed it.

"Yes," Mom agreed, wiping more tears from her face. "I'll pack some things after lunch. Kevin and Kat can take care of the house and business, right kids?"

Kat nodded and Kevin agreed. "Yeah. We'll be fine."

"Mom, Dad; I only ask one thing; Teagan's really hurting, and she's been dealing with Remi's illness for three years. I know you're probably angry, but please don't confront her or Jensen about any of this. We're dealing with it in our own way. I'll tell you the details eventually, but right now it's just too much to dig through."

"But what about—" Mom began.

"Roma," Dad chastised. "Leave the boy alone."

"I just was going to ask when we'd get to meet our granddaughter."

"Soon. When the doctors clear it." I answered. "Teagan and I agree that I'll be in her life, and that means, she's part of this family."

"Will it be a custody fight?" Kevin asked. "Obviously, you can crush him. You've got the dough."

"No. My name is on Remi's birth certificate, but she loves Jensen, so for her sake, I won't force him out of her life."

"Wow," Kevin said, getting up and walking back into the kitchen. "I'd have beaten the shit out of him, at least." He called behind him. "I mean, we all thought you and Teagan would get married after graduation."

"Yeah. Who said I didn't kick his ass, Kevin? It still stings, but going forward, we all have to put Remi first."

"How does Bronwyn fit in?"

"She's not fitting in." I flushed. "Like I said, it's a long story, and Remi is the focus."

"You're acting like a real man, Son. Life is hard, and a man is measured more by how he handles the bad shit. A man does what needs to be done for his family no matter the sacrifice to himself. You make me very proud, Son." My dad nodded his approval. His features were filled with admiration.

"Very," Mom agreed. She came to me and rose up on tiptoe to kiss my cheek. She patted my chest. "I can't wait to meet her. I'm sure I'll adore her."

"She'll love you, too."

"Come in and eat. I made your favorite."

"Chicken Parm?" I asked, already knowing the answer. I smiled and followed her into the kitchen.

"Of course!"

With the knot in my stomach now gone, lunch sounded good. I felt sure that when they heard the whole story about Teagan's father's threats and Bronwyn's deception, that they would forgive Teagan, too. One look at Remi and they'd be owned just like I had been.

Chapter 18

Teagan

Remi was in isolation up on the tenth floor and we'd been unable to see her since her radiation. She took it better than I did. The nurses played with her and convinced her the whole thing was like an adventure, so she went into it well, but it was the after effects I was worried about. The high-dose radiation was given to her entire body, so she would likely have side effects of vomiting and headaches, among others.

My heart ached because she'd be suffering and I wouldn't even be able to comfort her. There is nothing worse for a mother than for her child to be hurting and being unable to help. No doubt she'd be crying for me.

Jensen and I were with Chase in the outpatient center waiting room. The whole thing from prepping him until he'd be discharged would be six or seven hours. Remi would receive the new marrow before Chase was even out of anesthesia.

Jensen was more used to long hospital waits, and he'd flung himself into one of the chairs by the window with his legs sprawled in front of him as he fiddled with his phone.

"Is he okay?" Chase asked, nodding in Jensen's direction.

My eyes followed his lead. "Yes, I think so. He's always been so strong, but I know he's scared, too."

"I'm surprised he's here. It's to speak to Remi's doctors, isn't it?"

"That's part of it, but he's still your friend, Chase."

"Is he?"

"How can you forgive me and not Jensen?"

"It isn't that I don't want to forgive him; I'm trying. He was my best friend and he should have told me what was going on with you, not used the situation to steal you from me."

"There's plenty of blame to go around, I guess," I murmured. "Jensen is hurting, too. You care about him or you wouldn't have asked about him, and he cares about you or he wouldn't be here. Think about it."

"I guess."

It was a pretty big admission and one I hoped would help heal the rift between the two men.

"God, I'm so damn thirsty," Chase murmured, looking longingly at the bottle of water I was holding.

I flushed and shoved it guiltily in my purse. "I'm sorry. Are you hungry?"

"Yes, but it's tolerable. Not being able to drink anything is much worse than skipping a meal."

I smiled. "Remi has gone through it twice for the port. She never complained this much." I nudged him with my shoulder, and smiled, trying to lighten the mood.

He huffed out a laugh. "I guess I'm one big pussy."

Looking at him, I realized how he was putting his whole life on hold to be here. "Chase," I said seriously, leaning into him again and maintaining the contact between us because I couldn't help it. "Thank you."

He was leaning forward in his chair with his elbows on his knees, and he pushed back against me to nudge me back. "You don't have to thank me, Teagan. She's mine, too."

"I know, but I'm still grateful."

He was casually handsome in dark jeans, a light blue striped button down and white sneakers. Chase turned toward me. "Me, too." Those two softly spoken words lifted a huge weight from my soul. I didn't know what to say. What could I say that would be enough?

We hadn't had a chance to talk about his trip to Greenville or his parent's reaction and that was something I needed to know in advance. I had considered that they might already be in town. "Is your family coming to be here for you?"

"Just Mom and Dad. Any minute now, probably."

"Thanks for the warning," I said wryly. Inside I was panicking; scared of the inevitable confrontation. "How did they take the news?"

"Mostly good. I can see you're stressing. They won't bring up the past, Teagan. I made it clear that was between us, and I didn't want you fretting over it."

"Really?"

"Yes," he nodded. His green eyes roamed over my face in a caress. "It was a shock, but they handled it better than I expected."

"I'm glad but… I'm going to be sitting with them… for hours," I stammered. "Alone. Surely, they'll have questions."

"Maybe, but I promise they won't attack you."

"Did you tell them about Bronwyn's phone call? I mean, the real reason I didn't tell you about Remi?"

"Teagan, Relax. It's not their business."

"Yes, but I'm worried. I mean, without the facts they'll misunderstand my motives, just like you did. I can't have them believing the worst of me."

"No, I didn't tell them about it. It's personal, and it was too much to get into yesterday. You're free to tell them anything you want, but mostly, they'll want to know about

Remi. You should have seen my dad light up like a firecracker when he saw her picture."

The thought filled me with joy. No doubt, he could see himself in Remi's little face. Chase looked so much like him, and there was no mistaking her resemblance to him. "Her eyes."

"Yes. Oh, my God, he was beaming!"

"How'd your mom do?"

"She's sad that she hasn't known her, and that she's sick."

"I understand."

"Soon she'll be playing Barbies and dress-up with Remi like she does with Kevin's girls. What about your dad?" Chase asked. "I remember that you told me he tested to donate also, but you never said how he did with Remi."

"That's because I've barely spoken to him since he basically disowned me. He paid my tuition so I could finish nursing school, but we don't see each other at all anymore. He didn't want his political career stained by his promiscuous daughter. I only asked him to test because I was desperate, but we don't have a relationship anymore. Remi doesn't even know him."

Chase's face showed his deep concern. "That's sad, Teag. You're his only child and Remi is his only grandchild."

"I know, but in all of this misery, he's never even come to see her." I always got that sick, empty feeling when I spoke about my father. I had nothing for him but contempt and resentment.

"What a bastard!" He shook his head in barely disguised disgust.

"Over there, Roma. There they are!"

I heard Frank Forrester's voice behind us, and Chase stood to greet them. Jensen saw them too, and made his way over to our group. I was nervous and didn't know how to react, and I could see the same apprehension painted all over Jensen.

"Mom, Dad." Chase greeted them, hugging his mom and shaking his father's hand. "I'm glad you're here. You remember Teagan and Jensen."

"Of course," Frank said. He moved forward to give me a hug and then offered his hand to Jensen. "Hello, Jensen."

"Hello. It's good to see you. Roma," he greeted her. "How have you both been?"

"Hello, Jensen. We're fine, thank you." He hovered, awkwardly unknowing of what to do, until Roma held out her arms to him. Relief flooded his features as he took her up on the hug.

Afterward, my eyes skirted to her face. How would she treat me? Guilt was probably dousing me like a deluge. "Hello," I said softly. "I'm sorry." I blurted it out because I couldn't stop myself. I was emotional; on the cusp of tears.

Jensen's instinct was to put an arm around me and Chase noted it, and tension visibly coiled all over him. It was an innocent enough gesture. Jensen and Chase were both protective, and neither of them was to blame for their reactions.

Roma stepped forward and took both of my hands in hers. "Let's just worry about Remi, shall we?" She had such a gentle face and she and I had been so close while Chase and I were dating. My own mother had been dead for years, and Roma had made me feel like her own child. They'd treated both Jensen and I as if we were part of their family, and technically, I guess we were. We both spent many holidays and school breaks with them.

"I'm so very sorry," I said again, and squeezed her hands. I prayed she could feel how deeply I meant it.

"Hush. There is plenty of time to sort everything out." She still had that gentle comforting way about her. Roma

Forrester was the epitome of nurturing, and her kindness caused tears to rain down my face. "Chase told us enough for now. I trust my son and if he forgives you, then you must deserve forgiveness," she said simply. "How is that beautiful little angel?"

My heart soared at her words, thankful to see love and not hate in her eyes. I wiped away a tear or two that managed to escape my eyes. "Um, we're waiting for her doctor. He said he'd come down here to give us an update before Chase's surgery. She was irradiated last night, so I'm not sure how she is."

"We're all worried about her," Jensen added, "but anything would be better than more chemo."

"Chase explained it yesterday. Poor little thing." Chase's dad said before turning his attention to Jensen. "You're doing well. I see you all over ESPN, lately. You're practically the new Frank Gifford."

Jensen smirked and seemed more at ease. He rolled his eyes. "Chris Fowler, maybe. I'm getting there. I don't love the traveling, though."

"I can imagine."

We continued to talk and clock watch. I could see Chase's agitation as the minutes ticked away and Dr. Radar still hadn't made his appearance.

"What time do you have to do this, Chase?" Frank put a hand on the top of Chase's shoulder.

He looked at his watch. "Soon, I hope. It's all this goddamned waiting that drives me crazy."

We all sat down to wait; the men were talking together and Roma sat next to me. "We've missed you and Jensen, Teagan. It was like I lost two of my own children. I wish you would have felt able to talk to us."

"I didn't know what to do. I just—" I shrugged sadly as the memories of those first days after Chase left surfaced. "He was so happy about Arsenal. I couldn't ruin it. He wouldn't have gone. I couldn't take the chance he'd blame me, years later, for missing out."

Her gaze washed over my face, her expression filled with sorrow. "You can't know that's what he would have done. It was his responsibility, too."

I nodded and swallowed at the painful lump in my throat, looking down at my hands. "I know, but I thought, I'd finish school and then go over there, and it'd all work out. Then he could have both." Every word hurt as I said it. "I never expected my dad to be so awful." Part of me wanted to let her know about that fateful phone call, and another didn't want to cast any shadow over the image she had of Chase. "I didn't expect Jensen to go to him, either."

Roma's voice wavered. "I wish you would have come to us, darling. We would have helped you. When the little one got sick, you should have called us to help, too."

"I didn't know what to say or how to reach out, Roma. Jensen's been so good to us, I didn't want to hurt him, and I didn't want to dig up the past. Chase seemed happy."

"He was so heartbroken that he almost gave it all up anyway. He loved you, Teagan."

Chase told me he was heartbroken, but he never mentioned that he almost gave up his professional career. "I know, but I was so confused. My father's threats, and other stuff... I was a complete mess. Having Remi made life bearable. I concentrated on her, and that's how I managed to get through it."

Roma beamed at the mention of Remi. "I'm so anxious to meet her. Chase practically soars when he speaks of her. And the pictures! She's so beautiful."

"She's the light of my life. I'm so grateful that Chase came back. Remi adores him."

"Thank you for naming her after me, Teagan. I can't tell you how much that means to me. It's telling about your motives. We know you were thinking of Chase. Misguided," she patted my hand with a wry glance, "But, pure in your intent."

I was so grateful Roma was being so gracious and loving. She could have been accusing and judgmental, easy to think the worst. "I loved you like my own mother," I admitted tearfully.

"Oh, Darling!" Roma exclaimed and enfolded me in her arms. "You precious girl! It's going to be alright, now. You'll see."

We were both tearful; the moment was a mixture of joy, regret, and worry.

"Chase Forrester?" An orderly called from the door that separated the surgical suite from the waiting room.

"Oh," I was startled by the abruptness because we'd been waiting so long.

Everyone stood and Chase lifted a hand. "That's me." In a second or two he was in front of me. "I guess this is it. I'd hoped to speak to Dr. Radar before I went in."

"Are you going in with Chase, Teagan?" Jensen asked. Frank seemed surprised that Jensen would ask such a thing. There was still much to explain, but now wasn't the time.

"I was, but I thought Dr. Radar would have been down to speak to us by now."

"You don't have to. It's just a needle prick," Chase murmured, the corner of his mouth lifting in the start of a teasing smile. "It's more important to find out what's going on with Remi."

"Chase Forrester!" The man called again, clearly irritated by the delay.

"Better get going or that dickhead is going to lose his shorts halfway up his ass," Jensen added wryly.

Chase burst out laughing and laid a hand hard on the top of Jensen's shoulder giving it a squeeze. "No shit!"

"No. Definitely, *shit.*" Jensen grinned back.

I was elated by this little glimpse of camaraderie between Chase and Jensen. It was reminiscent of our college years, and it was a spark of hope that we'd all be okay. Chase's parents joined us all in a chuckle.

Chase's eyes locked with mine.

I moved in front of him not sure what I wanted, but needing something. "I'll come back as soon as Dr. Radar shows. If they'll let me through."

"Don't worry, Monkey" he said easily then cupped the side of my face with his big hand. He brushed across my cheekbone with his thumb. "Everything is going to be fine."

I wrapped my hand around his wrist. His skin was warm and he was strong.

"Chase Forrester!" The orderly called again.

"Gotta go before this guy has a coronary," he smirked boyishly.

"We'll see you in recovery, Son," Frank said as he started away, holding a hand behind him in a half-assed wave as he disappeared through the door and it shut behind him.

Jensen had a short haircut for his ESPN gig, but Chase's hair was long enough to reach his nape and had a slight natural wave in the tawny strands. He had a healthy tan from his hours on the soccer field and he moved with an easy grace that had every woman in the room turning her head as he passed.

"Now we wait, I guess," Roma said.

"Does anyone want coffee? Frank offered.

I couldn't help looking around the room and toward the hallway where I expected Dr. Radar to appear an hour before.

"I'd love some, dear." Roma's voice held the same soothing tone I remembered.

"What's taking Dr. Radar so long?" I wondered aloud, starting to pace.

"Don't assume anything, Teagan. He might be behind on rounds or something." Jensen was standing near me and offered his reassurance. "If anything was wrong, we would have been paged."

I nodded and ran a hand through my hair. "Yeah." He was right, but I was a nervous wreck. I wanted the update to settle all of us, but more, so Chase could know what was happening with her before they put him under. "I just want to know she's okay."

"I'll see what I can find out," Jensen began, but just as he turned to leave, Dr. Radar appeared. Jensen's steps halted as quickly as they began. "Here he comes."

Dr. Radar had on dark rimmed glasses and a white lab coat over his teal scrubs. All of us stood immediately and gathered around him.

"Dr. Radar, these are Chase's parents, Frank and Roma Forrester," Jensen introduced. "This is Remi's doctor. He is the chief of childhood cancer at the hospital."

The doctor shook hands with Roma and Frank. "It's nice to meet you both."

"How's Remi doing?" Frank's question was anxious.

"She's doing pretty well for as weak as she's been." His answer was full of caution and his expression stoic.

"What does that mean?" Roma was standing next to Frank, her attention fully centered on Dr. Radar.

I sighed heavily. It wasn't a resounding endorsement from the doctor, and I knew him well enough to know he was choosing his words carefully. Jensen stood silently at my side, drawing the same conclusion as I was.

"She's vomiting some, and it's been hard on her. We're giving her fluids through her port. Her infection tests, before the radiation late last night, showed we'd eradicated it, which is good. The sooner we can get Chase's marrow into her, the better."

"What's the process doctor?"

"As soon as it's removed from Chase, it will be tested for infection and impurities, but generally, it goes into a bag, like a blood donation and it will be administered to Remi in a similar fashion through her port."

"That's it?"

Frank and Roma continued to question Dr. Radar.

"Yes. I'm afraid Chase has the hard part. He'll be very sore for a while. We'll puncture his pelvis in four places to extract the marrow."

"How long will it take for the marrow to be replaced?" Frank asked.

Dr. Radar's eyes met mine over the top of Roma's head. He smiled, answering all of the their questions patiently. "Chase will be completely replenished in about three weeks. Remi, we're hoping, within a month."

"Do we have to wait a month to see her?"

"No. We'll watch her cell count and play it by ear. She's in a room that has a lot of windows, so technically, you can see her, but I'm afraid it will only agitate her. She'll want Teagan, Jensen or Chase in the room with her, and right now, that's not possible. It's better to let her rest for a few days."

"Poor little squirt." Jensen inhaled a deep breath and threaded both of his hands on top of his head.

Dr. Radar continued to converse with Chase's mom and dad. "Are you all from Atlanta?"

"Greenville, South Carolina."

"Well, at least that's not too far. It's pretty up there."

I turned to Jensen and spoke in low tones. "I'm going to go back and see if I can give Chase an update on Remi."

He nodded. "Okay. Text me and let me know what you're doing. I know we can't see her, but I still want to go up and talk to the nurses."

"Okay." I reached out and laid a hand on his bicep. "You're a good dad." He was a special person and I loved him, dearly. Not in the same way I loved Chase, but he had a big heart, and he never held back with Remi, and they were close."

"You sure about that?"

"Yes."

I walked to the surgery reception. "My name is Teagan Jeffers. May I go in and wait with Chase Forrester until they take him to surgery?"

"Teagan, Teagan, Teagan…" The thin young woman scanned the list of visitors approved to enter for my name. She slid a pen down the list that was clipped to the hard board she held with her other arm. "Teagan… Tessler?" She looked up with a smile. She was wearing surgical scrubs and her hair and shoes were covered as well.

"Yes, that's me. Tessler is my maiden name."

"Can I see a piece of ID please?"

I offered my driver's license by flipping open my wallet.

"Sure, this way." She led me through the same doors that Chase had disappeared thirty minutes earlier. "Chase Forrester. That name is familiar," the nurse mused. She led me into a big room that looked similar to an emergency room, with a row of smaller rooms on each side of a main aisle with a workstation in the middle. The tile was stark white and magnified the florescent light to an almost offensive level. It smelled of antiseptic and bleach.

I couldn't help but smile as the woman rattled on. "Oh, I remember. There is a super hot soccer player that plays for that English soccer club, right? But, I think he's from Carolina."

"Yeah. We met at Clemson."

She stopped abruptly. "This Chase Forrester is that Chase Forrester?"

To be honest, I was surprised we made it all morning in the waiting room without someone recognizing either Chase or Jensen.

I let out a light laugh. "The one and only."

"Wow. I hope he's okay. I mean, I hope he's not sick, or anything," she pried.

HIPPA laws kept her from asking directly, and I wasn't in the mood to share. "He's okay."

"He's in room six, right on this end."

"Thank you." I walked to the door and knocked on the glass.

The nurse was hovering, no doubt wanting a glance at Chase.

"Come in," his deep voice said from the other side of the door. There were three quarter length curtains pulled closed, so it blocked her view. I had to push through them, but closed the sliding door behind me.

"Hey, you," he said. He was on a portable hospital bed with an IV already started in his arm. "Did you hear from Dr. Radar?"

"Yeah. Your parents are giving him a run for his money. Hey, sexy. Nice dress," I teased gently.

Chase rolled his eyes. "This fucking thing. I'd rather be naked."

My left eyebrow shot up. "I'm sure that would make for happy nurses."

"Wouldn't it make you happy?" he grinned.

"Could be," I laughed.

"How's Remi?"

"Dr. Radar said she's doing okay. She's throwing up and has a headache. He said he's cautiously optimistic."

He motioned for me to sit down on the edge of his bed, and took my hand and brought it to his lips, brushing his lips across my knuckles. "It's almost over, baby. You just have to be strong for a little longer. It's all going to work out and Remi is going to grow up, perfect."

There were so many things still up in the air. When he went back to England, what would happen? Would he go next week when he was healed from the donation? The questions raced through my mind.

"I hope so."

"My dad told me that I win. I'll win this, too."

"Sounds good." I couldn't help reaching out to touch his face. He had shaved that morning, but there was already a light smattering of stubble on his strong jaw. His green eyes were clear and intense. "I know we have a lot to talk about." His thumb rubbed back and forth over the top of my hand and I never wanted him to let go. I needed him so much... for no other reason than I loved him. I wanted to be close to him, I wanted Remi to grow up having her dad, but I needed him like I needed air.

"Yes. I love you."

"That, and Remi to get better is all I need." He lifted my hand and kissed the inside of my wrist.

A knock at the door signaled a nurse's entry just seconds before the door slid open. "Okay, Mr. Forrester, we're almost ready for you."

"I was thinking maybe I should just get that local thing, instead, nurse. I want to be awake for my daughter."

The nurse shot him a skeptical look. "No you don't. Trust me. Those needles are more like sharp pipes."

I agreed with the nurse. I didn't want him to feel any more pain than necessary. "Chase, Dr. Radar said we can't see Remi for a few days anyway."

"I know, but I want to be up there close to her."

"You'll be awake in few hours." I tried to comfort him.

"But—" he started to argue.

"Chase Forrester. Shut up and take your medicine," I admonished with a raised eyebrow, which was met with a smile and a squeeze of my hand.

The nurse held up a small syringe. "This will relax you and you might feel drowsy. It's not the main juice. You'll get that in the O.R." She quickly inserted the needle into the IV port. "Okay, I'm off to hear the nurses blather on and on about this famous soccer star! It's all they can talk about." She moved to the door and pushed it open, shooting a smile in Chase's direction. "Good thing I'm not a fan of soccer." She left and the door shut.

"Kiss me," Chase demanded. "I've wanted to kiss you all morning."

I didn't hesitate and moved closer to press my mouth to his. He opened to me, and his tongue sought mine, both of his hands coming up to cup the sides of my face. It was sensuous and delicious.

When I pulled back, Chase's eyes drooped. "Holy fuck." He blinked, trying to keep his eyes open. "That shit is fast," he mumbled, his head lolling to one side as he fell asleep. "Love… you."

I brushed the hair back off of his forehead, lovingly. There were two faces I could stare at until the end of time, and his was one of them.

The door slid open a bit and the funny nurse popped her head in. "Is he out?" She smiled brightly.

I couldn't help but smile. I hadn't been this at ease in years. "Yep. Like a light."

"Good." She pushed the doors wide and came in to push a lever at the bottom of the bed with her foot. A tall male nurse followed her in and the two of them started to maneuver the bed out of the small room. "He'll be back in here for recovery. The procedure won't take more than an hour and half once we begin. He'll be fine and awake in no time. You're welcome to wait."

"Thank you. I think I will." I pulled out my phone to text Jensen, asking him to let Roma and Frank know that I was staying where I was until Chase was awake and to keep me updated about Remi because I could be up there in literally five minutes.

My heart swelled with hope for the first time in what felt like forever. The future seemed brighter and I was looking forward to good things to come. I had to embrace Chase's confidence that Remi would make a complete and full recovery. For the first time, I felt like it could happen. Really happen. After all, my baby girl was about to receive the stuff of champions.

Chapter 19

CHASE

Son of a bitch!

I couldn't open my eyes, but already, my entire pelvis and lower back were on fire.

"Chase." I heard Teagan's voice in a sort of fog and her soft hand stroked the side of my face. I struggled to open my eyes but it was as if they were weighted down with lead. My body wanted to sleep, but my mind wanted to wake up. "I'm here with you."

I reached for the hand on my jaw and held it. "Remi?" I managed to mumble. "How's Remi? Did she get it yet?" I didn't try to open my eyes again but reached out, hoping Teagan would take my hand. I was rewarded instantly when she held it in between both of hers. The familiar scent of her perfume wafted around me, a pleasant replacement from the sterile smell of the hospital. The antiseptic one that always smacked you in the face the second you walked through the front door, and only got stronger as you moved further in. Everything reeked of it.

"She has, babe. They took it up right away. Jensen has been upstairs with her the whole time so I could be here with you." She paused for a second. "I mean, he can't be with her exactly, but he's up on her floor so he can keep us informed of what is going on. We just have to wait now."

I nodded and swallowed. My mouth was desert dry and my head was laden with remnants of the anesthesia fog. I needed water. "May I have a glass of water?"

"I'm not sure." She patted my hand and then let go of it. "I'll ask. Be right back."

I could hear the sound of a door sliding open and a cool draft blew over me as she closed it behind her. Again, I tried to open my eyes, but it was difficult. I'd never been put out before, and it was as if only a second before, I was being wheeled out of this room and now, poof, the whole thing was over. The only proof of it was the awful throbbing in my hips and lower back. It hurt like a bitch. Logic told me the pain would get worse before it would get better. I was certain they'd given me pain meds in my IV and that was probably another reason I couldn't wake up like I wanted.

Swoosh! The door slid open and another cold draft blew through the room. The head of the bed was elevated, but still, I lifted my head and willed my eyes to open. Teagan entered with a plastic glass filled with water and one of those bendy straws.

Swoosh! She slid the door shut behind her, came closer, and held the straw to my lips.

"I'm not an invalid, babe," I said, trying to take the glass. My hands felt like they were filled with lead. "Fuck," I muttered, letting my head drop to the pillow and letting Teagan help me with the glass. I took a long draw on the water, and the cool liquid relieved the dryness in my mouth and throat. I sucked on it again until Teagan took it away. "Wait," I said, wanting more. I was parched. I hadn't had anything to drink for at least twelve hours.

"Chase, you can't have a lot to drink or eat yet. The nurse said general anesthesia affects people differently, and because this is the first time you've had it, they're cautious. She said some people get nauseous and throw-up. Heaving will make your pain worse, so let's take it easy, okay?"

"I can't believe this shit has me so wiped out. Isn't there some kind of medication to bring me out of it?"

"There's no rush. We can't see Remi anyway. The last text from Jensen said she was sleeping."

"Not at all?"

"Her room has a glass wall so we could look through it, but Dr. Radar is concerned that if she sees us, she'll cry and carry on. I tend to agree, as hard as it is. I don't want it any harder on her than necessary, even though I miss her so much."

"Me, too." I signed heavily. "I guess I'm so anxious to see if the transplant is working. I can't stand it."

"I can relate, but results won't show for at least a few days. We've been through two rounds of chemo, and waiting to find out if it worked was a bitch."

"I wish we could see her. My poor little princess." My heart was full of Remi and Teagan, and it was hard to imagine any future without seeing them both every day.

"Maybe we can go look in on her when she's asleep. Jensen said it's hard not showing her he's there."

"I'm glad he's close." As weird as it was, I meant it. The resentment I had for him was lessening every time I saw how much he did for Teagan or how much he loved our little girl. "Are my parents with him?"

"Yes. They are basically camped out in one of the waiting rooms. I spoke to your mom on the phone. Do you want to call her?"

"In a bit." Teagan nodded. "We have to do something for her, but they won't let her have anything from outside." I closed my eyes again because I had to. Talking with Teagan helped, but I was still very sleepy.

"I've been thinking about that, too. If she's in there for weeks, we'll have to get creative."

I listened to her soothing voice wash over me; the bright light of the room still invaded in a yellow hue through my closed eyelids. "Like what?" I wondered.

"When she's feeling well enough, we do a lot of dancing and singing to her favorite songs. It's her favorite thing. Maybe we can make her a video of the three of us."

"What, like Barney?" I asked skeptically. I didn't think I'd be able to pull that off with a straight face. Teagan and I used to go dancing a ton, and that was part of my life I'd sort of put away. I hadn't wanted to try to re-create the same experiences with anyone else. Bronwyn was the only woman I'd dated for more than just a few dates, and we were focused on working out and hanging out with the team.

Teagan chuckled. "What? Remi would be shocked you think she's such a baby. No, remember she likes Justin Timberlake, Pink, Katy Perry, Shawn Mendes, Taylor Swift; you know, the new stuff."

I smiled. "At least that's something."

"Will they let her have her tablet?"

"I don't know."

"Well, dancing is cool. I like dancing." I smirked and looked at her.

"I remember," she smiled warmly. "I miss that part of us."

"I miss the whole thing," I admitted.

The dimples in her cheeks appeared with a bright smile. She was gorgeous. She was dressed in a floral dress that swayed gently when she walked, and pretty, strappy white sandals.

It was quiet for a while and I could hear Teagan rustling through her purse, presumably to get her phone. I opened one eye to watch her type out a text.

"I'm asking Jensen what it's like up there. I'm wondering if there are a lot of patients up there in isolation, or if it's just a small part of one floor?"

I sucked in a deep breath and closed my eyes again. "Why?"

"I'm thinking we can do a show for her?"

The shock of her words woke me up fairly well. A show? I laughed in disbelief. "Like what?"

"She's going to be sad, so I don't know, something to cheer her up."

"Yeah, but you still haven't said what kind of show. Like a puppet show?"

"It depends. If the windows are thick, she won't hear us through the glass. That's why I have to find out what we can get by with. If it's a busy floor we won't be able to, but if it's just Remi and a couple others, maybe we can play music loud enough."

I smiled so wide my face almost hurt. Teagan was amazing. "You're willing to make a fool of yourself up there?" I goaded.

"No. But I'm willing to make a fool of you and Jensen." Teagan giggled softly.

I laughed again. "From what Dr. Radar said, it could be weeks before she was feeling up to anything."

"I know. That gives me time to whip you and Jensen into shape."

I crossed my arms over my chest. The IV was still embedded in the top of my hand and it was a nuisance. "I see."

"Will you have to go back to London? I mean, if it takes a full month for Remi's new marrow to take hold, I assume you'll have some games and tournaments coming up that Arsenal will want you back for."

Her question was hesitant, but I could tell that she'd just been waiting for the right time to ask. I'd been in frequent contact with Coach Noonan many times since I'd been in Atlanta and while they'd been understanding, the end of the season would come soon enough, and history was cruel. A missing forward in a few important games was the very reason they'd scouted me in the first place, and it hadn't escaped my thoughts. I hesitated to bring it up to Teagan for fear she'd think I was putting Arsenal before Remi, but long-term, I needed my career to take care of Remi. We still hadn't discussed the logistics of making everything work, and I didn't feel this was the right time.

"I may get in a few games if her prognosis is excellent and we're only waiting for her to get out of isolation. Until we figure everything out, I don't think it's wise to burn any bridges."

She seemed unsurprised by my answer, but I could see sadness she was not able to hide. "That's smart."

"I didn't want to discuss this when my dick is almost hanging out and I'm wearing a dress," I teased, trying to lighten the mood.

"Hmmm. I could have sworn you liked it when your dick was hanging out. Maybe I'm remembering wrong." Her response was dry and her expression flirty.

The drugs were finally starting to wear off and I leaned forward to grab her. "Oh, sassy, are we?"

Teagan squealed loudly as I hauled her on top of me. Both of us laughed happily until I started to kiss her hungrily. My heart exploded in my chest. I loved her beyond anything, and now that I stopped fighting this thing between us, and allowing myself to believe she returned my feelings, a huge weight had been lifted and the dark cloud that had been

358

inhabiting my heart for years was beginning to disappear. Since her confession that she and Jensen had already decided to divorce: any guilt I felt was gone.

We kissed breathlessly for a few minutes until Teagan pulled away breathlessly. "Chase, the nurses could come in any second." Her sweet breath washed over my face deliciously.

"Maybe they're spying on us through the crack in the curtains," I suggested, my lips curving up against hers. "Let's give them a show."

She pushed gently on my chest with both hands. I covered one with mine and pulled it up to kiss the palm suggestively, using my open mouth and tongue to hint at what I really wanted to do. Teagan flushed and her hips arched into mine with a small groan. I knew the move was an involuntary response, but it didn't matter. It felt amazing. "Chase."

"If you don't want my dick hanging out, why don't you give me a place to put it?" I murmured suggestively against her mouth. Her breath rushed out and her small pink tongue reached for my top lip. "Hmmm?" I coaxed.

Her dress gave me easy access to the smooth skin of her thighs and the curve of her hip. She was wearing a thong and that only made my cock even hungrier. I pressed her hips into mine so she'd have no doubt what I wanted. There was something about the moment that was intoxicating. I didn't even care if the whole world saw us, I felt ravenous.

"Chase," she groaned again. "Stop. We have to stop." She pulled back, leaning away so I couldn't reach her mouth with mine. "Chase." Teagan shook her head.

My hands curled hungrily into the bare flesh of her thighs in pure unadulterated frustration. "Uhhhhh," I sucked in a deep breath and sat back. "What do you expect? Bare legs, short dress... lace fucking thong? I'm not made of stone."

She offered a sexy smile as she climbed off of my lap and moved to the chair. She reached forward and wrapped a hand fully around my erection. "Are you sure? Feels like it to me."

I shot her a wry look. "Now who needs to stop? You're going to leave me in pain."

"You seemed to forget about your pain for a second there. The pain meds must be working."

The ache in my pelvis was still prevalent but my need to feel her body warmly sucking on mine, overpowered all else. "I doubt that's it." I waggled my eyebrows at her.

"Yeah, it's probably a bulge in the blanket," she quipped, her brown eyes shining. She was flirting and it was glorious to see her so euphoric and carefree again.

Pain shot through me when we both burst out laughing. I winced but it was worth it. Happiness was like a blanket that was wrapping me up with Teagan, even if she was sitting four feet away in the chair against the wall of the small room.

The door slid open and the plump nurse with the rosy face and gleeful disposition appeared, and instantly my hands fell to my lap to hide the evidence I was still sporting. Teagan bit her lips and her shoulders started to shake when she started laughing.

"How we doing in here?" the nurse asked, glancing from Teagan to me. I could have sworn she knew exactly what had been going on in here just a minute before.

I cleared my throat. "Good. We're good." I knew I sounded as guilty as hell, but there wasn't a damn thing I could do about it.

"That's great to hear!" She pulled out a packet of alcohol soaked gauze and opened it, setting it on the metal instrument tray that sat near the bed. She rolled up the round little stool and sat on it. "Ready to get this IV out?"

Within seconds it was out and she was putting a Band-Aid over the little ball of gauze she'd held over the small needle wound. My other hand was still lying on my lap because

I still had a bit of a problem. Not as much, but it was still there.

My clothes had been placed in a locker with my wallet, shoes and watch in the dressing rooms. The key was hooked to the hem of the gown I wore. "Do you need help getting dressed?" the nurse asked innocently, taking the key. "I'll be back with your clothes and a wheelchair, so you can get out of here."

"I don't think I need a wheelchair."

Her brows shot up and her mouth pressed into a thin line. "Is he always this difficult?" she asked Teagan.

"More," she answered smugly.

"Oh, nice, Teag. Thanks."

"I know you think you can move around fine, honey, but when you get dressed you'll see it's not so easy, and the pain meds we put in the IV are stronger than these pills." She handed a little white envelope to Teagan. "The doctor is sending you enough hydrocodone for two days. I'd suggest only taking it if you're going to sleep or if you can't stand the pain without it. It will clog up your pipes," she said matter-of-factly. "I'll be back."

"What if he has pain longer than that?" Teagan stopped her as she left the room.

"We're cracking down on narcotics scripts. If you need more, you'll have to call the doctor."

She breezed out as quickly as she arrived.

"I won't need the pills, babe."

"Well, I don't want you to suffer if it's not necessary."

"I know. I'll be fine."

"You're such a guy," she huffed wryly.

"As evidenced by the giant wood I had to hide from that old lady."

361

"Epic fail. Like she didn't see it. Please. Is she gonna find your sexy superman underwear in the locker?" she taunted.

"You know you're gonna get it later."

The nurse came back with the wheelchair and my clothes were neatly folded in the seat, amid Teagan's soft giggle.

"Okay, if you're sure you don't need help, I'll leave you in this lovely lady's capable hands," the nurse said and turned right around and left.

I eased myself gingerly to the edge of the bed, at the same time that Teagan made sure the curtains were completely shut. I pulled off the gown and looked down at my body. There were two small butterfly bandages on the top of my hips and I felt behind me and found two more a bit lower down. The doctor said there would be four small incisions to let the needles go in but there wouldn't be stitches, still, if they had to cut the skin before inserting those needles, they must have been monsters. I had a burning sensation start with the throbbing and there were dark purple bruises starting around the incisions.

"Uhhhh!" Teagan gasped when she turned around holding the folded pile of clothes in her hands. "Oh, my god! Chase, that looks bad."

I motioned for her to hand me my boxer briefs so I could start putting them on. I was more than sore, but damn if I was going to admit it. "Don't worry sweetheart. This is nothing." I winced out a smile as I pulled them up and started to repeat the process with the dark denim. Teagan helped me on with my shirt and shoes and I didn't argue with her. It hurt like a son of a bitch but I did my best not to let Teagan know how much.

It was good of Jensen to keep us updated via text but I wanted to see for myself. She opened the door to the room then patted the back of the wheelchair. She was already standing behind it, waiting to wheel me out. "Don't argue." Her voice and expression were stern. "It's too far for you to walk right after surgery. You might pass out."

"Wouldn't dream of it." I used my arms to lower myself gingerly into the chair. Pain shot through me like a lightning bolt. "Jesus," I hissed.

I reached out and hit the electronic button that would open the door to the waiting room so that Teagan could proceed through it. There were camera flashes the second the door opened, and several reporters and camera people met us.

"Ace! Could we have a moment?"

"Why are you in the hospital, Mr. Forrester?"

"Your fans want to know!"

They were all speaking at the same time. This is a surgical waiting room and they at least didn't yell, but it was still unbelievable. One of the nurses or doctors must have leaked it. I figured it would happen.

"What do you want to do?" Teagan had leaned down to speak in my ear.

I put up a hand to indicate I wanted her to pause so I could make a brief statement. If I didn't, they'd end up chasing us upstairs.

"Can everyone be quiet, please, and I'll make one statement. I don't want to answer questions."

They all quieted down, but the cameras kept flashing. "I've just donated bone marrow. I'm fine."

"Who was it for?" A pretty brunette in a bright pink suit shoved a microphone with a Channel 7 marker on it.

"I'm not at liberty to say."

"Will you be playing in the European finals with your team? Will you be well enough?" A thirty-something man whom I recognized as a local sportscaster asked.

"I hope to."

They kept firing questions at me and I put up both of my hands. "No more questions. Thank you." I turned my head toward Teagan. "Let's go. Excuse us."

Teagan started navigating me through the crowd of reporters and bystanders, toward the hallway that would take us out of the surgical wing and into the main hospital. We almost made it through the throng when another reporter asked, "Excuse me miss, aren't you Jensen Jeffer's wife? The commentator from ESPN?"

Fuck, my mind screamed. I should have considered the consequences of letting Teagan stay with me here. The last thing I wanted to do was shame her, but on the other hand, if we said nothing it was like screaming the answer.

"We're all friends from college." It was the truth without airing all of the dirty laundry.

"From Clemson?"

"Clemson: yes." I nodded. "Thank you," I said, effectively dismissing them.

Thankfully, Teagan kept moving and they let us leave. I couldn't see her face but she wasn't saying a goddamned thing. I wanted to crank around in the chair to look at her, but it hurt and the reporters would still be watching which would make it too conspicuous. The fucking thing was, I didn't want to hide anything, but it wasn't just about me. "Are you okay? Teagan?" She didn't answer until we were at the elevators.

"Yes," she said stiffly. "I shouldn't have been so stupid. I'm involved with two well-known men... of course, the press would pounce. I can't believe I didn't think about that."

"I didn't either. We've got Remi on our minds. All of us."

"I just don't want Jensen to suffer any fallout from this."

"Yeah," I answered as the elevator dinged and the metal doors opened. We waited for an older couple to file out, but there wasn't anyone waiting to get into it with us.

Maybe I was being naïve thinking that she'd be able to walk away from Jensen so easily and that no one would suffer any more collateral damage. Maybe I was selfish to think Teagan, Remi and I could build our own little fairy tale. Maybe I needed to rethink things.

The huge weight I thought had lifted during the amazing moments in the recovery room settled back down on me like a sledgehammer. In silence, I pulled my lower lip with my thumb and index finger, contemplating with dread what was the right thing to do. My heart dropped like a stone into the pit of my stomach. I felt sick inside, and the pain filling my heart was a hundred times worse than the physical pain I was experiencing.

Teagan wasn't speaking either, so I knew what that meant; she was thinking the exact fucking thing.

ONE *touch*
AND THE PAIN
melted away.

Chapter 20

CHASE

I wanted to talk to Jensen. I *needed* to talk to him.

It was one thing to hear from Teagan that the two of them were getting divorced, and another to hear it from him. It wasn't that I didn't trust Teagan, it was that Jensen might tell her one thing and be feeling another way. Teagan's explanation gave me a clearer perspective on Jensen's motivation to help her and despite the betrayal still sitting annoyingly in the back of my mind, I understood why things happened the way they did. I was still unhappy with the pain we all suffered, and the lost years, but perpetuating the anger wouldn't help anyone; least of all, Remi.

There was also Teagan's response to the reporters to consider. It gave me pause to wonder if she wasn't torn. We had this rush of emotion between us, and clearly, our behavior had demonstrated that we weren't exactly thinking clearly. No matter how much I loved Teagan and wanted to be with her, was it the right thing? Had too much happened and too much time passed?

I hated that these thoughts nagged at me. I hated all of the doubts messing with my mind and heart and the way it was ate away at my insides like acid, but the bottom line was that we'd all fucked up in a big way. Now, it had to be all about Remi, and Jensen was a huge part of her life. As much as I hated how it happened, it was the reality that had to be dealt with.

I could let myself fantasize about an idyllic life with them; flying high on the brand of happiness like I'd felt with Teagan in the surgery suite. I could even feel relief that knowing the whole truth facilitated the bloom of forgiveness deep inside my heart, but I couldn't lie to myself that there might still be residual feelings between Teagan and Jensen. He'd been with her longer than I had been and that alone, hurt, but nothing would be harsher than to reconcile with Teagan only to watch it fall apart. To lose her again and see it play out in front of me if she stayed married to him, would be the cruelest twist of fate.

Still, I needed the truth. Even if it ripped me to shreds all over again, I had to face it. As much as losing Teagan would destroy me, Jensen could face the same sort of desolation. One of us would be on the losing end.

My parents, Jensen, Teagan, and I had been up in the isolation unit all day waiting. We had no access to Remi, though we could watch her through a window that reminded me of a natural history museum display. The room was divided into two halves separated by glass.

The side we were on was living-room-esque where the family could relax and the other was a high-tech hospital room. There was plenty of plush furniture, a table and chairs, a private bathroom and a nice size television. It at least felt like we were in the same room with Remi, and there was an intercom system set up so we'd be able to speak with her when she woke up. It wasn't nearly as isolated as I feared. No, we couldn't touch her or hold her, but we could see her and talk to her, read to her, and stay with her so she didn't feel alone. If Teagan had her way, we'd be singing to her, too.

The isolation unit took up half of a hospital floor and there were ten similar suites, each one a private haven for patients and their families. It was hard to imagine that ten patients were going through something similar to Remi at the same time, but I supposed they weren't just used for radiation patients, but also those with infectious diseases.

Her nurses and doctors entered from a door on Remi's side of the room, which I assumed came from a sterile space behind it. Still, they all wore get-ups that looked almost like space suits with clear plastic windows in the hoods so they could see what they were doing. They were covered from head to toe.

And then there was Remi. My heart ached looking at her, so pale and hooked up to tubes and wires. Right after we came upstairs, there was an empty blood bag, which I was told was actually how the marrow was administered, still hung above her. She still had a full bag of slow dripping saline so they could give her medications and make sure she was hydrated, and an EKG machine that beeped out her heartbeat. I wondered why she was still sedated, but the nurse who was constantly with her, monitoring her progress, told us that the doctor felt it best to keep her lightly sedated so she wouldn't be scared until the family arrived, but that would wear off soon and we were all waiting with baited breath.

Teagan was curled up on a chair near the window, glued to it since we'd come upstairs, and I'd managed to maneuver out of the wheelchair and onto one of the sofas and was stretched out and laying as flat as I could. It was much more comfortable than the couches throughout the rest of the hospital, and for that I was grateful. I was still aching badly, my hips and lower back throbbing because the pain meds I'd received during the surgery were wearing off. It felt like I'd been hit in several places with a hammer, and each puncture site burned like a son of a bitch. I wasn't prepared for the burning.

"Are you doing okay, honey?" My mother vacillated; flitting back and forth between worrying about me and going back to stand beside Teagan's chair at the window. She'd been crying when Teagan and I'd arrived upstairs, shaking her head in disbelief. The precariousness of Remi's situation was upsetting her, but the steady demeanor of my dad helped to calm her down.

"I'm okay, Mom," I lied, but she saw me wince and concern filled her features.

"Are you telling the truth?" she demanded.

"No. It hurts like a bitch. Is that better?" The corner of my mouth lifted wryly.

"Stop being smart with me." She said, a wrinkle appearing between her finely manicured eyebrows.

I snorted. "What? You asked."

"I know, but parents don't like to see their babies suffer."

I knew what she meant. It was staring me straight in the face with my own child. "What do you think of Remi?" My fatherly pride wanted the answer.

"Oh my goodness, Son! She's so small, but so beautiful." Her voice cracked a little.

"Wait until she opens her eyes; then you'll see how beautiful she is. What's so incredible is that she's so happy, despite being sick. She's amazing."

My mother dabbed at her eyes with a Kleenex. "I didn't expect the poor little thing to have hair, but I'm glad she does."

"She's had a rough few years. I wish I could have been here to help her." Regret must have filled my face because my mother reached out and patted my hand.

"You're here now, and you have the rest of your lives to be together."

My eyes went to Teagan; she was still watching Remi sleep. "I hope so," I said softly, unable to tear my eyes away from her beautiful profile. I'd always wanted forever with Teagan, and my heart still felt the same way, and I wanted more kids.

"Have you made any plans?"

The answer to my mother's question was laced with unknowns. "We've talked about it. If I have my way, we'll be a real family." I kept my voice low because I still had to speak to Jensen and I didn't want him to overhear.

"So you forgive her, then?"

"I do. Her dad was a prick; he threatened to hurt my career, and refuse her tuition because Teagan wouldn't get an abortion."

"Well, thank God she didn't do that! He never liked you."

"I know. He didn't think I was good enough for her."

"Well, he was against you kids from the beginning. We always thought he was an asshole. That poor girl left with only him for a parent is a travesty."

"Yeah." My mother rarely swore and I was surprised. "She doesn't have much to do with him anymore."

"I hate to say it, but it's probably a good thing. What about Jensen? How did that happen?"

Air filled my lungs to capacity as I imagined the alternative reality if she would have complied. Maybe she would have been with me, but we wouldn't have Remi.

"He told her dad he was the baby's father to get him to back off of Teagan and me. I mean; it was brutal. I wish she would have just told me the truth so I could have been with them, but I'm grateful for Remi, and I'm grateful that Jensen has taken care of her as well as he has. I had all these emotions: I was completely pissed off and resentful, and I didn't want to dig it all up again. I mean it was killing me, Mom, but Jensen convinced me that I needed to hear the whole story, and he was right."

She looked at me intently. Her blue eyes full of admiration. "I'm proud of you, Son. Teagan told me a little of it earlier."

"Yeah, but now, as much as I'd like Teagan and Remi to move to London to be with me, how can I rip her away from Jensen? He's the only father she's ever known, and she loves him."

"But, yesterday you said Remi knew you were her father."

"She did. I'm grateful that Teagan showed her pictures, told her stories, watched my games with her, but Jensen has been here since she was born, and I can't ignore that."

"If Teagan had moved on, she'd never have done that, Chase. Teagan still loves you as much as she ever has. I can see it as plain as day."

"I know, she does. But she cares about Jensen, and I know she feels she owes him everything." I ran a hand over my stubble-covered jaw, feeling frustrated with the conversation.

"Are they planning to divorce, then?"

My jaw set. "As I said, it's not an easy answer."

My mother concentrated on my face for a few more seconds.

"What?" I asked, agitated.

"Remi needs her real daddy, and you need her, Chase. You'll figure it out."

"I have to." My eyes moved back to Teagan and my heart literally seized inside my chest just looking at her.

She was half lying across the arm of a big, plus chair that matched the sofas with her head resting on one bent arm and her knees curled beneath her. She had pulled her short dress down to cover her legs as much as she could manage, but she looked cold. I glanced around wondering if there would be blankets hiding in one of the cabinets along one wall by the sink where she'd found the pillow I was using.

Her eyes were trained on me like mine had just been on her. Her dark gaze was intense and intuitive. "Your pain pills are in my purse. Do you need one?"

I shook my head. My stomach reminded me that I hadn't eaten in eighteen hours and I knew the pill would put me out. I wanted to speak to Jensen, not take a nap. "No. I could use something to eat, though."

"Your father and I can run out and bring something back," Mom stated. "Frank!" she called.

Dad had been watching a baseball game with Jensen but turned his head quickly at the mention of his name.

"What is it, Roma?"

"Chase needs something to eat." She picked up the purse sitting beside one of the sofas. "Let's go out and bring something back."

My father's face looked perturbed at not being able to finish the game, but he didn't complain out loud and stood up obediently to do my mother's bidding. "What does everyone want?"

"No cheeseburgers," I said.

"Why? You love cheeseburgers," my dad said, frowning quizzically. "You must not feel well."

"They're Remi's favorite," Jensen answered easily. "If she wakes up and can't have one, it won't be good."

"Yes," I nodded, meeting my dad's eyes and pointed at Jensen. "That."

Frank smiled brightly, glancing at Jensen and me. "Okay. No cheeseburgers. What doesn't she like?"

"She isn't that picky, honestly. As long as it's not cheeseburgers, though, I think we're all good," Teagan said with a soft half smile. Her eyes were heavy and I was sure the relief of the transplant being over, and being able to see Remi, would allow her to rest.

"Mom, would you mind looking in that cupboard for a couple of blankets? I'd do it, but the pain meds are wearing off."

"Of course," she went to do as I asked, and returned with two of the white cotton blankets that were standard hospital issue. She spread one over the top of me.

"Thanks, Mom. Can you give the other one to Teagan?"

"Surely!" Mom replied and spread the other over Teagan in a motherly fashion.

"Chase, you said you didn't need a pill!" Teagan accused.

"I don't want to get all drugged up before Remi wakes up."

"I see. Okay. But please don't let the pain get out of hand."

"I won't," I answered as my mother went over and spread the other blanket over my girl.

"Thank you, Roma," She murmured, pulling the blanket close and snuggling in and then smiling in my direction. "That was sweet of you, Chase."

"I'm sweet," I agreed happily. It did my heart good to see her so relaxed and unstressed. I only wished I was able to snuggle up with her. I knew she was tired and would sleep if she felt warm.

"And also humble," she added with dry humor. Her eyes were closed, but a sweet smile graced her luscious mouth. I felt like love was about to explode every cell in my body. I felt protective, incredible, unconditional love and insatiable lust all at the same time. In my efforts to bury her in my past; trying to hate and forget her, I'd never been able to dull the love. It manifested as indescribable pain, and my regret at the loss of her had been profound and debilitating. I'd been miserable, and now, that same love was a blessing that could bring back every amazing memory like magic.

My mom followed the direction of my gaze and then bent and kissed my forehead. "We'll see you in a little while." She patted my cheek.

"Roma don't dawdle," my father admonished as he waited by the door. "The kid will starve waiting on you to get a move on."

"I'm coming, Frank. Good grief!"

Minutes after they left, Teagan was sound asleep and Jensen was still engrossed in the game on television. I hesitated only briefly before pushing back the blanket and struggling into a sitting position. I groaned, causing him to notice that I was getting up.

"Do you need help?"

"Nah." My muscles were working fine, but I felt like I'd been run over by a truck. The bruises were in the bone and the muscles. "They must have used a hammer and chisel. Fuck, it hurts," I muttered using the couch itself to push me into a standing position. I hobbled over to the sofa where Jensen was sitting, and gingerly lowered myself down to his level.

"Why didn't you just stay put, then? Or take the pain pills? If you wanted to watch the game, I could have pivoted the TV toward you,"

"It's not the game I'm after. I want to talk to you, and I don't want Teagan to wake up while I do it. I want to try to put what happened in perspective and talk man-to-man."

"Oh," he had the remote and seemed to consider whether he should mute it, but decided against it. "So talk."

"Teagan told me that you two were planning on getting divorced years ago but it all changed when Remi got sick."

"Yeah, that's true." He acknowledged without offering more. His blue eyes narrowed. "Where are you going with this? Didn't you believe her?"

"I believed her, but I'm trying to figure out if that's what you really want or if you're just making a noble sacrifice."

He huffed and leaned back, returning his attention to the screen. "What difference does it make? It's what Teagan wants."

"It makes a difference because as much as I hate admitting it, this fucked up mess is partly my fault. I'm ready to own it and I don't want to make it worse."

He looked at me, unflinching so I continued.

"I'm glad that Teagan and Remi had you. I know you love them both."

He nodded slowly, his expression cautious. "Yeah, so?"

"So," I tented my hands in front of me, concentrating on them hard. "As much as I want to believe we still love each other and we can be together finally, I don't want Teagan choosing to be with me out of some sense of guilt over the past."

Jensen sighed heavily. "She does feel guilty and so do I, but since we're being honest; I tried to make the marriage real, but her heart has never been in it. She didn't want to marry me in the first place, and we didn't until right before Remi was born. She was mad that I went to her dad, and she was going to tell us both to go screw off, quit school and follow you to England. But then the phone call happened and she lost it. Do you know about that?"

"Just. Teagan told me recently."

"Well, I've never seen someone so fucked up as Teagan was, over that. She cried all the time, and she wasn't eating. I think she was still hoping you'd come back, and she secretly refused to believe you'd ever betray her like that. It was as if finding out you were less than she thought you were was the worst thing that could happen to her. She worshiped you, man. No way I could compete with that, but I didn't know how to help her other than marry her."

376

I closed my eyes and leaned my head back on the sofa, hating that I'd made her feel that way for even one split second. "You could have helped by calling me. From where I was sitting, it felt like I was the one being betrayed and hung out to dry. All that stuff you just said she suffered was happening to me, too. When neither one of you would return my calls, I went crazy. I felt completely abandoned by the two people who I trusted the most."

"Teagan was so destroyed I thought a clean break was best. Honestly, Chase, it wasn't a malicious attempt to fuck you up. I was afraid she wouldn't be strong enough to resist calling you, and I couldn't take the chance that woman would answer again. I got new phones because I seriously thought she'd do something stupid."

"I know the feeling."

Jensen frowned at me and huffed softly. "Then you shouldn't have let that superstar bullshit go to your head. You should have known Teagan would find out you were screwing around."

"I wasn't screwing around!" I said vehemently. Jensen had been my best friend and he knew how much Teagan meant to me, so I was stunned that either one would think something so completely ludicrous. Hearing him question me made my teeth clench. "I have no idea how Bronwyn got a hold of my phone, but it wasn't because we were fucking, and that's the truth!"

His head snapped around. "So it was her," he accused. "I figured. How'd you hook up with that narcissistic bitch, anyway?"

"I didn't. Until last year."

"What?" Jensen seemed incredulous.

"She's been trying for years, but it took me a long time to take her up on it. I was trying to feel better."

"Where is she? I assumed she'd be with you for the surgery."

"Sent her packing a few days ago when I found out about the phone call."

"Oh. If this whole thing was a huge misunderstanding, we've all paid one hell of a price. Especially that little girl in there." Jensen used the thumb on his right hand to point at Remi, still asleep behind the glass.

"Sadly, I agree. I wish it weren't so."

"Seriously, Chase. This is the truth. I didn't try to steal Teagan from you. It's just that I did care about her and when I saw what you did—" He stopped to relent. "What I thought you did; I'm not gonna lie, I was furious at you. Teagan was so fragile and she was my friend; I felt someone had to step up to help her when her bastard dad cut her loose just because she wouldn't get an abortion. And after the phone call, I couldn't turn my back on her."

I covered my eyes with my hand as hatred for Teagan's dad exploded inside my mind and heart. "All you had to do was confront me and this whole thing would have been avoided."

"You're right. I should have caught a flight and beat the shit out of you."

Air whooshed out of my lungs as I huffed. The whole thing hurt because so much was ruined for nothing.

Jensen held out a hand waiting for me to take it. I hesitated just a beat before shaking his hand. "I'm really sorry, man. I hope at some point we can be friends again," he said.

"Me, too. All I ask is that you never tell me any of the intimate details of your time with Teagan. Ever."

"Understandable." He turned his attention back to the baseball game without denying they'd ever slept together, and that was more information than I needed. "All I ask is that I get to be in Remi's life. I love her like she's my own, and my parents would be devastated if we lost her. Teagan promised that wouldn't happen."

"Understood," I repeated, knowing I'd already figure that out for myself. "I'd never do anything to hurt Remi, Jensen. The more people she has around her who love her, the better."

"Except if you take them to England, I won't get to see her much."

Boom. There it was. It wasn't as if that very thing hadn't crossed my mind at least fifty times since Teagan and I admitted we loved each other. Was it selfish to want what should have been mine in the first place? My mind said it wasn't, but my new perspective made it harder.

"Teagan and I haven't made any concrete plans, J. You're still married, and Remi has a lot of recovery in front of her." I couldn't believe how hard it was to admit he was the one married to her instead of me. "I don't want to push Teagan into anything. I'd feel better if the divorce wasn't because of me."

"It is about you, Chase. It always has been. Even if you weren't here, we'd still be getting a divorce, and it still would've been about you." He didn't seem angry, just matter of fact. The baseball game was ending and he picked up the remote and began switching channels. "You need to wrap your head around that."

I was honestly surprised by how calm Jensen was. I thought he'd be heartbroken or at least, mad as hell. If he was hurt, he was hiding it well and I had no intention of provoking a deeper reaction by not letting the subject drop, there was one more thing to mention.

"By the way," I hesitated, "there were a few reporters in the surgery waiting room when Teagan and I came out, and um, they took some pictures and asked a few questions. When we were almost through them, one of the reporters asked Teagan if she was your wife."

"Yeah, I know," he nodded.

My eyes widened in surprise. "You do?"

"Pffft!" He dismissed with a wry snort. "It's already all over social media and my I've already had a call from the network."

"You don't seem upset," I observed.

"What good would it do? You handled it."

"Yeah, but after the divorce, if Teagan and I get together— it could be a shit storm."

Jensen interrupted me. "Yeah, yeah. They'll have a field day. What are we gonna do to change the narrative? Not a damn thing. One thing I've learned from working in media is that sensationalism sells and the gossip hacks are the worst of the bunch. Most of them have no morals. Better that it all comes out now while Remi is young and not when she's older and has to deal with it herself. The good news is, there's always new blood in the water a week later. "

My lower lip came out and I nodded as I deferred to his logic. He was one hundred percent right. It was better to confront it so we could all move past it. "Maybe I should do an exclusive interview with a certain ESPN commenter. You know, just to make sure the real truth gets told."

Jensen's eyebrows shot up and he grinned. "Maybe."

"Seriously, I'm glad you're handling this so well."

"I've had years to get used to the idea that Teagan and I would split up, Chase. It's not a shock. I'll be fine as long as I get to see Remi grow up. I know that if she gets to grow up at all, it's because of you. I'm thankful for that."

There was no way I could hold on to my resentment when Jensen had taken such unselfish care of both Remi and Teagan? Yes, I would have rather have known the truth, even if it meant giving up Arsenal, but this was above and beyond what any friend could expect of another. "Thank you for everything you've done for them. I can pay you back for a lot of things, but without the insurance…" I let my words drop off. Without insurance, Remi wouldn't have had the best doctors or the most advanced treatment. "No, I mean it. Remi might not be alive for the transplant if it weren't for you. I'd say we're even when it comes to saving her."

He shook his head. "You don't need to pay me back for anything, Chase. I'd do it all again in a heartbeat."

I didn't have words to express my gratitude and really none were necessary. I owed him much more than I could ever repay.

"Are you going back to England, soon?"

"My team needs me. The season is starting and I'll have to play as much as I can, so I'll commute back and forth for a while. I mean, you're here and it's in her best interest to see you."

"You're richer than God and there are several flights a day," he stated. "What's to figure out?"

"I guess you're smarter than you look."

"You're not," he returned with an easy smirk.

I was enjoying the light camaraderie that used to be so natural between us, but in all seriousness, it could be months before their divorce was final and though my heart wouldn't let me be anything less than optimistic about Remi's recovery, it wasn't a given yet, either.

Still, I couldn't think of leaving Teagan and Remi behind without having a plan in place. My leaving might dig up feelings of insecurity in Teagan, and I wanted to make sure she was reassured.

"I'm not sure what's the right thing to do."

"Well, what you would have done six years ago if Teagan would have told you the truth. Do that." His eyebrow shot up in a smart-ass taunt. "Jesus. Do I have to think of everything? I guess we're back."

Chapter 21

Teagan

The five of us were sitting around, munching on the deli sandwiches, chips and sodas that Frank and Roma had brought back for all of us.

The hard chairs around the wooden table were too much for Chase, so we were all scattered around on the upholstered furniture in front of the television. Chase was ravenous and silently accepted the half of my turkey and provolone on rye I pushed in front of him on the coffee table.

Roma and Frank asked if I would bring some of the photo albums of Remi since her birth to share with them. Normally, I'd love nothing more. She was my pride and joy and I loved showing her off, but I didn't want to hurt Chase and he would be conspicuously missing from every one of them.

Jensen and I were answering Roma and Frank's questions about Remi, and listening proved difficult for Chase. I could see hurt flash across his face for a brief moment before he managed to hide it, and it killed me. All I could hope for was getting Remi better so we could take new pictures and build new memories that he would be part of. I could think of no better way to heal the damage.

Chase forgave me for everything. I could feel it whenever he looked at me, and especially when he touched me, or kissed me… but I couldn't lie to myself that he wasn't in pain and it would take time and a lot of love to get him through it.

Likewise, I believed him when he said he wasn't with Bronwyn the night of the phone call, even though it was still a mystery how she had his phone. Maybe she palmed it during a training session; I didn't know and really all that mattered was the overwhelming love I felt when I was with him and how Remi adored him. He was amazing with her, and she beamed whenever he was in the room. We both had pain we had to let go, and I was confident we'd conquer it together.

"Huh, huh, huh!"

I heard Remi crying through the intercom and jumped up and rushed to the glass. Everyone else, followed, though it took Chase longer to move and his dad went to help him up.

"Mommy! I want my mommy!" She was screaming at the nurse; no doubt scared by the personal protection equipment she was wearing.

My heart jumped up into my throat. "Remi," I said as calmly as I could. "Baby, I'm right here."

She was sitting up in bed and the nurse in her space suit was near her and pointing at me through the glass. "Look, Remi, there's your mom."

"Ahhhhhh," she cried, obviously scared by the nurse's appearance. "Mommy!" She was crying hard and holding her arms out to me, beseeching me to come to her. "Ah, ah, ah, ahhhh!"

"Calm down, baby girl. You're okay, sweetheart." It was such a helpless feeling knowing I couldn't get to her. I felt like crying myself.

"Mommy!" She looked over at all of us with tearful eyes.

"Remi, Daddy, and Jensey are here, too. We're all here, baby," I tried to soothe her. "Do you see us?"

Jensen held up his hand. "Hey, squirt."

Frank had one arm around Chase's waist and Chase's was over his father's shoulder. They limped to the glass, and Chase released his father and put both hands flat on the window.

Roma stood next to me, both hands over her mouth, as she watched her granddaughter. "Poor little thing."

"Remi," Chase said; his deep voice resonating. "Baby, remember we talked about this. You have to be behind the window for a little while until you are stronger, but we're all here with you. It's only for a few days, but you're safe."

Remi hiccupped but her head snapped to look at her father and blinked, tears still rolling down her face, though she was no longer wailing.

"Remember? Until Daddy's marrow makes you better, you have to be in there for a few days. Pretty soon, everything will be easier, princess. I promise."

"Squirt, the nurse in that suit is Sally. Look at her face inside her hat. Don't be frightened, honey," Jensen added. "The doctors and nurses have to wear those funny suits. Aren't they goofy?"

She hiccupped again and nodded, letting her eyes skirt over Roma and Frank and then back at her nurse.

Sally moved closer so Remi could see her face through the clear acetate in the front of her hood. She put her hands out to calm Remi down. "It's okay, Remi. I'm here to take care of you, and Kari will be in later. And Dr. Radar, okay?"

My heart broke that I couldn't be in there to take her in my arms and ease her fears.

Remi sat in the middle of the bed, glancing around. While she wasn't crying as hard, I could see she was frightened.

"Oh, God," I murmured painfully. "I wish I could get in there."

Chase was standing to my right and his hand came down on my left shoulder and he kneaded gently. "She'll be okay, Teagan. You have to keep calm."

I nodded, still looking at Remi. I had her two favorite stuffed animals in a plastic bag on the counter, but if she couldn't have them in there, it might just upset her. "Remi, I have some of your books and we have your songs. I'll read you a story after you have some dinner, okay?"

"Or, maybe I can read to you," Roma suggested gently. I could see it on her face that she wanted desperately for Remi to know who she is.

"Who are those people?" She pointed first at Roma then Frank.

"This is my mom and dad, honey. They are your grandparents," Chase answered.

Remi's eyes were like saucers as she checked them out.

"Hi, pumpkin," Frank waved at her, grinning from ear to ear. "I'm your Grandad and this is your Nana."

"We've been waiting for you to wake up. We're so happy to meet you, Remi," Roma said tearfully.

"Then how come you're crying?" Remi asked innocently, forgetting her own tears.

Roma let out a small laugh. "Because I'm so happy, darling."

Remi's brow wrinkled and her lower lip jutted out as she considered this. "I only cry when I'm sad."

"Nana is silly, that's all," Frank added. "She's a waterworks. She leaks a lot."

Chase let out a sigh that echoed my own relief that Remi was calming down as Roma and Frank continued to talk to her and divert her attention from her isolation. There was a metal edge at the bottom of the window and he let go of me and leaned on it with a muffled groan. "Ughhh…"

Jensen heard it and quickly retrieved the wheelchair and pushed up behind Chase and bent to engage the brake. "Take a seat, gimpy."

Chase tried to glower at Jensen, but it turned into a grin as he lowered himself using only his arms. Obviously, the two of them were getting along and I wondered if anything was settled between them. "She looks like she's doing better. She has more color in her face, already."

"Agreed. I'm going to ask the nurse for an update," Jensen said moving away to the other end of the room and motioning for the nurse to come to the glass.

Chase reached for my hand and threaded his fingers through mine and then he kissed the top of it. His open mouth brushed against my skin in a caress. "She already looks healthier," he said.

"I'm afraid to think that yet. I don't want to jinx it."

My apprehension stemmed from the two rounds of chemo putting her in remission. I was afraid of too much early optimism leading to a huge letdown, but I didn't want to dampen Chase's good mood. All I could do was look at him in wonder. With my whole heart, I wanted to believe it was true.

His gorgeous green eyes were intense. "You and Remi are my world now. This has got to work."

The familiar combination of emotions of love, hope, & fear raced through me, but I tried to hide it. "I'll feel better in a day or two. Every hour that passes, the closer we are to being in the clear."

"Teagan," Chase's voice was filled with conviction. "I believe in miracles. Just look around. We're surrounded by them."

When he put it that way, I couldn't argue.

Remi was chattering away with Roma and Frank and it was good to hear her little voice coming through the intercom stronger than it had been in weeks. "You know, I gotta friend named Sally, too. Not this one." She pointed at the nurse. "She lives next door. We play dress up a lot when I can't go outside 'cause of the Leuky or mean medicine."

"Sally sounds like a very nice friend, Remi." Roma's happy expression only faltered momentarily at Remi's mention of her illness. She and Frank had pulled two chairs close to the glass so they could get to know the little girl and both of them were completely smitten with her.

"Yeah. She has a dog, and Jensey said I could have one when I'm better. Do you have a dog?"

"We have three dogs," Frank said. "They'd love you. We have a tree house and a big tire swing, too. There are a bunch of trees behind our house and your daddy and uncle Kevin built a fort back there. All of it is waiting for you to come and play. And you have five cousins, too."

"I would like to play with the dogs and stuff, but what are cousins?"

He nodded in her direction. "Just listen to that. It's music to my ears." Chase seemed tired of being confined to the wheelchair, and decided to stand up, but it wasn't without a grimace. "Come sit with me over here on the sofa."

I slid a hand around his waist and my other hand flattened on his hard abs beneath his shirt. "Are you sure you're ready to walk around?" He was moving slow and he seemed stiff as we settled onto the couch. "You should take some of the pain medication. You'll sleep better."

"It's only ten feet for Christ's sake. Why are you trying to drug me? If you want something, all you have to do is ask," he teased.

"Haha," I mocked, poking him gently in the ribs. Chase's arm lifted and wrapped around me and guiltily, I glanced at Jensen who, it appeared, was finishing up with the nurse. Chase followed my gaze.

"I had a talk with Jensen when you were passed out in the chair, earlier." He looked at me seriously, gauging my reaction. I'd seen that look a thousand times and I could read him like a book.

"Yeah?" I reached up and grabbed his hand. It was easy to lean into him and lay my head back on his strong shoulder and chest as I looked up into his face. "What'd you figure out?"

"To start with, everything is cool with us."

"Really?" I asked skeptically. Six years of shit was a lot to put away with one conversation.

"Well, yeah, I mean..." Chase searched for the words he wanted. "He reiterated everything you said, and I took my share of the blame. I think we're good. We both love you, and Remi and that's the most important thing."

Jensen approached and took the chair to Chase's left so the rest of this conversation would have to wait. I couldn't help pulling back from Chase guiltily.

"You don't have to do that, Teagan. We all know how it is between you two." Jensen said flatly.

"It just feels strange. I don't want to hurt you."

"I know that." Jensen looked me square in the face. His features didn't hold anger or sorrow. "I also know where your heart is. We might as well just get on with moving on."

Jensen was one of the most unselfish people I knew. His heart was huge and he deserved all that life had to offer, and I hoped that the deep friendship that he and I had forged since we'd been married would remain with us. I hoped that he and Chase would be able to get back some of the closeness and trust that they shared in college.

"I hope we can all to be friends again, Jensen. And not just for Remi's sake."

"I know that, Teagan. We'll be fine as soon as we get a divorce, and we can acclimate Remi to the changes. I want this to go as smoothly as possible, for her sake. It isn't like we weren't going to do this anyway, so stop worrying."

Over the years, I'd grown accustomed to Jensen's gentle, yet firm way of putting me at ease. Whenever there were problems or something upsetting, he had a quiet assuredness about him that calmed me down. He got me through the worst of my broken heart, he got me through the mess with my dad, he got me through Remi's illness... I could always count on him. "Thank you. I don't know what I would have done without you, Jensen. I want you to be happy."

Jensen nodded. "I know that, Teagan." He effectively turned the conversation to Remi. "The nurse said Remi's dinner had been ordered, and after that they want her to rest. She needs as much sleep as possible, but her counts are getting better, and the nurse said Dr. Radar's notes say he'll check in late tonight. They seem optimistic. She seems busy with your parents, so I'm going to run home and get a few hours sleep. I have a trip to New Orleans tomorrow and I need to pack."

"Do you leave early in the morning?"

"Mid-morning, but I'll stop in to see Remi on the way to the airport."

"Do you need me to drive you?"

"No. I'll just park in long-term parking. It's not a big deal. You should be here for Remi."

He stood and I got up to hug him goodbye. He embraced me warmly and my own arms tightened around his shoulders. I was hoping to communicate how much he meant to me. "Thank you," I said softly. "You're a good man."

He kissed my cheek, and half bent at the waist to shake Chase's hand. "Don't get up, I know you're hurting."

"Thanks for everything. Including the talk," Chase said, sincerely.

"You bet. Let me know your schedule, so we can work it out so one of us is always here."

"I agree." Chase and Jensen were easy going with each other, and I could see a hint of how they used to be as friends shining through and it filled me with relief.

Jensen walked over to the window. Frank and Remi had somehow manipulated the nursing staff to move the bed closer to the glass and she was sitting in the middle of her bed jabbering away at her grandparents. Her face was animated and she seemed to be feeling pretty well. Her cheeks were rosy and she was smiling.

I settled back on the sofa next to Chase and we watched Jensen say his goodbyes. "Come on, give Jensey a kiss, Squirt."

He and Remi leaned in to kiss the glass at the same time. It was the next best thing to a real kiss. "Mmwah!" Remi made an enthusiastic smooching sound. "Love you, Jensey!"

"I love you, too. Be a good girl and do what the nurses and doctors tell you so you can get better, okay?"

"I will, I promise." He said goodbye to Chase's parents and held up a flat hand to wave to us on his way out the door. Remi's dinner arrived and the nurse got her situated with it. Remi's demeanor was like that of any happy five-year-old who was the center of attention of doting grandparents leaving me to turn my attention back to Chase.

"Are you leaving?"

Chase wrapped a reassuring arm around me and pulled me close to his side. My heart stopped. I knew it was coming, but being faced with it was another thing altogether.

"Arsenal has a league tournament coming up in ten days and I'll be okay to play by then. I'd rather not leave, but the club has been accommodating about my absence, so I feel I owe it to them to be there. Coach Noonan doesn't think the team can win the whole thing if I'm gone, and I can't really say no."

"Remi will most likely still be in the hospital for a few weeks." It would be selfish of me to ask him to stay. I didn't do it six years ago when I was pregnant and I wouldn't do it now.

"I'm hoping she is at least out of isolation, but either way, I'll be back as quickly as I can. You can always hope we lose a few games, so I can come back sooner."

He was casually teasing, offering an easy smile and a nudge, but it was obvious that he was itching to play in these games. The European Championships were much more visible on the world stage than the league games his team played inside the UK, but those wouldn't be for a few months. I knew Chase, and he was driven to be the best, and his team counted on him. His dedication to his team and the game was part of who he was, and it was part of what I loved about him. "They'll want you back permanently, soon."

Chase's fingers played with mine. He nodded. "They will. It's presumptuous of me to ask you and Remi to pick up and move to England, Teagan."

Just hearing those words filled my heart with panic. "I know, but how else will we—?"

"Let's just take a minute. You and Jensen have a divorce to settle, and I don't want to get in the middle of that. Plus, Remi has to be completely well before we can plan anything else."

"Chase, I know I can't expect you to stay, and I don't want to be separated if we can avoid it. It feels too much like when you left six years ago."

"Except nothing is going to happen to rip us apart this time. We just have to work out the logistics so whatever we do is best for Remi. Those reporters today made me realize that we have to be careful." Chase's face was soft with contemplation, and the soft stubble that had now become scruff. "I don't want J to have any blowback from this. He doesn't need to be made a fool of, even if it's all made-up lies. I don't want it to appear as if I swooped in and broke up his marriage right under his nose. You and I have each other; we have our perfect little Remi, and the rest of our lives together. We can afford a little patience so Jensen doesn't suffer unnecessarily. We're both visible in the sports world and I want to make sure his pride stays intact." He pressed a kiss to my temple. "I owe him that, at least. It might be a little inconvenient for a few months, but trust me; you and I are going to be together like we were always meant to be. With Remi."

How was I lucky enough to have two such amazing men in my life? Jensen unselfishly making it easy for me to be with Chase, and Chase making sure Jensen wasn't hurt unnecessarily. Hope unfurled inside my heart. Jensen and Chase would be okay.

I looked up into Chase's face in wonder, unable to articulate the pride I felt. "I love you; so much it's hard to put it into words."

Chase reached out and ran a gentle finger down the side of my face. "I'm counting on it."

CHASE

We made it to the finals of the first league tournament, but Chelsea kicked our ass 5-3 to win. I was mostly healed, and the purple bruises were starting to turn an ugly yellow and green. I blamed myself for the loss because I'd missed the practices for six weeks, but it couldn't be helped. My teammates and the coaches were gracious, but they were obviously anxious about what my long-term plans were.

After the story broke that I'd been back in Atlanta for several weeks, an agent representing the US National Team had contacted me. I had a serious offer in front of me that had to be considered. As much as I hated the thought of leaving Arsenal and all of the friends I'd made in London, I had to consider what was best for my family.

I'd been in London for eight days and I couldn't wait to get back to Teagan and Remi. Remi was going to get out of the glass cage any day now, and I wanted to be there for that.

Teagan had been conspiring with my sister, mother, and sister-in-law to have a surprise party for Remi when she got out, which I thought was a brilliant idea.

I Skyped with Teagan daily, and most of the time she was in the isolation suite and she could hold up the tablet so I could talk to Remi. She was getting stronger and stronger, the bloom in her cheeks was healthy and she had a lot more energy. She liked to make up shows and do them for me over Skype and my heart filled with pride. She was missing two front teeth and that gave her a bit of lisp, but she didn't seem to notice or care either way. I was bursting with pride and my teammates were probably ready to sack me because I never stopped talking about my girls in America.

Bronwyn tried to corner me at my apartment right after I got back in London and though I tried to be respectful of her feelings, she put the moves on me, thinking that she could change my mind with sex and when I told her I wasn't interested, she wouldn't stop. I shouldn't have been surprised because sex was our main connection, but I'd hoped she would have moved on after Atlanta. She wouldn't back off and kept grabbing at me until I was rude about it. The twinge of guilt I had over my behavior went away the second I remembered she was the reason my relationship with Teagan went to hell. I requested one of the other trainers to work with me, and kept my distance from her, making damn sure my phone was in sight at all times. I wouldn't put a repeat performance past Bronwyn, and it was doubtful Teagan would fall for it again, but I wasn't taking any chances.

Teagan had been bugging me to learn some simple choreography to a song Remi liked because she wanted to surprise Remi during the party she was planning with Kat and my mom. I'd been asked to do a lot of things in my life, but this was new. The song was Pharell Williams' Happy. It had a fun, snappy tune and I could see how it was completely appropriate for a party, and given Remi's affinity for singing and dancing, how could I refuse?

It turned out to be great fun. My teammates started out making fun of me, but many of them knew the song and Ceasar Rommono, our goalkeeper, helped me learn the damn thing. When he suggested we make a parody and convinced Yosef, the team photographer, to take a video of me and some of the Gunners dancing around the locker room, on the field, in the parking lot of our stadium, and on the team buses.

Some of the shots were of the whole team and others of individuals dancing along. We even convinced Coach Noonan, the team doctor, and a couple of the trainers to join for a few frames. Of course, we were also lip-syncing the song and I was front and center. The different pieces were edited together in a mash-up just like the real video. It was completely goofy, but my friends and I laughed our asses off practicing with beer and Jack the second night I was back in London. It was heartwarming to see how supportive my friends had been and how willing and enthusiastic they had been to help me make it so amazing.

It was so much fun, it turned into a thing, and we did one for JT's song; *Can't Stop the Feeling*, too. I remembered how much Remi loved that song and I was sure she was going to love it.

I could hardly wait for Remi to see them. I was jumping-out-of-my-skin excited. Of course, it would probably outdo Teagan's surprise, but what the hell; I was making up for lost time.

I pulled out my phone as I waited for my plane to take off from Heathrow. I couldn't wait to hear Teagan's voice. For her part, she and Jensen had filed for divorce, and she was packing up her things and putting a lot of it in storage for the time being. Kat came up on the weekend to help her so Teagan could still spend most of her time at the hospital with Remi. It was five hours earlier in Atlanta than it was in London and it would be breakfast time there. It was 3 AM London time and I was hoping to sleep much of the almost nine-hour flight, so I wouldn't be dragging when I arrived. Jet lag was always easier to manage than when I traveled from Europe to the States.

"Hey!" Teagan answered. Her voice was jubilant and happy. We still weren't a hundred percent sure that Remi would be cured for good, but her progress and prognosis were good. Her blood counts were better than Dr. Radar expected for so soon after the transplant.

"Hey, Monkey." My words had to be laced with the love and anxious desire I was feeling. I was elated and it was catching. The flight attendants in first class beamed at me as they passed. I was smiling so hard the muscles in my cheeks hurt.

"Ace Forrester," one of them mouthed, pointing at me.

I still had on my sunglasses but she was still able to recognize me. My brow shot up and I nodded with a smile, but put a finger to my mouth, hoping she'd understand I didn't want my presence on the flight spread around.

"Got it," she mouthed again.

"Are you on your way home?"

Those words meant everything to me. It didn't matter where I lived, or even what team I ended up on, the only thing that had to be was that Teagan and Remi were with me. There was nothing that mattered more or anything I wanted more. Wherever they were was home. I'd miss my team, but more and more, I was leaning toward taking the offer from the U.S. National Team.

"I am," I responded. I was sitting next to the window, and in the time since I dialed the phone, a woman in a business suit took the berth across the aisle. I was thankful for the sleeping cubicles not only because it would help me really sleep, but because I didn't have anyone right next to me. Still, I turned a bit away so that my conversation couldn't be overheard. "I'm dying to see you. It feels like ten years."

Teagan laughed. "I missed you, too, but I promise, it didn't feel like ten years. It didn't even feel like six."

I was watching out the window of the plane, watching the baggage get loaded into the underbelly of the plane. I chuckled. "Yeah. Are you going to stay with me at the shitty apartment tonight?" We'd started to refer to the place that way. "If you don't want to, we can get a room at a hotel by the hospital."

"I'm not sure." Teagan's response was vague, but it still felt positive. There was a smile in her tone that she didn't match.

"I know you stay with Remi every night, but why don't you give my mom a call and ask her to drive down just for tonight. I miss you and as much as I love Remi, we need time together, too. I'd call her, but they are pushing back and this is the last call I can make."

"I know." There was a promise in her voice that couldn't be denied. If I weren't careful, I'd have a problem that would be difficult to hide. Thankfully, the woman to my left already had her laptop out and headphones in both ears, and anyone in front or behind me wouldn't be able to hear or see me.

"I splurged on the extra airfare for one of those new planes with those sleeping pods in first class, so don't expect me to be tired tonight if you know what I mean. I can't wait to get my hands on you."

"That sounds really nice." There was a sultry purr to her tone that caused a physical reaction in my pants. I pulled the plastic wrap off of the blanket that had been waiting in my seat and draped it over my lap to hide the evidence from the flight attendant passing out flutes of champagne.

"It will be, I promise."

"Mmmm."

"Okay, no more sexy moaning and teasing me until you can do something about it."

A musical laugh tinkled through the phone. "Okay, you poor thing," she taunted. "I'll change the subject. Did you learn the dance?"

"Yes," I said, purposely bemoaning. I wanted her to think that I hated every minute of it and I'd only done it because she insisted. "I learned the goddamned thing, but I suck at it." It was a flat-out lie, but I wanted Teagan to be as surprised as Remi. "I figured you'd threaten to hold out on me if I didn't acquiesce." I was so anxious to see her, it wasn't just the sheer happiness on my face, but my body was literally vibrating with anticipation. This was so different than the plane ride I took to Atlanta two months before, when my heart was fighting my head and when I was praying she'd be so different. Now, nothing could be further from my heart. I loved that she was still the same girl I loved in college. Only now, she had my daughter. Life was good.

"That's weird. You used to dance well." She was skeptical and I should have known I couldn't fool her. We went out dancing every weekend when we were at Clemson.

"I guess I'm out of practice," I offered as a lame attempt at a feasible explanation, almost cringing when I said it.

"Well, try to look like you're having fun, at least. Jensen and Kat are going to come to the hospital and do it with us, too. Since Remi can't come out yet, I just thought it would make her day if we surprised her by dancing for her outside that window."

I sighed deeply. The only thing dampening the homecoming was that Remi was still in that damn glass cage. "I know it's only been a little over two weeks since the transplant, but I can't help wishing she'd get out of there."

"Me, too, babe. She will, soon."

"I know. I just want her to be better."

"She is. She's amazing. She's got so much energy back and the bloom is back in her cheeks. I can't wait for you to see her."

"Well, it's not long now. I hate to go, but the flight attendant is asking me to stash my phone because they're starting those damn recordings."

"I'll pick you up at the airport."

"Okay, baby. I'll see you in nine hours."

"I'll be waiting where I was the last time so you'll know right where to find me."

"Can't wait. I love you. Tell Remi, too."

"I will. We love you, too."

I shut off my phone and took one of the flutes that was offered, downed it and reclined my chair almost to prone position settling in before the plane even got off the ground. Hopefully, sleeping would be easy and I'd be in Atlanta before I knew it.

ONE *touch*
AND THE PAIN
melted away.

Chapter 22

Teagan

"Mommy! Mommy!" Remi was so excited.

She was wearing a new dress that Kat had given her. It was a beautiful explosion of fuchsia, lime green, orange, and yellow floral on a bright white background that brought out the new pink hue to her now plumper cheeks. Her hair was in two high side pony tails with matching bows around them. "Are you getting Daddy, now?"

She was jumping up and down on the bed behind the glass gleefully, it was the most energy I'd seen her exhibit in months; since her last remission. We'd been able to bring clothes and toys in for her because the hospital had an ultraviolet irradiation machine that killed germs similar to how Remi's bone marrow had been prepared for the transplant. She was able to have her iPad, Bennie the elephant and Jewel the dog, as well as some of her favorite stories, coloring books, and crayons.

I couldn't help but giggle. Remi was beside herself and it was the most beautiful, amazing thing I'd seen in three years. For myself, I felt like I was flying. Kat was in town and Roma was more than happy to come down when I called her. No doubt Kat was teaching her the Happy dance already. Jensen was just back from another assignment and would have to sleep tonight, but with both women here to stay with Remi; making it possible for me to have the night with Chase.

I'd taken a lot of care with my own appearance, too. I was primping in the bathroom on the family side of the isolation suite, but the door was open so Remi could see me as I put my lipstick on.

"You look pretty enough, Mommy. Go get Daddy!" She jumped up and down on the bed, and the motion lights in her new sneakers glittered. Normally, I'd never allowed her to jump on a bed like that, but this was a special occasion and it would be a day of surprises.

I couldn't wait to see Remi's face when the entire group of us started dancing for her. The only thing that would make it better would be if she were dancing beside us. Lacking that, the best thing would be letting her dance along on top of her bed, so she'd be able to see us all. Two of her regular nurses from the oncology floor, Dr. Radar and Alissa, the nursing student that Remi had gotten attached to the last time she was a patient down there, would join us. Having Kat and Roma join in was even better.

After she got out of isolation, she'd have to be in the hospital for at least a week more, but when that day came I hoped to have the entire family in attendance.

"Mommy!" Remi demanded again. I looked at my face in the mirror. I had on blush, lipstick and a bit of eyeliner, but I was not overly done up. My hair was down because I knew Chase liked to thread his hands through it. I smacked my lips together to evenly distribute the lipstick, then turned back to Remi.

"Mommy!"

I laughed again. "Remi, settle down, honey. Daddy's plane lands in about an hour, so I'll leave soon. Why don't you watch TV or read a book while you wait? It will make the time go more quickly." We'd spent so much time in the hospital, I'd had a lot of time to teach Remi to read, and do basic addition and subtraction. She was well ahead for her age.

"I wish I could come," she said, jumping as high as she could, then pulling up her legs so she'd fall back on the bed on her bottom and she bounced a couple of times before coming to a stop on the mattress.

"I know. Nana is coming with Aunt Kat to be with you while I go to the airport. Maybe you can draw Daddy a picture while you wait?" I sat down on the big chair that was pulled close to the glass and facing Remi's bed.

"Okay," she said. "Mommy?" she asked thoughtfully. "Will we go on an airplane when Daddy takes me to the castles?"

"Probably, sweet pea, but we have to make sure you're all better first. There are a lot of germs and colds on airplanes."

She'd come to a better understanding of the reason she had to be in isolation during the engrafting of Chase's bone marrow. "Hmmm," she said. "Do you think Daddy will like my dress?"

"I think he'll love it! It's beautiful! Aunt Kat has good taste in dresses."

"Do you think it looks like a princess? It's not long. Princesses have long gowns."

"Princesses wear shorter dresses in summer," I offered. She seemed to accept my answer as a plausible explanation. "Is the sky blue at night, too?"

"That's an interesting question, Remi."

She jumped down off of the bed and started to twirl. "'Cause, my room is pink but at night it's dark, and I can't see the pink, but if you turn on the lights, it's pink. Is the sky like that?"

I was delighted by her inquisitive mind. "Well, that sounds logical, doesn't it?"

"Yeah, 'cause the sun is like a big light bulb."

"You're right, it is. A huge light bulb."

"Uh huh."

"Remi, be careful," the nurse who was attending her murmured. She was sitting in a chair, still wearing the protective garb.

"Maybe I can borrow one of those outfits to go on the plane." She pointed to the nurse. "Cept, I don't think it's very princess-y. At all."

"Where's my girl?" Roma called from the doorway of the room.

"Nana! Auntie Kat!" Remi was quite taken with Chase's side of the family. Remi ran to the window and plastered both hands flat against it.

Kat and David and Kevin and Jodi had visited with their kids last week, and Remi had a hundred questions about the dogs, the tree house, and fort. Jensen was an only child and she had no other cousins. The closeness of Chase's family was a blessing.

"My goodness! Look how beautiful you look!"

Remi beamed at her and twirled around. "Auntie Kat has good taste in dresses!" Her toothless smile was radiant.

"Right, because my skills are so honed from picking so many out for my boys," Kat smiled ruefully, taking a seat on one of the sofas. "I loved getting it for her. I loved picking out all of the little extras."

"You did a terrific job," I said. I crossed my arms and leaned on the arm of the sofa. Roma was already sitting on the chair nearest Remi. "She loves it. She hasn't felt good enough to care what she was wearing for so long, but she's been twirling in that dress all morning."

"We'll go on a shopping spree when you get out of here, Remi," Roma told her. "Your Mommy and you, Kat, Jodi, Mandi, Mellie, and Nana will take Grandad's wallet to the mall."

Kat rolled her eyes and looked at her watch. "You better get going, honey. You look great. Brother dear won't know what hit him."

I had a new dress of small cornflower blue flowers scattered over a cream fabric. The neckline was scooped just enough to show the top swell of my breasts, and it was lightly gathered below and an empire waist. There were small cream buttons from the neck to the waist. The bra and panties I had on beneath it were in soft ivory lace. I almost blushed thinking about Chase's reaction. I'd worn it to tease him. No doubt he'd be thinking about the thong I'd had on under the dress in the surgery recovery room.

"Yes," I agreed. "I can't wait to see him."

"Well, you're glowing." Kat winked at me.

"Kat, I'm so thankful for Remi's recovery, for Chase coming back into our lives, and all of you. For Jensen being so amazing about it all. I never dreamed life could be this good." I couldn't help the sting of tears at the back of my eyes and the tightness in my throat. "I mean, it's all so surreal. Two months ago, it was as if the world was about to end, and now, everything is amazing. The future is brighter than I'd ever hoped. The only thing that worries me is how Remi will do without Jensen all the time."

"Have faith in both of those men, Teagan. They're both doing right by you. Trust them."

Her words sank into my very soul. It was true. "Thank you, Kat," I said and hugged her. I walked to the glass. "Give me a kiss, baby girl," I said before pressing my lips to the glass.

She ran over and kissed it on her side. The giggled when the lipstick imprint of my mouth remained in pink lipstick. "Thanks, Roma. Chase says thanks, too."

"He can damn well thank me in person!" When she smiled, I could see Chase's smile. He had his father's eyes, but his nose and mouth were all his mother.

I put a hand on her shoulder. "Are you ready to dance?" I whispered with a saucy grin.

Her eyes sparkled with laughter. "No, but that won't stop me."

"Be good for Nana and Auntie Kat, Remi."

"And Nurse Nancy," the nurse said. "She has to eat her lunch."

"I don't like it," Remi whined. "It tastes yucky!"

"You have to get your strength up, doll face," Kat said to Remi, before giving me a blank, wide-eyed stare as she crossed her arms over her chest. "However, everyone knows health food blows," she added sardonically.

I gasped loudly, grabbing my purse. "Kat!" I reprimanded with a wide-eyed look.

"What? It's the truth!"

"Not always!"

"Ninety-nine percent of the time!" She was clearly enjoying taking Remi's side of the argument.

I wanted to distract the little girl's attention from Kat's remark hoping I could get her talking about the sky, the sun and airplane germs. "Remi, why don't you tell Auntie Kat what you learned today."

She giggled. "Okay. Health food blows!"

My mouth dropped open. I was speechless as I looked at my daughter. She was grinning from ear to ear, and her head cocked to one side.

Her precociousness was a sign she was getting better. "Remilia Victoria!" I admonished, sternly, biting my lip so I wouldn't laugh.

Remi burst into a fit of giggles. "Hahahaha!"

"Oh, goodness!" Roma let out a peal of laughter and the nurse rolled her eyes inside her plastic helmet.

Kat high five'd Remi through the glass. "Now, that's funny!"

CHASE

There she was.

Teagan was waiting for me in the very spot she said she'd be; the same place I'd seen her for the first time after six years of separation. She was simply stunning. I stopped for a few seconds to just look at her. Her long legs were bare underneath a white and cream baby doll style dress, and her hair was curling gloriously around her. She had on high heels that made her legs look even longer. She was slim and strong, and gorgeous. She was mine.

Teagan's teeth flashed in a brilliant smile when she saw me and then quickened her steps, shortening the distance between us. Though I would have been happy to just to look at her, I wanted to get her in my arms, so I quickly started walking her way. I was wearing a dark grey hoodie and my RayBans with three days growth of beard, hoping to hell I wouldn't get recognized. I had a black duffle with me but made a conscious decision not to take my team bag with the Arsenal logo plastered on the body of it.

It didn't take ten seconds and the bag was at my feet and I was holding her tight against me. I closed my eyes, smelling her perfume, feeling her round breasts pressing into my chest, and reveling in her hands holding the back of my head when I

407

bent to take her mouth with mine. She tasted delicious; like mint and vanilla, and Teagan.

I sucked in a deep breath at the start of the kiss so I could keep at it long and deep without the need to pause. Our tongues laved and tasted, plunging into each other's mouths as we feasted on each other. I didn't care if anyone was watching; the whole world could have melted away and I wouldn't have noticed. I lost myself in Teagan, in the sensations of having her in my arms, of tasting and teasing her lips with mine. My heart was pounding against her chest and I wasn't sure if it were mine, or hers. The kisses, that started out fast and desperate, lessened to slow, deeply connected, and languid.

"You taste so good," I said when we finally had to breath, burying my face in the curtain of her hair. Teagan still held me tight, unwilling to break the contact; one arm around my shoulders and another around my hooded head. "Jesus, I missed you."

I started to lower her to the ground, but she resisted moving out of my arms and held on for dear life. "Chase," she said softly, her mouth moved from speaking into kisses on my jaw and then my neck. "Oh, God."

I didn't want to deny her request and lifted her off the floor again. I was willing to hold her close as long as she wanted, even standing as we were in the middle of the airport terminal. "I wish you could monkey me," I said softly, kissing the side of her cheekbone and then her temple.

Teagan held me, and I knew she was crying. I could feel her hot tears drip on my skin, rolling down from my collarbone onto my chest. "I can't believe you're here."

My heart was exploding with love, and there was nothing in the world I wanted in that moment than to hold on to this woman. "Hush, my love. It's okay, baby. You're stuck with me," I said, smiling because I couldn't help myself. I knew she wasn't crying because she was sad because my own soul was fucking flying. My hand moved up her back to hold the back of her head and I kissed her again and again.

We clung together as Teagan cried softly in the circle of my arms. "Baby, it's okay," I laughed softly. "I'm not going anywhere." Her hands slid across my shoulders and up to cup both sides of my face. She opened her tear-filled eyes and gazed into my face. I met her gaze, though I had the sunglasses on and she couldn't tell. She bent and kissed me hard once more and tugged on my beard. "Is this supposed to be a disguise?"

I laughed and sat her down, bending to pick up my bag at the same time my other hand slid down her forearm to thread my fingers with hers. "Yes."

"It isn't working."

I laughed out loud. "Not with you, but something's working because I haven't been accosted for an autograph once." I shrugged. "If you don't count the flight attendant, that is."

"What if it scare's your daughter?"

"Will it?" I asked. "Because then, we might just have to get a room so I can shave before she sees me."

"I'd love that, hon, but she's waiting, and not very patiently."

"I'm stoked to see her. Last night on Skype, she looked so healthy. I can hardly believe the transplant is taking hold."

Her free hand settled on the inside of my bicep as we walked hand in hand out of the terminal and across the street to the garage. It was the same garage where I learned I had a daughter.

"I held my breath, afraid to stop worrying, but Dr. Radar said she hasn't rejected it and feels the prognosis is good."

"Did he say when she'll be able to get out of the tank?"

"Not yet."

"Ugh."

"Chase, thank you."

"No, thank you." I looked down at her as we walked the last few feet to her SUV. Teagan handed me the keys. I popped the hatch and threw the bag inside, instantly clicking the doors open with the fob. I held open the passenger side door as Teagan climbed inside, and all that bare skin was torture.

"I bet you've got some delicious little nothing on under that little dress. Are you trying to torture me?"

"Yes." Her eyes flashed sensually and she licked her lips. "Is it working?" She taunted me with my own words.

A grin spread across my face as I slid my hand up the outside of her thigh, seeking to discover what I already knew was there. My fingers slid up her leg and over her hip, finding a small expanse of silk and lace. "Yes. It's definitely working." I murmured the words against her mouth before regretfully closing her door. I walked around to slide into the driver's side.

I started the car and Teagan opened the glove compartment and pulled out the parking ticket. I retrieved my money clip from the front pocket of my jeans and threw it in the console. I backed out and drove through the darkened garage. It wasn't long until I'd paid for the parking and we were racing north along I-85.

I reached for Teagan's hand and pulled it up to hold it on my thigh. Glancing at her, I took in her profile. She was perfect. Sunglasses hid her dark eyes, but her cheeks held a beautiful pink blush and her lips curved into a happy smile.

"You are fucking beautiful!" I shouted as loud as I could in the inside of the car, startling her so bad she jumped in her seat. I pulled her hand off of my leg to kiss it.

"Are you crazy?" She asked, incredulously resting one hand over her heart.

"Crazy in love. I love you so much," I said seriously.

Her pink lips curved to expose her white teeth in a brilliant smile. "You scared the crap out of me."

"What's going on with Jensen?" I had purposely refrained from asking her while I was away. She was packing up her things and I knew he filed, but I didn't know what the progress was.

"He's been amazing. We won't need to go to court and we are using the same lawyer. All he wants are the same visitation rights any normal father receives in a divorce."

I nodded. I expected nothing less.

"How do you feel about that, Chase?"

"I feel... that she loves him and he loves her. He is my best friend, Teagan. I have a lot of friends in London, both on the team and off, but none like J. We just have to figure out how to make it work. I want to make sure to take any outstanding medical bills and to pay him back for the others."

"He doesn't seem to care about the money."

"I see that, but I want to make it right."

"I'm not sure he'll take it. He's trying to give me half of the house, but I want him to keep it. I figure he'll need it so she can come stay with him sometimes. ESPN will always be in Atlanta and he should keep it."

It was noble of Jensen to want to split the marital assets, but I had plenty of money, Teagan would probably go back to nursing if Remi went back to school. It didn't escape my logic that he'd married her to take care of her, and there was no way I'd let her take any money in the divorce. "I think that's a good plan. We have the shitty apartment, anyway," I mocked, amused. "Isn't that every woman's dream?"

Teagan and I both started chuckling as I pulled into the parking lot of the hospital and quickly navigated through it. I found a space on one end and smoothly parked the car.

I needed to talk to her about the USMNT offer, but we had time later. In that second, I was more interested in seeing my daughter. It was early evening and the southern air was warm and fragrant and it hit me as we got out of the car. "Wait," I told Teagan so I could hurry around and open the door for her. London didn't smell like this, and the air wasn't as soft. It was much cooler all the time, and it drizzled more. "My lady," I opened the door and bowed slightly.

She laughed softly and climbed out, taking the arm I offered her. She had her purse over her shoulder but her phone was in her hand, using speed dial to call someone. "Hey, Kat. We're here. Five minutes." She hung up the phone and shoved it back into her bag. "Are you ready to dance?" she asked.

"Oh shit!" I exclaimed. I'd forgotten the iPad in the bag and it had the two videos on it. "I forgot something in the car. Just a second." Leaving Teagan to wait, I ran back, opened the back, unzipped and pulled out the tablet from on top of my clothes.

"What was that about?"

"You'll see."

"Okay. So here's the plan when we get upstairs, Kat will start the song. We have one of those little blue tooth speakers on her side and one on the living room side, and her iPod is connected. She'll start playing Happy and we'll go through the door and surprise her, dancing to the song. Okay?"

I couldn't help the silly smile on my face. "So, I have to dance like a moron before I get to talk to my kid, is that it?" Teagan didn't know about the videos and I wanted to surprise her, too. I'd share them after I'd gotten to talk to Remi.

She nodded. "Not like a moron, necessarily. That's up to you," Teagan answered, tongue in cheek.

By now we were at the elevators and I pressed the button and when the doors opened, I pulled her inside. "Okay.

After we arrived on the floor, I waited while Teagan texted Kat. Jensen was waiting outside Remi's room, leaning up against the wall. "Ah, another dancing moron," I said. He smiled and nodded, with a roll of his eyes.

"Remi knows this dance from start to finish, so don't let me down." She was practically whispering.

Kat appeared at the door to the room. "Roma is in here with Remi, and doing a fine job of distracting her. Dr. Radar said he couldn't make it, Teagan, sorry."

"Awww!" she said and stomped her foot on the white tile. "That's too bad. What about the nurses?"

"Should be here any minute."

Obviously, it was going to be a bigger production than just four of us, and I thought it was awesome that so many people were going to do this for Remi. As if on cue, the elevator doors opened and out stepped two nurses and a student who I recognized from the first week after I'd come to Atlanta. They were some of Remi's regular nurses on the oncology floor. "When did you have time to teach everyone this dance?"

"Dude, only you had to be taught. The rest of us just watched Pharell's video," Jensen said drolly. "Jeesh."

Kat glanced at all of us. "Okay, are we ready? We'll line up and go in one-by-one every few bars, right?"

"This is gonna be freaking awesome," the nursing student said. "You guys are awesome."

"I'm going in first," I said. After all, I was playing Pharell, but even Teagan didn't know how much I was into it.

I was super excited to see Remi's face when I popped around the corner and started to dance for her. We lined up; me, Teagan, Jensen, Kat and the three nurses and when we were done, Kat took out her phone and in seconds the music was starting; Bomp! Bomp! Bomp!

I jumped into the doorway and started lip-syncing and keeping the beat, clapping. Remi's head had popped up when the music started and her face lit up like a lantern. She squealed and started giggling. "Daddy! Look Nana! It's Daddy! He's doing Happy!"

She was in a beautiful dress as vibrant as the expression on her face, and she started bouncing to the music with me, clapping and doing the steps right along with me. She was doing a great job at keeping the beat and she probably knew the steps better than I did.

I was laying it on thick, singing to Remi directly. I felt Teagan's eyes on me, certain that she was peaking around the doorframe, probably with a huge grin plastered on her face. When the chorus started, the rest of them poured in through the doorway and filed out around. Teagan went to my right; Kat and Jensen to the left and the nurses behind us in a second row. "Mommy! Jensey!" Remi shouted, jumping up and down. "Yay! Yay! Yay!"

Everyone did amazing and seeing that much life in Remi almost brought me to tears. It was such a change and it choked me up. I had to concentrate hard not to lose it. It was incredible that Teagan and Kat had this put together. I thought it was just going to be Teagan and me, but this was incredible. Everyone gave their all for three minutes of joy for my little girl. It was uplifting and inspiring. Teagan was laughing and crying at the same time and I wanted to hug her. Seeing Remi so well was a true miracle. I mean… it was.

The only thing that could have made it better was if Remi could be out here with us and I could have put her on my shoulders, but as it was, she was so happy; singing along with the song, dancing, and clapping. Her face radiating joy. It was priceless. It was our own mini flash mob.

And incredible as it was, my mother, stood up next to Teagan and joined us. Oh, my god, I wished this whole thing was being recorded!

When the song ended, everyone hooted and clapped, the women were all crying. I hugged Teagan and kissed her. "It's incredible. She's incredible!"

Teagan nodded, a tear slipping from her eye and she brushed it away quickly. My mother stood back with both hands clutched at her chest.

I turned and quickly knelt down to talk to Remi. "Hello, sweetheart." I placed one hand on the glass and one over my heart as I looked into her green eyes. She had a pink flush to her skin that was new. Deep in my heart, I knew she'd be okay.

Remi stepped up to the glass and placed her little hand up to mirror mine. Mine dwarfed hers. "Hi, Daddy."

I swallowed hard, blinking so I wouldn't lose it. "I missed you so much, Remi. You're so amazing! You're so beautiful, and you did so great!"

Remi was all smiles, though I couldn't help a tearful laugh. "I can't wait to hold you and play with you, all the time!"

"Remi," Kat said from behind me. "Why don't you show Daddy, Mommy and Jensey your surprise, honey?"

Her eyes grew into round saucers. "Oh. Wait!"

She ran off to a corner of the room near the bathroom and disappeared. I assumed she was getting something. I stayed on my knees but glanced up and grabbed the hand Teagan had placed on my shoulder. My mother sat in the big chair near me, and the two sofas were behind us, pushed back, I assumed, so there would be enough floor space for all of us. "What is she getting?" I asked with a quizzical frown.

"She drew some pictures of you playing soccer today," Kat answered.

"What's taking her so long?" Jensen wondered.

I looked at my mom and she winked at me. I turned back to the window, waiting for my baby girl. We were all waiting.

"Surprise!" Remi said from behind us. "Hahahaha!" Her magical laugh filled the room, but not on the intercom.

"Oh, my God," Teagan exclaimed, bending to swoop up the exuberant little girl as she ran into the room. "Remi! You're out! Oh, baby!" She was crying again, holding Remi tight and kissing her cheek in a succession of ten kisses.

I didn't know how it happened but I ended up on my feet, standing next to them with both arms wrapped tightly around them both. Remi had one arm around my neck and one around Teagan's. "Remi," I breathed, finally giving in to emotion. I kissed her silky light brown hair. "I can't believe this!"

Dr. Radar stood in the doorway, smiling from ear to ear. "We got'em good, huh, Remi?"

"Yup! We got em!" Her brilliant smile filled up my heart and looking at Teagan, I knew she was equally moved.

I kissed Remi again. It felt amazing to hold her and I didn't want to let go of her, but I noticed Jensen sitting on the edge of one of the couches, brushing away a tear of his own. The last thing I wanted was for him to feel like he was on the outside. I nodded in his direction so Teagan would see him sitting there. She nodded and let me take Remi from her. I walked with her over to where he was waiting and sat down beside him with Remi in my arms. "Baby, is there anyone else who you think needs a hug?"

Remi nodded. "Jensey!"

Jensen was as overcome with emotion as the rest of us when Remi went immediately into his embrace and onto his lap. "Hey, squirt." His eyes, full of gratitude, met mine over her head.

"Jensey, how come you and Daddy are crying?"

"We're happy, I guess."

She shook her head and questioned logic like only a five-year-old can. "I think it's silly to cry unless you're sad. You're not sad, are ya?" She frowned at him.

"No, honey," Jensen answered. Remi put a hand on his cheek and he kissed her on the forehead. "Far from sad! We're all just so happy you can be with us like this."

I stepped back to slide an arm around Teagan.

My mother was crying, but not interfering, and Remi herself realized it and scrambled off Jensen's lap and over to my mom.

"Don't cry, Nana. Are you just being happy, too?"

Mom stroked Remi's hair a couple of times and wiped away a tear. "Yes," she answered, gathering Remi into a hug. "Ecstatic! I wish your Grandad were here. He'd want one of these marvelous hugs." She was concentrating on Remi's expression and watching her responses closely.

"I can save him one," she answered simply.

At some point, the nurses must have left, but no one noticed their discrete departure. Dr. Radar cleared his throat. "Remi, are you ready to find your new room?"

Her face fell. "Can't I go home?"

"In about a week, I think," he answered. "Remember, we talked about this. I need to run some tests to make sure we're A-okay."

"Okay," she agreed sadly.

"That's okay, honey. It will give us time to make plans, and we'll all come see you and stay with you. Just like we have been," Teagan comforted gently.

"Can I have a cheeseburger?"

"Yes!" Four of us answered at the same time and bust out in a chorus of laughter.

"I'll go out for it," Kat murmured, getting up in search of her purse.

"Remi, would it be okay if I stay with you tonight in your new room?" Mom asked. "I'd love to snuggle with you and read you a story. We can call Grandad and tell him the news!"

"Sure, Nana!"

"Daddy has something for you, too, Remi. You and Nana can watch it."

Within the next thirty minutes, Remi was settled into her new room with her cheeseburger and fries, and we were all saying goodnight, with assurances we'd be back in the morning. Kat decided to drive the two hours back to Greenville to be with her family, so she left before the rest of us.

"Mom, do you need anything?"

"Get out of here, Son. This has been a big day and our Remi needs her rest."

Jensen was still with us and he and I kissed Remi and waited in the hallway outside the room while Teagan lingered.

"Jensen, I love Arsenal, but I love Remi, more. Don't worry about not seeing her. I'm doing what you said to do," I put a hand on his shoulder.

"What do you mean?"

"You told me to do what I would have done six years ago if I'd known about Remi, and that's what I'm going to do."

"I don't understand," he frowned.

"I've been scouted by the USNMT. I'm gonna take it. It's clear that Remi needs us both."

Jensen's head dropped and he fell back against the wall; his emotions making it hard for him to speak. He pinched the bridge of his nose for a good ten seconds, clearly overcome. "I don't know what to say. Thank you."

I held out my arms to hug him. "No. Thank you."

Chapter 23

CHASE

We ended up at the shitty apartment.

Teagan and I had been in euphoria about Remi getting out of isolation and the promise of being a real family. It was a sort of unspoken realization that all of it was happening. I had been unable to stop touching her all night and I couldn't wait to get her alone. I wanted her, no question. There was a sort of visceral hunger between us that was always there, but it wasn't just about sex; it was about the connection.

I didn't bother turning on the lights in the apartment. There was enough light filtering in from the streetlight, though the blinds were closed. The room was similar to a blurred black and white photograph and it was easy to maneuver through it.

I threw the keys down on the coffee table and led Teagan around the furniture and into the bedroom, by only her fingertips. A live current ran between us forming a circuit, and no words were necessary. Even though I missed her and my body was charged with need. I didn't feel the need to rush. Instead, I wanted to savor.

I tugged her toward the bed and stopped beside it. I let my hands run over her shoulders, down her arms and upward again until both of my hands were cupping the sides of her face. My thumbs traced the delicate bones of her cheekbones and jaw as I bent to kiss her. It was deep and greedy, but at the same time slow and exploring. I groaned from somewhere deep inside my chest and the sound was lost inside her mouth as the kisses continued.

Teagan had the same desire to touch and explore me; the feeling of her hands on me sent shock waves of electricity through me. Her fingers crept underneath the hem of my shirt until the muscles of my stomach contracted in pleasure and anticipation.

I pulled her close because I couldn't help it, my hands gathering up fistfuls of her dress at the same time pressing her hips into mine. My dick was already swollen with desire; throbbing within the confines of my jeans and hungry for release. I wanted Teagan to feel the evidence that I wanted her, as much as I needed the pressure in an instinctive move to ease at least part of the ache.

"Chase," my name left her mouth in a breathless plea. "Uhhhhh," she sighed as my mouth pulled from hers and down the side of her neck to the top of her shoulder. Teagan's head fell back in surrender, giving me the access I needed.

My hands explored her smooth body underneath her dress, inching the fabric up as my fingers found the tight, smooth skin. Her womanly curves called to every masculine cell in my body, but more than that, my heart worshiped her. The reason that my existence without her was empty, the reason every woman I was with left me unfulfilled, was because of her. I'd always known it, since the moment I laid eyes on her.

I pushed the dress up and obediently, Teagan lifted her arms so I could take it off and let it flutter to the floor. My hands ghosted over the beautiful swells of her breasts, curving temptingly above the delicate pale lace of her bra. I gently cupped them, teasing the nipples with light brushes of my thumbs.

My cock was ravenous; aching for release. I wanted to touch her, to slide my fingers inside her and find the hot, slick heat I knew would be there. I turned her around in my arms for easier access. I continued to kiss and torment her with light sucking kisses and small nips with my teeth on her neck and shoulder as my fingers slid into her matching panties and lower.

Teagan's body arched as my fingers parted her flesh, sliding down through the treasure I was seeking. My fingers slipped over her clit and into her body, thrusting deep, then pulling slowly out and up to repeat the motion over and over again. She was tight and hot and my cock was jealous of my fingers. The small mewling sounds and sighs Teagan made drove me crazy. I worked her body into a slow frenzy that was killing us both. I knew what I was doing; that the longer it took to give her the release she craved, the more intense her climax would be.

My own clothes felt like they were burning me. My cock was crying to be free of the confines of my pants and boxer briefs.

"Mmmmm," Teagan moaned. Her hands reached behind her searching and pressing; doing her best to stimulate me as I was doing for her.

Suddenly, she stepped forward; the movement effectively pulling my hand out of her. The loss of her body pressed up against mine left me wanton and bereft. Teagan's hand wrapped around my wrists and she stood on her tiptoes to kiss me, her mouth reaching for mine.

Both of us were panting and breathless, desperate and more frantic for each other, now. Our tongues and mouths melded intimately, and I felt like I wanted to devour her. I couldn't get close enough. Teagan's hands pushed the plaid button down from my shoulders as we continued to kiss over and over. Soon it joined her dress on the floor and she was unbuttoning and then unzipping my pants. She dropped to her knees in front of me and pushed my pants down just enough to finally free my rock-hard erection.

"Oh, God," I breathed, knowing her intention. She bit her lip and looked up at me as her hand closed around the shaft. "Teagan." Her name ripped from me in a low, guttural groan. "Jesus."

My body tightened, engorging even more. I felt like the skin on my dick would split like a grape, and my balls ached, as my eyes fell to her mouth. That amazing, sweet mouth would take me to heaven or hell.

Her hands worked me, pulling and pushing up and down, her thumb teasing over the head in circles at the top of her strokes. At the same time, she licked and kissed my nipples, her hot breath rushing over my skin as she moved down to my lower abs. Her lips were torturing me with slow kisses; she sucked on the skin and let her tongue lave the skin as she went.

My body started to shake and my knees felt weak. I sank down on the bed; my arms wrapping tightly around Teagan to pull her forward with me. I scooted up the bed and kissed her deeply.

"Are you sure you want to do this? I'm happy to make love to you all night."

Her answer was to simply push me back against the pillows and move to pull my jeans and shorts free of my body. I was completely naked, but Teagan's perfect body was still taunting and teasing in the beautiful lingerie. Instinctively, I understood it was new. "Did you buy that for me?"

"Everything's for you." Her little hands slid up my legs and thighs to converge on my cock. Teagan knelt between my legs to finally take the head into her mouth. My breath sucked in on a hiss and my head fell back as I let her take me over, losing myself in the delicious sensations.

"Ughhh," I groaned as her tongue circled and teased the head of my cock before she took me in deep and sucked hard. Over and over she tormented me with teasing licks and then long hard pulls up and down until I couldn't stand it anymore. "Jesus, Teagan." My fingers threaded through her hair because I had to touch her as she brought me closer and closer to the edge of release. "Teagan, slow down, baby. I'm too close. I don't want to come in your mouth. Make love with me." I couldn't tell if it was a demand or a plea, and it didn't matter.

"I can taste you," she almost whispered. "You're close."

"I know. It feels incredible. Stop. It's too much." She seemed more determined than ever at my words, her hand reaching up to splay on my chest as her mouth continued its torture. Involuntarily, my hips rose from the bed in a thrust and I knew if I didn't stop her, she'd push me over the edge.

I sat up half way and hauled her up my body, flipping her so I was hovering over her in one motion. My hand pulled down the cup of her bra and my mouth closed over her nipple to suckle hard at the same time, my hand moved down over her flat stomach and over the lace of her panties to knead her sex. I wanted to make sure she was ready, but I shouldn't have worried. Her panties were damp with her desire and heat radiated out of her core. I kissed her hard, pulling her lower lip between mine to suck it into my mouth.

I had both of her breasts free of the lace, and I was impatient now. My dick was going to explode if I didn't get it inside of her. I moved between her legs and she opened for me as I hooked the crotch of her panties with my index finger to move it aside. "Help me," I commanded. Teagan's hand grabbed my cock and guided it into her body. I pushed forward with a hard thrust and was instantly buried deep inside her. Teagan gasped, her hips arching up to meet mine, her inner walls clenching around me in pulses, perfectly timed with my thrust.

The pleasure was so intense I thought I would die right there.

"I love you, Teagan," I panted. "Do you know how much?"

I didn't want it to be over; it had to last. I wanted to show her the intensity of my love with every touch, every kiss... every thrust. Her hands pulled at my ass and back to bring me closer. I dug into her body with purpose, with deep slow thrusts as our mouths echoed the intimacy of our bodies. It was glorious.

"Teagan, I need to hear you say it." It was more like a prayer than anything else. This was the temple of our love, she was my heart and soul, and we were meant to be. If there were such a thing as soul mates, Teagan was mine.

"I know you love me. I love you, too." Her voice broke. "Forever."

The emotion between us was as intense as the desire; so intense I couldn't contain it. If we melted together, it would never be close enough. I pulled my mouth free to breathe, but words burst from me as my mouth hovered over hers. Our hips continued to work against each other, the pleasure still building to the point of no return. "I want to have another baby," I said, urgently.

"Oh, Chase," Teagan cried, her hands came up to hold my head at the same time as she raised her knees higher. I sank even deeper into the cradle of her body. She was crying softly as we made love, and emotion stung my eyes and made my throat tighten. It was like everything with Teagan; a combination of heaven and hell, pain and bliss, incredible pleasure and insatiable want. She was everything. We were everything.

"Say yes," I panted, in time with my thrusts. "Oh, God, say yes."

Her body arched against mine and she shuttered, her legs trembling. Her arms and legs caged me in as the intensity of her orgasm pulsed through her. Her body contracted and convulsed, sucking blissfully and mercilessly on mine.

Wave after wave of pleasure washed over me as I came hard inside her. She held me; kissing the side of my face as my body jerked against hers as I rode it out. I stayed inside her because I couldn't bear to separate from this woman who owned my heart, body, and soul.

I was breathing hard when I rolled to my side, pulling her leg up and over my hip. I pushed a tendril of her sweat-dampened hair back behind her ear and wiped at the tears on her face with my fingertips.

I bent to kiss her softly. It was gentle but intense. The salt of her tears landed on my tongue. "Teagan, I love you and Remi more than anything. Say yes."

Teagan cupped the side of my face, her fingers moved into my hair to stroke it softly over and over. I was dying, waiting for her to speak.

A soft, contented sigh filled the space between us. I ran a thumb over her lower lip and I could tell she was smiling softly.

"Yes."

ONE *touch*
AND THE PAIN
melted away.

Epilogue

CHASE

We spent the week at Disney World.

England, Scotland, and France to see real castles, but the enthralled look on her face when she saw Cinderella's Castle in the Magic Kingdom, was priceless.

Her grandparents went nuts and my mom had Remi, Mandi and Mellie decked out in different princess dresses every day we were there. We'd have to buy another suitcase just to get the damn things home. I laughed at the thought. It was one hundred percent worth it.

Kat's boys, Jackson, Jace, and Jalen were more rambunctious than the girls because they were a bit older. Thankfully, there were enough adults in the party to keep them all in line, and everyone had a great time.

My entire family was with us, including Jensen and his mom and dad. Somehow, we'd ended up closer than ever, and for that, I was thankful.

The kids were the perfect age for Disney, and Remi was having the time of her life. She loved her cousins and they had embraced her with open arms. She was healthy and happy and was about to finish kindergarten.

It was early April and my first season with the U.S. National team was behind me. Teagan and Jensen's divorce had been smooth and had happened within a month of Remi getting out of the hospital, and I'd given her an engagement ring shortly after, but we still weren't married because Remi insisted princesses marry princes in castles. I'd rolled my eyes at the time, but Teagan convinced me to go with the flow. It was tolerable, only because we were living as a family, and the whole thing was being planned. My mother and sister were totally on board with Remi's vision for the wedding. What the hell did I know of shit like that? I was just a guy.

The delay also helped put time between the divorce and our marriage, which I felt was the right thing to do. Jensen told me that he knew from experience it was a better choice to shut up and go with the flow and let media madness die down. It was easier, anyway.

After the week in Orlando was over, the rest of the group were taking a Disney Cruise, and I was taking Teagan to Turks and Caicos for our long-awaited honeymoon. Remi had Jensen and two sets of grandparents to dote over her, so we had no doubt she wouldn't even miss us. I was looking forward to finally being married, and adding to our family like Teagan had promised me last fall.

"Are you ready?" Jensen, dressed in a full dress black tux poked his head in the door. We were getting dressed for the ceremony in one of the rooms of the upper floor of the castle, and we were getting married in the East Pavilion of Magic Kingdom.

I chuckled. I was struggling to tie a black bow tie in the mirror and I glanced at his reflection. "Hell if I know. I'm ready to be married, but I'm not sure if I'm ready for the hoopla."

KAHLEN AYMES

He came in, already fully dressed. "Yeah. It was a trip yesterday. Remi was inviting everyone she came in contact with."

I nodded with a grin. "I know. I think Mickey, Minnie, and Goofy have front row seats." Many of my teammates from the U.S. team and Arsenal were here, too. "I guess it was a good idea to have it here. Everyone gets a vacation with their families, at the same time."

"It will be good," Jensen agreed. "Knowing Teagan, I'm sure it will be perfect."

He came in and sat down on a chair in the sitting room of the suite. I finally got the tie done in a way I was happy with and reached for my jacket, shrugging into it.

"I really appreciate you being here, Jensen. I don't want this to be hard for you." I never asked either he or Teagan about their wedding because honestly, I hadn't wanted to know, but I realized that asking him to be my best man might cause residual feelings.

"I'm fine, Chase. Teagan and I didn't have a wedding. We just went to the courthouse and the justice of the peace. Nothing like this."

In the months since the divorce, we'd fallen into an easy friendship that was reminiscent of our college days. Remi spent time with Jensen at his place, and we had chosen to domicile near the new national training center in Kansas City because it was much closer to Atlanta than the one in Carson, California. The new city was good because it was a clean slate for Teagan and me, and we were able to make a lot of new memories. I had to travel often for games and sometimes for training, but it was a hell of a lot closer to Jensen than London. It wasn't always easy, but we made it work.

"Have you seen Remi? How is she doing?"

A genuine smile split across my friend's face. "She's on cloud nine. It's all Roma and Kat can do to corral the girls. They're bouncing around like beach balls."

"It's the princess garb, undoubtedly."

"It is. I know I'm biased, but Remi is the prettiest. She's beaming." His expression was incredulous. "It's amazing that she's perfectly healthy now. It's like she never had leukemia."

It was a miracle that I thanked God for every day. "I'm not sure if it is the transplant or the princess dresses that cured her." My smile echoed Jensen's.

"It's neither. It's the tiara and glass slippers," my father said from the doorway. Teagan and I had purchased them for the little girls to wear at the wedding, and my father had delivered them to their dressing room earlier. "They're gorgeous!" he said, beaming.

I pulled at the cuffs of my shirt under my jacket sleeves and ran a hand down the front of my formal shirt. The tuxes were classic three-piece; black and elegant. Thankfully, I'd managed to talk Remi out of the Prince Charming costume.

I turned to my father. "How does Teagan look?"

"Beautiful. Like mother, like daughter. You're a lucky man."

"Yes." I nodded. There was no way I was going to argue.

Teagan's father was invited, but he wasn't in attendance. She said it didn't bother her, but I knew in her heart she was a little bit heartbroken. "Dad," I handed him a note that I'd written for Teagan. "Will you do me a favor?"

"You want me to take her this note?" He was looking dashing in the tux. It was quite a transformation from his usual dark pants, grey work shirt, and billed company hat that he wore almost daily.

I shook my head. "No." I put a hand on his shoulder. "Yes, but that's not the favor." I opened the note so he could read it and handed it to him. His eyes glassed over as he read the handwritten words on the white page.

Dear Teagan~

Thank you for being in my life. Thank you for blessing my life with Remi and giving me the promise of many glorious years to come. If I could, I would give you the world. Though I know there are some things beyond my reach, still, I will endeavor to try. I'm sorry your dad isn't with you today, but today and always... you can borrow mine.

I love you.

Always,

~Chase

"Will you be 'something borrowed' for Teagan, Dad? I don't want her walking up that aisle alone."

My dad wasn't one to show emotion easily, but his brilliant green eyes, so much like mine, were filled with pride and admiration. He moved in to hug me. "It would be my honor."

I returned the embrace and we both patted each other on the back. "I love you, Dad."

He cleared his throat before he spoke. "You too, Son. It would be my honor to walk Teagan down the aisle."

"Okay," I gave him another hard pat and then moved out of his arms.

"You make your mother and me so proud. I hope I'm around to see you walk Remi down the aisle someday."

I'd been ready for the day. Ready to marry Teagan, and I had been looking forward to it for months, so I really thought I'd have a handle on my emotions, but in that moment I felt raw and derailed as if I could lose it at any time. My father's words only emphasized that fear. Eight months ago I would have been hard-pressed to think of Remi growing up at all, and now we were talking about her wedding.

I blinked rapidly, trying not to tear up. "You will, Dad."

"Damn straight, I will!" He smiled brightly, tucking the folded note into the inside breast pocket of his suit jacket. "Let's go get you married off."

He went to the door of the suite and opened it, waiting for Jensen and myself to precede him through it. It only took us five minutes to make it down through the hotel and out into the garden of the pavilion. It was beautifully decorated, though it was only set up for about one hundred guests.

The chair backs were wrapped in satin bows, offset with a small bouquet of matching flowers tied on the aisle side. The very pale pastel color scheme was arranged according to the color spectrum, with lavender at the back, fading up through sky blue, mint green, yellow, pink and finally ivory near the altar. It looked like a watercolor rainbow. It was amazing.

It was sunset, and there were candles everywhere, and paper lanterns hung from the trees; everything was glittering. To one side, there were ten or twelve round tables arranged around a round wooden dance floor. Each one completely decked out in china, votive candles, and crystal, and also decorated to follow the softest pastel rainbow theme.

My father nudged Jensen, pointing to my mother wearing a soft lavender suit. She looked amazing and elegant and standing beside her in a very pale pink princess dress, was sweet little Remi. It had little cap sleeves over her shoulders, a very full and swirly skirt. The style was simple other than it sparkled from top to bottom.

"There are our dates," he said. "Boy, are we in trouble."

"I'll say," Jensen agreed, his eyes as drawn to Remi as mine were.

She was standing next to my mom and proudly greeting everyone. "Thank you for coming to Mommy and Daddy's wedding," she said over and over to each guest and offered her hand to shake it. The women commented on her beautiful dress. Her hair was professionally done up in a mass of curls that nestled the coveted tiara. It was adorable.

When we approached I leaned in and kissed my mother's cheek before Remi noticed me. "She's a little doll. She's eating this up."

"You look great, Mom." She had a linen handkerchief in her hand and an orchid corsage on the lapel of her suit.

Her hand reached out and touched the front of my shirt, lovingly smoothing it down, and patting my chest. "I'm so happy for you, Chase. You look so handsome."

I smirked, running a hand over my freshly shaved jaw with a wink. "Yeah, you got your way with the haircut, so you have to say that."

"Hi, Daddy!" Remi exclaimed when she saw me, and I bent to swoop her up and hold her up with my right arm.

"My, don't you look beautiful!" I kissed her rosy cheek. It was a little more filled out now that she was healthy. She was still thin, but not like she was when she was ill. I loved the healthy radiance about her. "Your hair is gorgeous!"

She leaned in and put her hand over her mouth in an effort to tell me a secret. I cocked my head to accommodate her. "It's just like Mommy's! And look!" She splayed her little hand in front of her showing off her beautifully French-manicured fingers. "And look at my feet!"

I used my free hand to lift the hem of her long dress just enough so that her tiny foot was exposed. The pretty little low-heeled pumps were made out of clear acetate that made them look like glass. Her toes were clearly visible and painted to match her fingers. "Wow!"

"Yeah, my toes had to be done too, 'cause you can see 'em through these slippers!" She was so excited she was practically jumping in my arms.

"You really are a princess! You're dazzling!" I hugged her close and kissed her forehead. Her little arms wrapped around my neck and squeezed.

"Come on, squirt," Jensen held out his arms for Remi. "Let your dad get on with business. Let's go get your flowers and get you back to Mommy."

"Okay," Remi paused to kiss me on the jaw and then held out her arms to Jensen so he could take her.

"Are you all done greeting guests, then?" Jensen asked her.

"Mmmmm…." She looked around and pointed. "Nana, can you help me? Those people over there need to be talked to."

My mom patted her cheek. "Of course, Darling. You go be with your mommy. You can see everybody at the reception."

Remi nodded and Jensen carried her in the opposite direction. "Daddy!" She called over his shoulder.

I turned at the sound of my name just in time to see her blow me a kiss. I pretended to catch it and held it over my heart with both hands.

I made my way around the room to speak to many of my old Arsenal teammates that I hadn't seen in months, who were there with their own families. Coach Noonan and Arsène Wenger were seated in the second row back on the groom's side. I shook both of their hands, honored that they'd made the trip.

"We miss you, my boy," Coach Noonan offered. "You're welcome back with your mates anytime."

"Thank you, Coach. I miss Arsenal, I won't lie."

"It's an open offer."

Mr. Wenger patted me on the arm. "The little one looks healthy. So beautiful."

"She's good! A little precocious, if I'm honest."

"All of the good ones are." He winked.

There was a string quartet playing classical music in the background and I took my place near the front of the altar. Kevin appeared a few minutes later and took his place to my left. "Is everything okay?"

"Perfect."

The sun was almost down and the sky was painted in brilliant pinks and violets behind the castle in the background. My dad escorted my mom to the front row of chairs and seated her right on the aisle. He met my eyes and then walked back up the aisle to wait for Teagan to arrive.

The music kept playing and at the back of the short aisle, my sister gathered with Kevin's two girls and his wife Jodi. Kat lined up the little ones and had them start walking. Mellie and Mandi were sporting tiaras similar to Remi's. Kevin beamed at them. They were sweet; each holding a basket of rose petals in the color of their dress. They threw them up in the air and walked through them as they fell onto the ivory runner. It was precious.

They came down the aisle in the same pastel rainbow; Melli in lavender, Mandi, in light blue. Jodi and Kat's dresses were ball gowns, with sparkling ivory bodices over colored skirts made from some floaty type of fabric I didn't know the name of. They were slightly shorter in front so their crystal-encrusted high heels were visible. Perfect. Jodi's dress was a very pale green, and Kat had a light coral, and both of them held tight bouquets of white roses that were tied with ivory and accent ribbons that matched their dresses.

A Cinderella carriage pulled by six white horses approached, and I could only assume it was carrying Teagan and Remi. It was out straight out of the fairytale, as six costumed and wigged footmen walked beside it. I strained to see inside it but all of the guests had risen and turned which blocked my view.

Jensen and my father were waiting at the end of the aisle for my girls to alight from the coach and the quartet started playing a new song. It was one I recognized, one that Teagan and I had decided would be our new song in the months since Remi's recovery. We'd made love to and danced to it many times. The lyrics told our story perfectly and the title suited the song to a T. It was about the inevitability of the one.

It was Ed Sheeran's *Perfect*. It was being played with string instruments joined by a single acoustic guitar soloist. Three of my old teammates from Arsenal left their seats and moved to the front by the instrumentalist. It was a surprise to me when they started singing in beautiful harmony. The lyrics were perfect. The song was amazing. Emotions welled up and made my eyes burn and my throat ache.

The coachman opened the door and Jensen stepped up to lift our little Remi down. He held her hand and walked her up the aisle toward me. I couldn't tear my eyes off of her, holding a bouquet that I knew was a smaller replica of her mom's. She was a gift and it was clear the man escorting her down to me, felt the same way about her.

Jensen lifted her hand and kissed it, bowing at the waist when they reached the pinnacle. She curtsied sweetly, holding out the sides of her dress, first to Jensen, and then to me. I held out my arms and she ran to me as he took his place next to my brother.

I lifted Remi and held her up with me as we watched her mother walk toward us with my father. Her little arm clung around my neck and her head was tilted to rest on mine. I could barely hold it together; my heart was exploding with love. The music and lyrics of the song were so fitting for us, and I found myself rocking back and forth with my daughter.

Teagan was stunning. Her dress was more fitted than the others and flared out toward the bottom. The deep V-neckline and sleeveless bodice were covered in lace that continued, unlined over her delicate shoulders. I could imagine the back of her dress was similar. She was luminous, and I was breathless. She looked like a princess. Her lace gown softly glittered in the candlelight and she was clinging to my father's arm. Her eyes were sparkling with tears. The long, gossamer veil floated around her was surreal.

"Oh, my God," I said under my breath. I was shaking. Her dark eyes were locked with mine and her chin trembled with her effort not to full on cry. I let it all sink in; me holding Remi, and how everything that should have always been, was finally coming together.

The aisle was short so the song wasn't finished, and after my father kissed Teagan's cheek, and offered her hand to mine, and tugged to pull her gently into my arms. "May we have this dance?"

Her face crumpled and she nodded. Kat came forward and took Teagan's and Remi's bouquet and Remi hugged her mom with her now free arm. I took them both in my arms and held on tight.

I closed my eyes as Teagan's forehead found my cheek. A small sob escaped her as we swayed together and my arms tightened around her and we danced together until the end of the song.

Remi's arms tightened around both of our necks. And Teagan's head fell to my shoulder and she was shaking. I kissed her temple, lovingly, unwilling to remove my lips from her skin for several seconds.

"Finally," she said.

My throat was tight, almost swelled shut, and tears slipped from my eyes. "This is my whole world, right here," I whispered. "My two princesses. I love you both, so much."

The song ended and no sound was made from the guests.

"Are we gonna get married now, or not?" Remi said in her normal voice. Everyone burst out laughing. I looked at Teagan through my tears and some clung to her lashes, too.

I smiled. "Well, answer the kid."

She laughed through her tears and nodded. "Yes."

I moved back and set Remi down, but she stayed positioned between us. She tugged on the hem of my jacket. "Daddy," she whispered. "I need to tell you something!"

I glanced at Teagan. Her eyebrows shot up and she shrugged, brushing away a tear. I looked at the minister and put up a finger to let him know it would just be a minute. "I'm so sorry, please excuse me for one second."

I bent down on my haunches to talk to my daughter. "What is it, Remi?"

She cupped her mouth and though I doubted anyone could hear her, I humored her and bent toward her. "I'm gonna be a big sister!"

My mouth dropped open and a hand fell over my heart. I was sure it just hit a full stop. My head snapped up to look up at Teagan, and she nodded her affirmation with a bright, tearful smile.

I stood, uncertain if what I was about to do was proper wedding etiquette, but I didn't care. I grabbed Teagan and kissed her full on the mouth. Her laughter joined the many chuckles, hoots, and gasps coming from the group behind us and the room burst out into applause.

"Really?" I whispered. "When?"

"In seven months." I kissed her again, and the minister cleared his throat.

Remi put one arm around my leg and remained steadfast between us. Teagan cupped her cheek with her hand.

"Please face each other, and join hands."

We did as asked but Remi stayed where she was.

My thumbs brushed the top of her hands with my thumbs over and over. I couldn't take my eyes off of her beautiful face.

The minister waited to give us a minute.

"Excuse me, sir, I think we can get married now," she told the minister. "Please."

The whole congregation burst out laughing, and there under the perfect night sky, with Cinderella's Castle lit up in front of us, we were married.

My heart was full to the point of bursting. I had everything a man could want and finally, everything was put right.

There would be fireworks later; in more ways than one.

The End

Won't you join me?

Register for bone marrow donation!

Visit **BeTheMatch.org**

Maybe you can save a life, like Remi's!

If you enjoyed
Chase, Teagan & Remi's story,
Jensen's turn is coming in March of 2018!

FINDING
Tomorrow

PRE-ORDER NOW
wherever eBooks are sold!

Additional Books
By Kahlen Aymes

The Remembrance Trilogy & Prequel
Prequel: Before Ryan Was Mine
1. The Future of Our Past
2. Don't Forget to Remember Me
3. A Love Like This

The After Dark Series
1. Angel After Dark
2. Confessions After Dark
3. Promises After Dark

The FAMOUS Novel Series
1. FAMOUS
2. More Than FAMOUS
3. Beyond FAMOUS

One Step Closer
A Standalone Stepbrother Second Chance Story

Available Now in Audio
The After Dark Series
The Remembrance Trilogy & Prequel

Available Now in French
The Remembrance Trilogy & Prequel
The After Dark Series

Available Now in Spanish
The Remembrance Trilogy & Prequel

UPCOMING TITLES

CONNECT with KAHLEN

Facebook: Facebook.com/kahlen.aymes

Goodreads:
Goodreads.com/author/show/5768062.Kahlen_Aymes

Twitter: @Kahlen_Aymes

Pinterest: Pinterest.com/kahlenaymes/

Instagram: Instagram.com/kahlen.aymes/

Bookandmainbites.com/users/15876

OFFICIAL WEBSITE:
For merchandise, signed copies, Julia's recipes, missing scenes, appearances & events, Kahlen's Blog, series playlists and more, visit **KahlenAymes.com**

Sign up for Kahlen's newsletter
http://eepurl.com/ruw4x

Kahlen is represented by
Stephanie Delamater Phillips of SBR Media, LLC
130 Citadel Drive, Conway, SC
Tel: 1-843-421-7570
Email: Stephanie@sbrmedia.com